PANDORA'S KISS

T.B. BOND

Chelsea,
I hope you enjoy!
♡ TB Bond

Vanilla Mocha
Publishing

Thank you to my writer divas and my editor. Without you, my words could not get out there. Shout out to my Martinis and The League of Extraordinary Romance!
As always, thanks to those who buy my books:)

Special shout out to Nana Hall. You were a tremendous help and so patient as I hand-wrote this and then typed it out.

ISBN: 9798843436131

Pandora's Kiss by T.B. Bond

Cover Art by T.B. Bond

Edited by Ryan Starling

Copyright © 2022 T.B. Bond All rights reserved.

1

 uyen

Present Day

I bolted down a dim alleyway, known locally as Traveler's Alley, at my fastest pace. My breath, when I could catch it, escaped my body in burning puffs. I was a thinker, not a runner, which was evident because my lungs were a hair away from bursting into flames and fire wasn't even my element. I was a water man, but that was under the bridge at the moment—which I would have preferred. My escape would have been less taxing than running through the urban areas of Richmond in the dark.

Wishing for a better situation would not change matters. I could not stop. Not until I shook my pursuers.

My kingdom for a levitation spell.

Except all magic use was out whether it be spells or concentrated applications such as active powers. The most powerful practitioners could use active powers and perform magic without the use of a spell, however, all of us could use spells. I wanted Obscura as blind as possible during my escape.

Obscura employed witches and wizards more so than mundane security. They would expect magic, not mechanical ingenuity. Their lack of diverse thought is why I and several others could slide into their stronghold, take some of the ancient tomes, and then destroy the rest. It would take them months to audit what we took versus what we ruined.

I cataloged as much as I could of the destroyed items for my collection. It was wasteful to destroy the ancient magic, but Obscura was too dangerous. We couldn't allow them to continue with their world domination plans.

I could not, anyway.

Matt Wesley, the Grand Magister, was my issue. With him, it was personal. I knew his personality and capability. He was my best friend before he turned against me and became a megalomaniac. I should have seen when his path turned dark. All of the signs were there when I thought back on it—the obsession with government, power, and the lack of compassion for mundanes. It was my fault for trusting him.

A flood of light shined fifty feet in front of me. I skidded to a halt just inside the umbra of the bright halo, then hugged the cement and brick walls forming my alley prison. It was likely Obscura. Somehow they managed to get ahead of me. They appeared to be closing in on the kill. My goose was cooked only a few dozen feet away from the salvation of a populated street.

The spotlight slowly moved towards my general direction in a standard sweeping search motion. I studied the light of doom for a few moments, then relaxed when they didn't immediately shine it on me. They didn't know I was there. It was a guess based on the general direction that I ran.

Matt's people were more intelligent than I gave them credit. They must have switched to a non-magical tactic, though not entirely since the light was a spell, and searched for each of us. I still had anonymity on my side. He didn't know I was with Camera, so he couldn't employ any of his knowledge against me, nor did Camera know my connection to him. I made sure to keep my identity ambiguous using a variation of my lesser-known middle name, Andrew. The world was aware of, vaguely, Quyen Duong, but not Drew D.

Camera operated with guerilla tactics and cell organizations. The world thought we were unorganized. They were inaccurate. We worked as many parts to protect the whole. It was the only way I would have been able to join with virtual anonymity. The members who knew my face were in my cell. With the exception of one, they knew nothing about me and my skills.

And there were less than five of them. We should have met up with another cell. I thought as the spotlight moved inches from the section of shadow where I hid.

BOOM.

A raucous shock wave of sound shook the building I rested against. Glass from windows and light fixtures rained down around me. The sting of my head spurred me into action. I held the bag that contained the spoils of my theft over my head to protect me from the fallen shards and pieces. The light spell darted off, presumably in the direction of the cacophony. The alley plunged into darkness.

Screams and car alarms filled the brief silence. I made my move. I couldn't remain in my hiding place. There was no telling if someone pursued me on foot or if the spotlight operators would continue their search. Either way, I was gone.

I didn't have to go far before reaching the end of the maze of urban stone and trash. The city was in chaos. People ran up and down 7th Street while some stood in groups watching the night sky glow orange. Embers of fire magic flowed in the air while the smell of burning chemicals permeated the ether.

I slid the strap of my bag across my shoulder messenger bag style. It was OK to hold the bag while I ran, but I had to blend in and appear casual in the crowd.

"What happened?" I asked a woman furiously texting on her phone.

She glanced at me, then frowned. "You're hurt."

She pointed to the side of my head.

I touched my temple. The sting of a cut greeted me, and blood stained my fingers. Great.

"Glass started raining from everywhere. It must have got me," I explained.

The woman dug into her purse. She produced a wad of napkins and handed them to me. "Yeah, my car windows were busted out by the explosion."

I thanked her and took a few napkins to try and staunch the blood. "Where did that happen?"

"I heard it was near the old city hall building. Police won't let anyone near Broad Street. Then the light show started. I think it was those rogue magicians that Obscura is always talking about. I wish the government would pass that law. They're supposed to protect decent law-abiding citizens. That's why we pay taxes."

I fought not to react to her recounting of Obscura's propaganda or the mention of the Witchcraft Act. Camera had lobbyists working overtime to keep the law buried, but a recent resurgence had occurred since a few of the battles between Obscura and Camera spilled into the open. If we weren't careful, the witch trials would come back, and neither of us would survive.

"Did anyone get hurt?" I pulled the napkin from my head. I applied enough pressure for the blood to stop for the moment. It would hold until I was out of sight, then I would work a spell to heal it.

"Probably, but I hadn't heard much besides to stay away." The woman shrugged then glanced toward the orange and purple sky.

It was dimmer than before, but it was still unnaturally bright.

"I'm moving away from Richmond. There are too many magic freaks around. If I were you, I would do the same."

"Consider me out of here. I want nothing to do with it." I nodded to keep suspicion off me. A bigot like that would remember a Vietnamese man that disagreed with her. Well, I doubt she'd know my ethnicity but use an umbrella term like Asian. Either way, I wanted her to relegate me to the background of the terrible situation without having to resort to a memory obfuscation spell.

Anyone could question her if she started making a fuss or thought

I had something to do with the City Hall attack. I was confident that she was right, and the explosion was magical. I didn't know if it was a coincidence or if Obscura drew one of my cell mates into a fight while they escaped.

"See about that head," she said before hurrying away.

Obscura and Camera had operatives everywhere, Obscura more so. I didn't want some random practitioners to get lucky and turn Matt in my direction. My plan to stop him worked best with him thinking that I was beaten down and weak. If he knew that I joined forces with Camera, the gentle war we waged would turn ugly. I knew what he truly was and what he planned. He may have most of the world fooled into thinking that he represented the side of good and wished to protect everyone, but his version of everyone meant only witches and wizards. Even a large portion of the magic community didn't know what Matt planned for those without power.

I doubt he would differentiate those from a family of magic but with no talent from a family with magic users. And those who disagreed with him, practitioner or not, would be cast aside.

Everyone was in danger. They just didn't know it.

2

50 A.Q.

"Here goes nothing," I said to myself as I entered the *One-Eyed Lion*. It was a dilapidated speakeasy that was a marketplace decades ago when people could safely go outside and didn't have to scavenge. The brick building with its boarded-up windows and cyclops lion was still a means of commerce. Instead of food, the owner brokered information and booze.

I didn't want to go inside. The place was huge and there weren't many exits, but beggars couldn't be choosers. I was on the run.

My pursuers would utilize various tactics for hunting me. The land was too savage for me to live off of after the Sphinx attack scorched the earth in a 200 mile swath of destruction that took out DC. Coupled with several other attacks at major cities worldwide. The attacks destabilized most of the world's influential nations, and Obscura swept in and saved the day giving birth to the United Nations of Obscura.

I wanted nothing to do with them. The organization wasn't the good guys. Everyone thought they were the saviors of the earth, with Matt Wesley, the Grand Magister, being a god among men. He wasn't. The Grand Magister was like every other powerful man I read about in school before the world fell—self-serving.

"Are you buying or selling?" A grisly man asked with a leer. "I hope on all that is Obscura that you are selling."

Why did it seem all the perverts ran the trading posts? It was bad enough that I had to dodge slavers and gang bangers at every turn while traveling the desolate parts of the UNO called the lawless zone. The least Obscura could have done was restore the world to where it had been instead of selecting the parts they wanted and letting everyone fend for themselves in some sort of apocalyptic nightmare.

"Buying," I said.

The man frowned. "Two inches of gold."

And of course in the lawless zone, bartering was the only system one could rely on… that and power. If one had nothing to trade or the ability to take what they needed, they were victims—which was nearly the entire population of the social and ecological wilderness.

"I haven't heard your information yet. One inch." I countered.

He gifted me a lecherous, yellow tooth grin. "For a fab chick like you? Suck my dick and one and a half inches of gold."

I wasn't about to pleasure him or pay more than one inch of gold for my information. He was unreasonable. I would have to take another tactic with him. "I will say this once more. One inch of gold for information."

The man's eyes narrowed. "Then you can take your tight little—"

I punched him in the throat.

He doubled over as the swish of blades drawing sounded behind me. I jumped across the bar, grabbed the broker by the hair then pressed my sword to his throat. "Tell them to put the blades away."

He gurgled a response. I cut the skin lightly so he would understand that I wasn't in the mood for games.

"Put them away," he said with a raspy voice.

"Now," I said into his ear. "For an inch of gold. Tell me if there have been any strangers in Bordertown and what was their business."

"You," he snarled. "Harassing honest business folk."

I fought not to roll my eyes. Even with a blade to the broker's throat, he still tried to be snarky. "Who else?"

"Just traders and a few bounty hunters."

By traders, I knew he meant slavers. That was nothing new here. Those assholes were always about in Bordertown and the lawless zones. If I came across them, I dealt with them, but then their cargo got captured again. It was a vicious cycle.

"What bounty hunters? Who are they looking for?" I asked.

"They-they didn't say," he stammered.

Lie. An information broker wouldn't allow bounty hunters to leave without getting intel in return. Otherwise, the well would run dry. It was his business to know all sides.

The hairs on the back of my neck raised. It was a trap. The *One-Eyed Lion* was a setup because they knew I had to come here for information or at least barter supplies before entering the lawless zone. "Where are—?"

A gunshot rang out in the speakeasy. The broker jerked at the same time pain blossomed in my shoulder. Obscura found me. The run of the mill creep couldn't afford the ammunition after ten years of lawlessness. It was why everyone carried knives, swords, and sticks.

I dropped the broker. He was probably dead anyway, and if he weren't, he would die for having seen me. Matt didn't want the information about my existence getting out. It was the one thing we agreed on. Another shot burst a bottle behind me. I dove to the floor. My shoulder burned from the abuse as my body worked on healing. I was low on magic energy after my last run-in with "bounty hunters," but I had enough to heal faster than the old fashion way.

The fact that they shot at me spoke to their desperation to catch me. I would use that against them. "Powers that be let me flee. Send my captors who like to chase an illusion to take my place."

A wave of exhaustion hit as a double coalesced into existence next to me. The doppelganger mirrored my appearance from my gazelle horned and eagle feather headdress to my leather boots. She winked at me, then jumped up and ran in the opposite direction. Gunfire and a stampede of footsteps followed her.

I wouldn't have long before they figured out my trick. Inching to the edge of the bar, I saw the entrance was mostly clear. There were a few patrons, guards, or whatever milling around as though they didn't know what to do. My best plan was to surprise them and bowl them over.

It's now or never.

I jumped over the bar and rushed through the entrance like a bull in a fancy shop. I knocked into the nearest bruiser. My shoulder burned as I burst past the unsuspecting guards.

"Come here you."

Someone grabbed the back of my headdress. I spun around with my backhand. My attacker released me, and I took off out of the metal doors. Outside several heads turned toward me. I waved my hand, "Wind, heed my call. Get rid of my enemies. Remove them all."

A dust devil the size of a tank zipped through the lot sucking up henchmen as it went. With my way clear, I ran forward to the motorcade. One of the bounty hunters had to have a vehicle. Obscura wouldn't let their agents come after me without a means to bring me to Matt. He furnished them with guns. He would make sure they had a—far out!

The bounty hunters set up their RV three-wheelers neatly in a row, with no guards or protection to get in my way, courtesy of my dust devil. Even with my cleaning efforts, the fact that the vehicles weren't looted or vandalized beforehand meant they waited for me a while.

And I strolled in like I didn't have a care in the world.

Stupid. Stupid. I should have seen it. Coming to Bordertown was too risky, but at least I would get a ride out of it.

I hopped onto the bike. "Spirits, conjure for me this vehicle's key."

A silver key materialized in my hand. My shoulder twinged, and the bullet fell onto the three-wheeler's dash. I snatched it up and placed it in my pocket. I couldn't be sure if the bounty hunters were mundane or practitioners. There was no way in hell I would leave evidence behind for another witch to scry for my whereabouts. They would have to find me the mundane way.

I put the key in the ignition. Screams and yells signaled in the *One-Eyed Lion*. The jig was up. I was out of time.

I gathered more of my rapidly waning energy reserves. As much as I wanted to use a spell, an active power would do my final clean-up better and faster. I glared at the bikes with white-hot fury—easy to do after getting shot in the arm, leered at, and nearly kidnapped. The remaining bikes caught fire as I drove away. By the time I reached the other side of the parking lot, the explosions had begun.

That would keep them busy for a while.

3

 uyen

Present Day

I wasn't a fan of DC traffic. Congestion manifested near the city proper no matter the day of the week. The mixing bowl—what the locals called the maze of entrance ramps, off-ramps, and bridges that converged then split into I-495, I-395, and I-95—was a horror story this evening.

In the past thirty minutes, I managed to inch maybe half a mile. We selected Sunday night as the most likely chance to catch the drop on Obscura. That part went well. We got in and mostly out when one of the initiates set off the alarm.

I still wanted the details on that. It was suspicious that everything went flawlessly until the end. My experiences had never been that lucky. It either went wrong the entire time, or the plan worked. All better be revealed when I got to our temporary HQ in the heart of

DC, which likely would take me an additional hour because of the traffic. The after-mission briefing would probably end by the time I showed up, then Tonya would have to give me the details.

If she made it back in time herself.

With all the chaos from the hit on Obscura, it was difficult to know who got out and who had artifacts. We all carried bags when we set out for our smash and grab. It was part of the plan to confuse the enemy. I also made slight deviations to my part since I possessed knowledge of Matt's intentions.

I went for his assistant's office. Lauren adored Matt. She would do anything to impress him. He worked her hero worship to the fullest. She would hide anything from precious to pertinent there, *and* she would hide the theft from him to prevent him from losing faith in her. I used that dynamic against him. Finally, a character flaw of his worked in my favor.

He was always like that, letting others do the legwork, then come in at the end and finish the solution. Matt couldn't be bothered by menial tasks as he called it. I would benefit.

I patted the bag in the passenger seat next to me. It was the gateway to Matt's plans and the means to stop or at least expose Obscura for what it was. I wanted to immediately go through the tome but first things first. I'd check in with my cell and turn over the artifacts I was assigned to retrieve. Then I'd go dark with Camera while I studied the ancient book and the heat surrounding the theft cooled.

No movement on I-95. Surprise.

It would be a long night. These were the times when radio silence became a problem. It required discipline, and it was inconvenient. I should have teleported using a summoning with the others. Then I wouldn't be in an I-95 parking lot. Except I was too paranoid for my comfort and the paranoia seemed to be leading me slowly through the mixing bowl.

"What's on the radio?" I asked no one because I couldn't stand the silence and the stagnation a moment longer.

I pressed the volume button, and the radio roared to life with jazz. I was more of an R&B man with occasional K-Pop. The person who rented the car before me must have been a jazz lover. I hit the "seek" button. The saxophone melody abruptly turned to static then turned to rock music. I knew the song but let it pass to the next channel in the hopes of the smooth, sensual vocals of my favorite singer, Diva. Her new album came out a week ago. The stations should be playing it in heavy rotation.

"—several bodies were found after a lethal carbon monoxide leak—"

Static.

"—station is closed while officials determine the cause of a gas leak—"

Static.

"This just in, a carbon monoxide leak kills several in Vernon Square Metro station—"

I hit the "seek" button again so I could listen further to the news report.

"It is undetermined how many are dead in this tragic event, but it is suspected that there was a failure in the exhaust system that resulted in the deaths of passengers and City Metro workers. We will continue to update you each hour with the latest information of this tragic event—"

I shut the radio off. For a brief moment, I sat numb with disbelief. Then anger exploded out of me as I slammed my hand on the steering wheel. The car's electronics went bonkers at my loss of temper. I closed my eyes to block out the radio blaring sound, the horn yelling, and the blinking interior light.

My mind is a river, calm and flowing. Sharp and focused.

The car quieted, and I opened my eyes as someone honked at me. Traffic moved another car link. I inched the car forward despite wanting to mash the pedal to the floor. Fear of drawing unwanted attention outweighed my need to destroy something.

My cell was likely gone. It was too much of a coincidence that the exhaust failure occurred while Camera occupied the metro station. If it were a mechanical issue, the five witches and wizards would have handled it. At least one of them would have had the presence of mind —Tonya would.

She was the most battle savvy out of the group and the only one I was semi-close to in our cell. I should have pushed harder for her to meet up with me and drive to DC. What if she—

I focused forward. No. Everyone knew the risks when we set out. We all had to consider the possibility that we'd fail, or that they captured and killed us. It didn't matter if it was in Obscura headquarters or out. As the last surviving member, it was my job to investigate and triage the situation. Someone may have gotten away. All didn't have to be lost.

I gripped the wheel and plotted my strategy as I slowly made my way through the mixing bowl and into the city of DC. Once I turned down 7th, I ran into problems. Police blocked off the entire area of the DC Convention Center from North to Mount Vernon. Police, fire, and EMTs worked the section from behind the yellow wooden caution barriers. Onlookers and boots on the ground reporters crowded the perimeter, trying to get the latest details.

I parked the car then hoofed it. Once I assessed the situation, I would work a spell to dim the First Responders' perception and do a thorough investigation. Stopping at a souvenir stand for a quick purchase, I slid my new cap over my head. It was a dark blue Nationals hat, the most nondescript item that they had. Between the hat and the crush of curious lurkers, I should get reasonably close before I needed my spell.

"Hey, did you hear what happened?" A passerby asked me.

"Yeah, some kind of gas leak or something."

The guy nodded. "I was right here about to go over to the pizza shop by Mount Vernon Station when sirens started blaring down the street and cops were yelling. It was crazy."

The police came first?

"Who called it in?" I asked.

The guy shrugged. "Someone probably found a body then ran out. All I know is it was chaos."

"Crazy," I said to the guy.

There was something off about the order of events. An entire station of dead people, which had to be about a hundred people at most, would have resulted in chaos and panic. I would have thought a pedestrian would have sounded the alarm which would have caused a crowd of people to fill the place. The account sounded fishy. The guy might be leaving out details. Or maybe Obscura called the police to make a point. Either way, I would know for myself. I started down 7th and joined the crush when someone grabbed the back of my jacket and yanked me into a darkened alcove.

I struck out in panic.

My assailant punched me in the stomach then shoved me back. I wheezed as the muttered curse of, "Damn it, Drew. You can't use my moves against me. I told you that," stopped me in my tracks.

I froze in the middle of my second swing. "Tonya?"

A cell phone's LED glow lit up in the alcove briefly enough for me to see an angry Tonya with a split lip.

"Yeah, and I'm regretting showing you any self-defense."

I yanked her to me in a relief that I hadn't realized was so strong. She tensed in my arms, then relaxed and returned the embrace. After a few breaths, she shoved me away.

"Don't go falling in love or anything. We tried that once," she said.

The pang of regret at hurting her echoed in her voice. We were compatriots. She was good in bed, but we didn't fit in each other's lives as more. I struggled with the level of intimacy we managed to salvage, but my isolation from everyone not part of Camera kept me from pushing her away entirely. "We both know love is a distraction."

She sighed. "It is, but so worth it. I look forward to the day you find it and hope you're smart enough to keep it this time."

The censure stung, but I allowed it. I let things get too far between us, and while I couldn't quite let her be, I wasn't willing to go the distance. "Considering you're my only friend, you'll be the first to know."

"I'm a friend now? Not a colleague or an associate? I've moved up."

Her tone was light-hearted. She was as close a friend as I would get. I cared whether she lived or died. "Tonight made me rethink certain things."

"It did, did it?" She grasped my arm then felt her way down to my hand. "Veritas. Tell me the truth. Did you have anything to do with the attack? Are you in league with them?"

A dull ache at her suspicion pained me more than I thought. In her place, I would have asked the same. I still did have to ask, but I didn't expect her accusation to hurt. I placed my hand on top of hers. It wasn't necessary for the spell, but I didn't want her running away. "Not to my knowledge. I am not colluding with Obscura. I want to destroy the organization."

She gasped then pressed closer to me. "That last part is a lie."

I ground my teeth. The truth spell was inconvenient at times. "Obscura has its purposes if guided by justice, but my main focus is on the Grand Magister. Now you. Veritas."

"I'm not colluding with Obscura," she said as I listened for honesty, a ringing sound in my ears at her statement. "I went out to get pizza and to see if you arrived when the attack happened. I found everyone and called the police."

All truth. So she called the police. That puzzle was solved. "Why were you waiting for me?"

She yanked her hands away. I held firm. "My reasons are private but not nefarious."

I heard the ring of truth in her words, so I released her. There was no point in pressing further. It would only create an awkward situation. Given that we were the remaining members of our cell, I couldn't afford it. "Did anyone else survive?"

"No."

There was anger, at least in her voice. I imagine that she balled her fists, ready to punch something with a cold brown-eyed rage.

"Did Obscura get any of the items back?"

"Everything but what I held and what you took," she answered. "Mitchell wanted to wait until you arrived before cataloging everything in case there was an obvious significance once it was together."

That sounded like him. He had a theory that Obscura planned something massive that would put them in a better political position. It was the other objective of our mission. "At least we have that."

"You sound like you have a plan. Tell me you have one. I'm too freaked out to do anything but attack."

Tonya knew me better than I realized.

"I do. We go dark and study what we have. Our cell leader is dead, so we're cut off until we can contact the others. And I don't know if you realize this, but I don't trust easily."

"No," she drawled. The sarcasm dripped from her voice. "I would have never thought that after knowing you for three years. Surprise. Surprise. Surprise."

"No need to be hateful."

"Sorry. I'm just angry and relieved."

"It's been a long night. Come on. I have a rental. It's three hours back to my house, and we need to get a barrier up around the artifacts before they figure out what's missing and scry for it."

"You don't think that they are tracking us already?"

I grabbed her hand, or at least where I thought it was. Jackpot. Her fingers clasped around mine. "I think they were searching for concentrations of magic. Obscura probably followed the group summoning. Otherwise, they would have found you and me."

We stepped out of the alcove. "A coven of class A witches and wizards is going to leave a bright trail."

"Damn, you're right. We should have driven back like you did. Mitchell should have listened to you."

I wish he did too. "I came across paranoid, which I am. There was no way to know for sure that Obscura would think of tracking us by following spell trails."

"It was still stupid. We underestimated them, and now everyone's gone."

Welcome to my world. "It's not over. We'll make them pay for it with interest."

She squeezed my hand. "Now that's an idea I can get behind."

I wasn't ready to let her go just yet. She was my last ally. "Good, because I need your help."

4

andora

50 A.Q.

I checked the rearview mirror for the umpteenth time in three hours. No pursuit. I thought for sure I'd have to dodge the bounty hunters even though I destroyed their bikes at *One-Eye*. Obscura must be running out of quality henchmen to do their dirty work. They were either second-rate hunters, and I missed something, or I would soon walk into a trap.

I preferred to think they were incompetent. However, I would remain on guard just in case. The idea that Obscura hired guns and came up with new tactics to catch me didn't sit well. I couldn't go back with them.

I wouldn't go back.

They would have to find another means to take over the world without involving my power. The same went for their enemy, Camera. It was their war, and they brought the rest of us into it. I had no desire to be caged by one group and used by the other. But first, I had to find shelter from pursuers and the slavers operating in the lawless zone.

The two hundred-mile stretches of land were nothing but grassland with the occasional copse of trees and crumbling buildings as far as the eye could see. It used to be the Richmond and DC metro areas where the vast majority of the government officials lived for months out of the year. This is where it all started—where it went wrong for me and everyone else.

Greed and politics changed the world from a reasonably safe place to the scene of a post-apocalyptic movie, including the dregs of society. They stretched their primitive muscles while claiming whatever and whoever they could take, and there were no peace offerings to stop them.

What's worse is I remembered how it used to be. Nearly everyone lived in a city or town. Open violence in the streets was rare, no slavers rounding up anyone who couldn't defend themselves. I even went to school with other children for a few years, learning about current events. Witches and Wizards were in the news. People witnessing the next evolution of humankind were mostly amazed, but there were a few asshats that feared magic users. Despite all the good that came from magic, some bigots wanted to leash all that practiced the craft.

That was when lawmakers put The Witchcraft Act into place.

And it went to hell in a handbasket.

I spotted a group of structures in the distance. Glancing at the sun —it was in the western portion of the sky—I had three hours of daylight at most. I'd head to the buildings to scope it out. There was no telling when I'd reencounter shelter or if a squatter occupied the area.

Upon close inspection, the buildings were the remnants of shops and homes. The brick shopping center was partially intact. The central portion still stood with a crumbling wall on the side and weeds growing up the sidewalk while the stores that once were attached were destroyed or had skeleton structures.

The busted-out windows were a sign that scavengers already looted the building. I doubted anything was left to scavenge, or animals and the elements ruined the contents the looters left. It appeared abandoned. There were no scurrying movements as occupants tried to hide. I didn't even sense someone watching me.

I may have landed on a shelter gold mine, but I wanted to investigate further. The corpse of a strip mall was perfect for hiding but challenging to escape. My recent scuffle at the *One-eyed Lion* reminded me to keep my options open.

I steered the bike around the back of the strip mall. The rank stench of death and decomposing bodies greeted me. Grateful that I had enough magic for active powers, I backed out of the strip mall alley. None of the corpses appeared new, but that could mean anything from no new victims to this was just a dumping ground. Either way, the shopping center was out.

I should have known.

I continued to the dilapidated and destroyed homes near the shopping center when I sensed a familiar presence of magic in the air. My heart raced, and I glanced about wildly. No one should detect or hear me with my cloaking spell in place.

It didn't feel like magic that Obscura tended to wield. The magic wasn't dark, nor did it seem alive. Magic generated from a person pulsed like a heartbeat. This was just there.

A magical item, perhaps—one I could use to recharge my magic for an emergency. *Especially if I was going to be shelterless.*

At least there would be one plus to my survey of the broken neighborhood. The homes would not provide safety for the night. None of them had four walls. It would be too easy to spot me while I slept and I would be exposed to the elements. I might as well find the magic source, recharge, then see if I could find a place to camp.

Moments later, the magical trail led me to a structure just outside the broken neighborhood. It was more like a pile of rubble with two partial walls forming a corner and a fireplace. There weren't many homes with fireplaces when I was a kid. This house—the neighborhood must have been a rich one, like those self-contained little cities where everything was right there—no need to leave when everything was at their fingertips.

We went from mostly spoiled to mostly destitute in 15 years. Only life in Obscura occupied zones hasn't changed.

And living there cost a hefty price.

I turned off the bike and pushed it around the rubble as best I could. My spell wouldn't shield it without my contact at my current strength. Leaving it unattended while I investigated would signal my presence, and someone would steal it. There was another in the neighborhood with me. My survival instincts warned me of that. I didn't sense the predator's gaze amongst the vinyl siding and bricks, but then again, they could not see me.

Someone stacked those bodies, and it may have been a killer. I could handle myself in a fight, magical or not, but battles drew attention.

I wanted boring.

There was a small railing partially buried under rubble at the back of the house. The magic came from underneath the stone, dirt, metal, and—was that a bathtub?

It must be a basement. Hopefully, an intact one that I could hide in for the night. I had two choices. Move on within an hour and hope I find something or wait until nightfall to lift the trash, then take my chances in an unknown basement. It was an epic win or an epic fail—no real in between.

Then there was the magic. It could be the game-changer. I fiddled with one of the feathers in my headdress as I considered. With magic in my arsenal, I could put more distance between Obscura and me and maybe even get to other Obscura-unfriendly countries like Texas or California.

I would go for the basement. It had possibilities. My other option just had danger and unknown. Nothing beats a failure but a try and all that jazz. I took a deep breath then sat on my bike to wait.

Waiting for the sun to sink in the western sky was worse than watching paint dry. Nothing happened as the sky went from azure blue to amber to purple. Not anything interesting anyway. Flies accosted me from time to time. A rabbit hopped through the clearing near me before scurrying off someplace else to become dinner for whoever hid in one of the homes. Perhaps they located a basement free of clutter to hide in during the day. My possible neighbor would have the hunt at some point. The night would provide some protection from anyone who wanted to harm them.

I groaned aloud, then clamped my hand over my fool mouth.

What was I doing?

My life was on the line, and I behaved like a bored privileged teenager. Those days were over. Not just for me but most of the world —and it was my fault.

Pain welled in my chest at the reminder that Obscura was a real threat. I couldn't let Matt Wesley get his hands on me again, or the world may not recover.

A wolf or coyote howled in the distance. It was officially night. I focused on the dark area in front of me. It was showtime. "Light as a feather. Let me pass then once I'm gone, drift slowly to the grass."

My heart raced as dark shadows of debris rose into the air. The spell winded me. I wouldn't be able to hold it long after hiding myself most of the day. The gambit better pay off.

There was enough moonlight to see several stairs, not the few I imagined, leading to the basement once the way was clear.

Great.

I couldn't leave the bike, and it was too heavy for me to get down so many stairs and open a locked door. It looked like I would have to use another spell. "Light as a feather. Lift into the air while I move down the stair."

My bike hovered a foot over the ground. A gentle push moved it with ease. The spell was not my finest work, but it did the job.

Sweat erupted on my brow. I held on to the railing for a moment while the world stopped spinning. My magic energy was the lowest I'd experienced. I wasn't sure I could do another spell.

Pull it together, Pan.

I rushed down the stairs to a heavy wooden door. I panted from the magic exertion. Just a little longer, and I would be inside.

I tested the door. It was locked, no surprise there. I took out my lock picks then set to work on the door. A fine sweat coated my fingers. The pick nearly slipped from my hand, but I managed to earn the click of success from the doors tumblers. I readied my sword and a mini flashlight, then burst into the room.

The empty room.

For once, things were looking up. I pushed the bike inside then shut the door.

Finally, I made it.

I rested against the only thing between an outside intruder and me. Not that it mattered anyway because I was too tired from my simulcast to fight. I just needed a few moments before the next crisis could start.

My racing heart slowed as both spells released. That was when I discovered I wasn't out of the woods yet. There was another set of stairs across the room. I had to secure it if I was going to stay the night or possibly use it as another means of escape.

I managed to drag myself across the room and up a short flight of stairs to turn the knob. The door didn't budge. I put my weight against it—an annoying *creak* was my reward. With it unable to open, circumstances would trap me in the basement. On the other hand, no one without magic or a bulldozer could get to me.

I shined the light around the room. There were two windows the size of two paperback books. Both were painted over with black paint. My flashlight would not draw attention, but I would be in total darkness, even during the day. A light switch caught my eye. I considered it for a second, then gave it a shot and flipped the circuit. Bright incandescent lights flooded the room. For several moments, I fumbled while my eyes adjusted. I wiped at them to clear the mist from them.

I hit the jackpot.

Not only did the electricity still work, but the basement was a shelter equipped with several shelves of canned food, MREs, a hot plate, sink, toilet, and a whole host of other comforts and essentials. Everything was dusty but otherwise perfectly preserved. There was even a cot in the corner. I could stay for several days while the bounty hunters grew frustrated and gave up for more accessible pursuits.

I tried the spigot. Dirty water and minerals poured out of the faucet. I left it running while I checked the toilet. I flushed it. The bowl emptied and refilled. I turned to the sink. The water was no longer brown but clear. I still wouldn't trust it without boiling it first.

But this would do.

With the critical survival information solved, I focused on what drew me to the oasis in the lawless zone. I moved to the stairs. Underneath was an alcove of drawers. The first was full of potions that I would examine later. The next one held magical implements for spells and scrying. I picked up a pink crystal. Energy flowed through me with intoxicating dizziness that brought me to my knees. The crystal fell from my hand. Its luster diminished.

I glanced at the tattoo of air current on my wrist. It was less than half colored in. My magical energy was back where I liked it—enough to do spells and use active magic without the danger of transformation. I kicked the crystal away from me with my foot. It was better that I examine the rest of the items visually for a while. I didn't want to overfeed my oya power with magic. Obscura would find me for sure if that happened.

I opened the last drawer. It was more crystals and magic tools along with a thick book. Considering the previous owner was a practitioner with the foresight to prepare an apocalyptic shelter, I guessed it was their spell diary. Hopefully, it gave some insight into a meticulous person that readied for a cataclysm as though it were second nature.

With the book in my hand, I removed my headdress then settled on to the cot. The sneezing fit caused me to pull back the blanket before I laid down again. I opened the book. The name Quyen Duong stared up at me in neat, meticulous handwriting.

I liked my benefactor even more.

Then I turned to the first entry and allowed the writer to clue me into their life.

5

 uyen

Present Day

I ran my hands through my hair and sat on the side of the bed. Tonya slept soundly behind me. I watched her sleep for a few breaths. Then guilt spurred me on to the spell room in my basement. With the Witchcraft Act hanging over practitioners' heads in the U.S., it was a matter of preservation for anyone with a modicum of talent to hide their circles, potions, and spell diaries. The stigma in recent years regarding magic dried the well of curious dabblers. The harassment wasn't worth it, especially if a person previously went untargeted by some sort of majority. So I hid my abilities, as did everyone that I knew with magic.

I grabbed my journal and the tome I took from Obscura. Within my basement, the book and the other items were warded from detection. My cloaking spells were good. There was no way in hell they would find it. And it would be likely weeks before they realized—if they even did—that the book was stolen and not destroyed.

Opening my diary, I saw the entry from two days ago. I still had to chronicle last night. The loss of our cell drove Tonya and me to seek comfort in each other's arms. As usual, it left my body sated, and my heart wracked with guilt. I was no saint. Good sex was good sex.

Sex with a friend that carried a torch, however, was just wrong. It was an asshole thing to do, but I didn't want to alienate her with rejection. And again, the sex was good.

Tonya was perfect. She had all the attributes that got me worked up. Soft brown skin, jovial almond-shaped eyes, a firm ass, and breasts that fit my hands just right. I had a type. I wasn't embarrassed to admit it. Teasing and denial in high school toughened me. I finessed my game in college and enjoyed the companionship my tastes craved at a Historically Black College.

I should love Tonya. We shared so much in common, but I didn't. I cared for her as a friend and sometimes lover. Nothing more. She deserved better, but as long as I kept giving in to her alluring body, she would hold on to hope. I saw it in her eyes when she trembled in my arms. It was almost enough to give me whiskey dick, but I soldiered on for the both of us.

"You got to do better, Quyen, or you'll lose her as a friend." I wrote in my journal.

"Tell that to little Quyen. he doesn't want to give up somewhat regular—"

Creaks in the floorboards upstairs signaled that Tonya was awake. It would not be long before she joined me downstairs. I put my journal away then focused on the Obscura tome.

The book appeared to be a hundred or so years old. It was leather-bound and treated with some kind of light oil, probably to keep the leather from cracking. On the front cover, there were three swirls enclosed in an intricate circle. At least thirty points along the circle's circumference were linked across the other side to create a pattern similar to a spirograph. The three swirls reminded me of the symbol for wind. It must be some sort of wind summoning circle.

Or a wind creature?

The markings were too intricate for a simple storm. A hurricane, perhaps? It begged the question, why would Obscura want to control the weather? That kind of magic was volatile and required balance to handle it properly. Just changing the direction of the wind too long could create a desert in one area and a swamp in the other.

"You started without me." Tonya padded down the stairs in her bare feet and one of my shirts. She leaned in as though she were about to kiss me but opted for speaking loudly in my ear, "Stop being weird."

I flinched then shoved the book towards her. "You're the weird one. Look at this and tell me what you see. "

She caressed the tooled leather cover with a light touch of her fingers. "A transmutation circle? Is this alchemy in origin?"

I shook my head. "All of the points are on the outside of the circle. This reminds me of a summoning circle that I once saw with Ma—someone else. We were in South Africa on a trip to learn nature magic from a holy man."

"You'll have to tell me about that sometime." She opened the book. "This symbol looks like wind currents. I guess Obscura wanted to summon a wind god."

"Or they were just using it as a reference," I said, looking over her shoulder.

Tonya delicately flipped through several pages of the book. "This looks like a complex summoning, and the entire thing is devoted to it. Oya? I'm unfamiliar with that term. It would be too much to hope for an internet search. "

"That's the last thing we could do." I took the book and turned a few pages. "Between the government and Obscura, we would sign a death sentence looking up occult terms on the internet. "

"We need to invent a magic net or something." Tonya narrowed her eyes. "You don't think that act will actually pass, do you?"

I thought back to the woman on the street in Richmond. "Salem Witch Trials, the Holocaust, Slavery, and the Japanese internment camps. Need I say more?"

She shivered. "Point made. Fear makes the sheeple run and do stupid things."

I nodded. "I look at it this way. If someone had a gun and I didn't,

I might be nervous. Especially if they waved it around in my face knowing full well that they could kill me if they wanted to. Think of all the bigots out there that know they have it coming because they terrorized a practitioner before they came into their powers."

"Yeah, and we're people too. We can be corrupted. Here's looking at you, Obscura."

Exactly. A well-intentioned organization that turned to shit in an instant. "Which is why Camera exists. "

"And we will protect everyone and avenge our cell." She punched her hand in her fist.

"But first, we need to make heads or tails of the information we took. Well, what we have left. "

She moved from the desk and grabbed our bags. Gingerly dumping them out onto the table, we examined the rest of our collection: a collar or choker of iron with runes etched into the side, another tome, a rose quartz orb imbued with magic. Then there were pictures from some scrolls that I took before we incinerated them.

"Someone did a little extra shopping." She shoulder bumped me.

"It was an opportunity that I couldn't pass up."

"Let's just hope it gives us an edge in the war."

"Hear. Hear." I muttered, sifting through the items.

Tonya picked up the choker. "This doesn't look special. Someone into Nordic BDSM, maybe?"

I snorted. "I'm sure leather would work just fine, but the other parts would rust when the person sweats."

"And how would you know?" She lowered her eyelids as though she wanted another round of hot sex with me.

I focused on the Oya book and steered clear of any innuendos. "I think the plan of attack should be divide and conquer. I'll research this Oya summoning ritual to see what it is, and you can dive into the other book. Then we can compare notes."

"Sounds like a plan." She plucked her book off the desk then settled onto the cot I kept in the corner in case I pulled an all-nighter.

I began to pore over the details. The author wrote the book in Latin and what appeared like ancient Egyptian. Latin reference books I had, hieroglyphics I did not. I would have to go out and purchase one.

Translating the ritual would be painful, but my gut instinct told me that the Oya book was the key to Matt's plans. It may be a crapshoot, but my instincts were rarely wrong. Obscura and I wouldn't be enemies if I had listened to them, and my reputation would still be intact. Besides, calling up an ancient god to do his bidding sounded like the type of hubris Matt enjoyed.

He always pushed the line. Whether it be ethics or deeds, he wasn't afraid to get in over his head. There were many times I cleared his messes. Hell, I still cleaned up after him through Camera. "It looks like I'm going to need to take a trip to Bibliotheque for a reference book."

"Discovered another magic language besides Latin?" She teased.

"Well, this book sure as hell wasn't written in English or Vietnamese, the other two languages I know." Tonya grinned at me. "Do you need anything?"

"I could go for some breakfast." She glanced at her watch. "Make that early dinner. We had a longer night than I realized. "

My face heated. "Yeah, the drive was a long one. "

Tonya gave me a long look, then sighed. "How long are we going to do this dance, Drew?"

"Until one of us finds someone." I wasn't a cheater, and I wouldn't lie to her. There was no point.

"Okay." She stood. "How about this? We call the friends with benefits thing quits since we're both all up in our feelings about it."

I wasn't a fan of the finality of her tone. It was as though she were cutting off more than just the sex. Little Quyen hated that plan, but I knew it was best for the both of us. "Stay in the guest room, and if we get through this alive and single, then we try again."

She crossed her arms. "That sounds like a failed plan. What are you doing watching romance channels? Either we are in or out. Our friendship is too valuable to play games with each other."

She hit me with the ultimatum—the one thing I didn't want. Do or Die. If I said the wrong thing, I would lose her, but if I lied, I'd have good sex then lose her anyway. My gut instinct told me no. Little Quyen said yes. "Tonya, you deserve better."

She rolled her eyes. "You're right I do. I've been thinking about this for a while."

I held out my hand. "Friends?"

Tonya stared at my hand, then at me.

"After we shower," she said, then grabbed my arm to lead me upstairs for the last time.

6

 andora

50 A.Q.

"He found the summoning for Oya?" I wondered out loud as I sat up in the cot. For the past few hours, Quyen Duong riveted me with his exploits. He founded Obscura with Matt. Then the grand magister ousted him over philosophical differences. Quyen's entire family and the organization turned on him then he joined Camera—another poor choice. He was in the asshole lottery and constantly won.

No wonder he isolated himself. Not entirely. He let Tonya into his complicated life. I stared at the date at the top of the journal. Fifty years ago, they lived a comfortable life in a home that would become a crater. His paranoia for protecting his magic, along with the diary, was all that remained.

Oya. It had to be the same as my oya magic, or at least related. It was fate. Quyen may have the answer to Obscura's downfall. I could learn from him and succeed where he failed or finish what he started. He and Matt were around the same age, I assumed.

Witches and wizards could live hundreds of years, depending on how powerful they were. Matt could be anywhere from eighty to one hundred and fifty, given his appearance and movement. The grand magister may fool the eyes, but he could not deceive the senses all the time. And I knew him more than I wished to. His movements were still of a man in his prime. I shivered. I could relate to Quyen being with someone he shouldn't be with and stuck in a cycle. Our paths were somewhat similar in that regard.

In my time, a magical creature, dubbed the Sphinx, destroyed the Mid-Atlantic and later, by cause and effect, the rest of the East Coast. Thousands of people were killed, injured, or displaced during the attack. The old US never recovered, and the UNO was born. We just didn't know it at the time. That was the day I lost everything.

I should have listened to my dad.

My father hated magic. I thought it was great that humans were evolving, and I would witness it, which is why I became an ally, not knowing I was a witch. He and I fought a lot the weeks before the Anti Witchcraft Act Rally. He grounded me. I went anyway.

Of course, my parents found out and tried to drag me back home when someone started shooting. All I remembered was running, screaming, chaos, burning pain, then darkness. That was when the attack happened and the Sphinx ruined everyone's lives. It was the last time I saw my parents.

Camera captured me when the debris settled. I woke up in their dungeon, jail, or whatever it was, naked with a pile of clothes beside me. Like any other sane person, I freaked out. The fact that I was a teenager didn't seem to matter. Someone tased me then my experience there became a blur—snatches of memories throughout my imprisonment, nothing solid except the faces of those who interacted with me.

One day a new face came to see me. He had short dark blond hair and gray eyes that seemed to bore into the soul. The first time I laid eyes on Matt Wesley, he appeared every inch the avenging angel come to rescue the princess from the tower. It was natural that I left with him and joined Obscura—stayed with Obscura. He never asked me to join the organization. Matt offered me freedom and help with mastering my powers.

We grew close. He tutored me in spell casting and the use of my active power—my oya. I learned that I could absorb magic from an item or attack. Once it was mine, the ability aimed at me went into my magical memory. As long as I had the energy, I could reproduce it. The first drawback—my second issue—my power made it difficult to replenish my magic energy. I couldn't rest and rejuvenate as other practitioners did. It took months for it to come back, so I had to take it. I was a magic vampire of sorts.

The other drawback and my major issue—if I took too much, I would transform into the Sphinx. As that creature, I was a rage incarnate. I destroyed everything around me until I ran out of magic. The Sphinx controlled wind magic, so an appearance disrupted the weather and brought about storms days to weeks after the attack. Any place I ran loose never ecologically recovered and later became a lawless zone.

Matt comforted me each time it happened. He said all the right words for me not to blame myself and train harder to gain discipline. Then one day, he kissed me. I was of age by that time, but I thought that romance was off the table for a freak like me, so I gave myself to him. And I was happy until I found out that my life with him was all a ploy. He planned my "uncontrolled" transformations.

While I learned my powers, he studied them as well. Matt knew how to manipulate an event or a training exercise into a horror show so that Obscura could sweep in and save the day, then take control. And I was his dog to eliminate any who opposed him. He didn't even—

Let it go, girl. Matt is no good for you. Even if he did love you, he wouldn't give up his power and prestige. And he'd use you in a heartbeat to protect it.

The weight of the lives that I destroyed with my oya already weighed on me. My only consolation was that I had been an unwilling participant. Being with Matt meant owning it as a choice and sacrificing my soul. That was too much.

"You and me, Quyen. You and me. We both suck at love." I sighed then turned back to the journal. It was extraordinary how much romance complicated matters. He wanted Tonya, but the emotional connection wasn't there.

Men are impossible. No matter the age.

I glossed over the part about their shower sex that left him rethinking the friends with benefits. I almost lost respect for him until I saw he followed through with not sleeping with Tonya the next night. She ended up staying in the guest room, like they discussed, while they worked on translating the tomes.

He lives up to his word, my kind of guy.

A part of me wanted to skip ahead to see if they got together. The two were the classic boy who doesn't appreciate the girl till he almost loses her trope. Except in real life, the girl and boy end up with other people or alone. The romantic in me wanted to see someone that was willing to change win.

I glanced around the basement wishing the rest of the house was intact. It was Quyen's personal space. He could have found love, and it wasn't evident by the magical man cave, but the cot in the corner wasn't quite big enough for two. Quyen must have ended up alone.

Just like I would.

Anyone I grew close to would be a fugitive. This assumed that Obscura or even Camera never found me or attacked me with magic. If they located me, I could accidentally kill someone close to me or by proxy when attacked. No one would chance that. No one could, except Matt.

Quyen and I were the perfect couple based upon our luck at love. He didn't exist anymore. I couldn't hurt him. The ideal relationship, friend or otherwise, was a ghost from fifty years ago—a literal book boyfriend—the irony.

Get a grip. You're supposed to be researching.

Self-chastised, I continued reading about Quyen and Tonya's findings. Quyen's book contained the legend of Oya, an African wind goddess and one of the Orisha. An Egyptian wizard captured her essence in a canopic jar after seducing her from her husband, Shango. Apparently, they had a tumultuous relationship, and the wizard took advantage. It was his attempt at overthrowing the pharaoh that went bad. The account was from his notes, the only thing to survive what happened when he tried to transfer all of Oya's power to himself. Oya never manifested as a goddess again. It's thought that her essence was still in the astral plane in an energy state, and the ritual would instill it into the proper vessel.

Wait. That can't be.

I set the journal down. The proper vessel. I didn't recall any rituals, but it made sense right down to the name. Matt named my ability and I didn't question it.

And the bummers keep coming.

The summoning must have happened when I was a baby. Then how did I end up with my mom and dad? My parents adopted me as an infant. There were even pictures and videos of the day they brought me home.

They were ordinary people with no magic. They actually didn't trust it. My father would rant about how witches would turn the world into hell on earth while wizards enslaved us all. It was uncomfortable whenever he got like that. I loved my dad, but he was a bigot. I disagreed with it, but I was too young to express it at first. I remained quiet while doing my research and forming my own opinion until I was ready to confront him.

I couldn't see my father adopting me if he knew I was a witch. My mother maybe, but not my daddy. I wondered how I ended up in their care. Perhaps Quyen could unravel some of the mystery, and I could destroy the possibility of another witch getting Oya's powers after me. I owed the world that.

7

$\mathcal{M}$att

50 A.Q.

I tapped the arm of my chair as James droned on with endless excuses about Pandora's escape from his trap in the lawless zone. With each moment that passed, his argument went from factual to ad hominem.

The bounty hunters were inept.

We should have used magic to capture her or at least Obscura agents since they are more capable.

Anyone who worked for me was Obscura, so the point was moot. Throughout his explanations, I said nothing. At some point, his speech grew less sure, he stuttered, and he sweated.

His mounting nerves as he tried to read my mood grated on mine. I purposely remained stoic to gauge his ability to report bad news under pressure. It was evident that his attempt failed when he walked into my office without her. Then I had to endure *his* excuses when I could have been convincing *her* to stay with me—a much more satisfying prospect.

"Grand Magister, please don't leave me hanging," He stood straight as if ready for a lash or strike.

In my petulant days, I might have been so petty. Having Pandora by my side tempered that side of me. I didn't want her seeing me in that light or have evidence of it. Besides, the fear of possibility worked far better than actually performing the act. My people knew what she meant to me. They were much more engaged to bring her back than they would ever have been if I doled out threats.

The fact that they failed me just proved her competence. I did train her after all. They were pretty much battling a less experienced version of me. I couldn't blame them for certain setbacks. If anything, the tactical diversion made me want her more. Her mind as well as her power were the reasons she suited me. Drew was the only other to come close, except he wasn't my type, and he disappointed me.

I thought he would come back to Obscura up until the end. But he fought. Obscura had been our brainchild, but I took it further than he ever could. Drew lacked the inclination to go the distance. I ruled most of the Earth. The parts that I didn't have under my control still feared me. There were no more talks of enslaving or persecuting practitioners of magic. We were not tools for the mundane. We were the future of humankind. I was the father, and she would be the mother to my dynasty.

"Grand Magister?" James wilted under my gaze.

"I'm not angry," I answered. "I trained her. Perhaps it was too much to ask to assign someone else to the task. She is mine, after all. I should be the one to pursue her. It's more romantic that way, I suppose."

He wrung his hands. "Women do appreciate out of sight stuff. It's where it's at."

"True." It was settled. I would hunt Pandora myself. I could use the challenge. "As for the future of your subordinates—"

He flinched then stood at attention. His dark eyes were flat.

"Add this experience to lessons learned in training. We could still use the strategy of handling my wayward bride to finish off the remnants of Camera if employed correctly. See to it."

James nodded his head vigorously. "Right away, Grand Magister."

He saluted me then left my office.

Once he was gone, I slipped my sketchbook from the drawer of my desk—a constant source of comfort through the years when I needed to clear my head. I flipped to my favorite image of Pandora.

When I first started drawing her, she was a figment of my imagination, my literal dream girl of the last fifty years. Then fifteen years ago I saw her for myself when I went to recapture the witch that possessed Oya's powers from Camera. Her eyes were the same. The rest of her held the promise of a beautiful woman. I only had to wait a few years to meet the nymph that plagued my dreams officially. What's more, I had a hand in her becoming the perfect mate. It was destiny.

She was also a distraction. Even though my plans came to fruition via alternative means, I was still behind with my progress on the timeless spell. Through it, I planned to change the fate of the world and gain intelligence from my enemies.

The Oya project was an experiment that one of my assistants pushed. Lauren was a historian of African magic, which I dabbled in from time to time. I prefer North American but was well aware of the benefits of other cultures' ideas. I didn't see the power of the goddess being my primary strategy the way Lauren suggested. Deities were tricky at best of times and females more so.

However, Lauren often produced results, so I let her have her pet project. I failed to see the harm. It was during her failed ritual—so I thought—that the dreams began. I thought nothing of them at first other than a base need for companionship. Then Pandora stole my focus while awake. The only way to establish discipline was to draw her when I had a dream then continue on my plans for Timeless and Obscura. Not once did I realize she was my means.

"Are you thinking about her again?"

Putting my book away, I met the wizened gaze of my oldest assistant. A non-practitioner, she appeared every bit of the eighty years she lived with her graying hair and smooth brown skin. She pushed up her glasses then gingerly sat down in the chair in front of my desk. Her cane rested against the arm for accessibility.

"Always." I leaned back. "Is there something you have come to share?"

"No. Can't an old woman visit her leader?" she asked. "I've served you for over fifty years. "

"And with potions, you could serve more," I replied.

I may not have finalized Timeless, but I made other strides in longevity and turning back the body's clock for a short amount of time. My life extension potion could benefit her.

"Your potion is out of sight but temporary. I saw the data trial notes too. At best, it would extend my life thirty years if I managed the headaches. Your best test subject, Ray lived to be one hundred and ten years old, then dropped dead looking like a twenty-year-old corpse. No, thank you. I earned my old lady title. I plan to exploit it." She laughed. "Besides, I look old enough to be your grandmother. We could use that against some of your political enemies."

Old or not, she was still better than most of my assistants, including the practitioners. Her outlook on magical problems as a mundane gave her an edge, which the others could not successfully duplicate.

"We're the same age," I replied dryly.

"And you're still in your prime as a wizard," she said. "You better be if you plan to keep up with that young girl and keep her happy. "

"That young girl is a grown woman. Her name is Pandora." I was more than capable of taking care of Pandora's needs, be they intellectual or physical.

"I meant no offense, Grand Magister, I was just giving you the low down. Don't listen to me. It's the jealous blabbering of an old friend who wants her younger friend to hurry up and get the girl before I pass on."

I snorted. "Sounds more like a mother."

"I'm the only one brave enough to say anything. It comes with seniority." She cleared her throat. "Just promise me that if she rejects you, you'll move on."

"She won't reject me. The world is scared of her, and I understand her. There was no one else for either of us." It was as simple as that.

Lauren sighed. "Another time then. While I was reviewing the video surveillance of the *One-Eyed Lion* mission, I noticed that when she was shot, she didn't heal quickly. Her magic energy is dangerously low. As a strategy, I suggest pressuring her with overwhelming numbers. I'm working on a wind cage that doesn't use magic but can still contain her since she is less adept at disabling the mechanics."

Someone with a solution. "I could kiss you."

"And give me a heart attack," she quipped. "Henry has been gone for five years. The excitement would be too much. "

She did it again. "Why do you remind me of your mundane nature?"

"Because one day I will be gone, and you need to understand that."

I growled. "I order you to take the potion."

She shook her head. "I know you too well. We both know that if you force me, that will affect my work, and results mean more to you than enforcing a small matter like my aging."

Damn it, woman.

"I will personally see to Pandora's return to my side."

Lauren grinned.

"So the seduction begins." She reached for her cane then stood with creaky knees. "I look forward to your victory, Grand Magister."

Then she left me to my plans.

8

 uyen

Present Day

I pinched the bridge of my nose and squeezed my eyes shut as the symbols swirled on the page. The eye fatigue coupled with the stabbing behind the eyes signaled a need for a break.

"I know that look." She joined me at the desk then pushed the book from my grasp. "Take a break. "

"You know we don't have time. Obscura is up to something. I feel it and—"

"You and I are two people. Unless you want to bring in another Camera cell into this, which, to be honest, we should, we are in way over our heads."

"We're not bringing in another cell." I leaned back in my chair.

"Yes. Yes. No one can be trusted, including me," she replied. "There's such a thing as too paranoid."

I gave her a long look then closed my eyes. There was no such thing with Obscura. We both learned that the hard way. "Do you remember the last time you said that to me?"

She sobered and nodded. "I'm willing to err on the side of caution considering your track record. But real talk, are we getting anywhere by ourselves?"

"Obscura was started by two wizards, and look what it became in a decade. Look at Camera. Until ten years ago, practitioners didn't band together. The mundanes picked us off one by one. Occasionally you'd see a coven but then they were wiped out. Now we're in great enough numbers that the government has taken notice and wants to register us."

Tonya shivered. "So they can do gene studies like that one facility we found in Langley. "

I remembered. The place still gave me nightmares. It was similar to the pictures of German internment camps that I saw in history books. A few of the captives were volunteers looking for a cure for their "demonic ways," and others were kidnapped after exposing their powers to someone untrustworthy. The volunteers made the rescue mission difficult until we promised to bind their abilities–a death sentence in the long run.

Binding magic disrupted who they were. It was tantamount to removing a secondary organ. We warned the volunteers that they would live a half-life.

They didn't care. All they wanted was to go back into their lives, passing as mundane.

The remaining captives became part of Camera or Obscura. Matt rode in on his proverbial white horse toward the end of the Langley Raid, but he made an impression on the vulnerable by taking down the entire wall of a building.

It was easy for them to see that their government betrayed them. The speech about taking the high road after being tortured hadn't gone well with them compared to forming a magical state of their own kind. He had been close enough to strangle with my power, but I couldn't risk petty violence, not when I was outnumbered, and there was a much longer game in play. And neither organization could risk an open fight between us while the government watched. Not with the Witchcraft Act as the new buzzword in the media and anti-magic sentiment on the rise.

I guess it was a good thing that the ones who chose to give up magic weren't able to use it against us.

It was a thought I hated to entertain, but considering the political climate, it was better to eliminate sheep that wanted out of the flock before they became wolves.

"Yeah," I said. "Langley changed things."

She swallowed. "It made you consider if you were doing the right thing, didn't it?"

I sat up in my chair so that I could meet her gaze. "I know I am. It's easy to just say the hell with it. I only care about myself. Or I'm superior because I can manipulate water. But then I remember that most of my family are not practitioners. What does that mean for them? Any political power that I have doesn't extend to them by association. Am I willing to watch Obscura do what I saw mundanes do? The answer is no."

"Leave it to you to make a crisis of faith simple." She leaned against the desk. "Besides, you're right. Obscura killed everyone at the Mt. Vernon train station to get at our cell. I put nothing past them."

"Exactly. Most of the world can't do anything about them, but I can even if at the moment it's just flooding their building."

"Oh, please, you can do better than that. You also have rhyming and theft in your arsenal," she added.

I smirked at her then reached for the tome. Break time was over. The stabbing pain in my eyes eased into a dull ache.

She placed her hand over the book. "What have you found so far?
"

It was a stalling technique I would allow. My head hurt, and technically briefing her was still working. She may even have another point of view that I hadn't considered. A second set of eyes—or in this case ears—could never hurt. "This seems to be part logbook and part manifesto. It starts out as the notes of an Egyptian wizard named Jannes that had an affair with the goddess of the wind, Oya. She wouldn't run away with him and leave her husband, so he stole her power and tried to transfer it to himself. The experiment failed, and someone sealed his notes and the canopic jars away."

"Okay, I don't recall seeing any tiny jars with jackal head tops on them, so we have the notes." She sat up. "Is it too much to hope they said who and how they stopped him?"

If only life were that neat. At least mine wasn't. "Yep, it is. Though I think Jannes failed because Oya's power was too much, and then his followers were too scared of the calamity and just buried everything."

"So Matt Wesley expects to succeed where Jannes failed based on what?" Tonya asked. "He may be the brains behind Obscura, but even he's not *that* good. I don't think we have to worry."

"I've been going through the sticky notes placed inside—"

She cringed. "Someone put adhesive notes in a book that's thousands of years old? And I thought we were bad at handling it with our bare hands."

"To be fair, we are not handling it with our bare hands. We're using a cleansing spell on them and there's a spell on the book." I pointed out.

She glared at me. She opened her mouth—likely to toss out one of her witty retorts, then paused. Her eyes flashed with an excited expression. She grabbed my arm. "A sticky note that uses glue and not magic? "

I saw where her thoughts traveled. "You think the researcher isn't a member of Obscura? Or is it a third-party?"

"A mundane. I don't think they would trust a third party, but it is possible that they could have some non-practitioners in their ranks. There are always sympathizers to any cause."

I knew they had at least one mundane, but I hadn't had the opportunity to drop that intel without explaining how I came by it. I planned to remain low-key in Camera. That kind of information would garner me a second look. Tonya coming by it on her own could be the chance to introduce it without suspicion by supporting her discovery. "It's a distinct possibility, but what does that have to do with anything?"

"Well, it's valuable Intel about the enemy organization, Mr. Cynical, and I have to wonder how important is Oya's summoning ritual if he has a non-magical working on it."

"Point." I hadn't considered that. I knew there was a mundane on Matt's team. I didn't know what her place was in it. He trusted her enough to assist him at least, but exactly how much did he trust her with his main plan? My instinct pointed to the ritual being critical. However, Tonya's theory had validity. And I couldn't see Matt allowing Lauren to steal his thunder. "So what are you suggesting?"

"That we keep an open mind." She walked over to the cot where she had been working the past three weeks. "This book is in reference to astral projection as well as various summoning rituals for demons."

"You think he is going to unleash the horde of demons somewhere?"

She shrugged. "We're looking at the pieces while missing the most important parts. Obscura is up to something. If I were to choose between power enhancement and demon summoning, I would choose the latter. What if Obscura is just trying to destabilize the government by using outsiders? You know, gain trust, then take it over."

The idea sounded up Matt's alley overall, but it lacked his flair for drama and humility. "How does he control the demon? History was littered with hell summonings gone wrong. It's banned for a reason. Working with outsiders just doesn't turn out well. "

"Oh?" She crossed the room then turned back to me. She held the metal and leather choker. "These are containment runes. Not that I want to try it out, but in theory, it should hold a non-human. Wanna bet that they are used for an outsider, or that it might give them carte blanche access to our world while they wear it?"

I backed away from her. Tonya wore a sickly expression that I could resonate with. The idea of fighting Obscura and outsiders. There were too many unknown elements. "So basically, we're nowhere."

"Which is why I think we should consider help despite the danger," she said. "We're making decisions that could affect all of our lives."

I sighed. "I think you have something, but I'm not convinced that the Oya theory is a bust. I'm going to stay dark and see this through.

You can take what you have to Camera. This way, there is brainpower on both tasks."

Tonya wrinkled her nose. She always did that when she thought I was being obstinate.

"What?" I asked.

"Nothing. I just—nothing," she said. "You know I'm going to have to report that you're looking into something to keep the suspicion off of you."

I figured as much.

"But they don't need to know the details until I'm successful or the theory is busted." I reached out to touch her then thought better of it. I remained guilt-free ever since we became "just friends." There was no need to muddy the waters with a display of affection. "Do what you have to. I trust you, and it pains me to admit it."

Tonya hugged me. "Cảm ơn."

There was no need to thank me. It was the truth. Especially since I knew she could not lie to me in this room, nor could I. It was part of the enchantment that I worked into my space to keep it hidden. No lies or deception could take place within the four walls. I didn't mention it to her, but then she never gave me a reason to do so. "You're welcome."

"You know I'll keep you informed of what's going on as much as I can, right?"

"I prefer it that way." She was my friend, after all. "So you'll leave for Woodbridge in the morning then?"

"Probably. I could transport the other books with the bags you spelled. After that, I will be at the tender mercies of the NoVa cell. I'm sure Bane would love that. He's been hounding me to join up for the past few weeks."

He contacted me too, but I wasn't interested. Bane reminded me too much of Matt except without the talent and half the charisma. He was too small-time to cause trouble, but I'd rather have someone trusted next to him so I could remain under Obscura's radar.

"He knows talent when he sees it." The Northern Virginia cell was aloof—as most Camera cells were—but they were talented. They'd have to be to remain so close to DC and under both the government and Obscura's radar. "You'll be fine. You're Southside cell. Just don't give up too many secrets. We want to have some leverage to encourage membership when we rebuild."

She pointed at me in a gesture of regard. "You know that's right."

"I do."

We laughed and lapsed into an awkward silence. If this were the last night, we would talk freely. Then I didn't mind taking a break. My research wasn't going anywhere pertinent at the moment. The history of the goddess and her wizard lover wouldn't solve the riddle of Matt's mind yet.

It was entirely plausible that I was on a wild goose chase, and Obscura planned to do precisely what Tonya suggested. Or worse, neither theory was correct. That would be my luck. However, the hinky feeling in the pit of my stomach drew me back to Oya. I would see it through.

"Hey, let's call it quits for the night. We can grab something to eat, then chill since you're leaving in the morning."

"I'd like that," she said.

Then we headed upstairs to get ready. Hopefully, it was not for the last time.

9

andora

50 A.Q.

I closed Quyen's journal then stretched. For the better part of two weeks, I poured over the diary and studied the artifacts in the basement. I never dreamed that I would find out so much from one source. Armed with the information, I wanted to find out more about Oya. There was a book out there that could call her that I needed to find.

The diary filled in many gaps, but it also created a whole slew of questions. I wanted to know how my oya power worked. I didn't sense another presence within me. Matt would have mentioned it—or exploited it if I did, so it stood to reason that I had a portion of Oya's power and not the goddess. That was one concern crossed off my list of many.

Was I the only one who possessed it?

Could the power be taken from me and passed to another?

How could it be removed?

The journal appeared incomplete. There was one entry about Oya's tetracontagon summoning circle, outside the recounting of the wizard's affair. According to Quyen's journal, the tetracontagon required forty-two willing souls to stand at each point. Once in place, the ceremonial spell was chanted by each of the points while the vessel stood in the center. I wasn't sure how that would work with the canopic jars. I guessed that the vessel held them, or they were in the center with the vessel. The whole plan was incredibly complex.

The ritual also had too many holes. There had to be another way to acquire Oya's power. I wasn't alive fifty years ago. It was hard to believe that Obscura had a successful summoning then or even thirty years ago when I was born. The first documented appearance of the Sphinx was me fifteen years ago, and the last six months ago. I understood Quyen's frustration. Maybe he was wrong about the book, and it had little to do with the summoning, or at least Jannes left out the critical parts that constituted its success.

"Aargh." I needed answers.

I tugged at one of my locks. The frustration was hair yanking worthy. I paced the floor. What I knew so far was that Obscura knew of a ritual that brought the powers of Oya to a person. Quyen appeared to work out the steps and that it worked best during the most potent nights of the lunar cycle, which were during the solstices. And also, the big one, the summons, needed forty-two willing souls to be sacrificed for the vessel. The number was significant. There were forty-two powers. *I did have the ability to use any magic used on me. There might be something to that.*

It still didn't change the outcome of the past. Evidently, the ritual didn't work because Matt was sans powers. I had them. The book verified that I had Oya's capabilities based on the description the wizard Jannes wrote about her. She always appeared to him as a half woman and half lion with the wings of an eagle. I assumed that she transformed the rest of the way for the sex part of their story—for the sake of my mind.

I snatched up Quyen's journal. The night of the ritual entry was missing—torn out by someone. From what I knew of him, he probably did it to keep the exact details from falling into the wrong hands. Except, I needed the information to free myself and keep the others from cursing the oya on someone else.

Quyen did much of the legwork. I would have to do the rest, but I couldn't do it from his basement. It was a sanctuary from the bounty hunters and parasites of the lawless zone, but it couldn't last. I still heard the shuffling of denizens forging for materials or food. There were at least three of them, though they never appeared together and they didn't fight. It stood to reason that they at least tolerated each other's general proximity. They were also active at night, where they picked around and gathered items.

At some point, they would find this basement to loot it or live in it. I glanced at the small pantry that I recently started using. There was enough food for at least a year or two if I counted the MREs. There was no rush, except I couldn't find the answers I sought sequestered in a bunker. The bounty hunters had to have given up at this point. Or at least were in a different part of the zone.

Who knew? I could have fallen off of Matt's radar, and he was preoccupied with one of his pet projects if he was even aware of their failure. He already had what he wanted from me. As long as I didn't directly oppose him, he may not put any more of his brain power into finding me. Meanwhile, I'd gather knowledge against him.

I glanced at the three-wheeler parked beside the door. It had about half a tank. It was just enough to get me out of the wilderness if I didn't run into any trouble, which was a guarantee that I would at least run into the local scum.

There was one plus on my side, Quyen's magic. He had enough in the basement for me to recharge at least twice. I could swing some serious workings as long as I didn't get into any battles. I'd have to be careful not to draw too much attention from Obscura or Camera. Both monitored strong magic as a matter of survival and recruitment, as they both snatched up practitioners for their armies.

I'm surrounded without many options.

In disgust, I flipped over the journal, and the words, "stand firm and take destiny by the hand" stared up at me. I ran my fingers over the etched words on the leather cover. It was written several times on the back, likely in the different languages Quyen grew up with, but I can no longer perceive because of my powers.

Xenoglossia—the ability to instantly read, speak, and understand all languages. It was one of the benefits of my oya, the absorption of magic and the ability to reuse it. I acquired that talent when a witch from Afghanistan used her xenoglossia on me to communicate.

Again it paid off.

"I will, Quyen. Because you—" A wave of power flowed through the basement, shaking the ground. Dust and dirt from above fell in grainy streams through the ceiling then stopped.

What the hell was that?

I rushed to the blacked-out windows when the pulse happened again. The pantry fell over while I was treated to another dirt spritz. My body hummed with the heady sensation of power. One thing I hated most of all was how good it was for my body to teem with magic. To do whatever I wanted. It was difficult to walk away from, but I knew the cost of pleasure for everyone else. I had to get away.

Someone channeled magic into the ground. Was it a coincidence or purposeful? Anxiety sent the contents of my stomach swirling in my belly.

No, I couldn't allow this.

Another tremor of energy passed through. The waves were increasing in frequency. Whoever, whatever, grew closer to my location as though they sensed me through echolocation but with magic.

Whether they tracked me expressly or whether the basement's magic attracted a powerful practitioner, I wasn't sticking around to find out. I glanced at my wrist. The tattoo was two-thirds of the way complete, and with the pulses growing stronger with proximity, I was in a world of trouble.

I held out my hand. My bag flew to it. I opened it then activated the levitation power I learned from an angry wizard who tried to cheese me when doing a training exercise. All of Quyen's magical research and MREs would go with me. The items circled with ease before settling themselves neatly within.

Far out.

My bag of holding was indispensable. It held everything I needed and more within its subspace pockets.

The best thing I ever—

Another wave tore through the ground. The wall where the pantry once rested cracked. My assailant was close.

I checked my tattoo. My knees nearly buckled. The swirls were almost complete.

There was no time to waste. I closed the bag then slid my arms through the straps of the backpack. There was no time for a last glance around my haven. Another hit, and it would likely collapse in on itself much like most of the surrounding buildings.

It's time to book.

I hopped onto the three-wheeler, then transported the bike and me outside. The brightness of the day blinded me, but I immediately erected a barrier bubble of protection. Being flushed out in the open didn't mean that I'd let whoever was out there catch me or easily fall prey to some lucky bounty hunter. The barrier would buy me time while my eyes adjusted since I couldn't fly or teleport without knowing where to go.

I squinted. Then a shot ricocheted off my barrier.

Obscura.

The magic quake shivered through the earth. The remaining walls of Quyen's house came down along with a few surrounding homes. My feet ached with power, but it was nowhere near as intense as when I was underground.

One less worry.

Pew.

The shooter had to know that I was powered up and pissed off. They were stupid to use magic to flush me out. Yeah, it exposed me, but it gave me options. I lifted into the air, bike, bubble, and all. To anyone who saw me, I probably look like an old-school snow globe— sans snow. It was a good time before the sniper fired another shot.

Pew.

To my right. I flew the bike towards the problem shopping center as though it were a badass broomstick. On the dilapidated roof, a woman with a rifle on a tripod rolled over and fired two handguns at me. Flashes of kinetic energy flared on my barrier with her assault. I swiped my left hand, and she slammed against the wall.

I hovered over her body. The woman's neck hung limply but not at a cock-eyed angle. Even though she shot at me, I wasn't interested in killing her. She might have information that I could—

A *sweee* in the air behind me sounded as a grenade exploded against my barrier, cracking it open. The heat from the blast broke my concentration, and I, on my bike, slammed to the ground. I screamed out as agony radiated through my lower body. The back of the bike landed on me. I shoved it away with telekinesis only to discover more pain from my right shoulder.

"Move. Move," someone bellowed. "Get to her before she heals."

I grunted as I sat up. My right leg was bent at an awkward angle, while my left ankle was sideways. It was excruciating, but the sight of the injuries made it worse. I leaned over and retched as magic knitted me back to normal. Another power I was grateful to have—the healing.

It was also expensive energy-wise. My tattoo faded from seventy-five percent to about forty percent. Another set of injuries like that— which I think they were going for— would leave me just physical defenses unless Obscura wanted me dead.

The pain in my limbs dulled. My ankle was straight again. I attempted to stand, then crumpled in pain. *Too soon.*

I crawled to the 3-wheeler. Liquid oozed out from a crack some-where. I should have been more careful when I threw it. If I hadn't been hurt, I could repair it and get out of there whole. I'd have to leave it. Quyen's magical items would give me a boost but not enough to do what I needed, and I might need them in an emergency.

I crawled over to my bag.

Damn, Obscura.

The *stomp, stomp* of feet near me, and some kind of ladder reminded me that I didn't have time to dawdle. "Wind, heed my—"

Something sharp hit me in the side of the neck. I blamed the pain from the healing along with the stress of battle. Either way, I let my guard down, and they caught me.

10

uyen

Present Day

"This was utter sacrilege," I muttered as I made my way through the forest of Fairy Stone State Park to the park's amphitheater after a three hundred-mile drive. Technically it was seventy miles since I used several spells to teleport to Greensboro, then rented a car and drove to the Virginian Park. I took a risk that Obscura wouldn't monitor magic more than fifty miles out by erring on the side of caution.

Gambling with my safety had never been my strong suit. Neither was trekking in darkened woods of the western part of Virginia dressed like an overgrown bush, but I finally cracked the mysteries of Oya's summoning earlier. There was no time to rest. The ritual was best performed at the start of the lunar cycle when the moon's energy was fullest. As the year wore on, it would drain. That meant the beginning of the lunar year was the optimum time.

My plan to counter the ritual, a foul-smelling potion. The potion was the essence of a skunk. Between the god-awful smell and runny eyes and nose that it produced, someone would break, if not all of Matt's people. Hell, he would likely cut and run as an initial response. I doubted he would sacrifice forty-two disciplined followers. They'd run.

The volunteers probably weren't even practitioners. It would make the situation more manageable in the long run if they couldn't sense the magic of the place. The park—the city of Stuart in general—was a natural magic hotspot. Any practitioner with a modicum of talent could practically taste it when they reach the city limits. If not, entering the Fairy Stone Park woods was a live wire of raw natural magic.

I had to admit it was the perfect place for the summoning of a goddess. It was out of the way. Mundanes wrote off all occurrences as myth or tourists getting into the romance of the area—Virginia was for lovers, after all. The Old Dominion had it all, whether it was nature, power, history, or plain romance.

And Matt tried to claim it on Tet of all times. I should have been at the Eden Center in Falls Church wearing my áo dài while eating bánh chưng and my favorite mứt dừa with everyone else. I always had a sweet tooth, so naturally, I gravitated to the cake and candied fruit. They were the only traditional dishes that didn't remind me too much of my family. They chose Obscura over me.

Grrr.

My stomach didn't seem to care that I infiltrated the enemy's camp and that I might have to battle my fellow witches, wizards, and the mundanes bamboozled into Matt's hair-brained scheme. My mundane relations sided with Matt out of fear of the practitioner side. Most people feared the unknown—especially when they shared the gene pool.

Obscura capitalized on that fact. They cultivated a small herd of people to the point of blind fanaticism to get forty-two people to give up their lives. Did they even understand what the ritual required of them and what would happen to the world afterward?

Or were they short-sighted, caught in their immediate needs and wants?

Sometimes, I wonder if I am an idiot. I fought with Matt. My reputation, career, and personal life suffered. If I just fell in line, then—

"I think I heard something," someone called out to a companion.

I ducked down in the bushes. One of the branches scratched against my neck and face as I tried to become one with the plant visually. I was reasonably sure they monitored magic near the ritual, so I wore a ghillie suit and green face paint. In the bush at night, it would be difficult to pick me out from the foliage. If someone caught me in the open, I would look like a sasquatch or some other forest creature, and I'd have a moment of surprise to take them out before they reacted.

"See anything?" The companion asked.

The other shined a light in the area. It passed right over me with no hesitation. "No. It must have been an animal."

"You think? And in a forest, no doubt," the companion chastised. "We have magic detection set up in the entire park, and we're in a national park. Besides a couple of mundanes we let out here for cover, the only thing out here is the animals. Relax, nitch."

"Why are you such an ass?"

"Cuz I'm stuck out here with a noob witch on guard duty instead of watching the Grand Magister's ascension," the companion snapped.

I braced myself for some sort of retaliation from the first guard. If they fought, I'd use it as cover to escape."

"Fine. I'll work the perimeter by myself while you drool all over the Grand Magister. I'd rather work alone than have you at my back judging me for trying to do a good job."

"You know what, nitch, I'll do that. There's nothing out here. You already said no to boning. I can afford to let you stew for a while. Don't screw up and set the place on fire," the companion advised.

The crunch of steps moving away signaled me that I had one opponent left. I glanced at the moon. The position was high overhead. I didn't have much time left. The remaining guard was new to power, but that told me nothing of her physical skill. She could be a Navy SEAL for all I knew.

Magic was too risky. All I carried were potions, and they were in limited supply. I had to be smart and plan my strategy.

The steps from the guard moved closer to my location. It seemed that the action would happen regardless.

"Don't be afraid to let them show," uttered the guard witch.

The Camera passphrase. I gave the countersign, "I see your true colors."

She sighed. "Stay hidden. I'm not sure my partner is far enough away yet. There's a ring of anti-magic near the ritual to keep anyone from countering. Five teams of guards are walking the perimeter. I've already taken care of the majority of them. They won't notice much. A warning, the Grand Magister seems agitated, not sure if it's nerves or something else. I suggest your team get in and out. Now I'm going to walk past here to continue my search. If you could hit me with a tranquilizer so I can maintain cover, that would be great. I'm not in the mood for a brawl. Good luck."

Then she slowly walked past me as though she were still sweeping her area. Camera had someone on the inside. That was information that would have been helpful to know, but then again, no one from Camera knew where I was. And the guard thought I had a team. Was that because Camera was on the move somewhere or because coming alone was such a stupid idea?

In hindsight, it may not have been my wisest operation, but I knew Matt. We were roommates for four years in college. He was powerful, but I could counter him. I knew the basics about him, the things that wouldn't change no matter how much influence he wielded. The plan would work.

I threw a potion cap at her feet. A small pop and blue smoke surrounded her before she succumbed to sleep. Once she was down, I left the bushes and continued towards the outdoor arena. Ten minutes later, I understood the guard's meaning by "they won't notice much" when I came across a trio of guards groaning in ecstasy while using a tree to brace their action. The second group and their grunts confirmed my theory. They were sexing in the woods instead of being a pain in my ass. The Camera guard must have given the guards an aphrodisiac to keep them busy.

They'd be none the wiser since it was guard duty in a forest at night. For some, hooking up was likely the plan the entire time, though the potion made the various couples incredibly dedicated to the task given the orgy of evidence.

That pun was so bad.

The guards were out of my hair. Perhaps it was my lucky night. It was Tet, after all. Fortune smiled at me at the start of the lunar new year. Just in case, I remained cautious while moving through the nature of the park while the occasional branch pulled at my ghillie suit. I avoided the enemy's areas based on the "faster" and "yeah" I heard when passing through.

I knew the moment I reached the anti-hex barrier. It was Matt's work. My flesh crawled, and a foreboding sense of vulnerability threatened to overtake me. The fact that he cordoned off such a large area terrified me. I hadn't accounted for him improving so much. If he were this strong, then with Oya, he would be unstoppable. What if I was too late?

Or was I wrong about my tactics? The potion mix. Was I right when I measured the ingredients? I should—

I stepped back through the barrier. My heart raced as though I sprinted the entire journey there. I could hardly breathe, but I was myself again. The moment I doubted my ability to measure a potion that I had been making since I thought girls were pests instead of the gems that they were, my instincts kicked in.

Centering my mind, I focused on my confidence in my plan. I spent months studying the ritual. It wasn't ideal. However, I prepared my strategy. The barrier was in place to cause doubt to any who pass through it. My purpose was pure, and my execution was sound. I would not allow Matt's trap to become a setback.

I can do this.

"Libero." I stepped through the barrier. My skin prickled from the magic trying to subdue me, but the overwhelming inadequacy wasn't there. For the battle, it was me two and Matt zero. Almost getting me wasn't the same as succeeding, but it did remind me of the danger in dealing with him.

The barrier spell had three functions: obscuring the ritual, preventing outside magic, and deterring onlookers. On the other side of the barrier, torches on six-foot poles circled the perimeter of the clearing adjacent to the amphitheater. The summoning circle was set up outside the area proper —a sunken bowl filled with wooden benches in a V-shape around a small stage with a podium. Behind the stage, an old white structure blocked the view of the lake that butted against the arena. It wasn't the epic scenery that one expected for summoning a goddess, even in the moonlight.

But it didn't stop Obscura from trying.

The benches were full of spectators and equipment for large gatherings—speakers, microphones, and cameras. They weren't necessary to the ritual, so they weren't used except for a few people with their phones out. They were likely to keep the ruse of benign intentions when it was daylight. Props went a long way when trying to appear harmless to mundane people, though I didn't put it past Matt to make some sort of speech afterward. For the moment, they were not my concern.

The real action took place in the zig-zag circle of people, soon-to-be sacrifices, wearing white and chanting the incantation. The ritual had already started.

I pulled out a handful of stink potions. I hurled some near the center and one near the amphitheater. A breath later, screams and coughs replaced the chanting. A second later, the formation scattered. It was chaos, but it did the job.

And the look on Matt's face—*That's right. Run.*

A bolt of lightning struck one of the trees. I had nothing to do with that. I threw more potions, not knowing whether it was another Camera team member or part of the ritual.

My heart soared as they stampeded away from the summoning, then it sank as a twister swirled down into the clearing. A thunderous wind stirred up dirt and leaves, blinding me and everyone else. I grabbed the trunk of a nearby tree to keep myself from blowing away.

I can safely say this went better in my head.

This could not be Camera. I doubted anyone could or would conjure up a storm of this magnitude. It was too likely to lose control, and the mundanes would notice a freak lightning storm and tornado in the middle of winter. It had to be something else.

Was I too late?

In my worst-case scenario, I failed, and Matt received Oya's powers then went back to the city before making his next move. Nothing like this ever crossed my mind. I had no idea what happened. I disrupted the ritual before it finished. Without the necessary energy for fuel, it should have failed then fizzled out with no dramatic displays. The last image I caught of Matt before the wind kicked up, he appeared surprised and terrified like everyone else. The magic didn't come from him.

This brought me to a different scenario. I should have seen it but didn't. Oya was released and allowed to take vengeance while no longer contained. She would have free reign to run amok until the astral plane drew her soul back.

There was nothing I could do. Everyone was out of place. There was no way to get a ritual back on course to capture the goddess.

Another bolt of lightning struck the ground nearby, followed by ear-splitting thunder. I gripped the sides of my head in reflex when the wind snatched me away.

Caught up in a twister, it was like I imagined being in a washing machine if there were tree branches in it. And it was held in a wind tunnel. All I could do was put my hands up to my face to protect my eyes as stings to my arms and legs burned my senses. If not for my ghillie suit, I didn't want to imagine what I'd feel, except I still had one more issue—breathing and the eventual landing when the twister spun out.

Both concerns were solved a heartbeat later when I shot through the tornado. For a breath, I flew through the night sky like a super-hero. Then I hit the lake. It hurt like a brick wall. My arm went numb, then I sank into the lake, and blackness closed in on me.

Well, it had been a good run.

uyen

Present Day

Someone setting my body on fire was the first thought that came to mind when I opened my eyes. I hopped out of bed—a mistake. My left arm burned from ripping out my IV, my other arm flared to life in its cast, and the long tube that protruded out of my cock kept me close. I didn't want to think about the agony that would have caused if I'd moved away from the bed. Then the rest of my injuries reported into my discombobulated brain when a nurse rushed into the hospital room.

A stocky man helped me back into the bed. "Mr. Dong. You have to stay in bed until the doctor clears you. "

"It's pronounced 'zoong,' and I figured that out too late," I said through gritted teeth.

"The pain is a bitch, I bet. You should be glad that you didn't rip out that catheter. Now that you're awake, I'll get you something to help."

I nodded, not trusting myself to say anything else until I could focus on something besides my aching, burning body. The nurse returned quickly with two small cups.

"This is six-hundred milligram ibuprofen. It will take the edge off the pain until the doctor examines you again. She may prescribe something else if we can't manage your pain."

I knocked back the pills and water. Then I closed my eyes. What seemed a second later, the pain went from burning shrapnel to a warm ache. I opened my eyes to ask the nurse a question, but he was gone. I didn't even hear him leave.

Someone knocked on the door then came into the room. A short woman with dark hair and a metal clipboard paused briefly when her glance met mine. "Mr. Duong, you're awake. Excellent. I'm Doctor Sean. How is your pain?"

She pronounced my name correctly so that was a plus. "I no longer feel like I'm on fire."

"Good," she said, studying the monitors hooked up to me and the IV bag. "You were pretty torn up when you were brought in."

At least I was alive. "Is Sean your last name or first name?"

She took out a penlight.

"Last name," she said. "I'm going to shine this light in your eyes."

My eyes teared at the brief brightness, but Doctor Sean appeared satisfied with the results. She moved to checking my blood pressure then fussed over my bandages.

"How did I end up here?"

"A camper found you drifting in the lake at Fairy Stone State Park," she answered. "What do you remember before that?"

Time to be creative. "That I was never following George's leads again. He wouldn't know a Bubo Virginianus from a Megascops Asio."

She frowned. "Excuse me?"

I settled further into character by rolling my eyes in calm fanatical indignation. I didn't want to oversell it. "Someone in my birding group claimed they spotted a great horned owl at Fairy Stone, so I drove to check it out for myself. I was walking around the woods trying to catch sight of the owl, then a freak storm popped up, and I don't remember."

She gave me a sidelong look. "You don't look like much of a birder, Mr. Duong."

"That's rather biased, doctor." I wasn't about to let her shoot my story full of holes because she was fond of stereotypes. My lie will become a teachable moment if need be. "What is a birder supposed to look like?"

The woman flustered. "Older I suppose, and..."

"White?"

She cleared her throat. "Well, I suppose the world isn't exactly that simple."

I nodded. "Yeah, fifty years ago, I wouldn't have taken you seriously as a doctor and assumed you were a nurse."

Doctor Sean flushed.

"Point made, Mr. Duong. I apologize." She cleared her throat again then put her metal clipboard under her arm. "Sorry about your spotted—"

"Great horned owl. Bubo Virginianus. This is a misnomer because while they appear horned, the 'horns,' I made air quotes with my left hand, "Are actually tufts of feathers on their head. They are the tigers of the sky and—"

"You should get some rest, Mr. Duong," Doctor Sean said. "I want to keep you one more night, and if you're still lucid, I will sign your discharge papers in the morning."

I nodded as though I was disappointed about her not wanting to hear more about owls. "Thank you. By the way, where are my things?"

She pointed to the metal dresser at the front of the room. "Everything we found on you is in there except your clothing and the ghillie suit we had cut off of you. The Red Cross provided clothing, and your wallet and keys are inside."

Doctor Sean moved towards the door then paused. "And no bird watching out the window. You suffered a concussion as well as other injuries. I don't want you walking around the room till morning."

"Not with this catheter in me." I pouted it for effect.

She shrugged then left.

My body hurt too much to make trouble. Besides, I didn't like the way she tried to catch me in a lie. Either she was an Obscura sympathizer, or she was a good old girl who expected me to be doing nails and working in my family's restaurant. Regardless I'd lay low and listen to my surroundings while I cleared suspicion—if it were possible—and heal.

I laid back in bed and let my sight unfocus while I turned my senses inward. The one thing about the hospital, there was water everywhere. Glasses of water, running water from the sink, and water coolers, to name a few. It was a water wizard's paradise. And apparently, it rained outside, which I overlooked earlier with my achy body.

Resonating with the water around me, I could focus the sound waves of everyone's conversations like my personal microphone. My reach was approximately two hundred meters in dry conditions. Rainy days double that. There would be no secrets from me today. I would start with the closest water to me then work outward.

"—want to talk to him. He may know what happened out there," the voice of male authority said. "Something funny is going on out there. And that grand magic guy was lying."

"Grand Magister," Doctor Sean corrected. "And my patient may not have anything to do with magic. He claims to be a birdwatcher."

"At night?" The voice sounded skeptical. "You know that lot. Besides only old ladies and sissies—"

"He was looking for owls. Which are active at night," she interrupted. "And my husband is a birder, I'll have you know."

"Now you know I meant no harm. We don't get many lone foreigners in these parts. You know that."

"He's a U.S. citizen, Deputy Wright." Her voice seemed laced with irritation. "And my patient. He needs rest, and you have nothing to charge him with other than being a stranger."

"Doctor Sean, you and I both have seen the news. Witches are coming back and stirring up the pot. Now, mind you, that Obscura fella seemed on the up-and-up, but he still does that devil craft. I want to know if that Dong fella—"

"It's pronounced 'zoong,'" She corrected. "And you are free to interrogate him once he's well but not before. Now please leave."

I heard a heavy sigh, then the squeaking sounds of rubber soles on the tile. The hospital was a veritable tomb—nothing of what I imagined from television. There were conversations in the halls, but all of it in low or regular speaking tones. Occasionally there was a peel of laughter, cry, or scream, but on the whole it was eerily quiet.

"What did the deputy do-right want?" A male voice asked.

"The same as yesterday," Doctor Sean replied.

"He needs to let it go. Everyone that doesn't live here is not the enemy."

"It's his job to make sure we're safe. He's just overzealous sometimes," she replied.

"Yeah, whatever you say." The male didn't sound convinced. "I just checked on Mrs. Anderson. Her BP is still running high."

"Increase the HCTZ from twenty-five milligrams to fifty milligrams, then check her blood pressure an hour later. I'm going to finish my rounds before Doctor Baner's shift starts."

"Will do."

I eavesdropped on the conversations near me a while longer, then grew bored with work gossip about who did what, horrible patient stories, and who slept with who. I extended my senses further. It had been a while, but I sent my senses to the rain.

The deputy mentioned Obscura. It was possible that some of them were patients in the hospital or campers in the park. I would even take employees on a smoke break.

"—background check on Quyen Duong. That's Quebec, uniform, Yankee, echo, November for the first name. And the last name is delta, uniform, oscar, November, golf. Give me his priors as well."

Priors? Why would he assume I've been in jail?

Overzealous, the deputy was downright paranoid.

And biased.

It was time for action. I may not have a record, but the last thing I needed was the police checking up on me. It may get back to Matt. I knew he would monitor the authorities in the area to ensure none of them would cause trouble for Obscura. That's what I would have done.

He was sure to put two and two together when a report came out. My best weapon against Obscura was my anonymity. They didn't know that they had an enemy—outside of Camera— and they believed that I was harmless. Besides, I had a goddess to find. My life would be so much easier if I remained invisible to law enforcement or anyone else that could cause trouble.

There was no other option than to leave. I removed the IV needle from my arm. Pressing the wound closed, I willed the water in my blood to clot the small hole. All that was left was to get dressed, and exit before a nurse checked in on me.

I threw back the covers from my bed then remembered the long tube coming out of my dick—a catheter the nurse called it. I took a deep breath and began pulling. Blinding pain erupted behind my eyes. I stopped and lay back in bed, breathing hard.

"Mr. Duong, is there something—" the male nurse from earlier rushed into my room. "Got yourself in a pickle, did you?"

All I could do was cough as a response, which I instantly regretted.

"You do not want to do that. It's lodged in your bladder. You could damage your piece and end up in adult diapers if you're not careful." He stood over me, shaking his head.

I grunted as the pain ebbed and uncomfortable throbbing began. He could judge all he wanted. The agony was enough of a deterrent.

"I'm going to check the placement and see if there is any bleeding." He sanitized his hands then examined me.

The memory of the pain was enough for me not to become embarrassed that a guy had his hands on me—even in a professional manner. I hated going to the doctor. Give me an apothecary and spells, and I was good. "Am I okay?"

He covered me back up then put on hand sanitizer from the dispenser. "Fortunately, it was still in place. The pain probably stole your resolve. Bet it was like razor blades shoved up it, wasn't it?"

It was like I was being torn from the inside. "Something like."

"Well, if you end up having to go to the bathroom, just let go. That's what the catheter is for. The tank will catch all the urine." He pointed to the area hidden away under the covers at the foot of the bed. "There's no shame in it, but it will seem weird."

"Why do I have one in?"

"It's the standard operating procedure when we don't know when someone's going to wake up," he answered. "Though if you were in a newer part of the hospital, you would have a shorter tube and a bag strapped to your leg."

"I want it removed." I had to get out of there and to the Sheriff's Office to disrupt their search on me.

"Doctor Sean has orders for removal tomorrow if she discharges you," he answered. "You're still under observation for that head injury. You may feel fine now, but if we let you go too soon and it was a temporary lucidity, you could do more damage. Besides, Deputy Wright will be more suspicious of you if you leave now."

"Take my hand." I stared at the nurse hard.

When he grasped mine, I sensed it. The familiar energy of a practitioner. It was similar to the sensation of static electricity, including shock—depending on the practitioner. Earlier I was in too much pain to notice—something to make a note for the future. "You're a wizard?"

He shook my hand then released it. "You're finally catching on. Some friends of mine found you in a large bubble floating in the lake. They alerted me about you and brought you here to Sovah instead of Patrick Community with the other storm victims. Patrick County draws a lot of us to the area, but there are unfriendly people like Deputy Wright."

Speak of the devil. "He's doing a background check on me. I have to get out of here so I can stop him."

"Don't worry. We have someone in the sheriff's office that will fix it so that he doesn't find anything of interest."

I glanced at his name badge, Maxwell Spellman. Talk about being on the nose. It was a prominent name of a magical family but so common most wouldn't consider it. "Nice to know, Maxwell, but I'd rather remain off the radar. There is more than just the deputy that I don't want to know about me."

"I hear you. I'm not a fan of big covens either." He sat in the chair next to me. Slipping his phone from the front pocket, he texted a quick message. "Isn't that a shame? Deputy Wright's request is going to be lost. And even worse, he's going to forget about it."

I eased my achy body back against my pillows. Maxwell was a straight arrow. My instincts told me that from the start. I would have to bank on them until I could handle the matter for myself. For the moment, I would leave it. I wasn't going anywhere until they discharged me. Besides, I wanted to know more about Max and his friends. "Thank you."

"We're in the same boat." He waved me off. "Just out of curiosity, were you part of that battle that went on at Fairy Stone?"

We may be in the same brotherhood, but that didn't mean he earned my complete trust, but I would give him as much truth as possible. "I don't know anything about a battle, but I was caught up in whatever happened out there."

Max narrowed his eyes. "That's a partial lie, but I get it—either way, the background check is taken care of. Doctor Sean will likely discharge you as long as you remain on the mend. When it's time for you to leave, I'll make sure Deputy Wright is elsewhere in case he gets new ideas."

Then I would take it from there. I'd pick up the rental car from the park if the company hadn't impounded or repossessed it. In the meantime, I'd lay here and plan. "Thanks, Maxwell."

"No problem. We have to stick together." He stood. "My shift ends soon. The charge nurse is a stickler for the rules and a sympathizer of Wright. Don't give her any trouble, and everything should be fine."

"By giving her trouble, you mean trying to leave?"

"Sounds like you understand just fine. Sleep and rest like a mundane patient. She won't think twice about you. I will take care of the rest. See you tomorrow."

Once Maxwell left, I closed my eyes. I was drowsy again. It wasn't what I wanted, but I didn't have the guts to rip the catheter out despite what he said. I wanted to have sex again someday—and go to the bathroom like normal.

I could wait one more day to track Oya. Using a mix of the summoning ritual and a standard one, I was reasonably sure I could find the rogue powers or the person who inherited them. It was just a matter of working out the details. Then all I had to do was banish it.

Easy Peasy. I thought as my mind drifted.

Then I would have saved the world from Obscura's latest scheme. *And for my next trick....*

Sleep claimed me.

12

andora

50 A.Q.

I stretched out on the mattress, threw my legs over the side, and sat up. It wasn't the best sleep, but I needed the rest. The dream I could have done without—wait. I shot out of bed then frantically looked around.

It was my room in Obscura Tower. The possessions I left behind were undisturbed. If I didn't know any better, I would have thought that I dreamt the entire year. Except someone folded and placed my clothes neatly on the nightstand near the bed. The leather-like material was ideal for the harsh micro desert of the lawless zone. I acquired it after my escape, along with my gazelle-horned headdress. The ensemble made me appear fearsome. It went a long way to deter some of the slavers that would have approached a loner in the hazardous area.

"You're awake," Matt said.

I spun around as he stepped from the shadowed corner like a villain from an old movie. "You were watching me sleep? "

"For a while, yes. I must admit I dozed off myself. I would have joined you in bed, except I didn't know how you would react."

Badly. I would have screamed if I woke up to Matt beside me like some doting boyfriend playing house. We were over and had been for the entire time he chased me. "What do you want?"

"You by my side." His glance drifted down my body. "I missed you, though I admit watching my people try to catch you passed the time. You were meant for me, which is why you're here now."

"I'm here now," I snapped my fingers to recapture his gaze, "because you almost blew my face off, and you drugged me, not some sort of attempt to get your attention."

He watched me for a few moments, his jaw tight. "You're in a bad mood. I'll come back later."

"My mind won't change. And you love my power, not me," I said. It came across needy. I would have to work on that.

"You and your power are the same," he replied. "I made a mistake once of letting you get away. It won't happen again. You belong by my side."

"I hear a threat in there."

He wagged his finger at me as though I were a naughty child. "You do not want me as an enemy. I want you in my bed, but you will share it with me. Cool your head and think about your options wisely. My love or my hate."

I wanted neither, but I knew that wasn't an option, so I ignored his statement and flopped onto the bed. I knew him well enough to know he had contingencies in place while my loyalty was in question. Magic hung in the air all around me. There was plenty to absorb. I was surprised that he tried to use magic to contain me and said so.

"No worries, Kitten. I somewhat trust you. If you break out, your zoanthropy will kick in, and the Sphinx will kill everyone in the building and the city. That would be terrible for your conscience and your family."

My heart sank. My parents died in the first attack, my first loss of control. I saw their names on the memorial. Mine was there as well. "You're lying. My family is gone."

"Not so, Kitten. Camera had them. They were going to use your parents as a means to lure you out when I rescued them. They are under my direct protection. No one else will touch them."

My body shook. And *there* was the threat. If I fought him, I would lose them again. "I want to see them."

"At dinner," he replied. "I want to celebrate your homecoming. Wear something that I like."

Then the bastard left. My only comeback was to lay on the bed gathering my wits. My parents were alive. And I was in a pickle, as my grandfather was fond of saying. I wished he were alive.

He was a wizard that could tell when anyone lied, and he was handy with potions. My grandmother didn't possess the craft, or if she did, she never mentioned it. It was why my father wasn't a wizard—it was thought that the ability passed from mother to child. I couldn't see my father having magic and turning away from it without reason. I never saw him or my grandmother do anything overtly magical, so I assumed it was jealousy or disappointment. No one explained. I wouldn't be surprised if my parents adopted me instead of having children as some sort of twisted way of making sure that I didn't develop powers.

The joke was on them. I was a witch.

My father must be in hell right now, having to consort with so much magic. I wonder if he knew about me. No, he knew. Camera would have told him that he was their leverage. If they didn't tell them, Matt would have as part of his tactics or out of petty vengeance against bigotry. I would have to face his disappointment. Not Mom so much. She was the peacemaker. But Dad—

Enough.

I ran my hands across my face as I ran down the circumstances of my current situation—caught by Matt and held hostage along with my parents. Magic surrounded me so I could absorb it to fuel a spell, but I'd have to choose carefully. Then what? Escape was easy. Remaining free was another. I did it for a year alone, but with two extra people, it would be impossible. Our flight was also contingent on whether Matt brainwashed them. Stockholm syndrome was powerful, especially coupled with a rescue. They were probably loyal to him like I had been —minus the whole sleeping with him part.

I hated that my experience with men was down to being the dog/mistress of a megalomaniac and fantasizing about my journal book boyfriend. At least Quyen wanted to protect everyone. He disagreed with Matt's practices and was not afraid to say so. Quyen's affiliation with Camera sucked, but then he didn't trust them either. He was my kind of guy and, even better, unattainable.

It's not like you can date anyway. Matt would kill anyone that tried.

Back to the subject at hand. My options were limited. Buying time by playing Matt's insipid games appeared as the best option. The Grand Magister was patient. As long as I didn't anger him, he let me have the time to figure out a way out of this mess. First, I needed to arm myself with information. I read through Quyen's journal, which ended at the ritual—I sat up.

The journal. What if Matt found it and read it? I stood casually and searched for my bag. The last thing I wanted to do was alert anyone watching me that my bag was important beyond sentiment. I relaxed when I saw it tucked between the nightstand and the bed. I opened it. The enchantment on the book was still intact. Thank the craft that I had the foresight to spell the tome weeks ago to appear like a romance novel. When I left the basement, I didn't expect Matt to catch me. I just had to be careful with how long I was in contact with the book and he'd be none the wiser.

I took out the book, propped it next to me, then cozied up against the pillows to begin my research. There was a strong chance someone monitored me. I'd start laying the foundation for my compliance by quietly researching and giving Matt a sullen attitude. He'd eat that up thinking he was on the path to victory.

Then I'd make my—I flipped to the area where I placed my impromptu bookmark—a piece of faded junk mail I found in the basement. There was a new page after the ripped-out one with the ritual.

It can't be. I know I was at the end of the journal. Why would a diary from fifty years ago add pages?

Does this happen each day, or am I weakening a security spell?

That doesn't make sense. Why hide the last pages? Quyen would have destroyed or hidden the entire book. It has to be something else. A time spell?

Enchantments aside, spells shouldn't have the power to cross time and space. Even a long-distance working required an anchor in the location to tie the magic between two points. I didn't want to imagine the type of anchor needed to bridge the energy across time. A spell like that would be too much to handle.

I closed my eyes to focus on the magic. There was no reaction other than a tingling in my fingertips that I barely noticed. The book itself was charmed. It seemed like a loose string going nowhere, but there wasn't enough power to do something like pull pages from another time. I must have missed the page in my haste to leave. At least it gave me a chance to study Quyen's power.

His magic was cool, like a glass of water on a hot day or satisfying swim. He probably had an active power from the caress of it. If I were to guess, I'd say he was an Elemental—may be water or ice. I could see why Matt allied himself with Quyen. A wizard with mastery over the elements was rare. Most of them died young due to an accident. Many practitioners from non-magical families died from either their loss of control or the fear they created in the mundanes.

That was almost me.

That was still me if I wasn't careful. I was in a dangerous 3D chess game—surrounded by enemies and without any allies. The sad part was that I was the greater enemy depending on the circumstances, and there was no clear path. Until I came up with something better, my research project with Quyen would continue while I worked Matt for information.

That was a silver lining to the problem—I didn't have to worry about Obscura lurking around the corner. I knew where they were. They knew where I was. I could spend my energy on my freedom, which I currently saw as a single solution problem: Matt had to die. I just had to make sure I didn't take out anyone I cared about as I did it or create more problems.

13

*M*att

50 A.Q.

Pandora may have been back home with me, but I left her to her own devices too long. While gone, she undid most of the work I put in establishing the best impression of myself to her. She saw the underbelly of the change I brought to the world, and it hardened her. I supposed it couldn't be helped.

The lawless zones were an unfortunate part of the government's destabilization of such a large country. In a few decades, I would reclaim them. I wanted the fear of them to remain a while longer in the minds of the east and west coast, which I controlled, and the remaining part of the former United States that I have yet to claim.

Ruling was eighty percent head games and twenty percent force. Too much deviation from the ratios caused people to either fear the ruler or easily follow another. Many great conquerors fell from power because they either squeezed their peasants too hard or they expanded too quickly. I would do neither. As a wizard, fifty years was nothing to me. I was still very much in my prime and remained physically unchanged to the masses. It was just a matter of strategic movements and establishing the legend about my Grand Magister persona. In a hundred years or so, I will run the country of my birth.

And they will let me because I was their savior. I protected them from disasters and monsters. All they had to do was place themselves underneath my authority. With Pandora back, I had all the cards. As long as she remained thus, my opposition remained powerless.

The pressing matter that remained—seducing Pandora, the woman.

I opened the live stream to her room. My woman was beautiful with her cinnamon eyes, thick curly mane of hair that she wore as a long mohawk, and smooth brown skin. She reminded me of the warrior witches Quyen and I encountered in the hidden village of Dahomey. I'd always been attracted to strong, powerful women.

Her time on the run made her rebellious, but it also straightened her in other ways. The restrained manner she fought me instead of flying off the handle aroused me which I hadn't expected. While the mindless hero-worship she once paid me fed my ego, the fire in her garnet eyes did more.

I fought not to kiss her and make her mine during our disagreement. The pleasure of turning her ire into ecstasy had its appeal. From what I understood, makeup sex was gratifying. We had a year's worth of pent-up frustration to spend. However, her mood didn't appear amiable. I didn't want her by force, but for Pandora to give herself to me—my cock tightened.

That would be the challenge. Those firm legs wrapped around me as I spent myself within her—the heat of her cinnamon eyes as she quaked under me. I looked forward to our subsequent encounter. Dinner was sure to spike another battle.

And perhaps a small victory?

When I unveiled that I had her parents, I saw the defeat in her eyes. There was no doubt she tried to develop a plan to counter me, and when it failed, she would be one step closer to being mine. She would probably try sex. It was a go-to for women, and we did have history. I wasn't above letting her seduce me into bed if she decided to go with that age-old scheme. It would wear her down to know that there was no one else for her and no place she could go.

I'd make her my grand mistress. We'd rule together and create more with Oya's power. Then our children would take the other parts of the world I was unable to manage directly.

"A year." I groaned as I shifted in my seat.

Perhaps I wouldn't give in to any seduction plans she attempted. Already she tempted me to take the matter into my own hand, but giving in to it would allow Pandora to rule me. We were in the last leg of our race. Little steps here and there polluted my purpose. She was essential to me so I had to have discipline. Running after her like a lust-driven idiot catering to her whims was the opposite of what I needed. Once I secured her, I would allow a certain amount of grace to keep her interest, but I would never allow her to rule me. That, too, was how some empires fell.

"What's in a year?" Lauren hobbled over to my desk.

My point. I was so distracted by Pandora that I didn't hear my eighty-year-old assistant approach.

I closed the live stream. "Phase one completion of a project."

Lauren's dark eyes narrowed. "I take it that congratulations are not in order? I thought her capture was successful. I heard that—"

"Pandora's back with me, but she's different from before, defiant."

Lauren leaned forward on her cane. "Ah, and you like that."

Too much if my assistant knew the direction of my thoughts at a glance. "It has its appeal."

She raised an eyebrow and gave me a long look. "Might I suggest a tonic to help matters along?"

"No. That would strengthen her resolve against me and cheapen the experience. She will come to me in time."

Lauren sat. "As you say, Grand Magister."

No debate or the various methods we could try should something fail? I observed her closely. A fine sheen of sweat glistened on her brow, and she was out of breath.

The top two floors of the tower were my private residence and lab. In Lauren's prime, she crossed the distance with no issue, but I had noticed that she moved slower over the decades. It wouldn't be long before she could not make it without assistance. Her mind, however, remained sharp. It was her intellect that I needed. The rest I would deal with in time. "You're not well. Rest. Tomorrow, I want a report of your projects."

She stood on wobbly feet. I rose, and she put out a hand. "I'm perfectly capable of getting out of a chair on my own."

Somehow I doubted that, but I would allow her her pride. "Take two days. Your assistant can brief me."

"When I'm dead," she spat.

For a moment, she reminded me of Pandora. They had similar features when Lauren was still young, but Lauren wasn't a witch. She was a brilliant mundane. We would have never had a future. They lacked power, and their lives were too short.

It was a matter of time before I lost my assistant. The others, while powerful in magic, didn't possess her level of potential. Pity.

"You will do as I say," I replied.

She pressed her lips together in a firm line of disapproval. "As long as you know that everything has been for you, every project and intention."

"Yes, I laud your loyalty. You're the only mundane in my inner circle, but it changes nothing. You are to rest." I would not indulge her this time.

"Then see you, Matt."

She hadn't called me anything but Grand Magister in decades. A coolness spread across me. Was she feeling sentimental or softening me for a blow for later?

No. Lauren didn't get emotional. It was one of the reasons I kept her by my side. Despite being a mundane, she understood the application of magic and its history. At its inception, she was instrumental in Obscura while working with Quyen and me. Frivolity wasn't in her nature. Even when she developed a crush on me, she managed herself until she grew out of it.

Strange as she behaved, it wasn't sentiment. There must be complications with one of her projects. I'd get the details and deal with it when Garfield debriefed me. It was unlikely to be detrimental, and she had at least two backup plans for everything. "Rest, Lauren."

I watched her leave. She smiled as the elevator doors closed.

She is not going to do what I asked.

I texted James to alert the guards that she was to remain in her quarters undisturbed. Then I opened the live stream and turned my attention back to my reluctant bride for a few moments before settling into work on my pet project, a time travel spell—Timeless.

14

andora

50 A.Q.

I brushed my fingers over the halter dress in my closet. Over a year passed, and nothing in my room changed. Someone maintained the area, keeping it dust-free as though they expected my return. It was immaculate and everything was in its place, including the dress I bought to wear for his birthday celebration. I remembered the day I bought the far out little black dress.

Stupid me had spun around in glee with the purchase while James stared at me in his usual cold shaded expression. Since he covered his eyes, slight twitches in his eyebrows and face were the only indicator of what he thought as he protected me from afar. The slight quirk of his mouth gave me his warm approval. After an hour of searching for the perfect outfit to surprise Matt, his silent agreement was all that I needed. It might have been his day, but he planned to take me on a trip following one of the old Orient Express routes. He was a fan of classic mystery novels and thought it would be an amusing European jaunt.

At first, I was shocked that he was willing to be away from Obscura tower for more than a few days, but I wanted to see the cities on his route, Paris in particular, too. Then there were the rumors that circulated that he planned to ask me to marry him. I wanted to look my best at his birthday banquet at the first stop, London, just in case he asked, and if he didn't, then I wanted him to wish he had.

One moment I was shopping during my personal time, the next, the shop emptied for privacy was under siege by five Camera terrorists. Defending myself with magic back then had been effortless. I wasn't trying to remain anonymous. All I was concerned about was not turning into the Sphinx. I froze all of the intruders at once.

I hated Camera.

They were the ones that had imprisoned me when I needed training for my power. They wanted to use me. I figured that turnabout was fair play. They held me for months in a drugged, confused state so I would gather any intel I could, then keep them.

I wasn't kind when I raked through their minds for information about their evil doings—and there were some. Camera was not the far out organization that they preached about in their recruitment meetings. I knew that. What I hadn't been ready for was they believed they were doing the right thing, and there was plenty of good done as well. I was the enemy, seen as the Grand Magister's war dog, a weapon that killed indiscriminately and without remorse. They feared me, but some believed that I could be reasoned with if I was isolated from Obscura.

They waited and watched my movements until the perfect scenario occurred, but the Grand Magister's threat to the European Union forced their hands. He promised to lay waste to major cities in Great Britain, France, Germany, Austria, Turkey—all destinations on our Orient Express trip. I remember nausea settling over me as I made the connections. One of the five had witnessed the Grand Magister's threat over the teleconference, so I saw first hand what they witnessed, the cold promise in his eyes that he reserved for enemies.

Matt had known I couldn't control myself when the Sphinx arrived. Even my allies were in danger if I lost my way, yet he planned to unleash me anyway, to add territory to Obscura, to him. That was the day I ran with my bag and the clothes on my back.

And this dress still made its way to my closet.

He always planned to bring me back - to claim me as though I went on some sort of vacation and not away from him. He still didn't get it. I wasn't his plaything in his world domination game—and I couldn't hide. The only way he would understand was to join the fray. Otherwise, I would have to look over my shoulder for Camera *and* Obscura.

Why couldn't I have been born fifty years ago, when all I had to do was pretend to be a mundane?

Who knew? Maybe I would have met Quyen or someone like him and lived a regular life, having everyday problems like where to live or whether to have kids instead of plotting political moves and extricating myself from the position as a pawn on the world's chessboard.

I removed the dress from the hanger and tossed it and a pair of black heels on the bed. Removing my clothes, I hesitated briefly, thinking that someone watched me, then put the thought out of my head. Matt was too jealous to allow someone to watch me while I dressed. He probably blurred out my privates with a spell, and if he didn't, I might be able to use it to my advantage. Embarrassment over nakedness ended for me in the lawless zone when I saw how the slavers treated anyone they considered a "bottom." It was their term for sex slave.

Guards lusting after me was nothing compared to what did and what could have happened in the lawless zone. I would have to prepare to use any manipulation to gain leverage on Matt and cry about it later when I won.

The hot shower was magnificent. Not even my basement haven had that luxury. Steam and the comforting stream of water over my face did the job of washing away the aches and dust from the previous days. The stress was more palpable when I stepped out of the stall and viewed myself in the mirror, my reflection in a towel and messy top knot, to keep my hair from getting wet, staring back at me.

I learned that intimidation was a survival tactic in the lawless zone after a few encounters, so I adopted the headdress and leathers. For added effect, I planned to shave my head like the Agoyji African women of old, but I was too vain to go through with it. I settled on my current style as a concession to vanity—a long curly mane with the sides shorn. The style also made it easier to blend in some towns.

My efforts kept me out of Obscura hands for a year. *And now I was back to playing the girlfriend getting ready for a date with her boyfriend and family.*

Later. I would get through the battle first. I consulted my reflection.

Even with less hair, it took forever to dry using mundane circumstances. However, with a lavender apple cider potion, it would be out of sight. I needed to appear attractive and unbothered by whatever Matt intended. His affections were the only leverage I had. Until I developed some other plan, my accouterments of war were a halter dress, sexy heels, and makeup.

It was a bummer that I was left with womanly wiles, but all weapons were groovy.

With that in mind, I dried off and put on my seductive armor, then strolled out of my comfy cage as though I owned Obscura Tower. James fell in step beside me after a few paces down the marble and glass causeway.

"You've changed considerably in the last year."

When I wasn't with Matt, I spent most of my time with the captain of the enforcers. James even trained me on hand-to-hand basics until Matt's assistant, Lauren, found out. That woman was always hard on me. She convinced Matt that learning physical defense would hinder my magical abilities because I would rely on it.

At first, I thought it was because she hated me. Later, I realized it was because she loved Matt and wanted him to have the best—me. James was the same way. So the two of them secretly trained me, her with magic theory and him with magical defense, while Matt took credit for all of it. Their devotion at the time bothered me, but I understood since I owed Matt for saving me. As a wiser woman, I knew it was misplaced fanaticism. The two of them would be another obstacle I would have to overcome. "I've become my own woman."

"I was going to say you're not the spoiled princess anymore, but we could go with that," he replied.

I didn't dignify his comment with a verbal response. The naive, eager to please person he insulted was dead anyway. "You're not the only one who doesn't want me here, but the Grand Magister went through a lot of trouble to make it happen, so we'll all have to live with it."

He grabbed me by the elbow. "Now wait—"

I pistoned my elbow away from him while turning my body into a favorable angle to defend against him. "Don't touch me."

James met my gaze with his dark one. His brow furrowed then softened. Slightly. He nodded his head. "I guess I did overestimate you by not hunting for you personally. I won't let you fake me out again."

A witty retort died on my lips. James was the head of the enforcers. He was a listener— a wizard who could read surface thoughts— devoted to Matt. Touch increased their ability to break into minds. Taking care of him wouldn't be easy, and then there was Lauren if she was still alive. The woman would have so many traps and protocols in place that I would pay dearly for it even if I did lose control. They were my obstacles *before* I could deal with Matt.

The less information I gave them, the better. Obscura already caught me. I would learn from that situation and use it while giving them nothing new about me.

I disciplined my mind. If I had nothing to give, James had nothing to read. "I'm hungry."

I turned away from him then continued to stroll down the hall.

It was a gamble since James was a bit of a hothead. I also knew that he wouldn't rough me up, at least not before dinner. If he became in charge of my safety again, then he might reinstate my training so that he could use sparring as his excuse. Either way, I would use every weapon and opportunity at my disposal.

A minute of listening to my heels click on the floors later, I arrived at the dining room. It was showtime. Once I went through that door, I would have to face Matt again as he continued to play the dutiful boyfriend, instead of who he was, a tyrant that held me hostage. Knowing him, he would want alone time to let me know his expectations and dangle my parent's welfare over my head. Maybe I would even get to see them.

Let's get this over with.

I moved to open the door when James grabbed it.

"You're to be his Grand Mistress. The least you can do is act the part." He gave me the side-eye as he opened the door.

I rolled my eyes then strolled through the entryway.

"Baby girl? Is that...you?" My father said at the same time my mother gasped.

And my heart dropped.

15

 andora

50 A.Q.

"**D**ad, I..." My throat tightened as I stood in front of my father and replayed the bitter argument we had—the last time I saw him, the day I ruined all of our lives by going to an anti Witchcraft Act protest despite him forbidding me from going. My parents showed up to drag me back home the moment the demonstration turned violent.

Shaking off the traumatic memories, I stepped forward. Daddy was still the tall, dark, and handsome man that raised me. The years had been kind except for worry lines furrowing the forehead of his bronzed skin. The hint of gray in his thick beard was the only real give-away of his age of forty-nine. His maple brown eyes were wide.

Before I knew it, he enfolded me in his strong embrace. My mother joined us, crying into the side of my neck. I couldn't maintain the cold badassery that I presented to James. These were my parents, the people who selected me and loved me as theirs. For me, they were back from the dead. I wanted to cherish them while I could before they started asking questions.

And before my father realized what he tied himself to thirty years ago—the very thing he hated.

Too quickly, my father's warm embrace ended. My mother continued to hold me.

"You're...you're a grown woman now." His voice was a whisper that I barely heard above my mother's sobs. "Georgia, please."

She squeezed me tighter. "No, you don't, Maxwell Trin Spellman. Our daughter has come back to us. I'm going to enjoy every moment of this miracle that I can before he takes her away."

And like that, the joy was over for me. Matt was probably somewhere enjoying the drama of the family reunion moment. It was something he would hold over them and me.

I did this to them. My parents are hostages because of me.

I would get them out of this mess.

"Mom." I rubbed her back as I glanced around the dining and sitting room.

A beige couch, several matching armchairs, and a glass coffee table furnished the lounging area. It was perfect for what I needed. The conversation was likely not going to go well, and I didn't want to ruin my relationship with my parents at the dining table.

I walked my mother towards the couch. "Dad, we need to talk before the Grand Magister gets here."

He stiffened at the mention of Matt's title, but he perched on one of the armchairs. "What does he have you mixed up in?"

I flinched at his no-nonsense tone out of muscle memory. It had been almost twenty years, but to him, I was still a fifteen-year-old girl easily influenced. At least that's how he saw it. I knew my mind the way I knew what was right. "Nothing any more."

His posture relaxed somewhat. "Then what does he want from you —never mind. It's obvious what he wants. I thought he was holding you the past three months, but then you strolled in here like you were the queen in the castle."

"Don't, Max." My mother relinquished her embrace on me to hold my hand while she squared off with my father. "We just got her back. I want to cherish this."

I squeezed her hand. "It's okay, Mom. We need to talk but I need to know what Matt—the Grand Magister told you about me."

"Matt, huh? You and that…" He glanced around the room then back at us. "Are you sleeping with the Grand Magister?"

I flinched. He put it out there. No dancing around the subject or ignoring the possibilities. My face heated. "No."

"But you have." His eyes hardened.

My mother went ramrod straight next to me. They were disappointed.

I wanted to lie.

"You always did focus on him whenever he was on the news." He rubbed his forehead. "This was my fault. I banned all talk of magic, and it drew you in like a moth to a flame."

"It wasn't like that. He and I are complicated, but it was before I realized—when I grew up. Don't worry about that. I will handle him alone. It was my mistake."

My father stood, and my mother's grip on my hand tightened.

"Little girl, I am your father. You don't—"

"I'm thirty now, Daddy. I had to kind of figure things out without you two." I held his gaze while trying not to wither under his authority. When he remained silent, I continued, "I need to know what you know about me so you can decide how you are going to proceed forward."

Mom raised our joined hands and kissed my knuckles. "We know you joined Obscura and that you deserted."

"And that you're a witch," he spat. The last word was rife with venom. His feelings had not changed on the subject of magic.

My eyes stung, but I remained stoic, at least I hoped. "I must have inherited it from my biological parents."

Daddy's jaw ticked, then he puckered his lips as though he sucked a lemon. The fact that he hadn't exploded gave me hope that I didn't deserve.

"It seems so," he said. "You can't help your genes, but that aside *we* are your parents. Witch or not, you are still ours."

My mother's grip relaxed.

"...I will have to...adjust, but I can't abide by your association with Obscura or Camera. They are two faces of the same coin. Even *my* father knew that."

Hearing mention of my grandfather, I took a chance. "We're in a pickle, Daddy."

He sank back into the armchair. "Yeah, we are, baby, and I'm calm now. Tell us everything. I mean it."

Cold shot straight to my heart. I dodged some of the ugly truth with them already knowing I was a witch. Now I had to tell them that they raised the destroyer of everything they loved and a killer of millions.

My father put his hand over my mother's and mine. "Baby girl, you are our world. We know what it's like to fall in love, and we know what kind of world this is. There is nothing you can do to make us stop loving you."

"You're father's right," Mom added. "I may not have carried you in my body, but I love you as much as if I did. If the world burns, you will still be ours, and I will fight anyone who says otherwise."

I blew out a sigh. "You say that now, but you don't know what I've done in the name of Obscura."

The tears escaped from my eyes. I placed my free hand over our joined ones. My father knowing I was a practitioner was one thing, finding out that I was the monster he believed all magic users were was another.

My mother kissed the side of my head. "It's been fifteen years. We all need to get to know each other. Tell me what you can, and we'll learn more next time."

"We will see you again, won't we?" my father asked.

"Yes." I would make sure that even if they hated me later, they would at least give me the motivation to entertain Matt's insipid games.

"Now tell us what you can," my father said.

"I... The Grand Magister rescued me from Camera about a year after the event."

My parents both closed their eyes as though reliving the memory. My mother shivered.

"Did Obsucra unleash that monster?" she asked.

I just shook my head. "It turned out to be an accident, and both organizations are still vying for control of the creature."

My father snorted. "From where I'm sitting, Obscura seems to have it."

"He had temporary control. Now he's trying to get it back." That was as close as I planned to get to the truth anytime soon. "I was raised in Obscura. I was... I was one of their most powerful members. The Grand Magister and I..."

My face flamed. Telling my father I was involved with a man should be easy. I was thirty years old, no longer a virgin. My dad understood the world even before I turned it into a level one apocalypse.

"I think I understand, baby girl," my mother said. "Your hero worship and the fact that he saved you made you the perfect bedmate for an egomaniac."

"Mom," I groaned.

"Moving on," my father grunted.

"I was the bad guy, too, but then I realized that Obscura was just as bad as Camera and I left, " I finished.

My father crossed his arms. "The Grand Magister doesn't seem like the type to let his toys retire or share."

"I'm not his toy, Daddy, but you are right. He didn't light up with joy when I left. I've been on the run the past year. He caught me a few days ago."

"So then *we* are the hostages," Daddy said as though he were talking to himself.

"Why would you be—?"

Matt strolled through the dining room doors in his spell casting clothes, button-down shirt, and jeans. It was an underwhelming dinner ensemble for a man who preferred to make an entrance every-where we went.

After all that talk about looking good for him, he barely made an effort for me. I don't know whether he's trying to goad me into preening for him or he's testing me.

Two could play games.

"We'll talk again," I whispered as we all rose to greet him.

I would continue "Operation Brickhouse" until I figured him out. I would make Matt want me while I ignored his overtures. No matter what, he always wanted what he couldn't have. That was his core, spoiled brat.

And like that, I slipped into a persona of cold indifference, and I prepared for our first battle over dinner.

16

*M*att

50 A.Q. - several hours before dinner

I observed as the test goat fell over as my spell lost energy. It lay there with its slanted irises focusing blankly as smoke and the scent of burnt hair emanated from the carcass.

Another failed attempt.

"Trial two hundred and thirty-nine," I said into the camera, recording my work. "It is suspected that the subject has brain death similar to the previous subjects. Smoke emanates from the body. However, there is no fire, and the body is otherwise unburned."

I tossed the blackened diamond onto my work desk.

"The spell requires an enormous amount of energy to sustain. Note to self, look into a diamond lattice to control the flow of energy to the subject."

"At least the goat didn't burst into flames like most of the other subjects." Lauren said from beside me.

It wasn't the real her, but a projection from a halo-crystal. The image was of her in her heyday when she was still beautiful and fit— when we met at Hampton University. Quyen introduced me to her, and she had been with me ever since.

"I gave you that crystal as a personal protection device not as a means to get around my orders."

She flashed her youthful smile. "I'm better by your side, even if it's just a projection while I lay in bed. Now, what happened with the human trials?

I picked up my grimoire. "You know perfectly well that Pandora would object to me using my enemies as guinea pigs."

"Ah, so you present her with a mask." Lauren clucked her tongue. "She should understand by now that your work requires great sacrifice. You're doing all this for her anyway. If you can go back in time, you could—"

"The keyword is if." I set the grimoire on my desk harder than necessary.

Lauren jumped then sighed. "So you had a few setbacks."

"Two hundred and thirty-nine of them. Though I stopped charring them at trial two hundred and thirty-five. Brain dead test subjects do not constitute success." I pinched the bridge of my nose. It had been a long day. I might not have moved forward with Timeless but there were other causes for celebration. "At least I eliminated the last productive member of the NoVa cell before I switched to goats. That cell was an unnecessary distraction. If it weren't for them, I wouldn't have wasted a year chasing My Kitten."

"Bane's gone then? Good riddance. The rest of Camera will fall into in-fighting. I don't know why they continued to call themselves that after she—"

I glared at her.

"—the Sphinx destroyed the area. They are out of your hair now and a shadow of what they used to be." She attempted to put her hands on my shoulder when she passed through me. "Damn it."

I moved away for effect. Lauren needed to understand her role. She was my assistant. "I don't need comfort. I need results."

"If *she* gave it to you, you would've accepted it." Her eyes hardened.

We both knew who "she" was. I thought Lauren had outgrown her jealousy for Pandora. "Of course. She is my intended. It's her right to see to my needs."

Her voice rose in pitch despite my subtle chastisement.

"Except she sees an idealistic version of her hero where everything goes sanctimoniously, and there are no hard choices. She's too much of a child to see that you're bearing the burden of changing the world."

"Pandora's soon to be your Grand Mistress. Be careful." I still needed Lauren's council, but not at the cost of Pandora. Her pointless idol worship would be one more thing that I would correct when Timeless was ready.

Lauren lowered her tone. "She has no idea how much you've done for practitioners. You stopped the Witchcraft Act, which would have allowed the government to enslave, legally, and kill practitioners under the guise of safety and regulation."

"I'm aware of my accomplishments," I snapped then held my hands together as I brought down the energy Lauren stirred within me. "We've been through this, Lauren. Pandora has never lived in a world without me, where her magic was a threat and not just a topic for political pundits. My Kitten will come around once she has more of a stake in my plans."

Lauren shook her head. "Or you could be with someone who already—"

"I want Pandora"

Lauren shut her mouth and shifted her gaze. I knew she didn't like my answer. It was my fault for indulging her crush on me when there were other ways to ensure her compliance. Though if not for her mundane nature, she would have been suitable. However, we both knew I wouldn't allow children of mine to be born powerless, which was all she could provide me. My plans went beyond where we were. Pandora was an essential part of my end game.

"Then you shall have her." Lauren met my gaze then averted her eyes. She gestured to the tome on my desk. "I'm tired now. I will leave you to cogitate over your findings. If I think of something useful—"

"Rest. I don't want to hear from you until you've followed my orders." Then perhaps I would have my clear headed assistant instead of a sentimental one.

She pasted a grin on her face that by no means reached her eyes. "Yes, Grand Magister, though I suspect you'll be too busy welcoming back your wayward bride to bother with an old woman anyway."

Not likely, but Lauren didn't need to know that.

"Goodbye." I picked up my grimoire then allowed her presence to fall away.

When fatigue settled in, and no ideas to solve my energy problem came to me, I glanced up from my infuriating failure to the timepiece. I froze. The analog clock on the wall couldn't be correct. The energies from my experiments must have disrupted its gears. It didn't seem like another eight hours passed, and I was an hour late for dinner. I opened the live stream of Pandora. She was gone from the room. There were several pieces of clothing strewn about on the bed, and the timestamp read 7:30 p.m.

Disgusted, I chanted a spell to activate the summoning matrix I built into the foundation of my tower. I could appear anywhere within my home. It wasn't something I often did to keep my methods a secret from the general population, but this was an emergency.

I still wore my casual button-down shirt and jeans and—hardly the uniform for seduction. But I could use it to my advantage. My behavior change would throw Pandora. She'd think I was unaffected by her, then try harder for my attention while feigning disinterest in me.

I opened the dining room doors in my residence.

Pandora's parents rose immediately with smiles on their faces. Her father's grin wasn't genuine. I knew his thoughts on magic. He made it clear when I rescued him and from my surveillance. If not for leverage over Pandora, I would have left him and his wife where I found them.

Fortunately for her father, he remained tolerant out of survival and love for his daughter. The two of us agreed on that accord. We both loved her.

"Grand Magister," they greeted.

"You're late," Pandora said.

"Pandora, please," her mother hissed.

I met her annoyed gaze. My love didn't disappoint me. She wore the black dress with the wrap-around collar and black heels, the sexy ones with the ankle straps that made her legs go on forever, the same shoes I imagined her wearing too many nights over the past year. Her long locks lay across her shoulder, begging me to touch them. I imagined wrapping my hand around the curly mass when her father cleared his throat, reminding me that we weren't alone.

Pandora sighed. "You're late, Grand Magister."

"Occupational hazard." I moved across the room to join her. "You look lovely."

She narrowed her eyes. "I know. I followed your instructions."

Her feisty attitude remained. At least my fantasies didn't color my reaction to her.

"Grand Magister, don't mind her. It's been an emotional evening, and my daughter gets easily overwhelmed," her mother said.

Pandora shook her head at her mother then glared at me.

"I know." Despite knowing that she was adopted, Pandora resembled her father with her crossed arms and hard-eyed gaze, including some of the attitude. It wasn't a strong resemblance, but I would have thought they were a family if not for my research into Pandora's history. It was amazing how much nurture affected a person. What would she pick up from me? "Not to worry, Mrs. Spellman. It's expected."

I noticed that her mother clung to Pandora's bicep while her father openly censured me with his eyes. Her mother mentioned an "emotional evening." They must have done quite a bit of talking while I was toiling away in my lab. Not all of it was Pandora singing my praises, either. It wasn't as if their opinions mattered. I wanted their daughter, not them. They were there at my grace. If they became a problem, I would explain to them their roles, but not before I got a feel for the situation. Loyalty and commitment went further than forced compliance.

I'd start with dinner.

I made eye contact with one of the servers waiting by the kitchen door, then nodded. They hurried away to begin serving the meal, and I turned my attention to Pandora. "Dinner will be served shortly. I apologize for keeping my Kitten waiting."

"Don't—"

I caressed her face. "—what?"

She tightened her jaw. Her cinnamon eyes glittered in the lighting while her lavender and vanilla scent enticed me. I leaned in close.

"Grand Magister, you're getting out of hand with my daughter." Her father wedged in between us. "I'm... grateful for your rescue, but you're forcing your personality on her."

His tone was pleasant, but his eyes were cold, and one couldn't miss the curl of his upper lip and the bearing of his teeth as he protected Pandora from me.

From me.

Patience.

I willed away the impulse for petty violence. Pandora would be mine when the time came. Showing her how rash she made me didn't serve me, and it ruined the seduction. Once we started having children, she and her parents would comply if for no other reason than keeping our progeny safe. Her parents wouldn't offer Pandora up to me if I couldn't behave. It was annoying but impressive.

I stepped back—for her. "You have a valid point, Mr. Spellman. I would expect those under my protection to have integrity. I should lead by example."

He relaxed. All the while, Pandora watched me. Did she expect me to do something foolish or provide an opening for her to escape?

No Kitten, I plan to keep you unbalanced the way you make me.

The kitchen door swung open, and the first dishes arrived. I motioned for all of us to sit at the table. "Pandora, I want you on my right."

I held out the chair for her then pushed it in when she sat. My hand skimmed the naked part of her back. It was the one concession to restraint, copping a quick feel of her satiny skin. She gave me a side glance but said nothing. The fire remained in her gaze.

So that was the new tactic: silence. It wouldn't work. There was more to her than words. It was in her stance and her eyes, the way they flashed whenever I asked something of her. Nothing about her nonverbals indicated compliance, and the way she gripped her father's shoulders when he stood up to me meant she still cared for her parents.

"What did you discuss while you waited for me?" I asked as an attendant placed salad in front of me.

"Oh, we just caught up with each other," her mother chirped. "Our baby has grown up so much. The last we saw her, she was a budding adult."

She was a mediator. I would use that.

"I'm sorry I missed out on your reunion. Did you let Pandora know you were living in the tower?"

"We didn't get around to that yet. There was too much hugging and admiring the changes in our baby girl," she added. "Though we hope she can visit our apartment sometime."

"Of course, once she settles in. There were several matters left open in her absence that required her attention." I took a sip of wine. The headiness of the sweet wine warmed me to my toes. Or was it breaking bread with my taciturn lover in the early days of our seduction? "You should try the wine, Pandora. It's Riesling, your favorite."

Anything to end her silence.

Her eyebrow quirked. "You remembered?"

"I couldn't forget, Kitten."

She took the glass. I expected her to luxuriate with it the way she usually did, not to toss it back like a shot of whiskey. "Glass empty. Anything else?"

"Pandora." Her mother clucked her tongue.

Her father put his hand over his wife's. "I was unaware you were in charge of my daughter's schedule. Her mother and I haven't seen her. If she wants to see us, I expect her to visit."

"You are welcome to expect that." I glanced at Pandora and her half-lidded eyes. Was she trying to seduce me so I would change my mind? It wouldn't be that easy, no matter how sexy she appeared fidgeting in her chair. We were well past the innocent act.

But damn it, she looks good. I would take a long cold shower after our meal to reorient my discipline.

"What are your intentions towards my daughter?"

I drained my glass then unbuttoned my collar. Her father's line of questioning was not unexpected though the bluntness reminded me of my Kitten. He was a greater influence in her life than I realized. I could use that in my negotiations with her. "We've been apart for the last year, but I consider her my fiance. Even though—"

Pandora's gasp drew my attention. We met gazes briefly until I lost focus on the cherry tomato that she luxuriated over before taking the entire thing in her mouth.

I tore my gaze from her tantalizing mouth to focus on her father's brooding one. "—it's our first night back. However, I thought it would be selfish to keep her all to myself the first night."

"I bet." He snorted.

"Pandora, honey, are you okay?" Her mother put her utensils down and rose.

"I'm feeling fine." She ran her foot down my leg from my knee to my ankle.

I shifted in my seat. My head ached as my thoughts went between taking Pandora on the table in front of everyone or under the table for some privacy. It didn't help that she moved from rubbing against my leg to my thigh and groin. All while using her sexy garnet gaze to give me those wanton looks that I missed. The same one that last time I viewed it, we ended up coupling on top of a pyramid.

"Are you sure?" her mother asked. "I think—"

"Never better, but all this conversation has brought something up that I need to speak to Matt about." Her voice was husky. "There are some things I need to get off my chest. Would you mind if we talked alone?"

"Sweetheart," her father protested.

"It will be fine," Pandora assured him. "Trust me. I know what I'm doing."

Her chest heaved as though she were breathing hard but without the duress. Underneath the table, her foot play grew more urgent. I wouldn't survive much longer. If her parents didn't leave on their own soon, I would make them. "I will be on my best behavior Mrs. Spellman, but we need to talk…immediately. I have a lot to say to her."

"Come on, Maxwell. Let's trust our daughter."

Her father glared at me. "Grand Magister or no, if you—"

"I get the point." My focus was on Pandora and how her chest moved when she took heavy breaths in that dress. I was a hair away from ripping it off and skipping right to dessert.

"Bye, Dad."

Her parents left, albeit reluctantly. I muttered a spell to lock the door after them, then I pounced.

uyen

Present Day

"Why in the hell didn't you contact me before you went out to Fairy Stone? Bane is all over my ass because…" Tonya stomped down my basement steps. I regretted giving her access to my security wards the moment her petulant rant turned to a homicidal glare at the sight of my cast.

I covered it with an old shirt that I used for potion materials then feigned nonchalance. "Hi, come on in. I'm not busy or anything."

"Don't try to play with me, Drew. I already saw the cast on your arm. I'm not blind." She growled, then tossed away the shirt so she could examine me for herself.

"I'm fine," I assured her while she fussed. "I just miscalculated, that's all. How did you find out?"

She continued to glare at my cast with her hands on her hips before sighing and meeting my eyes. "It doesn't take a genius to figure out a freak storm that involved key Obscura personnel that was within three hundred miles of this place would have you involved somehow. Ours was the only Camera cell out here, and I was with the NoVa cell, so that leaves—"

"The Chapel Hill cell."

She pointed her finger at me. "Don't make me hurt you."

"I wouldn't dream of it." When she relaxed, I gave her a half hug. "Does the NoVa cell know?"

"Yes, it's why Bane let me come back here to check in on you. What happened?"

"Not sure." That was the truth. I had been racking my brains the past few days since I got back home. "I disrupted the ritual, but I'm not sure if the powers were loose somewhere or if it blew up in our faces."

"How did that happen?" She pointed to my arm.

"Hard to say, but I think it happened after the tornado sucked me up and threw me in the lake. I woke up in the hospital this way."

Tonya cringed then went back to examining me like a mother hen. "I'm fine, thanks to the benefits of mundane health care and all healed with the help of a witch doctor."

She smacked my arm. "That's for making me think you were still hurt."

"I was in character in case authorities came to ask questions. So what about the NoVa cell, did they figure out anything about the outsiders?"

She shook her head. "No, the artifacts are leaving us clueless and we have not seen anything since the Fairy Stone incident. All Obscura activity has gone dark."

"Well, that fiasco at least accomplished something we can benefit from, though I'd rather the mundanes stay out of it."

"Yeah, the anti-magic chatter is increasing in the DC area. I heard there's supposed to be a protest near Mirror Lake in support of the Witchcraft Act." She grabbed a stool then perched on it. "The word is we have to keep all battles low-key or out of sight. Any more press on practitioners that isn't in a positive light is a no-go."

"And only Obscura seems to work that to their advantage. The mundanes who aren't afraid think Matt walks on water," I muttered. "He is making us look like a bunch of criminals."

"Matt? You and the Grand Magister are on a first-name basis now?" she chuckled nervously.

"Using his title just gives him power." I wasn't ready to disclose my relationship to him, even with Tonya. She would never understand. "Besides, you know what I mean. He's always one step ahead, and when we foil him, he still finds a way to come out on top."

Tonya put her hand on my shoulder. "You're not quitting on me, are you?"

"Hell no. Just pissed." I grabbed the Oya tome with my left hand. I flipped to the page with the circle drawing. "The forty-two point circle is the key to the whole thing. It's a universal number."

"More like it's a complicated number. What kind of circle has that many focal points on it? Five is enough for most workings, or even eight if you are willing to do some serious spell-slinging, but forty-two?"

I shrugged. "The ancients probably liked the complexity, but think about it. There are forty-two powers. It makes sense. The spell might have worked if each of the souls had power."

"How do you know they didn't?" she asked.

"There's no—"

"Before you, poo-poo on the theory, think about it," she said. "What if they were descendants of someone with one of the forty-two powers, then would it still work?"

I paused. She may be on to something. I knew Matt wouldn't sacrifice practitioners, but I hadn't considered their relations. If they were mundanes, he wouldn't have any qualms about giving their lives up to a ritual. "So they had a viable summon theory, but I disrupted it. Everyone was running everywhere, then the storm from the released energy or the rogue goddess started wreaking havoc in the park."

"There haven't been any more strange storms, nor did the Grand— Wesley. I can't bring myself to call him by his first name no matter what you say. He hasn't gained any powers from what we could tell, but there were deaths at the park from the storm."

My heart sank. It was my fault that the storm occurred. I should have stopped the ritual sooner. "How many?"

"Forty-two," she answered. "It's national news. That's why I expected the apocalypse from Obscura. Matt would have been a god and unstoppable, but everything has been quiet, and he's still playing nice to the public eye."

"You should have led in with that." It was my turn to be irate. I should have monitored the news for information, but I had been so busy researching. "This changes things. If the forty-two died and it was too coincidental not to be the ones standing in the summoning circle, the ceremony was likely successful. That's problem one. The second problem is the vessel. If it's not Matt, then who is it?"

She shrugged. "She might be loose, or maybe she atomized into spiritual energy since she didn't have a body. I don't know. That was all of the intel I had. That, and Obscura taking credit for saving two-hundred tourists and park rangers from the storm. According to the news, the incident was a tragedy but could have been much worse if not for Obscura's magical intervention."

I tossed the tome onto my desk then went to the rug on the floor. Pulling it back, I revealed a replica of the Oya circle.

"What is that?" she asked.

I couldn't tell if she was scared or excited, but I knew it was rhetorical. It was evident that I reconstructed the circle. She joined me in the center of the floor as she studied my work then stared at me.

"What did you do?"

"Nothing yet, but you got me thinking." I made a few changes to the circle with a piece of chalk. My additions resembled the eight-point circle that I favored for my "return to sender" working. "We don't know where the power went, so why don't we call it to us?"

Tonya gave me a dubious expression.

"And we do that, how? Sacrifice forty-two people like Obscura?" Her voice rose in pitch as she formed an X with her arms. "No, that's too far. I can't believe you'd do that."

And I couldn't believe she thought I would. No matter what Obscura did, I wouldn't resort to their means. It was campy, but coexisting was the best option for everyone. Otherwise, we'd just be right back in the same spot, but on the other side as the mundanes revolted under our heel. "Forty-two proxies should work since we're not trying to receive the powers, just find it."

She let out a breath then reached for my shoulder. I moved away to examine my handwork. "I wouldn't kill innocent people to get at Obscura."

"Just volunteers," she teased, but the edge in her voice had a dangerous undercurrent. I doubted that it was an actual joke.

I faced her. "Probably not even then. This war is taking a sharp edge with the government hanging enslavement over our heads, a goddess' powers in play, and the threat of outsiders. I'd like to say that I wouldn't, but it freaks me out that I may even have to make that decision."

Her gaze lowered to my feet, then back to my eyes. They had a soft but determined gleam. "I'm leaving Camera."

"I didn't expect that. Did something happen?"

She nodded. "It's too much. We're supposed to be the good guys. But too many of my supposed colleagues are spouting the same rhetoric as Obscura, except with Camera as the solution. I didn't sign up for that. I'm the only witch in my family. They don't know about... me, and I don't want them caught up in this mess when the dust settles."

She slumped onto the stool.

I joined her. "My family has several: my grandmother, parents, my aunt, my sister, and me. The rest of the family fear us on good days and try to weaponize us on others. Most of them are Obscura sympathizers—at least for what they *believe* the organization stands for, being the accountability of practitioners."

Tonya punched me playfully in the shoulder. "You never talk about your family, at least nothing of real substance, just safe things. I was starting to think you were ashamed of me or something."

"Well, *they* can be embarrassing sometimes, but it's mostly a habit. What happens in the family stays in the family." I quoted my parent's favorite maxim. It was a close second to "always perform your best."

"Drew," she said my name with an exaggerated pause. "Are you going to stay with Camera?"

"Not any longer than I have to." I met her gaze. "Defeating Obscura is personal for me, and I need the resources of Camera to do it. The rest will get figured out."

"What do you mean it will 'get figured out?'" she asked.

"Exactly that. Obscura wants to start a genocide just like the mundane but with themselves as the victor. I can't allow that."

She jumped to her feet. "And when they're gone, then what? There'll be a power vacuum. Camera will swoop in, and it will be the same flavor of mess."

Her fists shook with her devotion to the cause. She posed a valid point. Since I had a hand in the problem, my role was to take down Obscura. I was in no way qualified to lead. I put too much trust in Matt and his ideologies that I let the entire situation spin out of control. "Then I guess you should stay in Camera, work your way through the ranks, and run it when that happens or take over Obscura, which has a squeaky clean political reputation."

Her mouth dropped open. "Wha—What?"

"You heard me. It's easy to leave an organization when you disagree with the culture and say it's the organization's fault, but Obscura and Camera are made of people. Be one of them that makes a change."

"I-I-I well," she sat down. "You have a point."

"Pretty much always," I deadpanned.

"Whatever." She slapped my arm. "Thanks for the pep talk. Now it's my turn. I thought about what you said about the proxies for the forty-two powers. Even *if* you gather—sorry, *when* because I know you — the proxies, won't the spell return Oya to the location of the first summon?"

I rubbed my chin. The scratch of a couple of days' stubble reminded me that I needed to shave. "It might not, however since Murphy's law exists, it will probably return to Fairy Stone where the last successful one happened, which means I have to go back there. My brain hadn't caught up that far."

"Glad I could help." She smiled. "I'm going with you, by the way. This way, I can fish you out if you end up in a lake again."

"Ha. Ha. Ha."

She winked at me. I looked away. It may have been weeks since we became just friends, but I could still be lured in. I needed a girlfriend, a brown-skinned goddess with long legs that was funny, had magic, and a nice rack. I didn't need much. I'd take a handful.

"You're over there looking pervy."

"How does one 'look pervy?'"

She smirked. "For you, a stupid grin and fox eyes. It's comical and sexy at the same time. So who is she?"

"I haven't met her yet." I changed the subject. "When do you need to report to NoVa?"

"Tomorrow," she answered. "I have to make my report at the evening muster."

"Then we need to move fast. It's a two and half hour drive to Fairy Stone, and it's already three o'clock. There's no telling how long it will take to find the proxies for the forty-two powers."

Tonya pushed up the sleeves of her sweater. "Then let's get to work. I got dibs on the drive."

I shook my head. "On second thought, we may be able to use a spell. Obscura's out of the area, you have to get back, and I was there recently enough to have a mental anchor to the place."

I doubted I would forget the park so soon. It may have been a few days ago, but being sucked into a tornado and thrown into a lake wasn't something to fade quickly. Besides, the place teemed with magic. My senses recalled the feel of the area. The way the atmosphere energized me to the point that the hairs on the back of my head stood on end. Fairy Stone held too much potential to be forgettable. A travel spell would have no trouble bridging Fairy Stone to any place.

"Alright then, give me half the list, and we'll meet back here in two hours."

"Done," I replied. "You take the abjuration, alteration, conjuration, and divination schools while I take enchantment, illusion, invocation, and necromancy. We need an icon that represents each power within the school."

She patted my chest with a note of patronization. "Little known fact, I was listening all those times you were going on about magical theory. Don't worry about me. I got this." She ran up the stairs. "And by the way, you will tell me about this mystery girl of yours when this is all over."

"Maybe." I waved her off. It was dumb to let her think I moved on when I hadn't yet. It was even stupider to mourn the loss of a one-sided relationship that was wrong for her. If some other guy yanked her along the way I had, I would have flooded his house and car.

Leaving her alone was better for both of us.

Now I just need to live it.

18

uyen

Present Day

Two hours wasn't enough time when you had to scramble searching for representations of power. For the summon to work, I had to believe the proxy stood in for the item selected. When I set out, I thought the most challenging thing to find would be necromancy—which I was wrong about. The metronome reminded me of a beating heart, the pillar of necromancy power, with its rhythmic pendulum moving back and forth, marking the seconds. However, finding a proxy for a siren took thinking, some creativity, and a CD of my second favorite songstress Jasmine Simone—Diva's was sold out. I have gotten laid more times than I should have to her song "Say Yes."

"You're getting that face again," Tonya teased.

She was a good sport about everything, but I wouldn't push. I held up the CD. She gave me a knowing look. No words were necessary. "It will be sundown soon. Let's get to Fairy Stone."

We stood close to each other then joined hands. Since I knew the location, my power would drive the spell. "Spirits usher us across space, take us to my mind's place."

Traveling spells take getting used to—one moment we were in my quiet climate-controlled basement, the next the cold Virginia woods. The smell of pine and fresh dirt permeated then eased off as our brains adapted to the sudden change.

I glanced up at the sky. The sun still reigned supreme, but it was starting to lose. It was February, the dead of winter, and the way of things.

"I should have worn a thicker jacket underneath the suit," she murmured.

I didn't blame her. I underestimated the weather as well. The January weather had been mild, like the Southeastern portion of our state the last time I was there. Since then, the park embraced the bitter cold and a light dusting of frost. If we tried later, we'd run into snow and the possibility of Rangers asking questions. I considered it a good omen. "Walk faster. This spell heats up when it has to compensate for the change in surroundings quickly. Invisibility is a tricky business. I still have bugs to work out of it."

"At least you have two of them. Thanks for including me."

"Don't thank me. We have a mission." I couldn't bear to hear the gratitude in her voice. It was a backup suit. I fully planned to go out here alone again. She was with the NoVa cell. Tonya didn't need me. All I did and would do was complicate her life. She wouldn't move forward as long as she thought I was open.

"Well, I'm going to anyway." There was sass in her tone.

Why didn't I love her?

"..maybe the time is not right yet."

"What?" I spun around to where her voice sounded.

"I said the sun is still too bright. Maybe the time is not right yet," she repeated with exasperation. "The first ritual was done on the new moon, right?"

I knew what she implied, except we were weeks away from the

next new moon. "Yeah, beggars can't be choosers. Besides, we still have the circle. There's enough daylight to get to the amphitheater and draw. After that, we risk mistakes and discovery."

"I should have asked this before, but what if the area is guarded?"

"A state park is not going to guard a small area twenty-four hours a day. Especially since no one has attached value to this place outside of sentiment, anyone who trespasses will do it during the day. This is not like the side of the highway that's accessible with ease."

"And if we're surprised?"

Ye of little faith. I pulled a balloon out of my bag. "Then throw this."

"Now I feel better, and no, that's not sarcasm. I'm not in the mood for winter combat in the middle of a semi-dark murdery forest." She took the balloon, and I watched it disappear under the suit.

"Point taken. Though I will admit, it's more fairytale-like in the day."

"Says you."

We lapsed into mostly silence as I guided her from time to time with my voice. During the trip, we encountered evidence of people walking in the woods but no actual people. When we got to the amphitheater, the stage and seating close to the lake appeared untouched, but the surrounding area had broken trees, and the wooden fence was gone. They were minor barriers stating that the cleanup was in progress but no real deterrent. The park probably counted on the fact that few would travel to the park this late in the year. Also, the value outside of enjoyment of nature to mundanes was little. If we ran into anyone, it was likely another practitioner. "Since it's a gibbous moon, I will mark out the circle with a moonlighter."

"That's impressive." She whistled. "You know how to make that complicated monstrosity by heart?"

I did. As complex as the circle looked, it made sense to me. I saw it every time I closed my eyes for the past three months. Drawing it with ink only seen in moonlight wouldn't be difficult and the next day's sun would destroy the spell. "Once I finish, I will wait for the moon to shine on it, and we can place a power at each point."

"Get to work."

I took out a jumbo marker that I used as a stylus for my moon-lighter. Rune enchantments covered the plastic cylinder. I held it up to the quickly darkening sky. "Goddess of the moon here on my plate, allow me to capture your light. May it remain hidden in the day and show for one night all that I write."

The yellow marker glowed. It reminded me of a glow stick with its faint light, but I had confirmation my spell worked. I began drawing in the soil and grass.

"That spell never works for me," Tonya said as I worked. "You're the only practitioner I've ever seen that spell work for; usually an entire coven has to do it."

"Blame my grandmother," I replied. "I had to study magic just as diligently as my mundane studies. She was my magic teacher. There were plenty of incentives not to fail."

"Everything I learned about magic theory was from you. It's too bad there's no magic school. You'd be a great professor."

"Thanks, but I don't know if I have the patience for that. I can, however, recommend some reading material. If you have a moonlight lamp, everything by Michelle Gomez is good. She breaks down the fundamentals of magic in such a way that even if you don't have an active power, you can supplement your spell arsenal."

"Wait, the science fiction author? The one that writes the time-traveling series?"

"The same." I was about half finished with the circle. "Make a moon lamp, and you'll see what I mean."

"Why didn't you mention this before?"

I imagine her hands on her hips glaring at me or in my general direction since she couldn't see me. "You have not because you ask not."

"You're lucky. All I see is a floating highlighter dragging across the ground."

From the tone of her voice, I was fortunate she couldn't see me. "Be nice to me, and I will show you how to make a moon lamp."

She pish-ed. "Please, you'll show me anyway. I don't know why you're playing."

Tonya knew me too well. "Fair."

I finished the circle then sat in the middle so I wouldn't smudge the lines. The sky was dark now.

"Hungry?" she asked.

"Yeah, I should have brought a snack."

A candy bar appeared out of thin air. I pulled back the sleeve of my suit so she could see at least a shadow of my hand. The bar flew towards my hand.

"Guaranteed to satisfy," she said.

I sincerely hoped that she referred to the chocolate bar and not her. My mind was gutter trashy enough to imagine. It was enough to consider a spell to pass the lonely nights. I wasn't that desperate yet, but at the rate I went, it wouldn't be long. "Thanks for the candy."

"No prob," she mumbled around what sounded like a full mouth.

We ate in silence when I saw the dim glow of the circle shining. The moonlight streaming through the trees was enough for us to get started placing the proxies. I stood, then leaped out of the ring. "Let's get started."

"How about you explain what you're doing?" A tall, stocky figure stepped out from behind a tree. The voice was male and familiar, but I couldn't place it. He trained a gun in my direction. He shouldn't have been able to see me. Something must have given my location away. I frantically looked around then caught sight of the indent of my boot prints in the dark, frosty soil. The guy was close enough to see me in the dark, but he wasn't likely to see Tonya.

Before I could reply, the figure bent over with his arm at an odd angle. "Who are you, and who are you with?"

That was my girl.

"Maxwell Spellman and—" he grunted.

"Max? you're a nurse at Sovah in Martinsville."

"Yeah, how did you know that?" he asked.

"It's unimportant. Why are you here?"

"It's my shift to patrol out here. My cousin has been watching this place since the Obscura shitstorm. Duong? Oh, is that you?"

"Let him go," I said to Tonya and pulled back my hood to show my face. In the week leaving the hospital, I checked in on him using a few informal channels. Everything he said had checked out. His coven was on the network for placing runaway kids with power into safe homes. Max was a good person, but I didn't want him to be privy to this ritual. He was an outlier in the civil war.

"Thanks." He rubbed his shoulder. "Now, why are you out here? Didn't you get enough of Deputy Wright's brand of southern hospitality the last time?"

"I'm a glutton for punishment," I said. "Joking aside. I have something to do, and then we are leaving."

Maxwell stepped forward, then paused and looked over his shoulder. "You were smart to bring a bruiser with you this time, but you don't live here. Another stunt like last month will bring out the welcome committee, and they'll start patrolling this area along with other creative activities under the guise of protecting."

I figured something like that between what Tonya said about unrest in DC and the local news. A small-town isolated from multiple forms of municipal support would resort to vigilantism. It was as much the southern way as breathing. "I was about to prepare a barrier to keep out intruders or anything else."

Maxwell relaxed. "Thanks for being a straight shooter. I hate when people lie. So many do it for no reason. It pisses me off."

It wasn't the first time he said something odd about whether I was telling the truth or not. And I knew he was a practitioner, so there was only one conclusion to be made. "You have veritas?"

"Yes and xenoglossia, none of which helps defend, only spy, so don't give me a hard time. Please answer my question."

I wouldn't lie, but I wouldn't tell him either. "I'm trying to find the person who caused the storm. Obscura may be after them."

"Okay, that was true, but you're leaving things out. I guess that's going to have to be true enough for now," Max replied. "How can I help? And before you say no, I have to report to my coven, and there's no way you can get me to leave without causing a scene by alerting them or the mundane employees. So which is it—a collaboration or a fail?"

Irritation made me jittery. I didn't like surprises in my plans. Max seemed to be alone. From his tone, either he wasn't, or there were checking-in periods. Most covens were small, with less than five practitioners. I bet they wouldn't spare two members to be out in the woods at night no matter how magical the situation. There would be check-ins of some unknown frequency. It was easier to comply than to read-just on the fly. Besides, I knew *him*, not his coven. "You can place these barrier spells along the perimeter."

I gave him eight incense sticks.

"Do I light these?"

"No, they will light when the barrier closes. It's a ghost flame so that we won't burn down the park."

"Ghost flame? What is that besides not harmful to trees?"

"It's a flame that exists on the astral plane. It affects astral bodies and Spirits, not the physical." I glanced up at the sky then behind me. The circle was in complete gibbous moon exposure. "Let's move. We're burning moonlight."

Maxwell took the incense sticks then trotted off to place them.

"I hope you know what you're doing involving him," Tonya said once he was out of earshot.

I didn't. "It's not like we had a choice. Besides, didn't you say this was bigger than the two of us, and I should trust more people?"

"Yeah, but not the first random person you see."

The exasperation was evident in her tone. "I met Max in the hospital, and he kept the mundanes off me when they started asking questions. He's not random. My gut tells me he's important in this. And he passed my background check."

Tonya chuckled. "I have to say it's annoying, but I do love your paranoia. It saved my bacon more than a few times."

I bowed. "Why, thank you."

"Wow. That's so weird watching a floating head bowing. I wasn't sure if you fell over at first."

I could relate. It was even stranger talking to a disembodied voice. "It's the price of doing business. Let's set up."

We placed the proxies at each of the forty-two points. I wasn't sure how Obscura had them, but I deemed it necessary to group them by the craft school. The placement looked better to me with the grouping. It made sense to me since the circle was so precise. The points might as well have organization too.

When we finished, Maxwell announced the barrier was up. I observed the mist that surrounded the perimeter. Everything appeared as it should.

"And what's this?" he asked.

"The ritual," I answered.

"You know, for a guy who hardly talks, you're a smart ass," Maxwell grumbled.

"I reserve the right to get better," I muttered. "It's time."

I cleansed my thoughts.

"Goddess of the Wind, Oya of the Orishas, I name you. I seek the vessel of your power. In the Moonlight hour, please send right away my enemy's prey." I lifted my hand skyward. "Goddess of the wind. Oya—"

Wind swirled around us in a column of dirt and residue. Then shot skyward.

"What the hell was—" Dirt cut off Max's statement when it rained down over us.

I coughed. "—of the orishas I name you. I seek the vessel of your power. In the Moonlight hour, please send right away my enemy's prey."

My throat burned, but I had to remain focused. "Goddess of the Wind. Oya of the Orishas—"

A blast of wind knocked me to the ground and the breath out of me. I lost my enchantment flow.

Damn it.

I sat up as a figure hovered in the swirling gray wind. A confused set of garnet eyes met mine. Crimson eyes? Well, a reddish-brown, they were beautiful as was their owner. The woman or maybe she was the goddess Oya. She wore a tattered toga about her, though that was something I expected Romans to wear. I wouldn't ask considering the last documented time she was seen was during that period. "Who are—"

The wind abated, and she dropped. I threw myself forward in an idiotic attempt to catch her or divert some of the energy from her fall, but we ended up rolling in the messy tangle of limbs and fire until we came to a stop.

Then I blacked out.

19

andora

50 A.Q.

The sun shining in my eyes should have been the first sign that I was in trouble. I enjoyed the star as much as the next person but not in my face when I first awoke. Matt draped his arm across my waist as he pulled me closer to him.

Wait. What?

I shot out of bed. The thundering of my blood in my ears assured me that I was, in fact, awake. My pulsing head let me know I was alive just in hell. Matt, the Grand Magister of Obscura, lay bare on my bed. And I...

I checked myself. I don't know why I bothered with the confirmation. The lack of clothing and the ache in other parts of my body explained the entire situation.

Last night we ate dinner, and I wanted him with a hunger that should have alarmed me. I even convinced my parents to leave then—I cringed at the memory after the debauchery. He drugged me. I never thought he'd—I should have known better.

My eyes misted, and anger welled in my throat. He really wouldn't stop at anything. A red rage filled my gaze.

"You," I choked out as I dove on top of him.

His gray eyes flew open at my snarl. He caught my arms then threw me across the room with his power. I slammed the back of my head against the wall. Stars danced in front of my eyes. I blinked to remove them and found myself on the bed again. Matt examined me with a squinty gaze. I tried to back away from him, but his magic pressed me down.

"Stop before you make me hurt you." He growled, pinching the bridge of his nose.

"Or what? You won't bother making me want you. You'll just take it instead?" I grit my teeth. The stars were almost gone. If he kept throwing magic at me, I would find a way to overpower him without transforming.

"What? I didn't," he sputtered at a loss for words as he caressed my face. "I love you."

"Don't you touch me, asshole," I screamed, sending him flying away with *his* power. It was dirty using anything of his, but at the moment, I didn't care. My heart and head hurt. Stupid me still carried some sort of torch for him, as absurd as it was. I was an idiot—a naive idiot.

Released from his power, I grabbed the bedsheet. I didn't want him to see me. I would never be vulnerable to him again.

"Kitten— Pandora stop. I didn't drug you."

I reached for my bag. I needed my sword. He'd regret not taking my weapons from me for the brief second before I chopped off his balls. The moment I touched my bag, a circle formed underneath my feet. A wave of nausea washed over me.

What was he doing to me? My body refused to cooperate as I sank into the floor.

"You can imprison me. I'll escape, and I will kill you," I vowed as I fell through whatever trap he enabled.

The last thing I saw of him before it swallowed me whole was his desperate attempt to reach for me. Again with the acting. It was probably so he could play my savior again in a year and conveniently forget that he drugged me and had his way with me all night.

Dumb. I thought I knew how far he'd go with his little games. But I knew nothing.

A cyclone of dirt and who knew what else swirled around me in the darkness. Not quite the oblivion of being in a dark place, but moonlight shone above me. There wasn't a hole with my enemy staring back at me but the gibbous moon that peaked in between the trees. The Grand Magister must have banished me to the lawless zone. I would survive, and then I would hunt *him*.

I hovered in the cyclone with my sheet whipping about my legs when I caught sight of a man watching me. Great, the slavers already had a bead on me, and I was in the wilderness in a bedsheet separated from my bag. Then as if my day couldn't be even more far out, the cyclone just dissipated. I dropped to the ground and landed on something hard, then rolled across the way. My back and legs stung as sticks and stones cut into me before I rolled to a stop. A heavy weight lay on top of me, making it difficult to breathe.

We laid there for a few breaths. Neither of us moved. I wasn't even sure if I was conscious until the pain of my injuries started nagging at me. First things first, I needed to heal myself, then I'd deal with the rest.

"Are you okay?" The slaver asked.

He had me pinned to the ground. A chill flowed over me. I lost my sheet in the tumble, and he stood over me while I was naked and easy. At least that's what he probably thought. "Get off me, slaver."

"Slaver? Wait."

I tossed him away with my power and then jumped to my feet. It was freezing, I was naked, and slavers rarely traveled alone. They ran in gangs when they roamed the lawless zone. There was bound to be another one nearby.

Something punched me in the jaw, then wrapped one of my arms around my back, and the other locked around my neck while placing pressure. Worse than the slavers. It had to be Camera. Matt wouldn't send someone after me so soon after my banishment.

You also thought he wouldn't drug you, too.

Magic tingled my skin. The sensation was passive. A practitioner throwing spells and power at me was fresh air while this was the stale feel of a magical device. My attacker wore a cloak of invisibility. The longer they held me, the more magic I would absorb from it. "Release me. I will only ask once."

"Hell no," a woman replied, then tightened her hold over me.

I shimmered away from her grasp. Without knowing where I was, I couldn't teleport far—a few feet in front of her was all I could manage in the dark. From my new position, I observed my attacker, a partially visible person in some sort of gray suit. All I could see was a floating torso and one arm when she turned toward me, then charged.

"Wa-wa-wait," A familiar voice said. "We mean you no harm, but you threw our friend in a tree. Retaliation makes sense."

I growled, then turned sideways to keep my eyes on the floating torso and the stocky shadow man in my view. His voice reminded me of someone I couldn't place, but that didn't equal a friend. If anything, he was likely Obscura.

"Leave me alone, and this will end," I replied.

"Well, you see you kind of put us in a pickle when you threw Duong over there in that tree—"

"Grandaddy Max," came out of my mouth, then I hit the ground.

"Gotcha," Torso replied.

Something sharp pressed against my throat.

"Now get my friend down safely, or I will hurt you."

I focused on the dark figure struggling in a high tree. It hadn't been my intention to throw him up there, but it served my purposes. The guy could die for all I cared. I wasn't about to help Camera or Obscura, especially for lifting the memory of my dead grandfather and using it against me. "Eat shit and—"

"Let her up. She's going to get hypothermia with no clothes on. We need her, and you'll catch more flies with honey than piss and vinegar," the shadow man said. "By the way, your enchantment is wearing off. You're half visible."

"Not until she releases—"

I grabbed the Duong person from the tree then sat him down

beside us. It wasn't worth it to me to freeze to death. I needed to find my bag.

"Thanks," he replied.

He sounded dazed. Torso released me then pounced on him.

I shifted my attention when a coat surrounded my shoulders. Shadow Man sounded like Grandaddy Max. He used phrases just like his. It was too cruel, but I had to dispel the shadow man to reduce the hold they had over me. I touched his hand.

The energy of a practitioner flowed through him. He wasn't a construct or an illusion. I formed a small light orb so that I could see his face. It was a man in his thirties with dark hair and a stocky build. What drew my eye was the pushed-up sleeve that revealed a panther tattoo down the side of his arm. It was a few years old instead of the faded and wrinkly version I was used to seeing. "Grandaddy Max, it is you!"

I gripped him around the waist. Tears streamed down my face as I held him. I hadn't seen him since I was fifteen—and overall, a bad year for me. His death heralded the beginning of everything going wrong in my life. He was alive, and—I pulled away. "How are you so young?"

He stared at me with a puzzled look. "You keep calling me your granddaddy, and I'm not even a daddy yet."

I covered my mouth. I looked towards the lovebirds on the ground near us. Their attention focused on me. "What year is it?"

"2021," Duong answered with a pensive expression. "I must have worded the spell incorrectly. It was supposed to return Oya—The spell that was cast last, not bring someone from another time."

My heart fluttered. It couldn't be. Of all the places and time periods for me to end up.

"Did you—" I gathered myself. I could mess up the timeline to something worse if I just started spouting off who I was. "Are you Quyen Doung?"

Duong's eyes widened. "How do you know my name?"

"Quyen?" Torso asked. "What is she talking about? I thought your name was Andrew, Drew."

"It's my middle name," he replied, then stared at me. "Answer the question."

His dark eyes were every bit as brooding as I imagined they were from reading his journal. Quyen didn't trust easily. The best thing I could be was transparent. Besides, Grandaddy would know if I lied. I didn't know what kind of relationship Quyen had with my grandfather, but I couldn't afford them not to trust me. At least not until I could manage to take care of myself. "I won't get into the details, but let's just say, years from now, you are known."

Quyen glanced toward Grandaddy. I caught the subtle nod exchanged between them. I was vetted for now.

I kept the flow of conversation moving. "And you must be Tonya. You do have a great right hook."

She slid the invisibility hood back. With her head exposed, she was the top half of her body. "Nice to know that my rep precedes me."

"It does, though it was a little underestimated," I added. Quyen never had to be on the receiving end of her wrath. It made sense for his assessment. He tended to focus more on magic anyway. "Now, how did I get into the past? You said something about a spell?"

"We can talk once we get you out of the cold." Grandaddy Max held me by the shoulders. "You are shivering."

"If I had my bag... I have clothes in there." The world spun. I dropped to my knees.

"Easy now. You're going into shock." He steadied me, but his face fell back into the shadow as the light spell faded. Or was it my sight?

Either way, I knew no more—again.

20

*M*att

50 A.Q.

I slapped my hand over the void in the floor only to be met by a barrier. There was nothing to do but watch as Pandora fell out of sight. She was gone, and I couldn't follow. Heads would roll for this, starting with the inciting incident that left me open to attack: drugging the two of us with a love potion. There was only one person bold enough to do it... Lauren.

Her concession to my request had been too easy. I should have known. She thought she knew best for my life because she appeared older than me. We were both eighty-two. Appearance had little to do with wisdom. Lauren nearly cost me Pandora. I would have had Pandora in a few weeks and my bed within a month. Instead, I lost a tremendous amount of footing in exchange for a few hours.

Last night reminded me how much I craved Pandora's touch, the way her body wrapped around mine, how I missed the euphoric sensation of her siphoning off some of my magic as we moved together. She was addictive. Once I had her, giving her up was difficult, and now I had to go without because of Lauren's antics at matchmaking.

As though I couldn't secure my woman on my own.

It was a shit morning.

"Someone stole my woman," I bellowed.

Guards entered the room with their defenses at the ready. They averted their eyes. In my anger, I had forgotten that I remained undressed. I grabbed my pants. "Search the tower and the surrounding area. Someone stole Pandora away from me. Include the lab for any experiments that have gone awry. This was beyond Camera. Do not engage her once you find her but let me know. The kidnapper has made things complex between the two of us."

"Yes, Grand Magister," they said, then hurried away to carry out my orders.

I quickly dressed and stalked to Lauren's residence. As my assistant, she had the title of Magia Lectore and lived on the same floor as me. The only ones on my private floor were her and Pandora. It was a bit ironic. I placated Lauren because of my fondness for her intellect and ability to get around her lack of magic. Such resourcefulness deserved a reward. If she'd been a witch, she would have been mine, but the dynasty I planned on forging needed power which Pandora would provide. Though, I wouldn't have known my Kitten if not for Lauren... then the minx orchestrated it all to be taken away.

I wanted to know why.

Her assistant hurried towards me as I neared. It was not uncommon for my people to respond to my moods with alacrity. Word would spread that Pandora was not only taken, but I was angry. They may not know the details, but they would do their best to amend the situation.

"Grandmaster, I just heard from the guards that mistress Pandora was taken. I will begin immediately on this task." He bowed his head. "There's also one additional matter that you must be made aware of."

"What is it?" If something else went wrong, I was likely to snap. I held out my hand and centered my mind. Pandora was powerful. I trained her. She could handle her assailant until I arrived. Then I would repair the rift between us. It was a minor setback that would further strengthen our children and us.

He wrung his hands. "Magia Lectore passed away last night."

My heart dropped to the pit of my stomach. I knew Lauren didn't look well, but I had no idea that she was that bad. "And no one informed me?"

He turned bright red and began to simper. "You-you-you were heavily engaged, Grand Magister, and presented no opportunity to interrupt. Which is a testament to your stamina, if I may add."

"No, you may not. That is an awkward thing to say to stroke my ego. Don't mention it again. Where is she—her body?"

My new assistant cleared his throat. "She asked to be cremated right away. Since all of her family was gone, she did leave this."

I gritted my teeth and snatched the note he produced from his lab coat pocket. Annoyed, I walked to my office. When the elevator doors opened to my workspace, I grabbed a vase then threw it. The physical outburst was enough to dull the knife of my anger. Using my power, I slammed my desk against the wall. It *was* a shit morning. Pandora was gone, and Lauren was dead.

What in the hell was my next move?

I shoved my bookshelf over, sending books and papers everywhere. I grabbed the one that landed near me, determined to rip it to shreds, but it was an image of Pandora in the throes of passion. The drawing depicted her on a table, with hands boxing her in while she was in the mid-thrusts of ecstasy. It was as I remembered her last night. I turned the page, and the expression of accusation stared back at me. My gaze immediately went to the date.

February of 2021, when my dreams began. I hadn't dreamt of her since she became mine. There was no need. The reality was torturous enough, waiting for her to be of age then cultivating her interest in me. During that time, I never made the connection.

Eureka.

I flicked my hands towards my bookshelf. Papers and the desk and books picked themselves up and repositioned to the way they were before I threw them. The scratches and the breakage, I would contend with later.

The fact that I possessed an image of Pandora depicting our drugged lovemaking and her rage the morning after fifty years before it happened... This was a breakthrough. I laughed. "She was stolen from me. Technically I stole her from myself."

My experiment with Timeless must have been successful. I don't recall it happening in the past. But I must have done it. Otherwise, I wouldn't have been able to dream of her in the first place. I went to my whiteboard and snatched up a stylus. A circle appeared under Pandora before she dropped through it. It seemed familiar. I sketched it out then stood back.

The outer edges reminded me of the forty-two-point circle of the failed ritual or something. I must have modified the center with an eight-point ring. A ten-point circle would be much better for my purposes.

This is the kind of rigid spell Quyen liked to use. He would create ten enchantments when one would do. It was what finally killed him, his inflexibility.

Then it struck me. I did have a moment of weakness some years ago when I tried an out-of-the-box solution. In my memories, it didn't work. But what if I created an alternate reality where my time-travel spell worked? Pandora may be there. I could use the ten-point circle coupled with Timeless to follow her. While I was there, I would do things right, and since she was there too, I could rule with her by my side fifty years earlier.

"Lemonade for the lemons given to me." I gathered the materials needed for Timeless then set up my circle. I preferred a solution with more flexibility.

The spell was likely to drop me in the Fairy Stone Woods since it was the site of Obscura Tower before Pandora's first outburst destroyed the Richmond tower. Fairy Stone was more powerful because of its position next to the leylines. It was perfect as my seat of power. Landing there would not be an issue. My only concern was the paradoxical nature of the visit.

One of two things would happen: I would ally with my past self to accomplish my goals then continue fighting my past self for power and Pandora, or my theory of a soul traveling through time was valid, and there was no past self to overthrow. If the latter, I wouldn't have to worry about it because I would be destroying this timeline and living in a new one.

It was a risk experimenting on myself, but then letting my past self fail, or allow someone else to claim Pandora wasn't an option, neither was a chance that she disrupted the timeline without me being there to compensate. I would have to go. There wasn't enough time to consider all of that. It was do or die. Besides, with her gone, I would have to bank on myself, and that Timeless worked. "Deities of time and space, I implore you. Return me to the place I've been as it was before. Send my soul through time's veil to where my desire entails."

A wave of dizziness washed over me. I reached for—not sure what since I was in the center of my office when a soft hand steadied me.

"Are you all right, Matt?" Lauren asked.

She was the version I met nearly sixty years ago, with walnut-colored skin, hazel eyes, lovely dark hair. The shape of her face reminded me a little of Pandora, something I hadn't noticed before. That would be ironic if they were distantly related. They are both essential, and my rise would be poetic.

I stepped away to study her. Exactly as I remember. I crushed her against me.

"Now, I know you're not okay," she teased as she hugged me back.

What was I doing? There was no time for sentimentality. The spell worked. My calculations were off since I was in the old Obscura Tower and not Fairy Stone. The important part was that I was in the past and not a catatonic, charred version of myself. I could puzzle out the fine points later. There was no going back. This time I would do everything the way I should have, starting with Lauren.

I pulled away from her to reorient our focus. Ours was a platonic working relationship. It would remain that way. "I'm fine, Magia Lectore. We have work to do."

And a destiny to change.

21

 uyen

Present Day

I paced the floor of Maxwell's living room. It was safe to say that the summoning did not go as planned. I wasn't even sure it was successful. Trying again grew less possible with each moonrise of the waning year. It was difficult enough working the spell last night. The next time it would require even more power and have a higher risk of discovery. For what?

Currently, I had a sexy, tight-lipped time-traveling woman that knew me—well, of me. I wanted answers, but she was unconscious, and Max wouldn't let me go through the bag that fell through with her. Apparently, being called Grandaddy Max obligated him to protect her privacy and take care of her.

Max's wife walked into the room. She put a hand on Max's shoulder. He nodded, then kissed her hand.

"Our visitor is sleeping," he said aloud while signing. "Trina says she's resting, and confirms that she is telling the truth and her name is Pandora."

Now I had a name to go with the face.

"Confirmed? I thought *you* had the power to tell when someone was lying."

"I do, but Trina is a listener. I wanted to ensure that our visitor wasn't a pathological liar," he answered.

That made sense. That was the one drawback to Max's power. If the person honestly believed the lie or gave creative responses to questions, they could dodge him. His wife didn't look like any of the listeners that I encountered. The whites of her eyes were normal. Despite their name, they typically had black sclera when they used their powers. Mundanes usually took the whites of the eyes turning black as a sign of demonic activity, so many of them were killed. Peters, Obscura's head of security and another that joined around the time of my falling out, wore dark glasses to pass.

Trina's power was another wrinkle. As a listener, she could pick up some thoughts, usually impulsive ones. However, depending on how strong of a witch Trina was, she might be able to read another's mind uninhibited. Pandora was unconscious, and Trina was still able to corroborate her story. I'd have to be careful to keep my own secrets.

As if sensing my thoughts, which she likely did, Trina signed.

"Relax. I have to touch you or an object to get the good stuff," Max translated.

"Good to know."

"New powers. I'll be fascinated later. How are we going to fix this?" Tonya asked. "This is some crazy, next-level sci-fi madness. Did the ritual cause a time paradox? Is the world going to explode?" She made an explosive gesture with their hands.

Trina signed, and Max spoke. "Trina says that a paradox can't happen because only one Pandora exists here. We have to be more concerned about the butterfly effect."

"And that is?" I asked.

Trina signed, "Every action she makes here, no matter how minor, has a ripple effect that changes history. The fact that we know she's our granddaughter changes Max and I's history. We never thought we'd have—"

She caressed her abdomen. Max paused in his translation, took her hand, and she kissed him.

I turned away from the tender moment. The catch in Max's voice and the misty look in Trina's eyes told volumes. It also explained the protective vibe from him toward our visitor. Pandora was the promise of a family they didn't think they'd have.

Infertility was not uncommon with practitioners. Witches and wizards rarely had children together, and most of the time, we inter-married, making it more difficult to control our bloodlines and pass on knowledge.

Families like mine didn't occur often, and even with my own, there were only five of us. We were lucky that my grandmother's magic was more potent than my grandfather's mundane genes. Still, out of her six children, only my mother and aunt were witches. Of course, those with magic would have to monitor descendants for the next few centuries to see if magic developed within our mundane relatives.

"My bad. This is huge for you too," Tonya said.

The Spellmans nodded.

"I'm sorry too," Max continued translating. "I'm sure you can relate to our problems."

Trina glanced at Tonya and me.

"We're not together," she replied while I sputtered like an idiot. Max laughed, and Trina smacked them on the shoulder. He sobered.

"As I was saying, we have to be sensitive about asking her questions and learning too much, or we could destroy everything we love."

"Considering that I want to change most things, that's going to be difficult," Pandora said from the hallway.

We all turned to her. Clothed in some sort of leather desert wear from out of a post-apocalyptic movie, she walked into the living room. The headdress she wore gave her a sexy priestess appearance with an animal skull and gazelle-like horns. Long pieces of fabric and feathers adorned the back of the otherworldly hair ornament. Then there were those cinnamon-colored eyes. They could pierce through a person's soul.

Whatever future she came from haunted her. When her beautiful red gaze settled on me, I responded inappropriately—my body did anyway. My mind, thank the goddess, could run on autopilot.

"Then you should be open to explaining when and where you came from." It came out assholish, which was better than lusty. I did have a job to do.

"I come from a future where the Grand Magister rules the United Nations of Obscura after the destabilization of the American government. Much of the world is closed off and composed of destabilizing factions and lawless zones due to the Sphinx—that's what we call Oya's wild rampages. Obscura is nearly everywhere, but even he doesn't have full control."

The goddess destroying everything was not something I wanted to hear. I shouldn't have disrupted the ritual. Either Oya found a vessel, or she was running free. "And no one stopped them?"

"He briefly managed to control the Sphinx. Once he had it, no one could stop him except the size of his ambition. However, he can only be in one place at a time," she answered.

Max stood with his hands palms out. "Whoa now, let's pump the brakes on the doom and gloom here. I know we're in a pickle, but what you're saying sounds like it's hopeless. I don't believe that. It's just—"

"—a matter of turning the problem upside down, so the solution shakes out," she finished.

Max blinked. He rubbed the back of his neck. "I guess we're close then."

Pandora turned to him with a watery smile that grew at the sight of Trina. She took a step forward then paused before she began signing.

"It's good to see you both alive again," she said aloud for everyone's benefit.

"Okay. Okay. Let's get back on track. Obscura takes over the world, how?" I asked.

She cleared her throat. "First, politics created a divide between practitioners and their allies and those who wanted to recreate the Salem witch trials. Then thirty-five years later, the first Sphinx attack happens—"

There had to be more. I disrupted the summoning, and then the freed goddess waited three and a half decades to attack. Something was left out. "Hold a sec."

"Let her finish," Matt replied.

Pandora shook her head. "It's fine. I know him from his writings. He's onto something."

She focused her garnet gaze on me. I had her *other* attention. Her spicy, intense eyes... My mind went blank. I began to pace to move the blood from the southern portion of my body back north. I muttered under my breath in Vietnamese.

"Don't be frustrated. A breakthrough will come," Pandora replied in the same tongue.

Hearing her sultry voice in the language of my ancestors did not help curb the distraction.

"Get to the point," Max growled at me in the same language.

Way less sexy.

Pandora's eyes widened. "You have xenoglossia too, Grandaddy Max?"

He flushed then coughed. "How about G-max? I'm only thirty-one years old, and the Granddaddy title is a little bit much."

She nodded. "G-max and Nana?"

Trina signed vigorously then hugged Pandora.

"Okay." Tonya stood. "Look, this is complicated enough. How about we keep the languages to English until the facts are known? This is for the limited language people in the room."

"I can dig it." Pandora nodded.

Tonya tilted her head. "Did you just say..."

I put my hand on her shoulder. "Later."

"Here's the short version. I was pulled from my time, and since I'm here, I plan to set it back to the way it should be."

"Whoa there. We have to be careful." All eyes were on me. "I tried to summon Oya, and we saw how that turned out. Just because you look like some exotic, desert priestess that stepped out of an apocalypse movie doesn't mean you have all the answers."

Sexy as sin, though.

I left that part out, thankfully. "What makes you think that we can course-correct the future when we clearly failed the first time?"

The future sounded like it was a horrible, literal hell on Earth. I didn't want Matt to win, but I also was a realist. It's not like we would get multiple shots at the future. We didn't know how it happened the first time.

Pandora frowned. "You're more jaded than your writings. Did I do that to you when I told you about Obscura winning?"

My stomach fluttered at how quickly she pointed out my doubt. It was as if she knew me. I never fancied myself an author. I must have written some incredible work that touched lives in the future. "I deal in facts."

"Now, you have to deal in faith because I'm telling too much as it is. I don't want to reduce your use to me."

"Watch it, Pandora the Explorer," Tonya snapped. "You dropped into our lives, laid a bomb on us, and you thought we were going to buy whatever you say. Piss off, you don't know our lives."

"I know more than you think." She closed off the distance between her and Tonya. "I have everything to lose if I do nothing. Excuse me for ruining *your* day."

Tonya narrowed her eyes and balled her fist. I knew that look.

Stepping in between them, I said, "Both of you to your corners. Fighting amongst ourselves accomplishes nothing."

"It's far out. She's just protecting you," Pandora said before joining Max and Trina.

The seventies slang would take some getting used to.

"Let's start again," I suggested holding out my hand. "We haven't been formally introduced."

Pandora rolled her eyes.

"Quyen Duong, Tonya Jackson, Maxwell, and Trina Spellman," she rattled off. "Camera and Fairy Tail."

"Fine then, who are you?" I asked through gritted teeth.

She took my hand. The familiar zing of a practitioner was there. Her palms were more calloused than I would have expected, but the rest of her hand was soft. Touching her fed my lusty imagination. I must be worse off than I thought. *Get over yourself, man. Worst-case scenario, she's dangerous, and best case, she's someone's future kid's kid. You're just a perv to her even if you age slower than a mundane.*

She slipped her hand from mine. "Pandora Spellman, no allegiance or coven."

Max quirked his eyebrow at the last part of her statement. Coupled with the way she worded it, I suspected it wasn't a complete truth. I won't call her on it, not yet. "Well, I am more irate than when we started, so I guess introductions didn't matter."

Pandora sighed and sat on the floor. "Look, this is not my time, and I want to change one thing, not end all existence. I need your help, Quyen. I read your journal. You know the most about Obscura."

"Let's start from the beginning," Max said. "What is this Oya business? I keep hearing about it, but no one's explaining anything, and now it's time because we are at a point where this is getting too confusing."

I raised my hand.

"This is your chance to walk away. Both of you. You go any further, and you become a target for Obscura and Camera." I glanced at Tonya. "They will not like non-members knowing their secrets, and you'll be obligated to report me."

"So I have to leave after all." She shrugged. "Back to plan A."

"Are you sure?" I asked.

"Pandora, what does Camera do to stop Oya in your time?" Tonya asked.

"The Sphinx is too powerful for Camera. Obscura barely had a hold," she answered.

"Do they help people?" Tonya met her gaze with a stiff jaw and flat eyes.

Pandora shook her head. "Only if they have magic. They were considered rogues in my time, but they were just the opposite sides of the same coin. Both groups are selfish and out for themselves. The difference is Obscura lets you believe you are free and Camera does not."

Tonya turned away. "Then I'm in, but I'm staying with Camera. I thought about what you said earlier. We'll need someone on the inside, and no offense, Drew, they trust me more than they do you."

"Then they are smart. Besides, the feeling is mutual." I winked at her, then glanced at the Spellmans.

Trina signed furiously. Matt nodded in agreement.

"We are in, too," he said.

Trina glared at him then signed again.

"She said to try and leave us out, and she'll curse you," Pandora replied.

"So we're all in then," I said.

Now what? Were we a coven now? None of us knew each other. Secrets bounded us just as much as they surrounded us, but I wasn't ready to share everything. Our endeavor would fail if I weren't careful. It would stand to reason that whatever I said next sent us on the path to failure. Or was knowing enough to make a change in the future? I doubted we all knew our actions would lead to a certain point, not that it mattered since pre-knowledge was rarely a deterrent when a person was determined.

The question was if Pandora had remained asleep, what would have been my next course of action.

Interrogation and info gathering then go off on my own.

It was my M.O. My last collaboration created this mess. It was mine to clean up. Yet every time I turned around, these same people followed me. My instincts told me to trust them despite knowing I should go on my own.

"Quyen?" Pandora asked.

"Drew," Tonya corrected. "He goes by Drew."

"Sorry."

"It's fine. You can call me Quyen." Her use of my name cleared my doubt. The one thing I wouldn't have done if I continued unchanged was to operate in the open. I had to be honest—mostly honest by admitting my connection to Obscura. Perhaps that's why I failed to stop Matt, because I didn't leverage enough of the strength around me. *Or maybe he's just that powerful, and it was always going to lead to this.*

Either way, I was at a crossroads. One direction went to apparent failure and the other who knew where. "This could be the wrong move."

"It could, but I think with everything in flux and you at the center of it, it will be fine." Pandora opened her bag. She hesitated for a moment, then took out a black leather-bound book that disappeared in her hands. "What happened?"

"Paradox," Max answered, watching Trina sign. "Two items from different points can't operate in the same space."

"Damn, that makes sense. My bag is a sub-dimension where the rules of time wouldn't apply. It must have protected the book." Pandora shut her bag.

"What was it?" Tonya asked.

"My journal." A weathered version of it. I recognized the privacy spell etched into it. The fortitude of the magic wasn't as strong as I thought if Pandora could read it. Or was she that powerful? It explained how Pandora seemed to know me so well. She was privy to all my thoughts. Great.

"Yes, the last entry would have been today. I wanted to show that it started writing itself each day. The future's not set. We can change it, I'm sure of it. We stop Obscura, and it ends the future I come from."

"I'm not sure," Trina signed. "That is too big of a change even for now. All that will do is create a power vacuum for practitioners."

Right. We were at this point because we didn't have a voice, and we didn't want fear to swallow us. "We only need to stop the Grand Magister."

"And what about Camera? They are just as bad," Pandora said.

I glanced at Tonya. Again coincidence. The very conversation we had just hours ago circled back on us. "Well?"

She took a deep breath then punched the air. "I will rise through the ranks and work my brand of black girl magic when I take over."

"Then it's settled. We need to stop the Grand Magister." Pandora's eyes shined with what seemed like hope.

She was a mystery. I couldn't have that on the team. It was too dangerous. Instinct told me she was a valuable ally. Lust wanted me to ignore anything about her that didn't add up. Pandora knew all about me. It was time I knew the same.

"Before we begin our plans, there are several mysteries we need to solve." I began, meeting her piercing gaze. "What do you have to do with Oya?"

 andora

Present Day

I knew it would get around to Oya and me again. Quyen was too canny. He helped forge Obscura. Matt wouldn't have worked with him if he wasn't powerful. Nor would Matt have allowed a competent enemy to hang around to oppose him. Quyen was my best bet to stop the Grand Magister without relying on the Sphinx.

A bonus was Matt of this timeline didn't know about me or my abilities, at least in theory. I plan to keep it that way until I discover how to destroy Oya's connection within me. The power could go back to the Orishas where it belonged. Then I could live out my life in the past or disappear as my current timeline negated. The nightmare would be over, and everyone would have a fighting chance without my further interference.

"You want to know what I have to do with Oya?" I stared at my grandparents. Nana was either pregnant with my dad—my ironically mundane father who hated magic—or would be soon. With my oya powers gone, I wouldn't have to lose them. "Oya took everything from me."

My voice shook. I wouldn't lie.

The power was a curse, but it was also why I had the opportunity to fix things. I had the training from the most powerful wizard because of it and the influence of another. However, the cost was too great. The magician, Jannes, stole that power. It was likely why I went out of control as the Sphinx. I wouldn't be surprised if it were some kind of rebellious catharsis.

Quyen looked at G-max, who shook his head then turned back to me. "Not exactly the answer to my question, but I'll allow it for now since you didn't lie. How did you end up here?"

To me, he'd always be Quyen. It suited him better than Drew. Besides, it was a part of his distance from the others. I knew his mind. So I'd call him Drew around the others. My crush on him withstanding, I knew he and Tonya belonged together. I wouldn't interfere with their on-again-off-again romance. They'd find each other eventually. Besides, I might disappear when it was all said and done. I was seventy percent certain of it. Getting involved with anyone would just bring heartache and distract us.

"How did you end up here?" he asked.

I did owe him something. "The Grand Magister claims to be in love with me. He and I were arguing when whatever you did happened."

Tonya snorted. "Naked? Is that what they call it in the future, arguing?"

My face heated. I wanted to deck her. If she weren't important to Quyen, I would have. They played off one another well. I didn't want to disrupt that. Instead, I transferred my ire to my fist and squeezed tightly. "I'm just going to say this once, and then we're not going to talk about it again. He drugged me with a love potion. I was trying to kill him when I ended up here."

Her eyes widened before she averted her gaze. I heard her mutter "the bastard" under her breath before she quieted.

"I don't want to get into the details of his delusions, but I will admit that we were once together before I realized the truth about Obscura. He chases me for kicks mostly. He'll lose interest once he can't find me." I wrapped my arms around my waist at the memories of our night together. The potion made me forget my issues with him. My lust was over when it wore off. There was nothing between us but memories.

If there were any guy problems to have, it would be meeting my book boyfriend in the flesh, Quyen, with his intense eyes and sexy smile. I didn't count on him being so handsome. He was my latest addition to my charismatic but unattainable fantasy men. I hated withholding the truth, but they wouldn't trust me if they knew my role in Obscura's rule.

And my grandparents...they couldn't know.

Quyen put his hand on my shoulder. His jaw was tight as he met my eyes. "Not if he saw what happened to you. Did he?"

"Yes."

Quyen appeared concerned. "We may have a problem."

"I don't see how. It's not like Matt can instantly come up with a solution," I replied.

"He doesn't have to. He has all the time in the world, and he knows it's possible."

"You're giving the guy too much credit," G-max said.

"I'm giving too much credit to a guy with world domination on his mind that has at least two effective plans on how to do it, and we have proof that he partially succeeded?" Quyen asked.

"Sarcasm has never done anything but piss people off," Trina signed.

"Exactly. You attract more flies with honey than..."

"Piss and vinegar. We know, G-max."

"Don't you get hostile with me, too." He glared at me.

I cowed. My parents taught me to respect my elders. I didn't have to like what he said, but he was right. I should face the facts, not attack my allies. Matt would pursue me to the past.

Shit.

Time was relative. He could spend years searching for me, and it would appear as though he had just arrived. It wasn't like I would know the difference. Bummer.

I didn't want to believe it. "The Grand Magister has what he wants. I doubt he'd go that far to find me."

"I've known him for twelve years. He's never obsessed over anyone. He was only close to Lauren, his Magia Lectore, but she wasn't a witch. She was more of a magic groupie," Quyen said.

"You sure know a lot about the Grand Magister," G-max said. "You must have left out the part about knowing him personally."

"I'm telling you now," Quyen replied. "We're in the endgame now. I don't have time to babysit you so I can maintain my secrets. I told you to get out before we went any further, and you opted to stay, so now you're coven. This is what it means. We either succeed or fail. No what-ifs."

Then he turned to me. "Did Matt ever tell you he loves you?"

I closed my eyes. Great. Matt may have been serious with his twisted engagement and seduction. "Yes. We're in a pickle. He's probably coming after me. Adding to the fact that he can chase me into the past, he has a photographic memory and strong skill in illustration. Sorry—you already knew that."

Quyen's mouth dropped open. "I didn't know that. But it makes sense. He always could recall even the most minute details. I thought it was because he wrote everything down in his grimoire."

He started pacing and mumbling to himself. I tried not to grin. From his journal, I imagined him as a pacer, puzzling out his theories. It was nice to know one of my guesses was correct.

"So where does that leave us? My first impulse is to run before he catches up to me, but I know I can't take him on without turning the area into a war zone."

Tonya snickered. "Dramatic much?"

I wish.

"At times, yes," I admitted. "The Grand Magister wanted me for my abilities. I was his second for a time. To him, either you're useful, or you're not."

"You don't seem out of the ordinary," Tonya said. "Other than the outfit and the seventies slang. Really? The seventies came back. Are people wearing afros too?"

"I... didn't realize that I was using antiquated slang. Everyone talks like this except maybe Matt." I would let the comment about me being plain slide. It didn't bother me. It was better for her to underestimate me. Jealousy was an ugly thing.

I could understand why she was territorial about Quyen. He was handsome, loyal, intelligent, and powerful. She didn't have to worry. He watched me with clinical eyes. He didn't trust me. Rightfully so, as everything I said was either true or omitted. I may have admired him, but I knew where I stood, and I knew I couldn't stay.

Quyen glanced at Tonya. Even though he rolled his eyes at her comment, his eyes warmed when he looked at her. I wanted to avert my gaze from them, but the stabbing in my heart was what I needed to kill my fascination with him. Quyen wasn't for me. No one was. Even if I did stay in this time, it would most likely be perilous. There's no way I would stand out to him once the change we made happened.

"I think we are off-topic, love triangle," G-max said, then looked at Nana. They signed back and forth about her calling things as she saw it and how he better not dare censor her. Then he signed something sexy to her that was none of my business.

Well, if Dad weren't cooking already, he would be soon. Looking at the couples in the room, it was clear what I was.

A fifth wheel.

It was time for me to bail out and give them all some time alone. "It's late, and I think we've all reached a saturation point. I'm going to get some sleep. You all do what you need to hash out the chaos I caused, and we'll talk in the morning."

I picked up my bag and slipped out of the house before anyone could say a word. They were all so absorbed in their sexual tension— likely a consequence of the apocalyptic news I dropped on them—I could dig it. I did have some relationship experience. Besides, it gave me time to get my story together and look around the place.

Starting down the long driveway that I had only seen in videos and pictures, I breathed in the fresh country air of Appalachia. Magic flowed on the wind in an unprocessed form. It surrounded the area. In my time, Matt built his tower in Stuart where he collected magic and drew it underground where it wasn't accessible to me. Not that I needed it. Magic like this required effort for me to absorb, unlike magic processed with intention. It was a difference between cooked food and livestock on a farm, except less mess in the process.

I would do all that I could not to stage a battle here. My grandparents moved away from Stuart when Dad was five, and at some point, he grew to hate magic. Maybe it was the move away that triggered it. I could always convince—

No. Stay focused on Oya and Matt. Nana was right. If I change too much, the world may become worse.

Besides, the fact that a major event hinged on Matt and me was enough to blow anyone's mind. Matt would come up with another plan without Oya. He already has several, according to the journal. And for my personal history, he didn't know I existed until the first rampage.

I wanted to keep it that way. The less he and his cronies knew about me, the better. It was Lauren's idea in the first place, according to Quyen's journal, which lined up with comments and conversations that I observed. She worshiped the ground Matt walked on, and she hated me when he wasn't around. I'm surprised she didn't poison me the moment I got back.

Crap.

She would be here too, younger. Then again, she didn't know me or my oya power. Matt's not going to create competition with himself... wait. Matt can't exist because he exists already, so he won't physically be here, no matter the ingenious workaround he concocts.

At least some good news. Ghost Matt wouldn't be as bad. He'd have rules.

"What are you doing?" The sexy baritone that should have been in the house making up with his girlfriend asked.

"Taking a walk and giving you couples some privacy. Why aren't you taking it?"

"You read my journal. You know why."

I did. Seeing the chemistry for myself was another thing. They made a striking couple. It made me want to punch something, but it was no less accurate. "As someone who knows what you're thinking and has seen you two, I don't suggest dabbling too long, or you'll lose her. You two are good together."

"Reading my journal isn't enough to weigh in on my life. Now stop trying to distract me from the subject. Are you Oya?"

23

 uyen

Present Day

I waited for her answer with bated breath. And what would I do if she said yes? Case her? Kill her? Pandora was not what I imagined when I sought to stop Oya's summoning. She wasn't maniacal. Hell, she wasn't even showing with her magic. A goddess would have struck me, Tonya, and Max down without hesitation, or at least would have done more than throw me in a tree on reflex.

"My spell—"

"Is perfect?" She raised an eyebrow. "It couldn't possibly be wrong, I suppose."

"Not perfect. I followed the forty-two—"

"You sacrificed forty-two people? I didn't see their bodies. I can't believe—"

I put my hand over her mouth. "No, I did not. I used the forty-two powers to represent them."

She nipped at my hand. I tore it away on reflex more so than actual pain. "Don't you ever silence me again, Quyen Andrew Duong."

My heart tugged at each use of my name. It wasn't the attraction to her that affected my feelings. There was a mystical connection when she said my name as though we were bound in some way. "Say my name again."

Her eyes rounded, then she raised her hand. A sphere of glowing water formed in her hand. *Just how many active powers does she have? No wonder she was Matt's second.*

I covered her hand with mine. "I'm serious. I'm testing a theory."

Her eyes glittered in the moonlight then she sighed. "Quyen—"

The hair on my arms stood on end.

"—Andrew—"

My heart raced. Last time she invoked a mild reaction. With her focused intention, it was…

"—Duong."

Euphoric. My erection returned in full force as a mental image of us kissing filled my mind, then abruptly ceased as though she shut the door in my face. The moan followed by a sulfurous curse from Pandora suggested that I wasn't the only one to experience the connection. Did my summons somehow bind us together?

Perhaps an experiment.

"Pandora Spellman," I said with the same intention I reserved for enchantments. A blast of emotion drove me to my knees as a vision of us standing in a dining room obscured all other sight. She wore a black halter dress and I, a shirt and jeans. I swept my arm across a table of dishes knocking them to the floor. Then her eyes captured me, and I took her on the table.

"That's enough of that." She held her chest as she panted. "Let's get this out of the way. We have a connection and maybe a tiny crush, but I know how to behave. I won't interfere in your life."

"And what if I want you to," was out of my mouth before I could reel it in. This was not the conversation I was supposed to be having.

She was an unknown equation. Hell, she was Matt's ex-girlfriend. She didn't claim him. But he was undoubtedly going to come after her.

I would if she were mine.

Her mouth dropped open. "Wha-what? Don't say stuff like that to me. Life is complicated enough."

She was right. I wasn't above acting out her fantasy. Not when we had such a connection. She knew most of my secrets. A woman that knew the real me that didn't run screaming was hard to come by, *and* she was a witch. "You read my journal. Then you know what spell I used."

She shook her head, letting the subject drop rolling with a new one. "No, you tore the summoning out of your journal and the spell you used today—well, the time stream negated the journal before I could read the entry. I know that it requires forty-two people, and the circle has a point for each one of them, but that's it."

What she said lined up with what I'd do. Or should I say what I did? I burned the summoning page earlier when I was gathering my potion. "My spell summoned the forty-two powers. They represented each point in the circle."

"I can absorb magic." She gripped the strap of her bag. "The majority of the forty-two powers are within me."

I held out her hand. "Wait. Absorption is a rare power, but that shouldn't give you recall—that's impossible."

She rolled her eyes. "I didn't come here to be a goof and grandstand. Believe it or not, but get out of my way."

I grabbed her elbow. "That's a temper you got there."

She stared at my grip on her, then met my eyes. She extricated her arm from my grasp. "You have no idea what I'm like when I'm out of control. I'd rather not destroy my grandparents' house before my dad's born."

Pandora clapped her hand over her mouth. Her gaze darted behind me.

"I won't tell Max," I assured her.

"You should go inside. Tonya is waiting for you."

That was more incentive not to go, at least alone. Tonya and I made a clear break this time. I would honor it. "Come inside with me.

It's the middle of the night. What do you wish to accomplish out here in the woods?"

"Enjoying the solitude of a peaceful era. I'm used to the woods. They are a precious resource in the lawless towns. Well, some of them. There is one where it seemed like it was more forest and grassland, and you can sleep unaccosted by slavers."

"Slavers?"

Pandora nodded. "Pockets of society broke down in areas that Obscura didn't influence. About a third of the country is lawless, might over right rules, and the residents police themselves. It's chaotic in town areas where the local bosses rule depending on the leader, but most of the lawless zone is desolate with people trying to survive."

Our current way of life wasn't perfect, but at least some of us had a fair chance. It seems as though no one did without paying in blood and standing on the broken backs of others. "And you thought I was a slaver when we first met?"

"Sorry about the tree thing. I quickly learned that striking first is the best policy," she answered.

I could believe it. The slavers probably weren't choosy, but a beautiful woman like her with exotic garnet-colored eyes that could drown a person would be worth a lot. And she was a powerful enough witch to draw Matt's attention from the sea of witches that would vie for his attention as Grand Magister. "How did you and Matt meet?"

She sighed and walked towards the house. There was a stone patio with a fire pit in the front yard, off to the side. The moonlight was enough to make out the outlines of lawn furniture and not much more with the treeline so close to the cabin-style home. A ball of fire coalesced into existence in the palm of her hand which she tossed into the fire pit. A decent blaze formed within a few breaths that a regular person would have taken at least fifteen minutes to start. "Handy."

She tossed a few logs from an iron wood holder into the pit.

"Yeah, well, it was cold and getting difficult to see in the front yard." She put her hands out in front of the fire to warm them before sitting on a cement chair with a lime green cushion. "If we get hungry, there is probably some stuff for s'mores. G-max always made them for me when he visited. Though I may be a goof for assuming."

I nodded.

"And about my question?". I hated being a dick, but something didn't add up.

She stoked the flames with a large poker she pulled from the side of her chair. I stood watching her until she gestured for me to sit. I hadn't realized how on edge I was.

Way to lull her into a false sense of comfort to spill her secrets. I sat across from her. There were five other chairs arranged around the fire pit, but I didn't need to be any closer to her. Watching her from across a fire suited me fine.

"Paranoia, thy name is Quyen Duong," she muttered.

The shiver she caused in me was minor compared to earlier, so I could ignore it. "It has served me well."

"At least you're not trying to seduce answers out of me."

I wanted to, though. Of course, with my reaction to Pandora, the interrogation would yield satisfying but unhelpful information such as "what was my name" and "how much do you want it?" It was intel I painfully wanted to know, but I couldn't afford to pursue it until I cleared her.

The justice of my situation wasn't lost on me. A perfectly trust-worthy woman that I knew wanted me, and I lusted over the shady siren that commanded my desire with the slightest action. "Yeah, well, my penis doesn't think for me."

She arched her eyebrow. "Liar. He gets the better of you sometimes."

"I'm human and reserve the right to get better." I shifted in my seat.

I was still hard. It looked like it wasn't going away anytime soon. I knew what that meant. If discipline caused me pain, I would pass on the misery, especially since she could relate. "You're dodging the question."

"Matt rescued me when I was fifteen from a Camera dungeon, okay? Then he trained me—helped me understand my power, and once I was of age, he became my lover," she snapped. "Did you find out what you wanted to know? I admired him until I figured out what he was doing and knew I couldn't go that far, so I left him."

"Did you love him?" My fingers grip the cement arms of my chair.

"What kind of question is that?"

"A personal one that could get us killed." I stood. "We're about to take the fight to him. I need to know if you're going to break when the chips are down."

Her jaw tightened as the fire rose ten feet into the air then fell back to normal levels. "Yes, but it cost me too much, and it was the idiocy of a kid. That is in the past. I will do what is necessary to stop him. I spent a year in education over the repercussions of allowing him to rise to power and continue. In my time, he's only in phase one of his plan, and I won't be a party to the rest. It's too much."

The response was honest and what I wanted to hear for the most part. Pandora would do what was necessary, but I wouldn't hinge any plans on where she had to face off with him or back me up, for that matter. I couldn't afford for her to hesitate, but my instinct screamed that she was an ally.

And she could keep her secrets.

While I was like this, acquiring additional answers was too stressful. I preferred an edge in dealing with compatriots. An allowance for the complicated company that Matt kept was a must. I'd get the more complex motivations later. Everything pertinent that I needed to know put her in the clear. There were ways to utilize her talents while mitigating risk. I would just have to be careful around her.

Pandora had a lot of baggage. Again, I noticed the coincidence that she was Matt's ex, and of all things, I wanted her. He burned both of us with his ambition.

I scrubbed my face with my hands. I would have to do something about our attraction at some point. The question was, what?

I took that back. I knew I wanted to do, but kissing her senseless then interrogating her while I was inside her would be satisfying but counterproductive.

"Are you okay?"

"Yes, why?"

She shrugged. "You just had a weird expression on your face—kind of reminded me of a fox. I just didn't expect that response to my answer. So I guess you're kicking me out of the coven because of my history."

"No. That would be hypocritical. Matt used to be my best friend. We both loved him once and have scars." I joined her and put my hand on her shoulder. My fingers itched to touch her. The part of camaraderie would have to do.

"You two are cozy." Tonya opened the front door then walked down the porch steps. "Well, I'm done being the fifth wheel for the night. I'm heading back to the NoVa cell. It will be suspicious if I'm not there for the briefing."

Her tone and body language were agitated. I attempted to meet her gaze to gauge her emotions for myself, except she refused to look at me. She was mad at me. That much was obvious—the why of it not so much. We were still friends. It would not change unless she decided to end it. "Can I talk to you for a moment?"

"No time, besides we're talking now. I was already supposed to be on the road." She held up my potion orb. "I'll take this to get back to your place and lock up before I leave."

"Tonya—"

"I expect you to fill me in when I check-in and have a decent plan. Don't mess up." She threw the orb to the ground. A puff of smoke surrounded her then imploded, taking the vapor and her form with it.

Pandora touched my hand. I didn't realize that I still touched her shoulder.

Crap.

It was the first time Tonya had seen me with another woman. Pandora and I probably appeared together with my casual touch on her shoulder and all. Technically I still sported a hard-on, but it was too dark for Tonya to see that even with the light of the fire pit. It was at my back and—excuses didn't matter. The only way to know what Tonya thought was to ask her, and I would the next time.

"I'm sorry that I came between the two of you. I didn't want that," Pandora said.

Her words were sincere, but her touch was conflicted in the tense way she held my hand. I knew it somehow. Probably from the connection we shared or because I felt the same. Either way, it was difficult to ignore the attraction when we were alone. "The two of us are not together."

"But you could have been. I know you wanted that."

Not after seeing you, I thought, but aloud I said, "Should've. Could've. Didn't. What if isn't the same as is."

Then I leaned over and kissed Pandora. I had to know what I was dealing with on my side of our attraction. She was a beautiful woman with her arresting eyes, velvety brown skin, and soft demanding lips that hungrily connected with mine. Her tongue slid across my lips as we explored each other's mouths inch by lustful inch. A quiet fire burst to bonfire status between my legs when a moan escaped her.

I imagined more sounds coupled with screams of desire as we sated each other. Together our bodies would sing a lustful lyric like no other. I knew it.

I sensed it all—from her while I grew dizzy from her kiss.

Pandora broke away before I was ready, and I found myself stumbling forward for more when she put her hand between us. "Too much."

Her husky voice doubled my desire, if that were possible. There was nothing I wanted more than to rip off our clothes and take her right then and there with reckless abandonment. "I don't know if I can get enough."

I moved her hand. Her form shimmered in front of me, then she was gone. The lusty fog lifted somewhat. "Did you just shimmer?"

"Yes. You needed space."

Another of the forty-two, shimmering was the ability to translocate short distances. I saw the power once before. So Pandora wasn't exaggerating about her absorption talent. What else could she do? "I apologize for doubting your abilities."

"It's a lot to wrap your head around," she admitted.

"And for trying to push you." I rubbed the back of my neck. I'd have to watch that. My reaction to her yanked my self-control to the point that I focused more on myself than her. I understood addicts a little more.

"It's fine." She waved it off.

"No, it's not." I stepped forward then thought better of it and sat next to the chair she vacated. "I don't know what this is between us, but we're going to give in to it eventually, and I want us to enjoy it."

She gulped. "That was frighteningly honest. I-I didn't expect that, but I can dig it."

"You read my journal. You know me and what my principles cost me. You're the only one who knows." And likely the only one out there who could understand and not run the other way screaming.

"Where does that leave us?" she asked.

"Horny co-workers for the most part. We're going to annoy the crap out of everyone until we figure that out."

Pandora snorted. "You are so far out. Another reason I fell for you."

She *would* have a cute snort. Was there anything about this woman that didn't speak to my sensibilities? Everything about her drew me in to know more about her. Even her kooky way of…"Fell for me?"

She's sobered. All traces of mirth left her face. "I can use some s'mores. I'm going to raid the kitchen."

I rose.

"No. You stay here and watch the fire. I've got it. I've seen so many pictures of the place that I practically know where everything is. We can eat out here and then figure out everything else later."

I watched her take off the mundane way. If she shimmered, I would have felt an inch tall for carelessly speaking. We had a connection that bridged time through my journal. I started that one in college and wrote in it at least once a week. It was my mini tome of life. Pandora had intimate knowledge of me. She practically had a relationship with Journal me. It made perfect sense.

Perhaps my spell had been flawed after all. The question was whether it was a blessing or a curse?

24

*M*att

Present Day

I examined my face in the mirror of one of Lauren's barrier devices as I feigned studying it. There was nothing different about my face despite the reversal of fifty years. If not for Lauren's youth, I would've thought my time spell failed. Not only did I travel back into the past, but it appeared that I landed only twenty years away from where I planned.

It was still a pivotal time in my world domination plans. At this point, I had summoned Oya and failed it phenomenally—again. It wasn't something I wanted to revisit, but there were certain events I had to play out until I reached a pivot point. I hoped the ritual would have lined up our chance to meet again, but it did not, which stood to reason that I was destined to try again soon. It would not be long from my reckoning.

The spell that called Pandora would have dropped her in a similar period. It would have brought me to where she was if I hadn't modified it, but it was too dangerous to assume that I completely understood the spell seeing the aftermath of my experiments. Combining it with Timeless was best. Besides, it gave me the chance to acclimate temporally and plan.

Oya's failed summoning caused a large out-of-season storm that pushed Obscura into media attention. Fortunately, I managed to spin the event for the news and local authorities into a Good Samaritan effort with my "we're in this together" campaign. I could always use the positive press in the various news outlets. It kept the extremists from guessing what I planned and the others on the fence from fearing Obscura.

The mundanes feared the unknown. There was always something to take umbrage. If it wasn't gender politics or religion, it was skin color. As long as they didn't focus on practitioners with the intent of bringing back the witch trials, my benevolence would remain while I kept my eye on the few rotten eggs in the bunch.

My plan to protect partitioners worked best if the mundanes saw us as benign. If they focused on their greater numbers or put thought into thwarting me, the project would fall apart.

People would follow a friendly face into hell, even when the sign out front said "DANGER." History was riddled with examples. All one needed was a charismatic personality. Good looks added to the effectiveness of the political con. I was handsome by most standards, and in my thirties for all appearances—old enough for wisdom, young enough for innovation, and I possessed perfect timing with my actions.

Those were my mundane traits. As a wizard, I was powerful and patient. I was an able student of Quyen's when we were in college. His knowledge of magic and the intellection of it advanced my agenda considerably. It was a shame he chose not to stay.

I nearly dropped the barrier device. Quyen was still alive in this timeline. It was a second chance to win him to my side. He, Pandora, and I would be nigh on stoppable. Then I wouldn't have to settle for most of the US. My children would need time and strategy to take the remaining parts of the world. And he will outlive Lauren by leaps and bounds. The potion would extend her life twenty or thirty years at most.

Speaking of—I met Lauren's worried gaze.

"Your eyes," she said. "They are different."

I scrutinized my reflection. My eyes were the same gray that they always were. "They are exactly the same."

She shook her head and stepped forward. "They are... older."

"Well, I am eighty-two years old," I answered. "My soul anyway."

"About that." She moved closer. "You said that you got Timeless to work, but it sent your soul back in time fifty years. Why just your soul and not the whole body? More could be accomplished with two Grand Magisters working together."

Lauren was brilliant at research and arcane knowledge, especially for a mundane, but not politics. Her knowledge of fringe science was a more significant help than her delving into my plans' fine details and intentions. "I would say it happened to prevent a paradox. Besides, I doubt thirty-two-year-old me would be willing to work with the eighty-two-year-old me."

She wrinkled her nose. "Paradox? It's not like you used science. I agree that there is some crossover between magic and science, but you shouldn't have the same constraints."

I wasn't in the mood to argue the point when I had higher objectives to accomplish. The spell I cast didn't bring my body. Once I found Pandora, I could get the details of the enchantment used on her to refine mine. "Not everything can be escaped with the supernatural, just augmented. But for all intents and purposes, two people or objects cannot exist in the same space or timeline, magic involvement or not. At least it's my working theory."

"Then what happened to *my* Grand Magister?" she asked.

Lauren was loyal to a fault. Traveling back to our early years showed me the truth of her last act. The last thing I needed was more interference from her. She would react badly to the possibility of me negating my past self even though I was still the Grand Magister. "My younger self has been displaced until I succeed in my mission."

She grasped her chest as she let out a sigh. "That's good. Not that I don't like you, but you're a stranger to me. Even though I've known you the whole time, you're not my Grand Magister. Not yet. Does that make sense?"

*And **my** Magic Lectore is dead.*

We were of one accord as far as I was concerned. "Yes. I understand what you mean. I promise you will adjust. Now I want you to bring me everything you have on Oya."

Lauren frowned. "The failed experiment, you mean? At least that's what you've been calling it for the past month. It's nice to know that you let your disappointment at my failure go."

She made me sound like a petulant ass. "I'll be the one to decide if it was a failed experiment or not. It may be a case of a minor setback. Either way, there's something I need to find while I'm searching."

Lauren perked up. "How can I help? What are you searching for?"

I knew where this would lead in fifty years—a sultry night followed by Pandora's cold shoulder. The less Lauren knew, the better. "It's a personal project."

"Oh. Well, I'll be of greater assistance to you if I know what you were trying to find," she said, putting her hands in the pocket of her lab coat.

It amused me that she wore the coat even fifty years later—for the sake of professionalism, she told me once. Her same sense of loyalty might prevent me from achieving my goals. Pandora would not appreciate others helping me win her. Lauren's interference already set me back.

My assistant's zealousness and her youth would cause me even more issues or jealousy in my precarious relationship with Pandora. It wasn't necessary for Lauren to know all the details of my life anyway, not when she'd exit in a mere half-century. It appeared that traveling back in time further than I intended gave me more than one do-over. I straightened. "This matter requires my direct attention. However, there is something you can do for me—find Quyen. I want to know what he's been up to the past few years."

She pressed her lips together and narrowed her eyes. "Quyen? He's disgraced. You defeated him. Why would you need—I mean you never—"

"Do what I say, Lauren. I have my reasons. They will be revealed to you soon enough."

She stiffened then nodded. Her obvious displeasure didn't change anything. I listened to her opinion over the decades then she died on me. Her contributions were integral to my plans in my first run. Lessening the dependency on her would save me grief later. I needed Quyen.

"Yes, Grand Magister." She turned to leave.

"I want the information on Oya first," I added.

She faltered in her exit then turned to me. "It will take some time to gather the information between my archive and sort through what was stolen in the breach."

I frowned. I remembered the event. It wasn't of any significance until she mentioned it. There was something I was overlooking about the activities in the past month. "I want everything and summarize anything we didn't recover to the best of your ability."

I had a theory. The summoning circle that swallowed Pandora had Quyen's spell style on it. Then a spell spirited away Pandora that was reminiscent of the Oya ceremony. Both used forty-two-point circles. I was confident.

Quyen could have easily infiltrated Camera. Hell, he may be in charge of it. They would be all over it—the enemy of my enemy and all. I'd expect more intricate spell-casting along with personal attacks.

No—the raid on my building was quiet and not the usual guerilla-style tactics Camera employed. The attackers had a surprising subtlety in the way crime had been executed. If Quyen was involved, he was sloppy to think I wouldn't monitor local practitioners to ensure they'd never work against me. The large casting did them in, making it easy to catch up to them and deal with them. There were no survivors, including the mundanes.

He must be involved.

One thing he never was… boring.

Except, I knew what opposing me would mean for him in the end. I would bring him to my side earlier.

"Yes, Grand Magister, I'll get it done." Lauren left the room.

I noticed she didn't face me the second time I spoke to her. She gave me her back like a child—a testament to how much I overindulged her even in the beginning.

Not this time. No one would stand in the way.

25

andora

The smell of eggs and bacon stirred me from a sound sleep, as it should. Luxury like this was rare in the lawless zone. Most of my year on the run, I lived on wild onions, carrots, and meat that I hunted. There are no markets in the woods—no refrigerators either. Anything I couldn't preserve or carry was lost to scavengers of all kinds.

Eggs were even rarer because that meant a farm or fighting an angry mother with family plans. People from the past didn't know how good they had it. Of course, most didn't realize what they had until it was gone, be it a luxury of traveling down a safe street or even indulging in the past. "Field stew? Out of sight, I missed watching you make it."

G-max paused in his task briefly with a wide-eyed expression. "It's weird knowing that my granddaughter's the same age as me, and I'm not even a father yet. But then you say things that only someone who would know from spending time with me…"

His awkwardness made me want to hug him. It was an adjustment for me too. However, commiseration would worsen the moment. He shouldn't get used to me, not if my plan succeeded. Stopping Matt would change my history. At best, my adoption would never go through. At worst, my intervention would erase me from the timeline. There were many variables—any time spent with me complicated matters when I needed to be decisive. I allowed the nostalgia of seeing my grandparents alive to color my world.

My time with them was over. I had to accept that fact and hope that I would get a second chance in another timestream where it all worked out. "You're right, G-max, so I should probably call you Max."

He folded the stew in silence for a few breaths. It was not actual soup. He just called it that because he often "stewed" over the results. It was really a mix of potatoes, bacon, and eggs.

"It will sell the illusion better if we involve the others. We should tell anyone who asks that you're Trina's cousin. I don't care that you're adopted. You resemble her enough to pass that off."

"If you're going to strategize, I'm awake now," Quyen said, opening his eyes.

He never left the chair next to me after our kiss last night. I was just glad there wasn't enough room for us to lay next to each other. The temptation not to do more was hard enough as it was.

I met his gaze. He winked at me, then turned to Max. "Tonya left last night so she could check in with Camera this morning. She's going to report that I'm alive and uncooperative as always. They will make some sort of move. I'm not sure how desperate they are, so I can't be seen leaving my house. And my lab is there."

"What about a bridge from there to here?" I asked.

"You're losing me," Max said. He placed the hot pan on the wide lip of the pit. "Hey. Trina should be out here in a minute. She's baking cinnamon buns."

A nostalgic expression must have crossed my face because Quyen squeezed my knee then rubbed it. Max cleared his throat.

"We should wait until she arrives," he added.

The light sense of spice on the breeze greeted us just before Trina's arrival of cinnamon buns and orange juice. Max kissed her as she sat them on a small table, then retrieved the cups.

"You two look cozy," Trina signed. "Did you get out the sexual tension you two were harboring?"

My face heated, and I shied away from him while I signed my excuses. I didn't know which was worse, G-max's territorial behavior or her matchmaking.

Trina laughed.

"I need a translator," Quyen said. "If you're going to talk about me, I should be able to defend myself."

I signed to Trina as I spoke. "She asked if we got out our pent-up frustration."

She waggled her eyebrow then signed, "I could have heated my house with the two of you."

Quyen gave me a look that kind of said, "I told you so," then turned to her and shook his head.

"Too bad. Don't wait too long, or you two will become annoying," she signed.

Quyen broke into laughter.

"Thanks for the advice. Please, let's move on," I said for the benefit of both of them. Things were complex enough without my grandmother egging us on.

"What did I miss?" My grandfather asked, setting down with the cups, plates, and utensils. He signed the question again once his hands were free.

"Nothing," Quyen and I said in unison.

Trina laughed.

"Liars." He spooned out stew for everyone, or should I say his concoction of eggs, bacon, cheese, and potatoes. We ate breakfast in silence. It still smelled as I remember and just as good, too.

"Thank you for the meal. It was great," Quyen said.

"Yes," I agreed.

Trina put her hand on G-max—I mean Max's shoulder.

"Okay, tell me about this bridge you mentioned," he said.

"I want to know as well," Quyen replied. "I've read theories about what I believe you're suggesting, but it was accomplished with physics, not magic."

Trina's eyes lit up.

"Yes, it's based on the Einstein-Rosen bridge or just a bridge as we call them. It sounds better than wormholes, and I think it explains the theory better."

"Keep this on the low level, or I'm going to start going into the finer points of the body's digestive system," Max said. "I went to college too, but physics and I weren't friends."

Trina rubbed his arm then leaned over to kiss his cheek.

"Yes, sir. The point is I can anchor two locations together so that travel over long distances is possible. We can connect the cabin and Quyen's basement so that we can go back and forth."

"And Camera won't know that I'm here," Quyen added. "It's perfect."

"Let me get this straight. You can connect my house to *his* house?" Max asked. "That sounds like it'll take at least an entire coven to pull off, probably two or more. We don't have that kind of man—person power. Besides, I don't see the need to make such a grand display of magic."

"We want Camera to think that Quyen hasn't left the area or is not involved with whatever is going on here." Trina and Max frowned. I turn to Quyen. "You said that Tonya was considering leaving Camera. I'm sure they followed her to make sure she came back to them and watched your house in case she left to test her loyalty. It won't be a good look to see you come to your house when they never saw you leave."

"Finally, someone more paranoid than me," he said. "I figured they'd shadow Tonya once she started climbing the ranks and restrict her movements until then, but you posed a good point. She's new to the NoVa cell, and Obscura has been making serious moves."

I shrugged. "And they still may wait. Camera may not be strategic yet, but it doesn't hurt to err on the side of caution. She's the only link to you. From what you two told me about everything that led up to the summoning, they wrote you off until the ritual. I wouldn't be surprised if they spy on you and use Tonya to get to you."

He growled.

I fought against the cold that tried to settle into my bones. For all his talk, a part of me hoped—no sexual tension between us was fine. He and Tonya, or anyone from the same timeline, made better sense. They had a future.

They also didn't have to lie about themselves.

Quyen and others would be furious when they found out about me and Oya. I had to remain focused on the mission.

"We will have to play a careful game." I touched his shoulder.

"And how do we do that?" Max asked. "That bridge you were talking about sounds like a heavy resource spell. The more that I know…"

I got the point. "It's more of an intensive spell than average, but no more than warding a home. If two of us do it, then it will be fine."

Max reddened. "You two must be heavy hitters then. It took our entire coven of five to ward this home, and we refresh it every year."

My chest grew cold. "I didn't mean—"

"Don't worry about it," Trina signed. "We're fine. Mr. Territorial here will survive. Won't you, baby?"

Max gave her a sour look. Then he made a flirtatious sign about putting her across his knee and—I turned to look at Quyen. "We will need a piece of foundation from the basement to anchor the bridge. Since it's your home lab, it doesn't have to be large, and we'll need a piece from where we bridge here."

"How big of a piece are we talking? I don't want to gouge out pieces of my floor," Trina said through Max.

We turned towards the couple. "A centimeter or less from the corner of the door or by a wall is preferable. It needs to be somewhere a practitioner won't notice it."

"That's fine," Trina nodded.

"So the major obstacle with the spell is getting what we need from my house without being seen," Quyen said. "I have my potion, so I can use that and summon you there. Problem solved."

It wasn't much of an issue to begin with, but I'd let him have his moment. Our coven needed to win something. My grandparents started to get cold feet. I'd rather have them in the loop where I could keep an eye on them.

"And what about Tonya?" Quyen asked. "A bridge to her would help us all stay in communication."

I nodded my head. It would work for several reasons, including reminding me that they used to be together and I had a shelf life. "We can set it up when we meet up again."

"Okay, once we have the bridge thing, then what?" Max asked. "Obscura is powerful, huge, and dangerous. Where do we even start?"

"I'm going to refine my spell then try again to find where the powers went after the summoning. We still need to make sure Obscura doesn't try anything more at Fairy Stone, and the locals stay out of it," Quyen replied.

"Same as before. Got it." Max glared.

I understood his frustration. The assignment sounded like babysitting, but it wasn't. "Protection of this area is more important than you realize. Obscura has its base in the future, and the surrounding area is highly developed. They're going to take this place if you don't stand against it."

Max arched an eyebrow. "There you go again with those spoilers. You're just like your grandmother. That's why I don't want her to see a movie without me. She'd tell me the whole thing before it was done."

Trina smacked him in the arm.

Quyen gave a thoughtful look. "Actually, that seems like an obvious move forward, especially once they realize the ritual worked, if they don't already know, it was successful. Taking the area over would result in less press leakage."

Trina's eyes widened. She gripped Max's shoulder. He put his hand over hers. "Exactly when does that happen?"

I hoped I wouldn't have to tell them that their home was gone unless it was desperate. Besides, the more truth I told them, the more likely they would catch on to what I *wasn't* providing. "I don't know. Obscura was already here when I was born. Most of what Obscura does is subtle. I suggest having someone check land acquisitions."

"Taking the park will be difficult. If I were them, I'd offer assistance outright or through a foundation to take the pressure off the

Commonwealth," Quyen said. "Do you have anyone in the county office or in the city?"

"We do," Max said. "We will suggest it at the next Fairy Tale coven meeting."

"I think we should consider bringing them in on this. The information is already too big." Trina signed quickly. "We could easily get in over our heads. Hell, we are."

"It's too dangerous," Quyen said. "We possess a lot of information without knowing fact from theory or even time tables. What will we tell them? Pandora's your granddaughter from the future, come with us if they want to live?"

My grandparents snorted despite themselves. The tension must have gotten to them.

"All jokes aside, we should let them be aware that Obscura is on the move. I don't suggest details beyond that until we know more." Quyen stood and stretched.

Sunlight danced over his body. His stealth clothing made it difficult to see his features, but his reach for the sky showed a flash of flesh. I was mesmerized by the brief sight of buttery skin and the light dusting of hair trailing into his pants.

Quyen dropped to his knees to meet my gaze. He sported a fox-like grin, winked at me, then became all business. "Let's get started on that bridge."

I opted for the safer ground after being caught lusting after him. I turned to my grandparents. Max shook his head while Trina giggled. I was an amusement.

Great.

How quickly I settled into the carefree behavior people had in this time. "I suggest anchoring to a part of the house where we are not easily seen. And we can hide if possible."

"The kitchen pantry," Trina suggested. "It is large enough for five people. There's another door that leads to a bathroom we don't use, so you can stay for an extended time like when we are having a coven meeting."

"Or a light search by the constabulary," I added.

Trina frowned, then gave me a worried expression. "Deputy

Wright has no cause to come here. But yes, it will work if it comes to that."

"We're still in this with you, by the way. We're not about to turn our back on family," Max added. "So stop trying to scare us off."

My throat tightened. They wanted to stick by me even though I wasn't telling them everything. I loved my grandparents. They were the same as I remembered, even down to how they always tried to find ways to tie me to them biologically. I always thought it was because they wanted me to belong. It must have just been a part of their "territorial" nature.

Quyen put his hand on my shoulder. "We better get started on the anchor here."

"You're right. We have a lot to do." I gathered the empty plates while he grabbed the cups then we went inside the cabin—my dad's ancestral home. I placed my burden in the sink. The white-painted door by the refrigerator was my goal. I turned the knob and pushed my way into the room. Shelves of cans and boxes aligned the small room along with a broom and kitchen towels. I knew the door to the bathroom waited for me about six feet from me. It was perfect.

"Do you need tweezers or anything?" Quyen patted his hands over the many pockets running down the side of his leg.

I didn't notice until he reached for something. The man had a contingency for every situation. He and Matt were similar in that regard. It also explained something about me. I was a powerful witch attracted to wizards that could match me in mind, power, or both. If I were to get over my crush and move on, I had to own it.

I liked Quyen.

He was funny, intelligent, sensitive, and in-person sexy. I could relate to his failures, triumphs, and insecurities. It was also wrong to deter him from his destiny. I didn't belong in the same time as him. I wouldn't be his romantic disappointment or, worse, the untouchable ghost girlfriend that no other woman could compare to. It would feed my ego for about two seconds then depress me. I would not do it to him.

Quyen held a minuscule piece of wood in front of my face. "Now what?"

I blinked. "When did you—"

He waggled his eyebrows. "I got it while you agonized about something. You worry your lip when you dissolve into internal spirals. You must be quite powerful not to have been killed in your time. You have such an obvious tell."

My blood boiled. Did he have to call me out like that? "I-I-yes, I am powerful. No one can hold me for long, and I can heal fast."

"As long as I have the magic to do so," I added mentally.

There. Take that, Mr. Know-it-all.

"You lack discipline then." He smirked then sobered. "Pandora, the Matt in this time doesn't love you. He doesn't know you. This Matt won't be wearing kid gloves and playing games. He murdered everyone in a train station just to recover his property. I need to know where your head is."

He had a point. "Everything is copacetic. I know this isn't a game. I spent a year learning that. Any illusions I had about him went out the door when he drugged me to have his way. When the fight happens, I'll be ready."

The subject was closed as far as I was concerned. I gestured to his hand. "Repeat, 'Anchoram habemus portem' while infusing the splinter with intention."

He raised an eyebrow. "That's it? I expected more complexity."

"Dropping anchors is easy. Connecting them is the difficult part." I was still mad over his comment about my self-control. "We'll place this piece in your basement, then your basement piece here, then we can connect them with a spell. Like I said, about the same as a warding spell."

I went to the counter then grabbed a paper towel. I held it out. The tiny fleck of wood fell on the napkin. Once he tucked it away, he took out a small balloon.

"This is enough for me to get back home. I will call Max when I get there, and you can leave getting to my basement to me."

He underestimated my power. He didn't even suggest that I shimmer to his house. I mean, I've been there before. I lived there for several weeks while I was reading his journal. He didn't even ask me how far I could shimmer. True, most people can't shimmer more than a mile or two at a time, but I could, and he didn't ask me.

I had a lot of raw power that I needed to siphon off. I'd show him. "Okay. It sounds like you have a plan."

I stepped back as he threw down the balloon. A puff of smoke surrounded him then dissipated. I waited five minutes for him to disable any added wards in his home. Quyen didn't explain his plan to me, but I suspected that he planned to summon me to his basement.

Lack of discipline, my ass.

I could manage my travel. I focused on his basement. My memory was fifty years in the future, but I knew the current him. I added that to my mental picture based on his journal and the sketches, then used a good portion of my magic to shimmer to his location.

The slack-jawed expression on his face was payment enough for his earlier comment. I strolled over to a stool at the drafting desk, then perched myself upon it. " The call is unnecessary unless you're that gung-ho to talk to him."

A Cheshire grin spread across his face. He closed the distance between us. Placing his hands on either side of me, he leaned in. "I guess we'll have to spend the extra time another way," he said, then kissed me.

I wanted to say that his kiss was horrible, and I should have pushed him off, but it wasn't. I knew it was wrong. There was no way I'd be able to stay. The kiss would just complicate things, but I wasn't ready to let it go just yet. Besides, admitting that I had a problem was the first step.

And one time couldn't hurt.

26

 uyen

Pandora wrapped her arms around me as she returned my kiss. There was no questioning the demanding way her mouth moved against mine. Her hungry acquiescence fueled my lust for her. We were of one accord. I wanted to take her then and there.

She moaned into my mouth. I didn't think it was possible to increase my sense of urgency, but she managed it by wrapping her legs around my hips, urging me closer to her with all the enthusiasm that ran through me. I knew I was the one in for it.

I lifted her to my drafting desk. My journal fell to the floor with a plunk that made me reconsider. I carried her to the cot that I kept for when I needed a break or to remain close to the experiment. It was designed for one, but I would make it work.

I broke our liplock to deposit her on the cot when I noticed the layer of clothing between us—hers especially—looked challenging to remove. Pandora watched me with her dark cinnamon eyes. She grinned as she quickly undid the strategically hidden buttons. It was as if she enchanted my gaze. I was transfixed until the leather top released her brown mounds.

They stole my attention for longer than I cared to admit with their hypnotic heaving and later jiggling as she shimmied out of her tight pants. Then I was treated to the temptation of Pandora's triangle, a place I wanted to sink into and get lost.

I stripped out of my clothing in record time so that I could join her on the cot. Our lips joined the minute I was close enough to connect with her. I cupped her breast and kneaded the bud between my thumb and fingers. Her soft flesh, coupled with her kiss, put me into overdrive. I eased her legs apart as I moved to the side of her neck, placing a few nips here and there until she undulated beneath me. Her warmth pressed close to me, beckoning, and I planned to come. I met her gaze for the visual go-ahead.

Her eyes drifted shut. "Hurry."

Even better.

My patience was at its end. Though I wanted her eyes open as I took her—to watch those garnet orbs change when she reached her peak, I didn't want to play any more games. I rubbed my rock-hard shaft against her slit, then dived into her pleasure pool.

Pandora's eyelids flew open as her lips formed a lusty O. I'd sear that into my memory as our first conquest of each other. I began my opening move in our battle of senses, rolling my hips. She arched her back and let loose a moan that could only mean I hit *that* spot. I rolled against her again.

And again.

Until I found the right piston rhythm that dizzied me with the sensation of her while it left Pandora delirious. I was on the brink of my climax swallowing me. It was too soon. Her first. It was my one rule. No lover of mine would go unsatisfied. I wouldn't let go until she got hers.

So close.

"No," Pandora whined when I slowed my pace to an agonizing deep thrust. She wrapped her divine legs around my hips again. Her heels dug into my flank as if she were an insistent jockey on her favorite disobedient mount.

"You know what I need." I rolled my hips.

"I…" Her head fell back. "I…"

Her sheath gripped me with a sucking motion that would finish me soon, thrust or not. No more games. "Come for me."

I rolled another thrust into her.

She squeaked. Her mouth hung open. It wouldn't be long. A little more…

"Come for me, Pan." I allowed the urgency to creep in my voice.

"Quyen…"

My control was gone. I drilled into her like a madman. Somewhere in my insanity, she gripped me and let loose, but I greedily pushed forward. I mined her ecstasy until the throes of my orgasm stole my breath. For a second, I thought I died of pleasure. Then life rushed back into place. I wanted more.

Later, I need to clear my head.

I meant to lay by her side. Instead, I kissed her languorously as though I prepared to start a fire with our heat—or in my case, a tidal wave, then laid next to her. It was a tight fit until I rolled us over, and she lay on top of me.

"Glad we got that out of our system," she croaked.

"I need to have you several more times to determine that for sure." I kissed the side of her head. "So unless your runaway plan involves sexing me into submission, keep at it. I'm very stubborn. You're going to have to take me several times."

She slapped my chest lightly. "You know, when you're thinking perverted thoughts, you get like a cartoon villain. Next thing, you'll rub your hands together and waggle your eyebrows. Such an obvious tell is a lack of discipline."

"I'll show you a lack of discipline." I did just that—waggled my eyebrows, then tickled her.

Pandora laughed as she wiggled in my embrace—my naked embrace with her equally unclothed body. I was ready for her again. "You have a beautiful laugh."

She's sobered. "Thank you."

I kissed the side of her neck. She shivered against me. Her sweet center nestled near mine—warm, wet, and waiting. It would take the slightest shift to be inside her. Except we were supposed to be working. "We have to finish the bridge."

"We do." She sighed.

I cupped one of her breasts. It didn't help the situation, but I had trouble thinking straight with her naked on top of me. I'd much rather explore her than do research. Little Quyen was in charge, and getting him to back down was turning into a monumental task. "Which one of us is going to be the strong one?"

"Good question." She ground her triangle against me.

"Woman, you're trying me." I wasn't in there yet, but my shaft would be if she continued.

Ding dong.

Pandora froze, and I closed my eyes. The person ringing my bell had perfectly rotten timing.

"Someone's at the door." I kissed her then lifted her off me. The decision to stop was out of our hands.

"You're not answering that are you? What if it's a trap?"

I loved that there was someone more paranoid than me out there. Her worries were sound. However, the person at my door didn't have dangerous intentions toward me. I had security wards for that, too. "It doesn't happen often, but I do get packages. That was probably one of my neighbors. It's cookie time, and I always buy a couple of boxes from the two scouts on my street."

I grabbed my pants.

"You're going to put the shirt on, too, right?"

Her tone had an air of command and a hint of, dare I say, possession.

"Worried that some delivery person is going to get an eyeful? I got the impression you were going to taste and run."

"Or maybe I'm worried that you were about to traumatize some little girl by giving her a vision she is too young to have."

So I misread her.

She frowned, then growled. "You're an ass."

Aha, I *was* right. Pandora wanted more of me.

I tugged up my pants then grabbed my shirt. "Don't worry. Whoever is out there will be safe from my sexy ways. I can't say the same for you."

Her cheeks darkened at my statement.

"We don't have time for this," she said, pulling a pillow in front of her body.

Okay.

I expected a flirtatious response, not a cover-up. Maybe she really would taste and run, taking us back to horny coworkers—me for sure. I thought I laid it down well enough for her to at least claim a sexual relationship. I was either out of touch, or she was more stubborn than me.

Gasp.

Ding dong.

I started up the stairs pulling my shirt on as I climbed. My bare feet slapped the steps as I walked up the staircase. "I'll be back."

Ding dong.

I hurried through the kitchen and the living room to the front door. As I passed through my house, I noted that everything was as I left it. Any infiltration of my protective wards was unlikely but not impossible, especially since Tonya was the one to raise them. The architect of a spell always had a stronger affinity than the person replicating the magic. It was a reason I wanted a hand in the bridge smell —that and blatant curiosity.

It had been a while since I had seen a new concept for a spell.

"I know you're home," came the muffled voice of my guest through the door.

I froze with my hand on the knob. There was no longer a reason to look through the peephole. I unlocked the door and opened it. "Hello, Thuy. Did something happen to my grandmother or my parents?"

My sister was too stubborn of a witch to die. There was no need to ask about her.

"Hello, Quyen," my cousin answered. "Everyone is fine."

"Excellent. Thanks for the update." I moved to shut the door when Thuy wedged her combat boot in my door.

"Rude, much?" She pushed her way inside my house.

I allowed it. The last thing I wanted was for her to draw added attention to me or my house.

"Not as much as you." She stood in my doorway dressed in all black as though she were about to do some breaking and entering. Thuy would have been in for a shock if she tried. "Why are you here?"

She kept her back to the street. I hated when my family did that—hover in my threshold so they could leap out of my house at the first sign of trouble. It wasn't even as though I had invited her in the first place. Thuy probably had someone out there watching in case I got rowdy, but out of sight so I wouldn't counter them with my "wizarding ways." The majority of the family behaved that way unless the need for magical help arose. Then it was "auntie this" or, in my case, "cousin that."

Thuy crossed her arms as she observed me with her shrewd almond-colored gaze. She smirked. "I'll make it quick so you can get back to your company."

I didn't expect that comment. "I'm alone."

"Your shirt is inside out, and your hair is a mess," she replied.

I faked a yawn. "I just woke up."

"Please, I went away to college. I know the 'I'm in the middle of sex' face versus the 'just woke-up' face on someone. Though, I'm surprised you answered the door. It must not have been that good."

I fought to remain expressionless. The longer I engaged with Thuy, the more she could gather intel to use against me later. "What. Do. You. Want?"

I saw no point in confirming or denying. If my family disowned me for my politics, they certainly wouldn't be fans of my dating preferences. I wouldn't let them ruin a good thing.

Thuy grinned. "Obscura is looking for you. That's got to be worth something."

Matt hadn't so much as scoffed in my direction since we parted ways. I couldn't think of why he would suddenly have an interest. It couldn't be about the robbery. He wouldn't need a PI to find me if he knew I had something of his. He would track the item instead—which I blocked. There was no reason for him to seek me out unless...

The hairs on the back of my neck stood on end. No, he couldn't have tracked Pandora to me. If anything he would have tracked *her*. Something must have happened or changed. I'd have to watch my back while I figured it out.

"What makes you think that, Thuy?"

She narrowed her eyes. "I work at *Lee & Associates*. It's a premier data collection agency."

"That's a fancy euphemism for espionage and private investigation. If the purchase order is already established, then it's already too late. Not that I have anything to hide. I just want to live in peace."

My tone came out cold even to my ears. Inside, my heart pounded. I didn't need both Camera and Obscura sniffing around me. They would make Tonya if this kept up. We would need to make a bridge to her as soon as possible.

I couldn't let both organizations find out about my association with each other. It was another problem I didn't need.

"Your P.O. hasn't been assigned yet. It just so happens to be hung in the approval phase. You have the damnedest of luck."

"I do. It must be my year. So I'm going to ask again, why are you here?"

Thuy tightened her jaw but didn't edge out of my house. "I kept up with you after uncle and aunt disowned you and your fall from grace three years ago. You've done well with the magic thing, even on your own."

I knew my financial profile. I invested well and lived modestly. My life would span centuries. Money management was a survival skill on par with self-defense. A practitioner needed resources to disappear and remove obstacles. "You have a point?"

"Give me $10,000, and the most incompetent, self-important jerk will receive your case. He will likely inflate costs with no results for at least six months before the case is taken from him. A year if you're lucky."

"You're ridiculous. Ten thousand dollars?" I closed the distance. "You and the rest of the family turn your backs on me, and then you try to extort money from me? Get out."

Thuy trembled but remained. In the periphery, a man lurked outside with his fists clenched. A cowardly bodyguard?

"Who's out there?"

"My husband," she answered. "Don't hurt him. It was my idea to come to you."

He sounded like a winner. "He's out of danger from the crazy wizard relative while you take chances? What a coward!"

"Don't you dare," she growled. "I did this because I had no other choice. We needed the money for my—forget it. Are you going to pay the money or not?"

"I don't give in to terrorists. Get out of my house or I will hex you."

Her eyes widened. "Bastard, I hope they get you."

She stomped out backward, and I shut the door in her face once she crossed my threshold. I rested my head against the heavy oak door. I took out my phone and wired the money to Thuy's email address. Bitch or not, she was family. I caught the desperation in her eyes. She was at the end of her rope.

"You're a softy."

I turned to see Pandora watching me with her soft cinnamon gaze.

"How so? I kicked her out."

"Parts of my world may be in the dark ages, but I do know about wiring money and cell phones. You sent her that money anyway, even though you didn't secure her compliance, and you said you wouldn't."

It probably wasn't the wisest decision I could have made, but Thuy must have needed it if she came to me with her extortion scheme. Most of my family was too afraid even to try it. "I couldn't trust her to hold up her end anyway."

Pandora shrugged. "That may be, but you're rewarding bad behavior. She may come back again."

I shook my head. "I doubt that. She probably thinks I'm way too loose of a cannon to take a chance. Who knows what I might do next time?"

Pandora wrapped her arms around my neck. "You do know that I know your mind. I read your journal from beginning to end. I read your successes, failures, and fears. You can't lie to me—at least not convincingly."

I did know that. It was part of why I wanted her—the *me* that appreciated her mind and heart and looked past her satiny brown skin, long legs, and nice rack.

"I can dig it," she said, well, moaned on account that I squeezed her breasts in her partially clasped shirt. She placed her hands over mine. "You're trying to distract me when we have a bridge to finish. I have a feeling that we won't be able to get any work done until we have a little more fun. Is that right?"

"Maybe. I'd like to explore all my options thoroughly before I make a decision."

She grinned. "I'm down."

Then she kissed me, and I became putty to her will for the rest of the afternoon.

 andora

How in the hell did Tonya have the strength to walk away from sex that good? I wondered as Quyen and I walked down the basement stairs holding hands. The warmth of his touch reminded me that what passed between us wasn't a dream. I was in his time, away from the devastation of Obscura's rule. I could heal and prevent the future that bore my horrendous power in this paradise of sorts.

A better question was how would I?

I squeezed Quyen's hand. He was a fantastic lover. I knew there was no way I could work closely with him and not give in to our chemistry, not to a man that remained disciplined in nearly every aspect of his life but then made love like it was his last night on earth. That kind of passion was challenging to ignore.

"What are you thinking about?" He kissed my hand.

Nothing that I wanted to deal with at the moment. My mind was supposed to be on fixing the future. "Haven't you had enough?"

"Work first, play later," he teased.

It came across as playful, but I knew he was serious.

"I wasn't the one who lifted me on the desk then took me." I gave him a mock chastising look.

He grinned. "Correction, I took you on the cot, and against the front door, and then in the shower."

"You make a fair point." My heart quickened at the mention of each encounter as phantom thrusts and squeezes had their way with me. He did that on purpose, the ass. "And I believe my oral appreciation was more than enough."

He gave me his foxy expression then wagged his finger at me. "The spell."

His voice was a deep, almost growl full of unspoken promise. It was heady wielding power over him, and the fact that he seemed to hold it over me was a new experience. The domination tug-o-war where sometimes I ruled and other times he did was pleasant, balanced.

And it can't last once Oya's powers are destroyed and he realizes that I lied to him.

I shook the thought out of my head. That was a problem for later. Besides, as long as the mission was a success, Quyen wouldn't have to know my secret. I would disappear from his memory, or the power would go away, then I wouldn't have to witness him changing his view of me or the power tempting him.

Quyen's gentle caress eased me out of my thoughts. Power hummed from his touch that gave me twice the high I usually got from a strong practitioner. Instead of the buzz of energy, my whole body warmed. It made the sex that much more intense. It was almost as though power within me adored him as much as I did—even more reason to keep the information from him. The one thing that kept those who sought to use me at a stalemate was that no one could control the Sphinx, including me. If he managed to...

Tremendous power tended to corrupt. I couldn't bear to see Quyen's thoughtful brown eyes turn cold, become more about revenge than the overall good for everyone—to become what he hated.

I wouldn't allow it.

"Are you okay?" he asked.

I covered his hands with mine, nodded, then regained my discipline. The longer I remained a bummer, the longer the mission would take, and the potential to lose him increased. I already gave in. He was mine for the taking. I would enjoy him until I disappeared from existence and my claim could no longer stand.

"Once we drop anchor here, we can form the bridge," I said.

Quyen held my gaze another moment then went to the door that led outside. Quyen hid the door behind a shelf full of books and magical implements. The basement lab was just that, except I knew later with Obscura running amok, the once safe space would become a shelter to wait out the apocalypse more than a place for experimentation. I shuddered.

"Cold?" He plucked a splinter of wood from the corner of the door near the jamb.

"No. I was thinking how similar the basement was in my time. It's the same but different." I wanted him to have as much truth as possible. I owed him that.

"Fifty years is plenty of time for me to want to reorganize my lab. I'm set in my ways but not that set." He reached for my hand. "Why do we have to enchant the piece instead of the entire doorway?"

"Security. If you need to destroy the bridge quickly, it's easier to pluck the piece out than take out the area. Also, if someone destroys the area and the piece is still intact, the bridge will continue to work."

He wrinkled his nose in studious consideration then nodded. "Makes sense. Who came up with this process? I've never heard of it. Just theories."

"I'm not sure. Once the US and a few other countries destabilized and Obscura 'rescued' them, it was necessary to quickly cover large distances. Camera may have something, but this is the Obscura process with some minor tweaks that *he* taught me."

Quyen squeezed my hand. "You know I'm not like him."

"Most definitely not," I purred.

He grinned. "Work first."

The way he said it under his breath made me think the reminder was more for him than for me. I didn't push. The subject was awkward enough without spending energy on it. "Anchoram habemus portem."

The splinter glowed briefly, then he released me to put the anchor back in place. "And now for the bridge spell."

I went to his desk for pen and paper. The spell was too complex for him to remember instantly. His work area was still in disarray from when we almost had sex on it. I gathered a few items and placed them on the surface. He could organize them to his liking later. His leather-bound journal was among one of the fallen items. I touched it reverently—missing the one from my time – when the book's existence flickered. One moment it was a thick leather journal, worn but still somewhat new, the next, a well-worn one of fifty years remained in my grasp.

"What the hell?" Quyen asked.

I dropped the book then scrambled backward. Was everything an illusion? Or was it a dream, an elaborate satisfying work of fiction to keep me contained? I warily watched Quyen as he studied the journal. He picked it up.

Nothing.

"That's odd." Quyen turned toward me, then frowned.

"Are you an illusion?" That was stupid to ask. Of course he would say no. "Don't answer that."

He took a step towards me. I scooted backward and raised my hand palm outward. He flinched.

He held out his hands. His palms faced outward and pointed at the floor. "Why would I be an illusion?"

"To control me."

Quyen jerked back as though I slapped him. "He did that to you?"

I ignored his question. The appalled expression and innocence could be part of the act. I had to know. There was only one way I could think to break the facade besides attack. "Who's more powerful, you or Matt?"

"In raw power, Matt, but in the manipulation of magical theory, me. It was why we were a good team." He stretched out his hand.

I breathed a sigh of relief and accepted the aid.

"I take it, I passed."

I kissed him. There were two purposes to it, one last test. I knew Matt's power. It was bold and spicy when it flowed over me. That's not what I experienced. Quyen's magic was subtle then consumed me. The sensation was akin to a slow heat turned inferno. The two could be no more different. I ended the kiss when he caressed me underneath my shirt and his need pressed against my belly. The feeling was mutual.

"Yes," my words sounded breathy in my ears, "you passed."

"You are hell on my discipline," Quyen muttered as he pulled away from me. He grabbed the sides of my face, kissed me one more time then stepped away.

I fought not to grin as I moved to the desk. The journal changed back to its present-day appearance when my fingers left contact. "We'll have to ask my grandmother about that since she knows the most about time travel theory. Do you mind if we take the journal with us?"

I kept my focus downward. My composure still needed gathering, and if I saw Quyen's tented pants or his lusty grin again, I'd jump him. It was a new wrinkle to my situation, but I didn't mind...too much. For once, it was a normal response. It had nothing to do with politics or end of the world stakes—well, not with politics.

"That's fine," he said from across the room.

I grabbed a pen and scribbled on a scrap of paper. It was Matt's spell. Annoying as it was, the ones I wrote never sustained a bridge for long. The imagery never matched my intentions the way his wording did. Perhaps that is why few outside the two main factions could accomplish the work.

Or I didn't try hard enough. It's not as though Matt was the most incredible wordsmith in existence. Maybe I just needed to do more without pressure.

I guess it didn't matter if the spell was my own or someone else's. If I couldn't power the enchantment, it was just a rhyme.

"Here." I faced him.

He took the paper and shrugged. I caught a slight purse of his lips when he read the spell, but I didn't ask him about it. Quyen worked with Matt for years. They were close. It was even a little confusing reconciling Matt from college, the one I knew, but reading the journal, I saw the progression. Absolute power corrupts absolutely. " Ready?"

"Yes."

I grabbed his hand. "Touch the shard. Then we'll say the spell two times."

He placed his hand on the old door. "Anchors of mine, heed my voice, coordinate my will. Bridge together a commonplace, connecting them despite the space, any anchor that I drop. Become a door from which I hop, with the password pop-pop."

I glanced at him on the last part about a password but managed to stay a second behind him. His change was not worth ruining the spell, but I was curious. The next spell cycle, the basement anchor, connected to the one in Stuart with a low buzz of energy that I sensed from most items. We were successful.

"What was that adlib about?"

He gave me a thoughtful look. "I thought about what you said. If either place is invaded, we don't want our enemies to use the bridge against us, nor would we want to destroy it. The password gives us options."

"That's…" It was brilliant. I never considered protecting the bridge via spell. "… a good idea."

"Thank you. Time to try it out. Pop-pop."

Magic surrounded us. Then we were in the Spellman kitchen pantry. I cracked the door open to see if anyone was in the kitchen. My grandmother stood at the sink washing dishes while Grandaddy— I mean Max—dried and put them away. It was heartwarming to see them together doing ordinary chores and surreal seeing them perform them at my age. I knew Grandaddy Max was a wizard, but Nana— Trina – that one caught me off-guard. Everything didn't add up to me. If anything, my father should be a practitioner since both of his parents had power.

Let it go, girl. It's a moot point now. It's not like you can ask your parents, nor does it matter since you are adopted. It's not like it affects your personal line. Daddy will probably adopt some other kid. Focus on Oya.

I knocked on the door. My grandparents were startled into a defensive stance, Trina with a knife and Max with a gun. "It's Pandora and Quyen."

They relaxed.

"Come in," he said.

I opened the door all the way. Trina gave me a tight hug. It was different this time. The warm buzz of her magic was there, along with something else.

"Glad you made it back." Max patted my back then touched her shoulder. "Give her some room, Trina."

She released me, leaving us all staring at one another in an awkward pregnant pause. I hated that. "The bridge to Quyen's basement is complete. To activate it, focus your intent and say the word pop-pop. And no, that was not my selection."

Quyen snorted. "It's not my best work on the fly. I'm much better when I'm prepared."

He tapped my nose playfully.

"Aren't we sure of ourselves?" I swatted his hand away.

"At least I thought of a password and enhanced your spell. We don't have to worry about enemies and innocents chasing us. You're welcome."

"Uh-huh, whatever."

Trina smirked as she gestured at the two of us and signed, "It looks like you two let some steam out while you were working."

My face heated. Max raised an eyebrow. I started to sign my excuse when Quyen put his hand on my shoulder.

"I gotta learn ASL, but I think I can guess what she said, though I could use the confirmation."

I didn't know which was worse, seeing her comment when she made it or having to explain it to Quyen. "Trina remarked that we appear to have let off some steam while we were working."

He faced Trina as he spoke. "I prefer calling it being an attentive lover, but yes."

I covered my face with my hands as my grandmother's grin widened.

"Really, y'all? I feel like you are trying to embarrass me. I don't know what to do here... This is just... Wow." I put my hands on my hips. "You know what? I'm a grown woman. I'm not going to take this. Yes, we are sleeping together. End of story."

My grandfather continued to scowl. "Yeah. Congrats on you two making me feel conflicted. I can only imagine how complicated parenting is going to be."

"Yeah, I heard that. How about a subject change? We discovered something interesting on the way here." There was no way I was continuing the conversation.

"I bet you did," Max said.

"Journal," I replied, ignoring the snide comment. He and I would hash it out later. Quyen placed it in my hand and the small tome aged fifty years.

Trina gasped and signed. " What the hell happened to that?"

"It turned back into the version that I am used to." I made sure she could see my mouth. "The one that disappeared from yesterday. We were hoping you could confirm my theory."

I held out the journal to her. When she took it, the book changed to the present-day version. She handed it back to me and it changed again. We did this a few times among the four of us to ensure it only happened with me.

"It's got to be temporal displacement," Trina signed. "Two objects can't exist at the same time. I told you that before, so the journal you showed us merged with this one. That's pretty cool. I would never have figured that. I expected it to be obliterated, but it makes sense. Matter cannot be created nor destroyed. Since you're from the same timeline, it appears when you touch it. But it begs the question of how are *you* here? You shouldn't be able to theoretically jump further than your lifespan, which is a solid hypothesis given the journal's behavior. And it's not like I'm pregnant or anything so—"

"Actually..." I let my sentence drop for effect. Anything to steer the conversation away from me. Besides, it was exciting news. I sensed an additional magical soul within her, which raised more questions because I didn't remember feeling magic from Daddy in our last encounter. And my grandparents' older appearance in my time—I was still puzzling that out.

"What?" Max asked.

Trina put her hands on her abdomen. Tears formed in her dark eyes as my grandfather's rounded. He crushed her to him.

I was at a loss at the emotion of the moment. "I'm sorry to surprise you, but I did tell you that you were my grandparents."

Quyen pressed me close to him. "I think you caught them off guard. Your announcement wasn't exactly subtle. You just tossed it out there."

I watched my grandparents holding each other, laughing and crying as though I was an outsider. Their happiness at becoming parents was humbling. I wished I had used more care in my declaration. Quyen and I are more alike than I thought. "Maybe we should give them a minute?"

Max turned to us. "Get over here, you two."

He held out an arm for us to join the hug. I went to him, yanking my reluctant boyfriend behind me. Quyen tensed at first, then settled into the group embrace. I missed Spellman family hugs.

After one more squeeze, it ended.

"We thought you meant that we adopted. That was what was in your mind when Trina checked you. After so many tries, we didn't want to get our hopes up. But we should have known. You favor Trina so much, and you have my mother's eye color, I thought..."

I lost the rest of his words as the world turned dark.

28

att

I closed the last treatise on ancient gods when a large stack of books materialized on my desk. My eyes were dry from the endless reading the past two days. I was no closer to answers than before I arrived. It was a wonder the ceremony even worked. I remembered Lauren's plan sounded solid enough to devote resources.

I wouldn't have risked so much after rereading proposals, theories, and research myself. But fifty years ago, I didn't know the payoff. I had even had another team working a summoning for controlling outsiders. If choosing between the two, I'd rather use Pandora, as it was less likely to cause a headache and she came with benefits.

She was my missing link. The Spellmans adopted her either as a baby or a small child. I wasn't certain. She was with them for as long as she remembered. Kitten was thirty-one, leaving an unknown gap in her history. I didn't think her past would become important, but then someone took her away from me and left me with mysteries that required traveling to the past to solve.

I still wanted to know more about the spell used on her. Unlike me, Pandora didn't have a tether to this time, and the spell took both her body and soul. It bared much study.

"Grand Magister." Lauren slammed her hands on my desk.

The frown on her face—a rarity—reminded me of Pandora. Except I knew Lauren would marry one day and die childless. As far as I know, there was nothing magical about her, but I didn't like the coincidence. The United States's troubled history with slavery created many distant relatives that were unknown to each other. Still, the resemblance between Lauren and my Kitten seemed too coincidental for my comfort. "Lauren, do you have any children?"

Her eyes softened and turned sad. "No. There's only one that—no."

She crossed her arms across her chest.

I was a fool. Of course, she didn't have any children. Even her marriage to Henry was a sham to draw my attention. Her crush on me was absolute at this point in our timeline. She needed to move on. I only slept with witches. The seed of my people was too precious to waste on a mundane, and I was too territorial to leave a lover alone. I wasn't easily swayed by lust that I couldn't handle on my own. The comingling of magics during pleasure could not be reproduced with non-practitioners. Then there was life span. Lauren was a dried version of her former beauty and physical prowess while I still had another century of mine. "You know my preferences and why."

She's stiffened. "Yes, I do. It doesn't change anything for me. I will continue to serve you the best way I know how."

No wonder she was my favorite. I smiled when the image of her older version saying goodbye to me and sabotaging my chances with Pandora flashed in my mind.

With a calm head, I saw that my Magia Lectore's final act of defiance was to give me a night of passion that I wouldn't have to take myself. Lauren thought she knew my needs better than I.

She was wrong.

That was one of the matters I planned to correct. "I need you to do what I say and not interpret what you believe I want. You are not privy to all my plans."

She flinched, but she didn't gainsay me.

"Is that all you require from me?" she asked. "The research?"

"For the moment, I'm still wading through the information."

She turned to leave when I recalled the other matters I left in her care. "What about Quyen?"

"I have a firm looking into the matter. They assured me their best is on it."

"Good, and keep on the lookout for a witch named Pandora Spellman. She has long, wavy hair, brown skin, and cinnamon-colored eyes. Do not engage. I will deal with her myself."

It was a basic description, but something in my tone implied more than professional curiosity because Lauren's eyes narrowed.

"I don't recall any such witch in Obscura, yet you seem very familiar with her. Anything I should know?"

I wasn't going to entertain her tone or explain more than necessary. Once I secured Pandora's compliance again, I would reinforce the boundaries between the two of them regarding me. "She's dangerous."

My assistant held my gaze for a moment then said, "As you wish, Grand Magister."

Her steps were heavy as she exited. I considered confiding in her. My plans would likely accelerate with her input, even if she didn't possess magic. Summoning Oya had been Lauren's proposal. I allowed her to pursue it even when the chances of success appeared low. She turned out to be successful despite everything. Lauren helped advance my agenda in ways I could appreciate, but I had to reduce my dependency on her knowing that it couldn't last.

She was mortal.

I need Quyen.

A reconciliation with him would set my course back in favor. He loved puzzles. The idea of searching for Oya would appeal to his nature. The sooner the firm found him, the better.

I grabbed the top folder marked "Fairy Stone Summoning." The file was a recent accounting of last month's attempt at harnessing the goddess's power. I casually flipped through the document packet when I came across a highlighted portion and Lauren's writing next to it. She indicated that I should send agents to the area to infiltrate the local coven, Fairy Tale. I touched the familiar scrawl. The woman could not leave well enough alone, but I heeded her advice.

For the past five years, my past self bought real estate in the surrounding counties and within Stuart. Any opportunity to own a business, property, or influence the local government past-self did. There were a few small covens in the area, but only one with more than four practitioners. The Fairy Tale Coven—I wasn't sure if the name was ridiculous or clever—was composed of the marginally talented. They were the strongest in the area.

My informant in the sheriff's department reported that a stranger washed up at Fairy Stone's lake the night of the summoning. No information was found about the stranger when searching. My guy expected the stranger, Andrew Duong, to be a wizard with Camera. The informant also remarked Andrew seemed friendly with a member of Fairy Tale.

Andrew Duong.

A memory of our first encounter at Hampton University as roommates flashed into my mind. It appeared that fate smiled on me yet again. I found him—his trail. It was a place to start. I grabbed my coat then left my office. It was time to check out Fairy Stone, starting with the local peacekeepers and ending with the hospital staff. I never properly ingratiated myself for their assistance with the disaster last month. It was high time I corrected that matter.

29

 uyen

Panic froze my being when Pandora's eyes rolled upward. Minutes ago we were part of an awkward group hug to celebrate Trina's pregnancy when she started convulsing. She slumped into my arms, dead weight and utterly boneless. Each beat of my heart thudded in my ears. My world slowed to molasses as I eased her to the Spellman's kitchen floor. Max pushed me away, then shook her.

"Pandora." He leaned in close to her face then pressed his fingers to the side of her neck. Max signed furiously. "She's breathing and her pulse is steady. We need to get her to the hospital. Trina, call 911. Quyen take the truck and wait by the highway. Guide the ambulance to the entrance and alert us when they turn down Deer Haven. The keys are by the door."

Trina shot to the large phone inlaid into the wall with a giant screen and keyboard.

"You can't take care of her like last time?" I asked.

Max continued to gingerly examine Pandora. "I know what happened last time, this time I don't. Hell, I don't know that not taking her to the hospital the first time didn't result in this. We can argue one she's treated. For now just do as I say."

"Obscura is looking for me and Pandora isn't from here. She doesn't—"

Max shook his head. "We will take care of it, Quyen. I need you to do as I say. Her breath is slowing, which means she's getting worse. I have to stay here with her."

My world then sped to a blur at his words. It seemed one moment I stood amongst the panic, the next I drove down the semi-dark road to the main highway lamenting that Max and Trina lived in the middle of nowhere. I could lose Pandora when we just found each other. And there was nothing I could do—I slapped my head. The bridge. We could have carried her through, then called 911. Then we'd have to deal with the Newport News authorities and hospital system. I didn't have any connections at Riverside to alert any of my enemies. "And then we'd be into a different fire."

Max was right. Stuart was the best. If I wasn't so involved, I would know that. I wasn't nearly as freaky when I thought Tonya was in trouble, but the idea of Pandora being hurt fried my brain. I fell for her way too fast, but then our personalities matched. Not to mention she was a gorgeous, powerful witch. There was nothing I needed to hide about my past from her. I wish she afforded me the same courtesy. Something that hadn't been disclosed ate at her, likely her role in Obscura.

She made it seem shallow despite being Matt's number two and being his—it was in the past.

And I'm way too territorial for a woman I've known for a day. No matter how good the sex was, acting clingy would send her running back to the future quicker than anything.

A day. It seemed as though it had been a lifetime. Then there was the huge problem of defeating Obscura's plans. There was no telling how long that would take or what would happen afterward. I had to focus on the facts. We had as long as it suited us but we wouldn't have anything if we let Matt continue unopposed.

I reached the end of the road and pulled off to the side so the ambulance could pass me when they arrived, then waited by the highway, bathed in the headlights and the comforting sound of the truck idling. The winter evening moon hung over me. I leaned against the Deer Haven street sign straining to hear sirens.

Where were they?

Each moment of engine idling and animals rustling in the woods put me on edge. I was on the verge of attempting to summon the EMTs—not that it was possible—when I saw red and white lights in the dark blue expanse. I waved my arms and gestured towards the entrance as they approached me. The driver acknowledged me and turned down the road towards Pandora.

I ran to the truck, hopped in, and tore after them. There was no way I'd miss another moment. I was in the driveway when I remembered to alert Max. He'd have to forgive me. No civilian was one hundred percent in a crisis. I may practice the magic craft in defense, but I was by no means as hardened as a first responder, or even the second tier. It was apparent I would be the partially scatterbrained loved one who became a timebomb in certain circumstances.

I wasn't even sure I managed to shut off the truck when I rushed up the steps. At least I had that much awareness to question it, but it all went out the door when I saw Max performing CPR on Pandora. One of the EMTs watched while Trina hovered with tears in her eyes and her hands over her mouth. Max held her a moment while the EMT took over chest compressions. "What happened?"

"She convulsed again and stopped breathing," he answered. He made a fist then rubbed his chest a few times. "Sorry. I don't know what's wrong, but I'm glad we didn't handle it on our own. They will get her stable enough to get in the ambulance then take her to Sovah since it's closest."

Pandora coughed. We all stared at her, expecting her to open her eyes. They fluttered once but no joy. I would take it. Anything was better than watching them fight to save her life.

"Let's get her to Sovah," one of the EMTs, a stocky white woman with a stern expression, replied. "Lift on three."

The other EMT, a willowy black woman with a wide-eyed expression, nodded. She moved to Pandora's feet.

"One, two, three." They lifted in unison, placed her on the gurney, then raised it to normal height.

"I want—"

"No, ride with us," Max said. "You don't want to be in the way."

I glared at him. Then I caught the hint in his expression. He was right.

Calm, Quyen. You freaking out over your girlfriend doesn't help. You lead this operation. Deal with your downed team member, the ill one from the future.

I mentally chastised myself.

"Good point. I'll drive so you can have your hands free."

We followed the EMTs then jumped into the running truck. I glanced at the gas gauge, then Matt's exasperated expression. "Good thing you have a full tank."

He opened his mouth to argue when Trina butt in. She grabbed both of our hands. The moment we made contact, I sensed another in my mind. I swerved in the driveway.

"Sorry for the hamfisted intrusion, but it's not the time, guys. I touched Pandora when she convulsed. I connected with her mind before something kicked me out," she said into our minds.

I kept my eyes on the road/driveway. Red and white lights were the only illumination. I tugged down the visor to shield my eyes from some of it. The contrast between the flickering emergency flashes and the near-complete darkness was too harsh. "So her problem is magical in nature, and we handed her to the mundanes?"

"Ease your tone," Max warned.

"Not sure," Trina replied. *"It may be an issue with the spell that summoned her, but it does change the fact that it almost killed her."*

"Point taken." Turning on each other was counterproductive. We all could have done something different. None of us had significant magical healing abilities, and the craft wasn't the all-solving fantasy television, books, and bigotry portrayed. It was more like science. There were rules and limitations. While we lived three to four times longer, we were still human, just with more than our hands for defense. "You said something? A possession?"

"*Possibly,*" Trina said. "*It happened so quickly, but it didn't feel foreign. Pandora hasn't explained a lot about her powers.*"

"She can absorb magic." I wished we did more talking about her powers. She avoided the details. Given what Matt did to her, I didn't blame her. Except now, our ignorance was a hindrance. "My working theory is that the summoning that I used grabbed a proxy for Oya since I used symbolic representations of the forty-two powers."

"A stand-in for a stand-in?" Max asked.

"Exactly."

"*I need more information. I'm not following,*" Trina said.

"The Oya ritual requires the sacrifice of forty-two people with each of the forty-two powers. I used items to represent—"

"*I get that,*" Trina scoffed. "*Pandora has one power, though rare. How does that justify the other forty-one?*"

"Once the magic is absorbed, she can recall it." I gripped the wheel. What if Oya sought a host and found her? I brought her here without care. It could be that I created what I tried to prevent.

Trina shivered. "*What are you thinking?*"

"It may be Oya that has her."

"*Or it may be temporal complications,*" she pointed out. "*It could be anything.*"

"Don't borrow trouble," Max added. "Besides, it happened almost six weeks ago. I doubt an ancient goddess's spirit hung out in the forest camping until the right body came along, not when the Grand Magister and others were there on arrival."

"Also possible." The goddess would need a vessel after being separated from her body. "I did say working theory."

"*Pandora's a Spellman. She will be fine,*" Trina said as we entered the hospital's campus. "*Let's focus on keeping the authorities off her.*"

"The story is she's your cousin like we decided before, and I'm her fiancé." I ignored the grunt from Max. "We came to meet her family today, and I discovered that I know Max, déjà vu and all."

Max sighed. "Got it. Oh, and you got your cast removed early. Dr.

Sean is on call tonight. She's going to remember you and expect a cast."

"Great cover story, except the lack of ID part." I let go of her hand and opened the truck door.

"You panicked and left without her purse," Max said.

I was about to argue the point when I saw Trina place Pandora's bag on the floor. He nodded at Trina then opened the door. It was her idea then.

I made sure she could see my mouth. "Good catch, Trina."

She flashed a smile, touched her chin, and pushed her hand away, palm facing inward. I assumed her sign meant "thank you."

"That will keep them off us until billing becomes more insistent," Max said.

I nodded, following his train of thought. "Her fiance will be responsible for the medical fees. Nothing shuts bureaucracy up faster than letting them know they don't have to be accountable for a problem."

"Done this before, have you?" Max snorted. His pithy retort eased the tightness in my chest.

"A time or two." We faced the emergency entrance. I gave Max and Trina a look. "Ready?"

"Always," Trina signed.

"Then here we go."

We headed to the bright entrance in the darkness. I expected chaos. There was some. The staff rushed about as we came in, but the waiting area was a sedate tableau compared to my expectation. Patients and loved ones sat in chairs waiting for a doctor to see them—injured people—not folks waiting for an exam. One boy had an obvious broken arm. Another man held a compress to his face.

How long did I wait when they brought me in last month? I didn't remember anything until I woke up in the room already treated. The pain had been unbelievable. I could only imagine what these waiting people endured.

Max marched up to the check-in desk. "Hi, Elenore, we need to check in."

"Oh no, sweetie, is Trina okay?" The older nurse peered around then relaxed. "She looks fine to me."

"No, it's our cousin. She was brought in." He thumbed in my direction. "She and her fiance were visiting when she passed out."

"That's terrible, bless yall's hearts. Here. Check her in, and I'll let you know when Dr. Sean sees her."

He took a clipboard from her hands then passed it to me. We were moved to the waiting area when I heard a familiar voice.

"If it isn't Mr. Duong. Back for more, I see."

Shit.

I turned then faced Deputy Wright. "So it happens."

"Mind if I ask what you're doing back here?" The deputy put his hand on his hips near his sidearm.

The veiled threat was exactly what I wanted to avoid. The officer was gunning for me, and as luck would have it, I ran into him again. I might as well lay out the cover story. "My fiance was just admitted. Now would you get out of the way? I have paperwork to fill out."

I stepped around him then went to the waiting area. Trina and Max joined me a breath later.

"I'll contact Beth to keep an eye on him," he remarked.

"We should do more than that." I focused on the clipboard in front of me. The deputy's gaze seared my senses. I didn't have to check. I knew he stared me down, searching for some nefarious reason for my visit. "He knows something, or we should be sure he doesn't."

"He is just peculiar about strangers," Max said.

"His ass is racist," Trina replied. "Don't cover for him."

Max sputtered in his translation.

"Though he seems unusually hostile," she added.

"Even more reason to watch him."

"Alright, I'll see what I can do but keep in mind our coven is less than five people."

"Size doesn't matter. It's about utilizing resources," I said, "but noted."

Then I settled into busying my mind with the paperwork and my next move. First and foremost, Deputy Wright had to leave the equation before becoming a danger to Pandora. The last thing she needed was Matt finding out about Pandora fifty years early through me.

30

 andora

I gasped for air and awoke to a stormy gray sky on soft, wet ground. The idea of falling asleep outside and waking up in a pool of—I didn't want to know. I was mostly dry. A fine mist covered me and the cushiony thing.

At least the slavers didn't find me while I was...

I sat up. My cushion was a cloud, surrounded by a mirror-still lake. Not a river. It was a winding snake-like body of water. A border of craggy rocks and large, green trees formed a backdrop and separation to the endless mist.

"Welcome, little one," a disembodied voice thundered.

A bolt of lightning shot out of the placid water. I shielded my eyes from the sudden flash. Technically it was too late, but I couldn't stop the reflex. I saw lightning streak afterimages for a few blinks before my vision cleared. A woman rose out of the water perched on a throne made of metal-plated bones. A better description was coalesced out of the flat surface like an apocalyptic ruler.

Clad in a horned headdress of feathers and ribbon, she wore my brown leathers. It resembled my entire lawless zone garb, right down to the leather boots. The woman even possessed intense garnet eyes that appeared to read and judge the soul as she glared at me from her throne of bone and copper. She tapped an armrest, a literal skull, as though *I* wasted *her* time.

She stole *my* appearance. I deserved the right to take it in and be intimidated like everyone else. It was why I chose the ensemble. When I wore it, I felt like I could take on anyone. Seeing it used against me, I decided well.

I wish I wore my leathers instead of jeans and a sweater. At least I still had the boots. I could stomp ass in them at a minimum.

A large ox with long curved horns lay beside her. He glanced at me before closing his eyes, unimpressed.

"Hey, we look the same. Just different outfits."

The woman laughed. "Dayo is unimpressed with your fear, little one. You should know better. Water buffalo can sense it and become stubborn."

I prepared a flippant answer, then remembered. I was on a cloud in the middle of a river. The witch had power along with a stalking problem. Pissing her off or getting into an unnecessary magic fight could strand me wherever the hell I was. "I moved up to needing to impress cattle. I better gather my composure then."

"She's insouciant, isn't she, Dayo." The witch rubbed the buffalo behind the ears.

The cloud was sturdier than I suspected. When I stood, it steadied underneath my feet—for the most part. "Not to be rude, but why are you looking like me, and where is this place?"

Her eyes narrowed. "Look deep, little one. You know me better than any mortal has or will."

My heart quickened. Oya. She can't be.

I thought I only endured her abilities. Why was it hard to believe she was sentient? Especially since I learned about the goddess summoning. Nothing was ever simple.

Grabbing the meaty part of my arm, I pinched hard. Pain shot up my bicep. The scene before me wasn't a hallucination, at least not like the ones I previously experienced. "Oya, where are we?"

She sat back petting the brown creature, the water buffalo, next to her. "This is not how I expected our first conversation to go. I spent years whispering in your ear while you ignored me, then you finally opened your mind after finding us a suitable mate, and you're *boring*."

She huffed.

"Oya." It came out as a gasp that perfectly mirrored the exasperation of my insides. The moment I said her name, the churn within me stopped. She grinned, then my heart sank. The situation was more complex than I thought.

"You're catching on."

I doubted that. My mind raced with information to the point of panic. I barely knew if I was coming or going, except I did it on a floating nimbus raft in front of the goddess that possessed me.

"Possession is such an inaccuracy for what we have, little one. What we are requires a story. One that you will have to return to the godscape again to comprehend. For now, let's discuss our mate."

My knees buckled. I hoped she meant Quyen and not Matt, but even that was too much. Quyen and I matched well. But it was too early for a happily-ever-after and unlikely for the two of us, given that we weren't from the same timeline. "I'm sorry—"

A bolt of lightning etched across the sky a second before raucous thunder boomed around us. "Don't play with my emotions. While a competent lover, you know I do not mean that arrogant son of a spider. He is of the same ilk as the one who trapped me: all charisma, power, sex, and faithless."

My heart leaped in my chest at her complement of Quyen. I understood what she meant about Matt, except the faithlessness part. As far as I knew, he never took another lover besides me unless she referred to power being his mistress, and that I could dig. The lure of his strong personality was difficult to ignore when I was younger. Matt was a powerful wizard, and all I had to do was follow his whims like an obedient dog, ignore my conscience, spread my legs for him, and I could have everything.

The world, for the price of *me*.. "Yeah."

Oya's face softened. "You learned before. He had too much of a hold on us, but then you found a mate who would shield us from that one's whims before we could become tempted."

"I don't need Quyen to fight my battles." My inner fighter chafed at needing him to protect me from Matt.

"But of course. However, even the greatest warrior needs a shield in battle. A male is a complement to the soul, not a crutch. Even *you* must know that." She leaned forward conspiratorially. "What is bothering you? Quyen pleased us thoroughly this afternoon, yet you shy away."

I almost covered my face like a child, but worked up enough badassery to stare her down instead. "What do you mean by *us?*"

She waved her hand. "That's a topic for another time. I want to discuss Quyen."

I failed to see what there was to discuss. Apparently, she was there for the entire afternoon. It was too embarrassing.

"Oh, yes," I moaned.

Hold up.

The river became a giant reflection of me pressed against Quyen's front door. His face was close to mine, flushed with exertion. Dark locks falling over his brow swept at my own with each thrust into my body. Phantom tingles between my legs accompanied the reminder. It was difficult to tear my eyes away, but I met Oya's gaze. "I was there. Thank you for the reminder. What is your point?"

The memory continued to play, though the volume of my pleasure lowered to an acceptable level for discussion. *Like that's not distracting.*

Oya stretched on her throne as though she were a cat stretching after a nap. She smiled at the pool, then back at me. "I approve of this match. Don't endanger it by concealing the truth about me. Quyen brings balance to us."

The one thing I dared not do. It was a story of my life. "You of all should understand after spending centuries as you are. I have limited time here. I want to enjoy it with him, not become a slave to another power."

"You know him better than that." She tutted and raised her eyebrow. "And what happens when he finds out?"

"He won't. I will stop Matt, and history continues without the Grand Magister and me to ruin it."

"Well and good, but then what?" she asked. "We're abandoned in this time alone?"

"With the timeline negated, I should fade or be sent back."

Oya studied my gaze. She made a slight frown.

Her throne sunk into the lake. "We'll talk again."

What was that supposed to mean? She gave me the stank eye as though I said something dumb. I wasn't a goddess. It wasn't as though I possessed thousands of years of magic, physics, and whatever time travel knowledge she had.

And what was all that freaky deaky talk about Quyen being my mate? The pornographic memories—well, that part was as exhilarating as it was embarrassing. Then there was the "our" business and "we."

As far as I was concerned, *we* didn't share anything. Oya was an unwanted guest that I planned to banish. Well, planned to set free since she was conned into the whole situation by a man who wanted her for her power.

She was right. We were similar in that way. I would free us both. First, I had to get out of the godscape. There was no telling how much time passed outside or how my grandparents and Quyen reacted to my sudden disappearance.

"Some warning next time," I shouted into the ether. My voice echoed off the nothingness, which shouldn't happen. Then again, I floated on a cloud raft down a river. Why should science apply here?

"Fine then, have it your way, little one," Oya's disembodied voice replied.

The nimbus raft collapsed under me. I plunged into the warm water with a gasp, sucking in water. Clawing my way to the top for precious air seemed futile as my body grew heavier and my lungs burned. The goddess killed me or was in the process.

Despair nearly won out as I sunk further no matter how hard I tried to swim upward. Was this it?

Oya brought me all the way here just to play head games, watch porn, and kill me? There had to be more. She could have gone straight to that. It didn't make sense.

Have it your way, little one.

The automatic response won out—I took a lung full of air, not water. I was still underwater, sinking further from the surface, but I no longer drowned. It wasn't real.

The sensation of slowly descending and general wetness appeared authentic, but it didn't follow the rules like the cloud. I wonder if it followed the laws of magic. Clapping my hands together, I thought of my spell. "Part for me spirits of water, send to the surface your daughter."

I always had an affinity for water and air magic. Hopefully— no, it was about to pay off. I spread my hands apart. At first, nothing stirred, then a whirlpool formed around me while a force below pushed me up.

"Yes." I punched the air when I shot out of the river.

Oya sat on her disturbing bone throne, tapping one skull armrest and stroking her animal—who snorted at me as though my accomplishment was nothing.

Everyone was a critic.

Oya, on the other hand, grinned. "You are stubborn. However, I chose well."

"And that means?"

"That our time is over, and the next time you appear in the godscape, it will be as an equal."

A straight answer. That was a surprise. "I'm just a person, one with lots of questions that I would like you to answer. So how about now? Starting with this 'as an equal' business."

"There are some matters for you to attend to." She gave a casual flick of her wrist, and I stared at a white ceiling with gray speckles. I sucked in a breath when someone squeezed my hand.

"You're awake." Quyen smiled then kissed the side of my mouth. "Good. We need to get you out of here."

31

uyen

I squeezed Pandora's hand to keep a grasp on reality. She was unconscious for almost twenty-four hours. In that time, I performed every divination spell I knew to figure out if there was anything wrong and turned up nothing. All I could do was wait and watch, which went a long way in solidifying my cover story with the hospital staff. They kept Deputy Wright off me as he tried to interrogate them about my intentions. He eventually laid off, but he was not far.

Thanks to an early morning rain, my water divinations showed him monitoring the hospital exits. I would worry about that asshole once Pandora awoke, which I hoped was soon because I could stand seeing her lay there.

As if hearing my silent plea, eye garnet eyes flutter opened.

"You're awake." I kissed her.

Her coloring was a little gray in comparison to her normal brown complexion, but her eyes were clear, alert, and she didn't blow the hospital up with some sort of supernatural tantrum the way I expected a recently escaped goddess would. She was in the clear which meant Trina was likely correct and I borrowed trouble. All I cared about was that Oya hadn't possessed her, the doctor couldn't find anything medically wrong with her, however Deputy Wright hung around. I wanted to get us out of there as inconspicuously as possible. Unfortunately, I would require at least another day since it was early evening again.

Pandora was in a coma for twenty-four hours and I wanted to know why.

"Where am I exactly?"

"Sovah Hospital. Max is a nurse here."

A gentle smile graced her face. I rubbed her knuckles affectionately.

"I forgot he was a nurse. He was retired by the time I was old enough to ask him too many questions. That was when I saw them once a year for our camp out. Where are they?"

"Max is on duty. He should be by on his rounds any time now. Trina went home to shower. She's going to be pissed at me because I just convinced her to leave fifteen minutes ago, but I'm glad you're awake."

"Yeah, sorry about that. An unexpected side effect of magic. How much suspicion did I rouse?"

My face heated. "I played the role of the worried fiance well enough that the hospital thought you were pregnant, which you're not. Given that we had sex recently, they wanted to check again if you didn't wake up."

A rose flush brushed lightly across the tops of her cheeks. "Well, that's embarrassing."

"It is, but it kept them from doing too much prodding and injecting you with medicine. The clearer you are, the more likely they will discharge you."

Pandora narrowed her eyes, then frowned as she read something from my expression. "Deputy Wright is here. Great."

"How did you—"

She held up our joined hands. "Listening, Trina's power."

"Handy."

"That and you're wrinkling your forehead as though you're bothered by something. He has nothing but suspicion. If we act guilty, he will continue to latch on to you. The deputy is just bored and biased. We will play the role and if he comes near me, I'll use my power to encourage other pursuits."

That should have been my plan not freaking out. *Get it together, Quyen.*

I leaned over to kiss her. "Excellent plan."

She moaned as the heart rate monitor beeps rapidly increased. "Probably shouldn't do that."

"Probably shouldn't do a lot of things." I gave her a quick peck then settled gently in my chair by her bed. "So what happened?"

Her eyes clouded. "I saw Oya."

I knew it. The goddess tried something.

I was out of my seat again, and she pushed against me before I could form coherent thoughts. "What the hell? Did she do anything to you?"

Pandora's eyes softened. She shook her head. "I'm fine, but we both need to remain focused, or we won't be able to work together."

"You're my girlfriend, damn it. I'll be a machine after I know you're okay." Not caring enough came between me and my cellmates. They all died, except for Tonya, and I couldn't bridge the distance. My heart wouldn't do it. I refused to do it with Pandora, not when I had such an easy connection with her. She was my fantasy come true. I lost too many people in my life to hesitate.

She gave me a pleased expression. My gamble paid off.

"Girlfriend? We slept together once. You're quite clingy, aren't you?"

There was no annoyance in her playful question. She was teasing me. I tossed myself out there, and she was giving me a hard time. It made sense to give right back. "I haven't heard you deny the claim. Besides, you started it when you seduced me most of the day and forced me to cover up my assets from possible prying female eyes."

"You are such a goof." She squeezed my hand. "That is the point I was trying to make before you suckered me into your madness. I don't want to leave us open to danger because we're mooning over each other."

"Then I won't assign us on team missions unless it is strategically necessary." Simple enough fix.

Her lips pursed in a smile that made me want to kiss her, but instead, I asked, "What did Oya want?"

"I'm not sure, exactly." She rolled her eyes. "She dodged all my questions."

That sounded par for the course. I doubted an ancient goddess that snatched the consciousness of a human without warning would be so kind as to allow Pandora to interrogate her. "Did she say anything that we can use?"

Her brow furrowed slightly, but she didn't say anything.

"What?" I asked.

She shifted her gaze downward before meeting mine. "She talked about you."

"Me?" A cold sensation trickled down my spine. I had the attention of a goddess. There was no telling if that was a good or bad thing. It did make sense. I was the one who tried to summon her the second time. Well, track her. "What about Matt?"

She wrinkled her nose. "She detests him. He reminds her of the wizard that imprisoned her."

Handy to know. Oya was less likely to join Obscura. "Then, at a minimum, she isn't their ally."

"Not from the impression I got from her."

"Why did she select you?" My throat tightened as I waited for an answer. If she even had one. Pandora already said that Oya wasn't forthcoming, but it didn't add up to me. If the goddess had an issue with me, she should take it to the source, not my woman.

Damn, neanderthal much? Pan may be your girlfriend, but there was no telling how long that would last or if she could remain in this timeline.

Another problem added to my list after dealing with Oya and Matt, keeping Pan by my side. I let one great girl go. I wouldn't the second time.

"This is embarrassing." Pandora took my hand. "Don't you dare laugh, but she likes you and me together. She wanted—"

I snorted as laughter bubbled up in me. Of all the scenarios I expected, even feared, curiosity was not one.

"I told you not to laugh." Pandora squeezed my hand then crossed her arms.

The pout on her face added another dimension to my impression of her. I lifted her chin. "I'd rather have supernatural curiosity than her stealing you from me."

Her cinnamon eyes softened. "The whims of a goddess and all. But it has changed the game."

A lump formed in the pit of my stomach. "Yeah, it has. You have an in with Oya that seems only you can work unless you think she would be willing to talk to me."

Pandora's eyes widened. "No. If she wanted to talk to you, she would have instead of me."

Interesting response.

"You know you don't have to assume all of the risk?" I caressed the side of her face. "Let me rephrase. I won't let you carry this alone. There's no need for me to be circumspect, not with you."

She kissed my palm. "You're... I don't know what. I've got Oya for now, but there's still Matt. We both know you're better equipped to handle him."

Damn her and her logic. My girl gave me a dose of reality that I couldn't ignore. "Point. Keep me in the loop about Oya. I wouldn't be able to take it if I lost you to her."

"Got attached quickly, didn't you?" she teased.

I did, and I wasn't ashamed.

"As a man who has lost nearly everyone in one form or another, I know what I want when I see it. I don't always agree with the whims of circumstance, but I recognize them. You, Pan, are inconvenient." She bristled. "You steal my focus and give me something to look forward to when I need to be cutthroat. You also bring me anxiety because I know when this is over, I'm going to want you to be my wife, and you might not dig that. And I love you—thought I'd throw that out there while I'm running my mouth faster than my brain can catch up."

"Quyen, I..."

I shook my head. "I'm tossing out facts so we can plan around them, not to obligate you. My decisions are biased because of my feelings, but that doesn't mean they are worthless. You handle Oya. I will take care of Matt, as you suggested, but don't forget that you have to make it to the end of this. I trust you."

And there went the last of my secrets. I embarrassingly exposed all of my cards.

Pan's eyes misted. "Quyen, there's something—"

The door opened, and Max rushed inside with a wild-eyed expression. "Great, she's awake. We have a problem. The Grand Magister is here with the hospital director, and he's heading this way."

It was too much of a coincidence running into Deputy Wright in the emergency room and then Matt showing up. I hadn't considered it, but the deputy might be in Obscura's pocket, or someone in the office is a leak. It was probably the former. An unlikely spy in a bigot like Wright was Matt's style, the whole hiding in plain sight adage. It looked like the jig was up.

Matt found me.

 att

The Fairy Stone area wasn't impressive in and of itself unless one was an earth magic user or loved nature. The location was mountains and green forests with pockets of civilization mixed into it. The natural setting was peaceful enough. It was full of solitude and the pulse of magic was enough to set one's soul on fire if they lacked discipline.

It was a wonder that another practitioner hadn't claimed the area, but many before me lacked vision. They hid within their families and covens, guarding their secrets, not progressing in their craft as they slowly became targets for mundanes.

The only person to understand the struggle was Quyen. We may have differed in our manifestation of practitioners' futures, but we had the same idea. The man was nearly as good as me. Letting him go slowed my progress in ways that only hindsight could process.

Quyen and Pandora, were the two keys to everything. "No man

was an island entirely of itself," John Donne once wrote, "every man is a piece of the continent, a part of the main."

They were part of my main, a capable general, and a powerful mate to sire my future. They made the difference between marginal success and world domination. Both would require a seduction of sorts. Quyen needed an appeal to his passé sense of morality and Pandora desired absolution. Neither would deny me once I fulfilled the requirements and I had just the cause to settle both.

She would follow me and share my bed. There I would worship her body until she bore my children and harnessed the power of a warrior goddess. Quyen would assist me in ushering in a new era where those with magic would not be burned for their talents or enslaved for political gain by the machinations of the current government. We were the next level and evolution, not aberrations. The mundanes would learn.

I gained wisdom from my past and a second chance to implement with greater efficiency with my pieces of my main at my hand. But first, I had to win Quyen back to my side before finding my wayward bride.

"Grand Magister, we're here."

I glanced away from the city-town nestled in the mountains that passed by my car window. "Where is this again?"

"Martinsville."

"Ah, yes." The little counties in the area bled together when compared to the fountain of power in Fairy Stone. It had been slow going, but I succeeded in buying large portions of the surrounding land. Still, I was far from outright owning it all in this timeline. "And now for the show to begin. Are the gift baskets and pizza ready?"

"Yes, Grand Magister. Along with the salads and a variety of drinks. A member of the hospital administration is waiting for you."

The door opened next to me. Peters nodded reverently as I plastered a smile on my face just in time for a starry-eyed man in his fifties to reach out his hand.

"Grand Magister, I'm Chief Medical Director Hobbs. It's a pleasure to meet you. I've seen your speeches on WNN and EBC. Your ideas about the evolution of the human race are enlightening. We are humbled that you'd visit our facility way out here in Martinsville."

"Director Hobbs, it is I who is humbled. It was your medical team that saved the lives of my people and the campers after that terrible storm." I took his hand and pumped it a few times. The tingle of low-level talent surprised me. This one's name did not appear in a dossier of the area. I would have Lauren oversee it next time. It would keep her busy, and she would do it right. "As a token of gratitude, I have gift baskets and a meal for your entire staff. I know they're busy saving lives and curing ills, but I would appreciate it if I could visit each floor to share my gratitude since it would provide the least interruption."

"Thank you. Of course." Director Hobbs gestured inside the hospital.

A portion of my detail followed as pre-planned while we prattled on. The rest oversaw the gift baskets and meal delivery while watching for Quyen. The tip I received this morning from one of my informants indicated that Quyen showed up at the hospital yesterday. They could not ascertain why, other than to accompany another who fell ill. He arrived with two unknown local coven members, and it was his second appearance in the hospital in the last sixty days.

I didn't believe Quyen was in the area just on tour. My old friend fell in with the local coven, probably to discern my intentions with the area.

It wasn't as though he had a choice. I left him without access to influential practitioners. His only option would be to join the delusional idealists in Camera. They were siloed with their cell structure to be more of a nuisance than anything practical. Besides, the moment the government seriously decided to put forth the Witchcraft Act, the majority, if not all, would flock to me.

No doubt Quyen got involved because of the death in the storm. I should have directed someone to hide a portion of the corpses in the other areas, but I couldn't resist the simplicity of a natural disaster serving as a clean-up. It was a little Act of God. Either way, it ended up making it easier to track Quyen and saved me weeks of effort, a sign that fortune favors the bold.

Now it was a matter of who paled from fear when I arrived and what action they would take next. And this time, mundanes did not have a reason to have an overtly hostile response to me. I expected a passing interest or apathy from the majority of them. Any practitioner would be eager like the doctor, unless someone informed them otherwise. They were the ones I wished to seek out—the rotten eggs in the basket.

So far, the tour was run of the mill. The facility was impressive for a rural area. I'd have to expand it once I moved Obscura out here. I made a mental note to place Lauren on the board of directors and cultivate Director Hobbs. I greeted the staff at each point with flowery gratitude that most people responded to, while I received awkward "you're welcomes".

At least none of them behaved as though I bothered them. No doubt due to the lack of political interest in the area.

If they only knew the value of the land. They were there for nature or philosophical reasoning, but power in the ley lines that formed Fairy Stone was not one of them.

"This is our step-down unit," Director Hobbs announced as we stepped off the elevator and into yet another area. "Patients here require immediate care and are not quite ready to be moved to the floor."

There was a small group of five standing about a nurse's station. Three wore lab coats, and two were in scrubs. They all watched as we approached with pasted smiles on their faces, the very picture of patronization of the boss and visiting company.

"Dr. Sean, Dr. Thompson, Dr. Paulson, and nurses Benson, and Benn, I would like to introduce you to The Grand Magister of Obscura. He's visiting us and is grateful for our work in the storm crisis last month."

Each of them shook my hand. The group was a mixture of curiosity at a VIP and resigned fate of placating the Medical Director's guest. It was a brief lull in the greeting of a female doctor who seemed fascinated by the practice of magical medicine that I heard a sound—a combination of a gasp and a groan. I shifted my attention to a stocky male with a shaved head moving quickly away from us.

The behavior in itself meant nothing, but something about it itched the back of my throat. Peters touched my shoulder. The touch of his mental magic wrapped upon my senses.

"Is there something wrong, Grand Magister?"

"I may have a lead, the male nurse walking away. I'm preparing for my next move. Alert James and tell him to be ready."

"Director Hobbs, will it be possible to visit any of the patients on this floor? I'm sure that they could use a little bit of cheer."

The man grinned. "If the patients are willing, I see no reason why not. It can be lonely convalescing."

"Yes, it can."

"I suggest starting from that end," I pointed in the direction the man in the scrubs went. "then work back towards this direction. I find that approach more methodical."

"Oh, I see. That makes sense." He ushered me past the nurses' station down the hall.

While we walked, I went over the information the informant provided. I didn't recall anything in the report indicating any names other than Quyen's. "Members of the local coven" were the only identification of his associates that I possessed. I should have placed someone in their ranks sooner or at least had a more detailed dossier on them beyond their marginal low-level talent status. With Quyen in their midst, they could become a nuisance if they meant to do so.

Another task to keep Lauren busy.

When we finally reached the end of the hall or near it, my heart tightened at the name on the dry erase board outside the patient's room. P. Spellman.

I didn't believe in coincidences. Someone spotted Quyen in the area, and there was a patient with a similar name to Pandora. They must have discovered her nature and they called him to recruit. If she was hurt then, why wasn't she with a healer? Even more importantly, why didn't she heal herself? Something must have happened, or she didn't have enough magic. Pandora needed me. Nursing her back to health would be the first step in winning her back. "Let's start on this side."

"Wonderful." Director Hobbs knocked on the door then poked his head inside the room. "Ah, nurse Spellman, is your relative up for visitors? The Grand Magister would like to spread a little good cheer—"

Spellman?

I knew it. This had to be her. I pushed past the Director and entered the room. "Apologies, but I believe that I may…"

Pandora lay on a gurney hooked up to machines. A blanket was thrown haphazardly at the end of the bed. A tube running from under the bedsheets bulged awkwardly. The quick beeps of the heart monitor echoed my fast paced rhythm. Finally, our eyes met, her beautiful cinnamon eyes wide.

I stepped forward when Quyen and the nurse—a relative that I didn't know—cut off my gaze.

"Grand Magister," Director Hobbs sputtered. "It's against policy to barge into a patient's room."

"I know the patient. Forgive me. I've been searching for the occupants in this room and was overcome with joy. If you will give us a few moments to reconnect."

"What a coincidence," he brightened. "Sure. Sure. Let me know when you are ready to continue."

I nodded to Peters to wait outside. He shut the door behind him, leaving the four of us alone. I spread my hands, and my telekinesis power pushed the two men apart so I could get to my Kitten. At her side, I felt her forehead and took her hand. She shied away from me.

"Excuse me, do I know you?"

I froze. In my shock and haste to find Pandora, I tipped my hand. In this timeline, I wouldn't know her save through dreams. I wasn't ready for her to know that I traveled back to find her, not until I sussed out her intentions here, and thwarted her plans. I knew her well enough to know she'd try to change our future, but I didn't know how far she succeeded in radicalizing Quyen and others against me. "I apologize, but I feel like I do. You come to me in dreams. Then I find out that you're real and with an old friend of mine."

Quyen wedged between us and shoved me back. "What the hell are you doing?"

"Fancy meeting you here." I kept calm. Allowing the concerned fiance to come out would negate any advantage I had in the situation. "You were the one in my dreams. It must be a sign."

He narrowed his eyes. "And why would you dream about my fiance?"

My world shrank to a pinprick of light and my body appeared surrounded by molasses. Far away, I heard speaking. Quyen droned on. Then her beautiful clarion voice brought the world back.

"Are you okay?" Pandora asked.

"Fine," I answered. My focus was on Quyen. "You're engaged. She must be quite a catch to get past your many rules."

His eyes lingered on her for a moment, then back to me. "What can I say? It's love. You shouldn't be so surprised. It has been years since we last spoke. It's not like you know me any more."

"I didn't expect such a milestone for the both of you. My dreams didn't reveal much, but you are right. We've been estranged."

"You turned everyone against me and became a politician," he snapped.

"An unintentional side effect of our public disagreement, but that is in my past," I said diplomatically.

Quyen frowned. "For you."

I was flailing. Seeing Pandora in the hospital bed with machines and mundane medicine bags hooked into her put me off my game. As for Quyen's role as her fiance, it had to be a ploy to stay close to her. It wasn't his style to get that close to certain women due to family pressures. The antiquated idea of the preservation of ethnicity didn't matter as long as the magic of the joining was strong. His family wasted opportunity by turning away potential strength and pressuring him to do so. "You're right."

His face slackened, but he remained in his position, between Pandora and me. "What are you doing here?"

"Seizing an opportunity, but this is not the ideal setting." I glanced around, my gaze resting on the man in scrubs with the perpetual surprised expression. The resemblance between Pandora's father and him was uncanny, as it should be. Though her father's skin tone was darker, he was the spitting image of the man in scrubs.

Interestingly, I didn't sense power from Pandora's magic-hating father. Even though she told me she was adopted, there was a faint resemblance around the mouth. There was also the Oya's dormancy for twenty years, despite a successful summoning. It was high time that I delved into the current Spellman line and verified Pandora's parentage for myself. The stronger her pedigree, the more powerful our children.

I held out my hand. "Matt Wesley, Grand Magister of Obscura."

"I know who you are." He took my hand. "Maxwell Spellman, and you're interfering with my patient's recovery."

His grip was firm and carried the familiar buzz of a practitioner. Coupled with subtle posturing, it stood to reason that he knew something of my adversarial relationship with Quyen and possibly the bad terms in which Pandora and I parted. "You're right. I apologize, but it's not wise for practitioners to remain in the hospital when other means are available. Allow my healers to finish the recovery process for you."

"No," Quyen and Maxwell said in unison.

My blood boiled at their refusal, Quyen's more. Something about it was more territorial than protective. I didn't like it, but I didn't know the situation...yet. And the refusal gave me the opening I needed to counter them. "Allow me to elucidate. It is the perfect opportunity to get away from prying mundane eyes and for me to catch up with Quyen. I also have to admit that I am curious about this entire situation. The fact that you are with the woman of my dreams made flesh and bone. As her relative, you should come. I will consider it discourteous not to accept my offer."

I preferred subtle terms as a means of persuasion, but the situation was perfect. Both of my quarries were in the same location at a disadvantage. Pandora would indeed run and warn Quyen about me. She had no idea that I came to get her as long as I didn't tip my hand any further. Letting any of them roam free at this point would work against my plans.

Quyen's jaw tightened. He moved a step forward when Pandora grabbed his wrist. I fought not to storm over to them and slap him away from her, especially when his treacherous eyes softened. It was a resigned expression. She was too familiar with him. And I didn't like it.

How long has she been here?

"You sure you don't mean as your hostage?" he asked.

Pandora rolled her eyes and sighed.

My heart sank with her exhalation of breath. I would deal with whatever their relationship was later. "You were never one to mince words, but you'd be my guests. I meant what I said when I mentioned that I wanted to talk to you about the curious coincidence."

Maxwell dragged two fingers across his palm. Pandora relaxed and released Quyen's wrist. I readied my power. If they thought they could overpower me, they were mistaken.

"He has a point," Pandora said. " We should get out of here so we can talk. I'm feeling better now, and anything else can be dealt with later."

"Are you—?"

"We accept," she said to me, causing both Quyen and Maxwell to sputter. "This is the perfect opportunity to answer all the questions that we have and for old friends to catch up."

"There's my Kitten," I murmured. She was never one to miss an opportunity to gain an advantage. I could use that.

"I'm sorry, what was that?" she asked.

"I was saying that it was great that someone had sense. Maxwell, would you accompany me to make the arrangements? As a medical professional and a relative, you best know how to handle matters."

The man briefly hesitated then walked to the door. I joined him, sensing the heated glares of two capable practitioners on my back. Neither would make a move while Maxwell was with me, and they would follow through with leaving. While I wouldn't harm Maxwell for fear of destroying Pandora's possible timeline, she didn't know what I would or would not do. Neither Quyen nor Pandora would leave someone behind to escape.

They would leave the hospital with me, and I would get my answers.

And my girl.

33

andora

The door closed behind G-max and Matt with a finality that made me dizzy. Everything had been going well then—bang! Oya hijacked my consciousness for supernatural girl talk and Matt found me. We were all captured because of my power. The sooner I got rid of the goddess the better. "So what do you have besides fighting our way out, because that's all I have at the moment."

"It's partially fleshed out and it depends on Trina, Tonya, and whoever else they round up to help."

My heart lifted. Leave it to him to come up with something sensible. I forgot about my grandmother. "Good thing she left or he'd have her too. Did you buy that dream business?"

Quyen nodded. "It's strange, but he's too arrogant to bother. And if he got better in the last few years—which he hasn't—then I would still know him well enough to spot an outright lie. The closest I've seen him get with any competency was subterfuge."

I threw my head back on my pillow. "Damn it. That's all I need to know that his obsession with me started before I was born.

Or to know it really was about me and not simply Oya's power. It was easier not to have any empathy for my enemy.

"Getting second thoughts about us?" he asked.

"No." The answer was out of my mouth without a second thought. A weight I didn't realize existed lifted from my heart. Matt may have been my past, but Quyen was mine for as long as I could hold on to him. "But I still have trouble maintaining bitter hatred for him when he shows human sides of his personality."

"It just means you understand the grays of life, but that doesn't—"

I touched Quyen's wrist. *"We should keep the rest of this telepathic. Move closer to me like we're kissing. The sentries posted at the door will notice the quiet and look in on us. If they see us engaged, they won't figure out that we're planning."*

He caressed my cheek then pressed his lips to mine. *"Won't they be able to listen in? He has several listeners in his employ."*

I thought about James. He was likely to be around or about to join Obscura. Either way, I had an edge.

"Trina's magic is a special application of listening. She can only control it through touch. She creates a kind of network between her and the person that an outside listener would not be able to intrude on. And I have her power, so we're safe."

"A perfect power for someone who's deaf."

"Her power is why she is deaf instead of partially blind like most of them," I replied. It was supposed to be an internal comment, however the tightening of his lips against mine let me know he heard me. My grandmother's magic would require more practice to make sure I could separate shared dialogue from my private thoughts.

"I've never heard of that."

"And I will tell you more about it after you tell me your plan. Matt's bound to come back here once he is sure Max is secure and I can be released."

"True. He's too much of a micromanager to allow me out of his sight for long, or you." Quyen licked my lips. *"The plan."*

His thought sounded like a reminder more than a statement, not that I blamed him. I wanted part two of our sexfest to begin, too.

He tugged on a lock of my curls, and I focused.

"Do you have an imprinting power?" he asked.

"Yes." It wasn't one of my go-to powers since it was passive. The ability to sense the feeling and history of objects was more of a ticking time bomb than anything helpful. It had its moments. The power gave me a greater understanding of Quyen coupled with his words from his journal. *"I don't see how reading an object's history is going to help."*

"I want you to write on an object. Trina used that blanket to sleep last night. Imprint the memory of what happened and contact Tonya on it."

I never considered using the power to leave messages. He was brilliant. I puckered my lips. *"As a listener, she'll hear my thoughts, but what makes you think she will touch the blanket? That's leaving a lot to chance."*

"I'm banking on what I picked up from her personality. She's curious and likes to be prepared. Did you see how organized the pantry was and the trays of food? I thought it was Max until she came out with a similar setup ten minutes after him."

"That is so weird that you noticed that… and sexy too."

One of his hands drifted to my chest. *"Good thing that was the last of my plan because you're distracting me."*

"No, it's a good thing I'm hooked up to this machine."

The heart monitor's casual beeps increased dramatically.

He sighed, then took his hand away. *"Yeah, because I'd get my hospital sex pin otherwise."*

"You wouldn't." The idea had some appeal, but he didn't seem like… then again, there was that morning. No, it was yesterday.

"The catheter is the only thing stopping me. Without it, I'd be inside you."

Gulp. Like I needed that fantasy taking up real estate in my brain. It was distracting enough as it was. *"Once we get out of this and take Matt down, we'll get your hospital pin and talk about others we can collect."*

"Deal." He kissed my nose then moved away.

He grabbed the blanket and laid it across me. I laid my hand on it then focused on the message. I left a memory of what happened in the hospital after Trina left. It was a gamble, but I wanted any Obscura foot soldier to assume that the blanket just happened to carry an impression and put it down before the message occurred. If they didn't, it would reveal our conversation about Oya.

Another risk. Matt behaved too friendly towards me for my comfort. And dreams—he had dreams about me before we met? I was his dream girl. If that wasn't taking the obsession up another notch, I didn't know what was.

"Done." Then aloud, I said, "Do you know where my clothes are?"

Quyen closed his eyes. "They were cut off when you were brought in."

Of course they were. I came in non-responsive. They weren't going to undress me casually. That didn't happen even in the lawless zone. Except there removing clothes was not all that would happen to an unconscious person. "My bag. Did you—?"

"Trina grabbed it when we left, but we left it in Max's truck."

"That's okay." I took his hand in mine. "Think about where you saw it."

Through our contact, I listened to his thoughts—the conversation in the truck as they followed the ambulance and Trina's plan to leave the bag in the truck so there would be plausible deniability about my lack of identification. I focused on the bag while calling to it. It was the best way to describe conjuring items and transporting them to other locations. For me, I had to call the place or object to me.

The gentle weight of the bag on my legs signaled my success. I released Quyen's hand. "Thanks for your help."

"No problem," he replied. "I can't get over the fact you can... You amaze me sometimes, but then that's what being a fiance is all about."

Good save on his part. Obscura still eavesdropped.

"You're so sweet." I reached into the bag for another pair of jeans and a sweater.

He touched my shoulder to reconnect our mental network. *"Sorry that I almost slipped."*

"Don't worry about it. You caught it in time."

"Yeah, but the less information Matt has about you, the better. He's way more interested in you than he should be."

"I caught that too, but I'm still going to play the innocent card until I can confirm any suspicions I have. Besides, it will help me baseline him in case future Matt shows up and makes a trade."

He cringed. *"I don't want to think about the idea of there being two of him. And if there were, I doubt they would last long. I'd lay odds that they both have a 'there can only be one' mentality."*

"And you'd probably win. I can't see him cooperating with his past self," I agreed.

"Or maybe he merged like the journals."

I shuddered. *"That sounds like that would make him demented, as bad as he was."*

Quyen tilted my chin upward. *"Hey, you know I'm going to do everything in my power to stop him. I won't let it turn out as it did before."*

I saw the resolve in his dark eyes. He meant it, but there was no way he could enforce his promise on his own. Still, his words warmed my heart. He would try. It was my job to make sure he succeeded.

"Thank you."

Knock. Knock.

"We're back," Max announced, cracking the door. He glanced around then came into the room—alone.

"Where's—"

"In the hall with his people," he whispered. "I'm going to take her catheter out," he said aloud before signing, "I hope you have a plan because I'm fresh out of ideas."

"Okay." Then I signed, "I'm leaving a message for Nana to contact Tonya. Meanwhile, we stay calm."

"Weak plan," he signed, then shooed Quyen away. "Would you wait outside while I help her?"

Quyen gave a curt nod then left. The moment he left, the two of us broke into a flurry of silent conversation.

"We have to get you out of here. I've only seen the Grand Magister on the news, but the that guy's aura is off the charts. Nearly everything he says is a partial truth or an outright lie. The paranoia is giving me hives. I can't stand him," he signed.

Aloud he said for the benefit of those who could hear us, "Since you're my cousin, I already know your identity, so there is no need to validate your date of birth. I'm going to remove your catheter. You'll feel some pressure on your bladder, and it will likely feel weird pulling the tube out of you, but it will be fine."

"Okay."

He lifted the bedsheets. "Bend your legs as though you're squatting in the bed."

I stared at him as self-consciousness settled in. He was a nurse and my grandparent. This was not a field dressing or a bleeding cut.

"What's wrong?" he signed.

"Freaking out that my grandfather is going to see me exposed. It's stupid," I signed.

"No." He dropped his forehead and index on top of his lowered thumb. "You're human. If it makes you feel any better, it's weird for me too. You're my future granddaughter and having a family member as a patient makes me hyper-protective."

I hadn't thought about his feelings. I assumed professionalism would shield him. "You're right. Go ahead."

"Not if you feel uncomfortable. I can get Nurse Benson to remove the catheter. It could buy us extra time since Grand Magister is arguing with Dr. Sean on whether you can leave before you void your bladder naturally."

My heart raced. The soft beeping of the monitor picked up in pace.

"What's wrong?" he signed.

"The longer I stay here, the more likely Nana will show up and get caught. Then Tonya's on her own," I signed.

He growled. "What do you want me to do?"

I lifted my hospital gown. All traces of my embarrassment were gone—temporarily. My modesty was not important in the grand scheme of things. There was no time for it. I brought my knees up to my chest while keeping them spread. "Get this out of me, and then I'm going to drink that pitcher of water while I work on a spell to cause a traffic jam without killing anyone outright."

He shook his head as though he were exasperated when he lifted a syringe. "Don't worry. It's not for you. There's a balloon inside you that

I'm going to deflate. It keeps the catheter inside the bladder. Ask your boyfriend what happens if you try to pull it out without deflating it."

I cringed in sympathy as he removed the catheter from me. While a strange sensation, it wasn't painful, just uncomfortable. Max took care of the contents and tube.

"You might want to start drinking," he called over his shoulder before he left the room.

I was alone. Part of me was surprised that Matt didn't try to steal his way inside. I don't know how it happened, but something about his behavior was familiar. The whole dream thing sounded hokey, but it was true—mostly. When a person lied or told a partial truth, Max tensed. It was slight, but he still did it. Matt told the truth but obscured parts of it. I bet that he was the Matt of my time. I had to be careful. If I were wrong, I'd give an already strong enemy more strength.

And if I was right?

Then we already lost the majority of our edge over him. Either way, I would use the lemons handed me to make lemonade and find out all I could to use against him.

After I peed.

uyen

I sat in a beige and blue patterned round-back armchair built for discomfort despite being placed in a waiting room. Matt fumed in his chair across from me after Dr. Sean won her argument of not discharging Pandora without proof of a functional bladder sans catheter.

I hated those things.

But I loved seeing Matt off balance. It was rare that he couldn't talk his way into a favorable situation, but Dr. Sean wouldn't abide by it. She gave me the evil eye as she glared at my castless arm. I moved it for her as a demonstration of my functional health. She wasn't impressed and remarked that it was fortunate for me that I was no longer her patient before she went back to her argument with Matt.

"We will be awhile if Pan has to use the bathroom before she can be discharged," I opened. "I know why I care about her well-being. Explain yours."

Matt snorted. "So obvious and lacking tact as always. Oh, how I missed not having to mince words with someone."

"Nostalgia? Come on, I know you better than that."

"And I know you didn't just pop in to visit the hospital staff and happen upon me." I met his eyes to see what I could glean from his body language. Surely most of his tells were the same. He couldn't have changed that much in a few years.

"Lady luck has always been on my side." He folded his hands then relaxed in the chair. "Is it a bitter pill to swallow that I ran into you, or are you still angry because I beat you in a battle of politics?"

I tightened my jaw. His betrayal did sting, but the conversation wasn't about that. I couldn't let my emotions sway my purpose. "I admit that pissed me off, but what can I do about it now?"

Matt leaned forward. "This is different from what I expected."

"Me admitting that I lost to you the last time?" I had his attention. What would I find if I put pressure on him? "Nothing like the love of a good woman to help a man move forward."

His lip curled in an almost snarl before he reigned his response. Bingo. Pandora was a hot spot. I could use the concerned fiance route to ferret out his intentions. When he burst into Pandora's room, he seemed surprised to see her there, which meant he was there for another reason. The question was, what?

"I wouldn't know. Obscura is my primary focus. Taking your eyes off the prize is how you lost in the first place. What happened to the Quyen that wanted a world where we could practice our craft openly?"

"I'm still here. Just older and wiser," I answered. "I know tolerance can't be forced. It has to be normalized by all parties."

Matt sneered. "Please, when was the last time you've seen a mundane stick their neck out for us?"

His point didn't matter. I didn't interact with every mundane person on the planet. There was no way I could judge them all. It was silly to base my experiences on a sampling, especially when the consequences were so dire. I hated it when they did it to us. I wanted nothing to do with being the opposite side of the bigot coin. "How's Lauren? Is she still your Magia Lectore?"

Matt's jaw ticked. "All cards on the table?"

I gave him a nod of my head. "That's the way I prefer them."

"You and I go back, but along the way, the path became muddled, and Obscura is not what it should be—"

That was an understatement.

"—and it went wrong when our friendship fell apart. Hell, you have a fiance, and I didn't know anything about it. Obscura was our dream."

"*Was* being the operative word. I have a new dream now."

He snorted. "You sound whipped. You're one of the most powerful practitioners out there. Coupled with your knowledge, you could do great things. Does this girl even know what you are and what you've done?"

The "this girl" comment centered my focus. Matt tried too hard to minimize Pandora as though he didn't spend thirty minutes arguing with a doctor to release her early, and immediately moving to touch her as though he had the right. The more he talked, the more confusing his behavior was. "Leave Pan out of this. She knows what she needs to know about me."

His eyes narrowed. "Now I understand the dreams. They were a warning that you've grown soft. Did you know the Senate is voting on the Witchcraft Act next week?"

No, I hadn't. My shock must have been evident on my face because he continued, "I have people on it, but there have been stirrings that Camera is going to attack the U.S. Capitol building. We both know what that will do."

"Camera would never get involved in terrorism," was out of my mouth before I could reign it in. Tonya hadn't mentioned anything— no, she considered leaving them. Perhaps they cut her out of their planning. She would never buy into an attack on the government and if she didn't go along with their plans...

What in the hell was Tonya walking into?

"Camera is fractious on the best of days, but the activity of some of its cells has increased dramatically, especially the NoVa cell. If you were still a part of Obscura, you'd know that."

"Then stop them before they drag us all down with them," I suggested.

"Hence why Lady Luck blessed me. Your help would benefit Obscura—all of us in the long term."

I walked into that one. I was damned if I did, damned if I didn't. "That's rich. *You* need *my* help."

"No man is an island," he replied. "I understand that now. And this is bigger than our past. We both know what will happen if Camera attacks the Senate under their guise of a peaceful protest, which we know is false."

"No, *we* don't know that," I added.

He gave me a touché type nod as he conceded the point. "Then do your research. The incidents involving practitioners have gone up dramatically. A Camera cell even raided my building—"

I knew all about that operation and his response to the slight. "And you played the innocent victim and let justice take over?"

He raised an eyebrow. "You know me better than that. I handled the matter in the way I saw best, though I admit it may have been a bit heavy-handed."

"You call killing an entire station of people a bit heavy-handed?" I growled.

"Ah, so you're more attuned with the murmurings of the people than you let on. Huzzah, this will not be so hard for you then. And to answer your question, I did mention that I made mistakes."

Again, I walked into that one. "You say Camera is planning on attacking the Capitol. What makes you think that?"

"I know people, and I deal with information. The NoVa cell has had an uptick in activity the past few months, and the attacks have grown aggressive. They are the reason the mundanes in the government are making moves. The government fears another young wizard or witch losing control in their school."

I closed my eyes. Two years ago, a kid struggling with their powers, bullied by mundane kids, blew up the school. It had been all over the news. Since then, most of the obvious suspicion and hate had calmed down, but it still lurked heavily in people's minds.

And it didn't help that I did notice the number of Obscura and Camera skirmishes increased to the point of spilling out in the open. "The way I see it, both sides are at fault."

"I agree," he said quickly. "I want to stop the hostilities, with you at my side. You are more diplomatic than I, being you've been out of the fray. You may even have more appeal since you're in the process of becoming a family man."

We were back to Pandora again. "She's not part—"

"How long do you think she can stay out of it? She *is* a witch, isn't she?"

I was a slightly better liar than he, but my tells probably didn't get better in my years of near isolation. "She is."

"Then she has every right to join us, even more so. There is no reason to leave her out unless you're not serious about her. Has she met your family?"

No and she wouldn't. That door shut years before she came along. It made things easier considering my feelings. There was no doubt in my mind that I wanted her in my future, but Matt was too comfortable driving the conversation. "Speaking of my fiance, what kind of dreams have you been having?"

"Confusing ones of all kinds. Some where she works with Obscura and others that appear casual in nature. The dreams are enough to make me think that someone in my line may have actually had the gift of prophecy."

It was not uncommon for some practitioners to have weak active powers that they couldn't control that they inherited. Matt was a first-generation wizard—so he thought. The last thing the world needed was for him to become more proficient at prophecy. He was difficult enough to depose—damn, that might be why.

If his power was so instinctual that he trusted.... I didn't want to think about it. "You saw Pandora working with *us* or *you?*"

His lips twitched. "It was a dream, well, some dreams. I don't want them to be the focus. Not when we have greater objectives to consider —the Witchcraft Act and Camera's radicalization to violence."

"That is a problem, the Witchcraft Act, if that's true." I didn't doubt Camera's internal issues. Tonya could help influence Bane, or I could if it came to it.

"See for yourself." He pointed to the television behind me. It was an anti-craft protest. Several protestors were holding signs. One of them had a witch Halloween decoration on a noose as they shouted. The closed captions read, "Ding dong, the witch should be dead," while a bright red bar of color with white text displayed, "Supporters of the Witchcraft Act protest those who oppose the bill."

Great.

Of all the rotten timing.

Matt shook his head. "It always amazes me the creativity of bigots. It's always the same no matter what they are against."

We both attended a Historically Black College. We understood direct and indirect racial tension when we saw it, both from those who decided we shouldn't be there and from those who came to the defense of our fellow students. The world at times was no picnic, but that didn't mean we all couldn't be better or do better. I just hated that Matt made sense. My instincts warned me that it was a trap.

"Pandora's ready to be discharged," Max announced as he wheeled her into the waiting room.

I glanced at my watch. Three hours and no Trina? I was sure she would be back and caught. Unless she slipped by everyone, got to them, and slipped out. Obscura personnel were staged throughout the hospital. I doubted she could have accomplished the op at a moment's notice.

So what happened to her?

Neither Pandora nor Max looked distraught. Well, Pan appeared tired. She must have drunk a gallon of water to get her bladder full enough to pee in half the wait time allotted.

I stood then knelt before her, taking her hand. *"Is everything okay?"*

"Yes, I just feel like I'm going to float away with all the drinking I did. Max even found lemons to add to it. I wasn't up for a spell after stopping traffic for the past three hours. We have to get out of here before Trina shows up."

I kissed her hand. *"And we have another problem to discuss."*

"I have a car waiting downstairs," Matt announced as he lifted me by the elbow. "I'd hate for you two love birds to lose track of time."

That was one. I glared at him, which he met openly.

"Boys, are we leaving or not?" Max asked.

Matt coughed. "But of course. We can get to know each other on the way."

If by "get to know" he meant to figure out how he could win Pandora from me, he was in for a disappointment. Still, I could use the time to study *him* and figure out a way through the Obscura-Camera mess that I was in the middle of—*we* were in the middle of. Then perhaps we could take them both out with one stone.

Or worse, I end up back where I started.

35

 andora

G etting out of the hospital and the last dregs of the traffic jam took less time than I thought it would. The entire time I kept my senses on high alert for Trina. There was no telling how effective my spell to hold her up from getting to the hospital would work or how resourceful she was. I always saw her as an older woman and a cherished grandmother. Coming back to the past showed me that she was more than that, and she was a witch—both of my grandparents. They lied to me.

Or they were made to lie.

My father did hate magic for some reason. He never spoke well of it. When I think about it, he never spoke ill of practitioners as a whole unless one abused magic. He believed it corrupted people, and the craft led down to villainy. Never once did he deviate from that stance, and once I started sympathizing with practitioners, our relationship got worse.

He must have seen it in me.

Going into the past created more questions. It wasn't like I could ask my parents or even my grandparents. I went back too far—just my luck.

When it rains, it pours, I thought as I turned my attention to a problem I could solve.

Quyen, Max, and I traveled to Obscura's office in a town car. He said it would take an hour to get there with the traffic, which was my fault even if he didn't know it. That meant spending the entire time sitting across from him, allowing him to study me. If it weren't for the fact I could observe him as well, I would have balked. As it was, Max and Quyen flanked me on either side with their usual "save the female I care about" nature. It was equally annoying and thoughtful. I would decide which one if fighting occurred. Until then, I'd let them be while I listened to Matt's explanation about the Witchcraft Act.

I tried not to shiver. It might arouse Max and Quyen's protective instincts, possibly Matt since I was his dream girl and all. I still struggled with that. If that were true, I'd have to give him credit for his restraint with meeting me as a teenager, and his behavior with the love potion didn't add up. He wouldn't take a chance on messing up with me when he believed we'd end up together. Maybe he really did have nothing to do with it like he said.

Why in the hell did he have to make his behavior less black and white?

"Pandora, you've been quiet," Matt said.

It wasn't like I could say that I was busy questioning everything I thought I knew about my history or that I may have been in the past before to delay the Witchcraft Act so that when I was fifteen, I could attend a rally protesting it and destroy the east coast. That would not go over well with my allies. I glanced out the window to his "office building" as we turned off Trail Road and onto one of the private ones. It was more of a compound in its layout on the outskirts of Fairy Stone. Morgan Le Fay Nature Reserve Research Center was on the brick and wood sign. "I'm surprised that you have a place in this area of Patrick County. It's the most crowded of the surrounding counties."

Matt shrugged from his seat across from us. "I own almost all of the county and parts of Stuart anyway. So it's not that outlandish of a thought. My love for privacy must be more evident than I realized for you to be so perceptive. Is it your power?"

Something about that question was off. It didn't seem like he wanted an answer or needed it—there was no curiosity in his tone. I turned to Quyen. We tried to sell a low-key image of me and the best way to keep it was to exchange a look when Matt said something odd. Responding that way often would confuse him and make it harder for him to read my actions.

"Matt knows you're a witch," Quyen said.

I narrowed my eyes to appear annoyed before I smiled hard. "Oh, I see. That explains why he included me in this and talked openly about your plans. We will have to discuss that later, dear."

"Don't blame him, Kitten, I know him well—"

Kitten? Crap. It *was* future Matt. So that dream business was a clever lie. That-that—

"Son of a spider," Oya whispered in the back of my mind.

Another issue I would have to save for later.

"My name's Pandora," I corrected him, then glared at Quyen to keep from panicking or wringing Matt's neck. "Is Kitten the name of some girl from your past?"

"Not mine." Quyen put his arm around me. "Relax. You're the only one for me. I know the day has been stressful, but you can rest soon, and then we can talk."

I snuggled against him. "Okay."

"Get a room," Max muttered.

Matt said nothing but his white-knuckled fist on his lap was evidence enough that I was right. We had to be on guard. His use of that childish nickname and his response to me touching Quyen told me everything I needed to know. He *was* Matt from my time. I knew it. The slip in the hospital and then again in the car made sense, but I couldn't acknowledge him. The moment I did, playtime would be over, and he would try to lord over everyone instead of pretending he was incapable of doing so.

He might try to kill Quyen.

"Who? Matt?" Quyen asked. *"You think he might kill me?"*

Damn it. I did it again—telegraphing my thoughts. *"Don't react, but that's the future Matt. He managed to find me and slide into his old life. You saw what happened with your journal. The 'local' Matt probably was destroyed."*

He laced his fingers with mine when Matt growled.

"So I'm going to address the elephant in the room, Grand Magister," Max said. "We've made nice-nice in your fancy car, but it doesn't change the fact that you have put us in quite a pickle kidnapping us. And I have to know, are you an enemy? And how in the hell did you hide your nature reserve from the locals?"

"Saved. We should glean what we can from his answers, but we can never let on that we know who he is."

"Are you sure it's him? He seems different, but—"

"Trust me. It's him." I lifted my head from his shoulder. "Max."

My grandfather shrugged.

"I don't believe in playing fancy word games when straight from the hip works better." He turned to Matt. "Well?"

Matt chuckled. "You're refreshing, Maxwell. I spend most of my time with politicians as I remain close to the goings-on with the law governing practitioners' rights. It's nice to speak plainly."

"Then how about a plain answer," Max suggested.

"I would like to know why you dragged Quyen and me into this as well," I said, taking Max's cue.

Matt sighed from his side of the car. "The Senate is about to vote on the Witchcraft Act, and Camera is planning a raid on the Capitol building in protest. I need Quyen's help."

"My Quyen?" I touched Quyen's knee for effect.

Matt bristled at the contact but didn't attack. As I thought, he was fully committed to whatever plan he concocted. I would have to stay on my toes while I tried to figure out his motivation.

"Your Quyen was once my partner. We formed Obscura together," he answered.

I met Quyen's gaze. "Is that true?"

He nodded. "Yes. We met in college, but Obscura was a place for us to practice openly, share knowledge, and be safe. We differed on what those terms meant."

I turned back to Matt. "Fine, you two have a past. Why the strong-arm tactics and that dream business?"

Matt flushed. It was an honest reaction to my question. Even *he* wasn't that method with his lying. His reaction was likely the only complete truth I'd get out of him.

"It's in the past. I'd rather not discuss the details, but we don't have long until the vote. Less than a week. When I saw the two of you, I didn't want to pass up the chance to mend my ways and correct my path forward."

"You call threatening us to make trouble 'mending'?" Max snorted.

"Fair," Matt replied as we arrived at a brick and tan building. "You are not a hostage. I hoped to link up with the Fairy Tale coven with this endeavor, but I understand. I would be asking you to stick your neck out."

"Just me, huh?" Max crossed his arms. "We're a matched set."

Matt smiled, and the hairs on the back of my neck stood on end.

"I figured that, which is why you're here now. How about this? Stay as my guest and hear me out. If you don't want to help keep Camera from getting us all enslaved—"

"Now cut that out," Max growled. "I know the government can be a pill sometimes, but they're not going to let a bunch of bigots scare them into doing something stupid. We're citizens too."

"A country of scared people is nothing more than a mob. Fear is the mind-killer. Have you read the bill that they propose?"

"Well, no, but—" Max sputtered.

"Then I suggest you research it on our business center or even on your phone, then we can discuss." Matt nodded to the person waiting by the car door. They opened it. "James—"

I nearly rolled my eyes at the young man that bowed to Matt with a flourish. Wow. He still does—I guess he always did that. "Please make sure our guests are comfortable and let Peters know I want to talk to him."

James nodded. His bald head—another thing that was the same. Dark glasses and clad in all black, the man hadn't varied his overall look in fifty years.

There were no additional threats there unless that's the seventy-five-year-old James instead of the twenty-five-year-old one. There was no telling how many Matt brought with him to the past.

It was way too stressful.

"As you wish, Grand Magister." Matt walked past him, and James focused his purposeful gaze on us. He didn't bow, but he extended his arm outward to exit and join him. "This way."

His glance barely brushed us individually. Not future James.

If it had been him, his focus would have lingered on me. We trained together for years. I knew a dismissal when I saw one. This James didn't know me. That was a plus in my threat assessment—his interference would have hindered me. He wouldn't learn I was a threat if I played my cards right until Matt was out of play.

We left the car and joined him on the steps of "Le Faye House," as the moniker announced. The building looked more like an office than a house with its tan brickface, industrial glass, and metal doors. Inside the lobby, two guards in dark blue uniforms with infinity loop badges—the symbol of Obscura—sat behind a reception desk.

"These are the Grand Magister's guests," James announced to the desk guards—battle mages.

One of them stood with a box device. The battle mage seemed familiar while the other I couldn't place. "If you would hold still while we capture an image and aural signature for cataloging?"

Obscura has come a long way. The Obscura I know would scan you at the door without asking. It was quick and didn't depend on making contact with everyone as they came in.

Magic tingled on my skin then the box caught fire. The guard dropped the scanner while the other grabbed an extinguisher.

"What the hell?" Quyen moved closer to me.

Max hovered by my arm.

"The scanner shorted out. We should probably stand further apart," I suggested.

James focused his sentinel gaze on me. "You seem knowledgeable about magical devices."

"I had an able teacher who had an even better one." I smiled at Quyen.

He winked, then stared at James. "Tell Lauren that adding a quartz matrix will keep the scanner from combusting when recording too many large auras. That's intermediate magical theory. Matt can vouch for my skill."

James's eyebrow twitched. "Scan them individually so they can rest in their quarters."

The guard that scanned us initially looked frazzled, but he gathered his composure with a dutiful nod of his head and pulled out another device. We stood apart from each other as if on cue. I assumed we were on the same accord that burning the place to the ground was not on our agenda. The car ride and the conversation were enough for me to realize that the problem was more profound than just the elimination of Matt. I wasn't sure how far I could go once I found Oya's vessel, but Obscura couldn't disappear. Practitioners needed an advocate, just not a power-hungry one.

"It's done," The guard grunted. He leaned over to the other guard, and they both watched me. It wasn't the cold stare of a threat. However, I was a person of interest to them.

"What is it?" I asked before James could usher us away. I added authority to my tone, hoping they would answer before James interfered.

"Nothing. You have a low aural signature on the monitor and the others... We were wondering why the device blew up. The aura of that guy," he pointed to Quyen, "is massive, but not enough to short it out."

I almost said something snarky about not being like other girls, but I didn't want to make them curious about me. "I guess my aura is weak from my recent illness in the hospital. The Grand Magister offered to let me convalesce for the evening."

The guard's expression brightened. "Then that explains it. Rest well, ma'am."

"Thank you."

"Now, if you'd be good enough to join me," James asked with all the impatience of someone tasked with a nuisance.

The James of my time I knew took pride in the study of all visitors up close so he could assess them for threats. He would have kept me from moving forward until my aura was figured out and cataloged unless Matt intervened. I guess their technology was not advanced enough to capture me yet.

Quyen slipped his hand in mine. *"What was that all about?"*

"I lowered my aura too much, so I had to give them something so we could move on."

"It was unavoidable." He kissed my hand.

"You may want to lay low with public displays of affection until we leave. It was antagonizing him."

He gave me a side look. *"I'm not scared of him."*

"Neither am I, but he is my ex—oh wow, that hurt my brain to say that." I shivered. *"The situation has grown complicated, and I've been watching you. You're considering taking his offer of temporary alliance."*

"Point." He swung our joined hands. *"There you go being logical when I want to enjoy a brief moment."*

"You want to be petty, and you're better than that. Besides, I don't want to inspire Matt's creativity to break us up."

"I don't see myself leaving you." He grinned. *"And I'm pretty stubborn. You're stuck with me."*

"You're a goof." I shook my head as we entered a large conference room. His sentiment was sweet, but I had a deal-breaker hanging over my head that seemed more like a noose. Oya was right. I should have told him and my opportunity passed the moment Matt found us. The only saving grace was Oya wouldn't gloat at my realization. She was probably too pissed and worried.

"Please wait here while we ready your rooms. It should be an hour. Someone will bring refreshments in the meantime." James gave us a once over then left—no bow, for which I was grateful. I didn't miss the Grand Mistress affectations that he delivered.

We sat in silence at the large table—Quyen by my side and Max across from us. I guessed that each of us was trying to figure out how to counter whatever Obscura used to surveil us. The conference room was basic, a large V-shaped table with a wooden top, dark armchairs all around it, and a little computer station at the back for presentations. I didn't see any video equipment, but that didn't mean there wasn't any. We should divide and conquer. It was a solution Matt wouldn't expect. I met Max's gaze and held up my hand as though I were about to indicate the number five. Max gave me an odd look but fortunately said nothing. I brought my thumb, forefinger, and middle finger together in the "No" sign, then put my hand down. I pressed my lips together dramatically.

When I was a child, he and Trina would do the same with their lips when they wanted me to be quiet. I took a gamble that it was something that they did with each other and not something they invented for me as a child.

He blinked at me then gave a slight nod but did not speak.

Excellent.

I leaned my head on Quyen's shoulder as I faked a yawn and placed my hand over his.

"What happened to not wanting to antagonize?" he asked.

I could sense the pleasure in his voice, so I'd answer honestly. *"I couldn't think of a way to connect us while Max was in the room that wasn't obvious."*

"Doesn't he have a catalog of your powers? I can't see him not knowing which ones you have and don't."

"I'm sure he does, but I picked up some refined uses of some of them in my time away from him. He sent Obscura after me at first, then bounty hunters. He doesn't know everything that happened to me."

"He sent bounty hunters after you? He's such an ass."

"He is, but he never met my grandparents. My grandma died when I was twelve and Grandaddy when I was fifteen during the Sphinx attack, with the other millions." I couldn't bring myself to refer to them by their first names. I was fortunate enough to see them again even though I knew how their histories turned out and that I was responsible for one of them leaving too soon. My parents were supposed to be part of the fallen, too. While my grandfather might have been alive somewhere too, I doubted I would be lucky a second time. The only way to save him was to change the timeline.

"That's right. His listeners can't hear us and he doesn't know how to counter it. You're brilliant."

"Thank you." I tried to slow my racing heart. Quyen's compliment pleased me way more than it should. It was simple gratitude, no more. I should relax. Instead, I snuggled closer to him.

"Business first. I've wanted you close, too. Something about fighting next to you is turning me on—Anyway, I noted the shine of a camera lens above the table's apex. There's probably one opposite to give both views of the room."

I missed those. It must be Quyen's placement in the room. *"I sense a magical field of sorts around the room. I'm not sure if it's a protection enchantment or if it's surveillance. It's kind of icy hot. Usually, protective magic is cool to me, and this is warm."*

"It may be both. Can you counter it without destroying the enchantment?"

An illusion would be best, but without equipment, a spell would not hold, and maintaining it would require too much concentration to keep an image while we talked...unless.

"Yes." I glanced around the room. There were no windows. *"If I could cast an illusion of darkness, they won't see us."*

"How long can you hold it?"

"For as long as I can keep my eyes closed. We'd have to sign, and I'd have to link through you to see Max's signs and to feed you mine."

"I don't see how that will work."

"By denying my physical senses. When Trina listens to minds, she's not hearing with her ears but through someone else and their interpretation of sound. It will be the same for us."

Quyen kissed me on the mouth. *"That is utter genius. You are so hot to me right now."*

"Down, boy. We need to start our plan. Go to the lights, turn them off, then turn them back on, and we will talk."

"We need to make it short. I give the battle mages three minutes at most before they will be on us." He stood then went to the door.

The light went out, and I closed my eyes. I waited for Quyen to move but heard one or two swishes before his hand touched my shoulder. I signed to Max, "We have maybe three minutes. We have to get a message to Trina to abort the rescue. There are too many unknowns that we have to sort out, and we may be able to leave on our own."

Max signed, "I still have my phone. I say we take a chance and text her. I can write something vague in case they are monitoring messages. Of course, that is if she even got your message in the first place."

"I'm sure she did. She will investigate and assume we left a clue when she finds out about Matt's visit. You know she can't resist a mystery."

"Yeah. Yeah. Trina's nosey as hell," he signed. "I'm doing it now."

I watched Max grab his phone and text from Quyen's gaze. It was surreal staring at him from a standing position while I sat. My stomach rolled in confusion. I would note this if I ever had to use someone's eyes again.

A few seconds later, he nodded and put his phone away. I opened my eyes, and a breath later, the door opened. James stood in the threshold, his chest heaving as though he rushed from where he was. He glanced around the room, then straightened. "I forgot to ask if any of you had food allergies. We would hate for a guest to become ill."

We shook our heads.

"Thanks for asking," Quyen replied, then took up his position beside me.

"Do you know when those refreshments will arrive? I missed lunch, and my patient hasn't eaten today," Max added.

James gave a curt nod with his shaded gaze. "I'll look into it."

"Much obliged," he replied as James left the room.

I was surprised he didn't find a reason to linger. No wonder he wasn't head of security. This James wouldn't last in the lawless zone or within future Obscura with such a lackadaisical attitude. I couldn't blame him. I could get into the peaceful vibe, even if all it did was make one soft. It was a vacation from a hell that I hoped no one else went through. I would enjoy it as long as I could.

"So what now?" Max asked.

I glanced toward the flat screen monitor on the wall by the presentation station. "We were offered the opportunity to research. I say we do it."

"I can dig it." Quyen smiled.

He teased me.

"You're a goof," was all I said before we began our exploration of the computer or television on the wall. Given his response time, I expected James back any moment to check on us, then the actual research would begin. Next we'd have to decide whether we would enter a truce with Obscura or not.

 att

Damn it. Damn it. The conference room feed returned to normal when James entered. Pandora, Quyen, and Maxwell all watched my vice-captain as though they hadn't hidden their plans under a curtain of silent darkness. Everything appeared normal in the room, but I knew it wasn't.

I hadn't earned their trust after all. I thought the Senate vote problem would give me at least a week before Pandora and Quyen went back to not trusting me. Everything about running off to keep the peace had Quyen and Pandora written all over it. At a minimum, she couldn't resist making sure that I wouldn't capitalize on the moment for my benefit. Their little blinding me stunt meant one thing —they found me out.

It had to be the slip in the car. I tipped my hand, calling her Kitten. Watching Quyen touch her, comfort her, and be her lover —ahhh!

I allowed my feelings to get the better of me on the drive. The only saving grace was that it happened at the journey's end. I thought I caught a hint of the recognition in her eyes that it was me and not past me. She hid it quickly, then her guard went up.

It all made sense. I saw it in Pandora's movements. She even tried to test me with more overt displays of affection to *him*. She must have done it to confirm a theory.

"Grand Magister?"

I glanced back to the scene in front of me from the safety of my office. My Fairy Stone office was a safe space to strategize without everyone watching me while I remained close to the local ley lines. Not that power mattered where Pandora was concerned. She was all that I needed.

No, I also need a clear head.

"I'm here. Did you see anything amiss in the conference room?" I asked into the com device as I watched Pandora, Quyen, and Maxwell through my scrying crystal. It connected to the crystal lens located in my conference room. Typically, I brought civilians to that room to uncover their intentions.

"Nothing was out of place," James assured me. "But they *did* expect my presence. They seemed to anticipate me coming into the room as though they were testing me."

Or they were testing me.

Those three were up to something. It was circumstantial evidence, but I knew it deep within every fiber of my being that plunging the room in darkness was not innocent. Those three didn't trust me. And they shouldn't, not yet. I piqued their curiosity and perhaps their morals, but none of those things garnered enough trust for them to come when I called upon them to "help" again after the vote. Until then, I was a half ally.

"They are to be treated as guests until otherwise noted."

"Yes, Grand Magister."

I placed my handheld radio on my desk and studied the trouble trio.

I missed something. There was more to their acceptance of my hospitality. I knew it.

"What are you up to, Kitten?" I asked the screen.

The darkness didn't make sense. They didn't leave the room. They just sat in the dark. Recon in the conference was something that I've always done, so it was a toss-up as to whether it was Pandora or Quyen that came up with the silent darkness plan. It seemed like Quyen's style more than hers unless—wait.

They were trying to keep me from seeing what was said. It was standard tactics to have someone who could read lips with proficiency, but then there was the silence. Which meant they were signing.

I slapped my desk. I had been estranged from Pandora for a year, and I already forgot. She knew sign language. She taught me when she became my lover. I wanted to encourage her to be more than just plea-sure. If I remember correctly, her paternal grandmother died when she was twelve years old, but she learned to sign from her. The whole family knew how to sign, and there was a Maxwell Spellman in the conference room that appeared—hell, it didn't matter. Maxwell was a practitioner. He could be thirty or a hundred years old, but it explained Pandora's father.

Her father must have been born without power and resented Maxwell. Pandora never mentioned magic within her family, either that or they must have hidden it from her. I had to teach her about her powers and magic theories from the ground up. If it weren't for the fact that Camera held her for years, she probably wouldn't have known she was a witch. And I doubt her magicless father failed to notice his daughter exhibiting magical traits. I enjoyed the irony of the bigot having an adopted magical daughter. However, I was choking on all the coincidences I had come across lately—my understanding of them anyway.

I sat up. Maxwell had a wife, or will have one. Deputy Wright reported two members of the Fairy Tale coven. Huzzah. I needed to find her. I'd lay odds that she resembled my Kitten, and if she did, Pandora's father was a practitioner, and he lied about her adoption. He must have bound his aura so no one could sense it. *But then that would cut off his abilities. That was tantamount to losing one of his senses. No practitioner would ever do something like that.*

Then again, he would have grown up with a deaf mother. That might have offered a different perspective that most would not consider. I wanted to know more. "Keep your secrets, for now, Kitten. I have another puzzle to solve that will get me back in your good graces."

"That sounds quite personal," Lauren commented as she entered my office.

In my concentration, I didn't notice her standing in the doorway. She was one of the few brazen enough to enter without acknowledgement. The other, James, would only do so in a catastrophe. "You don't appear dying and the evacuation alarms are not sounding. More importantly you're here in Virginia and not in DC. Why is that?"

Her eyes rounded, then went blank. "I was researching, and I came across information you should know. Quyen—"

"I read your notes in the file, and you could have called."

She held herself. "You never interrupted me before and you always took my advice. Why won't you just trust me with what you have going on?"

"And you did as I asked before," I snapped.

Lauren pressed her lips together then sighed. "I have your best interest at heart. You should trust me."

"You still haven't answered the question." I wasn't in the mood for more insubordination. How in the hell did I handle her in the past? The answer came to me instantly, except I could not cultivate Lauren's feelings while chasing Pandora. I knew where that led.

"I'm your Magia Lectore," she answered. "You asked me to locate Pandora Spellman."

"And you started here?" I searched her gaze.

Lauren put her hands on her hips. "Yes. When I found Katrina and Maxwell Spellman, who are also confirmed members of the Fairy Tale coven. It couldn't be a coincidence. Pandora's from the future, is she not?"

Impressive as always. If only she would listen.

"You are correct. Good work. But as fortune would have it, I found her, Quyen, and Maxwell Spellman."

She clapped her hands. "I knew I was right. Katrina and Maxwell are her parents. What are their powers?"

"You're partially right. They are her grandparents, and I'm unaware of their skills." I sat back in my chair. At least Lauren progressed in her assignment. I had names to go along with my information. Her success deserved a reward.

"We assessed the local practitioners as marginal talents," Lauren remarked, joining me at my side. "I find it interesting that such low-level talents created such a powerful witch—" Her breath hitched slightly when she viewed the scrying crystal. "Are she and Quyen together?"

For now.

"It appears that way," I answered.

"She is pretty." She chuckled. "Good for him. Maybe she can loosen him up."

"He's fine as he is."

"You don't seem so happy for them," she said.

"They are up to something." I didn't trust myself continuing with the subject. Controlling my anger was difficult enough. The two were cozy, and I didn't know where the spell dropped Pandora in the time stream. She could have been in the past weeks or months ahead of me. Initially, I thought she arrived with the storm and the summoning. However, she and Quyen appeared so comfortable with each other as though they had known each other for years. He didn't easily trust. I was his college roommate, and it took two years just for me to find out he was a practitioner.

"It must be bad with the way you're furrowing your forehead." Lauren put her hand on my shoulder.

I eased away from her touch. The sex potion incident was too raw. Pandora should be by my side, not with Quyen. "An hour ago, they shut off the lights in the conference room, presumably to communicate some sort of plan or decision."

"That sounds dramatic, even for Quyen."

"Pandora and I, much like Quyen, have not always seen eye-to-eye, so this does not surprise me that they are trying to keep secrets."

"I see. That's why you listed her as dangerous." Lauren continued to watch the crystal. "The other day you asked me about—"

The alarm klaxon cut off her words. I turned to the video monitor display. Several cameras on the property's periphery were static pictures with "signal lost" displayed across static, while others showed personnel scrambling to meet an unknown threat. I glanced at the conference room. My three guests stood close together, forming a triangle with their backs facing each other. Their expressions were just as startled as my people until Maxwell said something that calmed the others.

Was it a spell?

He only said one word. It was possible. I encountered some practitioners that used one-word enchantments. They were better in combat unless the practitioner had an active power. Perhaps Maxwell's talent was underestimated as marginal. I would look deeper into the file to see if there was an application that had uses for me.

A *boom* rocked the building.

"Stay here," I said to Lauren, then left the room. For good measure I locked it. I heavily fortified my offices from threats. No one would get to her and if necessary, she could evacuate from there. My office was one of the safest places to be in a skirmish. I wasn't ready to lose her just yet.

Out in the hall, chaos attempted to overrule my authority as my people moved in a combination of panic and purpose.

"Grand Magister," one of the non-combat staff members called out to me.

Her badge was blue with a water drop despite not wearing a battlemage uniform. It wasn't often that elementals were not in my guard.

She wrung her hands as she watched me with hopeful gray eyes. "What do we do?"

"Yes," another said.

Others surrounded us, waiting for my answer.

"Ren," I said, reading her badge. "I need you to remain calm and lead the other non-combatants to the muster areas as we drilled. Use your powers to contain any fires that you encounter. We don't want a fire blocking the escape path."

She nodded as she looked around us. "Yes, sir."

I stalked towards the conference room. It was several hallways away in the front portion of the building. Those around me either fell in line or moved to their muster stations as I walked, another process that Quyen implemented during his tenure that I kept.

His sense of preparedness made it easier to function in a crisis. The drills gave everyone something to do and a place to go—out of my way. His skill at seeing the smaller picture views and how they played out in the grand strategy could not be allowed to get away or be lost.

It wasn't clear who attacked, but I wouldn't lose track of Quyen or Pandora. I know they had something to do with this debacle, and I wanted to determine their intentions. If they ran away, I would have to use a different tactic when I caught up to them. Actually, it could very well be a rescue attempt as easily as it could be an attack. If they had no association with the attackers, they would fight with me. Either way, I would know.

Or I would once Peters gave me an update.

I reached down to my side. Nothing.

In my haste, I left my radio in the office. Peters was my second in this timeline, and James my third. They were likely having a conniption with my radio silence. I held out my hand to one of the battle mages. "Radio."

The one on my three o'clock placed a palm-sized device in my hand. "*Audire me primus et secundus.* Peters or James, come in. What's the situation?"

My spell connected Peters and James's devices to our channel. It was too costly in terms of resources to put all of the battle mages on it. *Perhaps Quyen would have a better idea of how to get around that.*

"Thank the goddess, Grand Magister. I was worried that we had lost you. It's Camera. They breached the property from the research section. I'm holding them off while James is countering them from the forest in the front of the building," Peters reported.

"How many? Do they appear to be after anything?"

"Unable to determine. Right now, it looks like five practitioners that are battle mage level two down here."

He and James were level threes. It must be another objective besides a simple rescue. Quyen was important to me, but I doubted Camera knew that. He wasn't aware of their plans to attack the Senate. He had that twitch he got when someone blindsided him, and he was pissed. I was sure he was associated with them otherwise. Why the betrayal by their idiocy?

It was his M.O. to work with them and do so clandestinely. No surprise there.

On the other hand, Camera was using the type of muscle they would need for their attack on the Capitol building.

So why waste it?

If it were my time, I'd say they were after Pandora or me. Except Camera would never be so bold as to attack me or think she would go with them. They would be too afraid of the Sphinx—future Camera anyway. There were only two travelers, me and her. The attack was sheer stupidity and rashness, even for them.

If it is just them.

All the more reason for me to get to Pandora and Quyen.

I reached the main area when the ruckus intensified. A bolt of energy whizzed down the hall in front of me. The battle mages tightened formation around me.

"We need to move forward," I told them. "I will hold a shield around us. Then we'll advance. Peel off into the side corridors and the rooms from back to front. We need to make it to the conference room then—"

"Go. Go! Move," Quyen yelled from the corridor.

I stalked forward, my shield at the ready, to the juncture. Pandora plowed into me—well, my protective barrier. Instead of bouncing back the way most would, she froze briefly before absorbing it and then fell into my arms. Max stumbled after her while Quyen kept his attention behind them. He held his hands outstretched, readied for defense or attack.

"What the hell," I began.

"Later," Quyen shouted. "We need to get to a better defensible position. I deterred them enough to fall back for now, but they'll be back."

I motioned for my battle mages to get ready as I righted myself. I glanced at Pandora's tattoo. The wind swirls were dangerously close to fully formed. One of my better ideas was the spelled ink that indicated her magic levels. I developed it after her third transformation. By the time she showed the physical traits of the Sphinx, it was usually too late.

A transformation would be inconvenient and thirty-five years too early. Camera did deserve it. However, I was not prepared to keep her power directed in a way that would suit Obscura. Accidental destruction before the vote would brand every practitioner a monster in the eyes of the mundane extremists, then witch hunts really would come back in style, and that was assuming she didn't kill her ancestors and negate herself.

No. I would not allow her to run amok.

I grabbed her arm as she stood under the guise of helping her stand. "You're too close. Sit this one out before you change."

Her eyes widened, then she glanced at the tattoo, then back at me. "What are you—?"

"Not now. We'll talk about it later."

She glanced at Quyen briefly, then shook her head. "No. I'm not going to hide somewhere while this attack is happening, not when I can do something."

Mist filled the air. It was Quyen's power. I knew it anywhere. He grabbed the two of us by the shoulders. "While you two were playing catch-up, the rest of us were getting shot at with magic and bullets. Fall back."

"And hurry," Maxwell added.

We made a tactical move to a previous hallway juncture where we engaged a few more battle mages guarding the area.

"Peters, what is the situation?" I said into my radio.

"We're still pinned down here," he answered. "The majority of this area has been emptied for evacuation. Once the rest are clear, we will retreat to your location."

Damn. The situation was out of hand. Pandora was close to changing. I needed to end this soon and send a clear but private message to Camera's leaders.

"We've got you surrounded. Drop your weapons and power down your magic, or your Grand Magister dies," a voice yelled out.

I froze. The screamed demands came from behind me on the right.

I saw a few weapons hit the floor as everyone focused behind me. I hardened the shield around me then raised my hand.

"No," Pandora called out.

She grabbed me around the waist and tackled me to the ground. There were two assailants behind me. I managed to knock one of them against the wall. "Get them."

"Stop," Pandora barked. Her voice sounded like mine—mimicry.

She used her power to gainsay me. "What the hell are you doing?"

"She's pregnant with my dad. Do you want me to disappear because he can't adopt me?"

I stopped. Considering I had doubts about her parentage, I didn't comment. I was pretty confident her father was her biological parent, but it wasn't the moment to share the traumatic theory. I needed her to stay disciplined. "Explain."

"When I figure it out," she said. "For now, you owe me for what you did."

"I had nothing to do with that. We both know you'd never forgive that. It was the meddling of a dead old woman, but I should have seen how far she had gone."

Pandora gave me a narrow crimson glare, then rolled her eyes. "Then I'll take it up with her in the next life. And before you get your hopes up, I meant what I said. We are done. I'm with someone else, and if you harm him, I will—"

"We'll see." I stood and took back control of the situation. Quyen hovered over the woman I threw against the wall while Maxwell held the other. The woman watched me with groggy, droopy eyes. "Quyen, do you know these two?"

"Yeah. I think this is a horrible rescue attempt." Quyen helped the woman to her feet. "Though this is overdone as a distraction."

That was because there wasn't one. It was the type of battle I expected from Camera in the time where I ruled. In Obscura, my enemies knew the potential of my wrath even if all they could effectively do was annoy or slow me down. This skirmish was overkill and would draw mundane attention. Camera had to be put down like a rabid animal before they became a greater problem. "More like an opportunity that will draw unwanted notice."

"I'll handle them. I'm partly to blame for this." Pandora glanced at her tattoo.

"I own a part of this too." Quyen stepped between us. "And what are you going to do? They have guns and a variety of magic that they are throwing out there. I'm not sure they even know their allies at this point."

"I'm not their ally, so no worries there."

Quyen took her by the shoulders. "I'm serious, Pan. We have our people, and law enforcement is probably on the way. We should get out and regroup. I don't want you to get hurt."

"You should save your bleeding heart for Camera. She can take them." I stood next to them. I wanted to knock his hands off of her. His point was still valid without him touching my woman. "It's a more peaceful solution than I'm prepared to give at the moment. We can handle the mundane peacekeepers later."

"Except it was my plan that led to this. I knew Camera might have been involved, but I didn't think Bane would go this far."

Bane. I didn't recall him being reckless in the past. No matter, I will handle him first when I cull the herd.

"Camera is only concerned with the short term." I put my hand on Quyen's shoulder and drew him away from Pandora. "I vote to let Pandora loose on them. Between her and—"

"Listen to him on this one." She shot me a look. "I'm going to let off a little steam."

I caught her meaning. She planned to unleash her magic reserve to keep the danger of transformation down to a minimum. It could work as long as Camera didn't get too aggressive.

"Then I'll back you up since you seem hell-bent on doing something unwise." Quyen glared at her.

Bile rose in my chest at the thought of them going off into battle together. I knew more about Pandora's capabilities and power than he did. If necessary, I could direct her energies to an appropriate target. "Three is better than two."

Pandora rolled her eyes then shimmered away, leaving Quyen sputtering. "Surely you knew she could do that."

He shot me a look. "She can't get far. She's never been here before."

Sharp as always.

"The conference room," we said in unison.

He shot off. "Take them to the muster site and treat them. I will give further instructions when I get back.

I hurried down the hall with my shield ready. Quyen may have darted ahead, but that didn't clear obstacles for me. He was the strongest water mage I had ever encountered. When he remained focused enough, he could turn parts of his body to water while still using other applications of his magic. Following him meant I had to watch for bullets and blasts passing through him and speeding towards me.

We weren't that far from the building entrance when the cacophony shifted from the thumps and crashes of breaking materials to screams of panic. Quyen met my eyes, then nodded. I hardened the air under our feet then pushed us forward as quickly as possible without draining too much energy.

"What?" Quyen wobbled as he tried to keep his balance on my airway.

I didn't hold us too far over the ground. It wasn't as if we were covering a significant distance and Quyen wasn't used to this application of my magic. I developed my air slide during the Sphinx rampage while trying to escape with as many people as I could carry. He was athletic enough that he wouldn't fall over, but I could drag him along without much effort if he did. "It's something new."

"You're moving the air underneath us."

I did my best to keep the mystery of my power. The more my enemies underestimated me, the better my advantage over them. Most of my allies didn't know that I was an air elemental. For Quyen to pick up on it, I didn't know whether my skills worsened or if he was more observant. "You just noticed that? I thought you were better than that."

He pursed his lips. "I always suspected you were an elemental and not a telekinetic, but there was never any wind when you used your power. The fact that you managed that level of control over a small area is unusual. No one would have caught on to what you were doing."

His eyes gleamed. I managed to arouse his intellectual curiosity when I needed his tactical prowess. "Pandora should be up ahead."

"Right." He looked toward the rushing entrance. "When we get to the lobby, you go left, and I'll go right. Be ready to duck and swing."

We burst into the lobby and jumped into silence as we dove in the directions we agreed.

"What are you two doing?" Pandora asked. "The coast is clear."

I stood in the chaos of broken furniture, glass, and a pile of bodies. All four walls remained intact. Given the noise and tremors throughout the building, I expected more damage. I could handle glass for the doors, windows, and new furniture, especially since I planned to take it out of Camera's hides. "You killed them?"

"No, they're asleep." She rubbed at her tattoo. "A compulsion. They should be down for at least two hours. Long enough for us to settle—"

"You," Bane screamed. Flanked with a contingent of practitioners, he pointed to Pandora. "Throw everything you have. That's the Grand Magister's Sphinx. She'll destroy us all."

37

andora

I held out my hands and shook them as I readied a shield to protect
me from Camera's assault. "No, no. You've got it wrong."

Well, they had it right but I didn't know how the leader knew
that. He seemed familiar. Obviously, he was with Camera. I made it a
point to avoid those people after they held me in a dark cell for a year,
and when I couldn't do that, I attacked. There was no getting to know
my enemy. I wasn't fond of head games, diplomacy, or intrigue like
Matt and Quyen. I got in and out for the most part, which served me
well until some unknown attacker recognized me before I could
get out.

"There is always wisdom in knowing our enemy," Oya whispered in
the back of my mind.

Her words were disturbing, but she made sense. I would make a
note of the leader for when we crossed again. He had a lot to explain,
starting with how he ended up in the past. I doubted Matt would have
shared knowledge with anyone outside of his trusted circle, least of all

an enemy. Yet their leader gestured toward me like a terrified madman, as though he had reason to be afraid.

And the first thing he did was attack—typical Camera.

"Kill her," the leader screamed.

Bullets smashed against the barrier along with several blasts of energy and fire. Their leader must have also traveled back in time after Matt. It was a regular futurist convention between the three of us. And he outed me as the Sphinx. Quyen would put two and two together when the skirmish was over.

I'd lose him.

No, I would trust him. He'd be pissed, but maybe he'd let me explain.

"Shield up, Quyen, or the ricochet might—"

A yowl from Quyen chilled my blood.

"Aim at the Grand Magister and the other one. She can't hold a shield on both." The leader yelped as he was lifted and knocked against the wall, courtesy of Matt. The Camera asshole crumpled in a heap. Most of his battle mages dropped their weapons to help him. It was my chance. "Sleep—"

A blast of heat hit me from the side. "This is for Bane," the fire mage yelled.

The flames surrounded me then seeped into my skin. Another blast hit me before a cry of pain stopped the flow of fire energy into me. My vision swam, and my body grew light. My enemies sought to hinder me, but all they did was stoke the fires of my power. I could do anything. Every hit of their meager magic was a step closer to the suffering of our wrath for their insolence, starting with their leader. His aura was not from this time. Both he and that son of a spider followed us through time, except this one—Bane—dared to harm us. I knew that name. He was the leader of Tonya's Camera cell.

This was *her* doing, no doubt, to test my claim to our mate. Quyen was *our* mate. Bane was also a spear in our mate's side. He constantly tried to recruit Tonya and him to his cell. *Because he's from the future, and he fears Obscura.*

More fire nourished my insides along with light energy. We wanted more.

"I'm hungry," We yelled. "Give me more."

"She lost control of Oya," the son of a spider called out—the one who called himself a grand magister. How dare he spill our secrets for all the world to know? Our mate will not be pleased to find out about us without a preamble. It was time for this interference to end. "Winds of the west heed my call—"

"Pandora, stop." Quyen stood between the infidel and us.

"You defend him?" Our indignation was clear based on his flinch. As though we would ever harm him. "The trickster who stole your mantel and turned your kin against you?"

Our mate's eye ticked.

"He has a lot to answer for but not this way and not at the cost of everyone. Look." He gestured around us.

The cement walls that once surrounded us were piles of rubble, and we had unadulterated access to the sky. So I destroyed the infidel's lobby. By our grace and protection—not for the infidel, he had his power to protect him—we stood unharmed, surrounded by piles of concrete, glass, rebar, and the bodies of those who attacked us. They were still breathing. He should be happy with that.

The infidel built it with our mate's blood, sweat, and tears, along with countless supporters. He even cowered behind our mate when he should be bowing to us. "What of it?"

Quyen's dark eyes hardened. "You're hurting people when the battle is over. Camera has surrendered. Matt is no threat to you."

A lightning bolt struck the forest near the building, followed by the *boom* of thunder. The infidel of a grand magister's eyes widened as he watched the trees catch fire. "See how afraid he is of our magnificence. He was never a threat to us, not even when he manipulated us into his bidding. We will destroy him and everyone that opposes us, then you can rule by our side."

Quyen held a trident of water in his hand. Magic swelled his aura three times the size it usually was. His handsome face was battle-hard —a magnificent warrior for our taking.

"Don't make me do this." His voice was quiet.

"You have to drain her of magic, or she'll become stronger," the infidel called out.

We swiped at him with a blast of wind. Instead of having the grace to fly out of sight, he caught himself and landed safely out of the field of debris. Clever. We briefly forgot that he would have been a potential mate if not for his arachnid way of slipping in and out of faith. I knew his kind. He wished to use us.

No. We were beneath that.

Perhaps a reminder of my power was in order. "We will burn this world, then start anew. He will understand proper respect and bow to our feet. Stars from the heavens, wind from the earth, bound together —" Pain burned through our chest, forcing our attention from the spell and to...Quyen.

He held the long spike of rebar that protruded from our chest. Agony flared through us with each breath. However, our heart hurt more as it labored to keep us functioning while our mind sorted through his betrayal.

"I had to stop you, and I couldn't do it with magic." He pulled the spear out of us. We fell over, but he caught us before hitting the ground. His eyes were soft and misty. "You can heal the wound. Heal yourself and come back to me."

We reached up to him when pain seized through us. My world erupted in white, and we were in the godscape by the River of Reflection. We crawled to the edge of the cloud raft to peer into it. Blood gushed from the open wound as we slowly separated.

I passed out. That was the only way to describe it. One minute I couldn't tell my feelings from Oya's, and the next, I was me. The pain grew less excruciating as my magic worked on healing me—or should I say us, for her wound repaired as quickly as mine.

And I finally understood what Oya tried to tell me. We were one. I could no more separate myself from her than she could me. To destroy her meant destroying myself. I genuinely never thought it would work like that. At most, I thought I would lose all my power but still exist as a mundane. I even believed that I wouldn't care as long as I was free from Oya. Having been faced with it...I knew what had to be done. We both had to go.

"That is a foolish plan. What about Quyen?"

"He's not going to trust us after this. I lied to him."

"We did try to warn us,"

"You did, and I didn't listen. It changes nothing. Everything is a mess."

"Then perhaps full disclosure of what we know will help."

"What do you mean by that?"

My reflection grinned back at me. *"While we have been together for three decades, our godhood has existed much longer. It's the reason we can exist in this time. The temporal flow is like this river, and the soul is the raft. Mortals can only travel as far as their raft exists. No more. There is much about our history that is known, but **we** do not. Therefore a reckoning must take place for understanding."*

I doubted it would change my mind, but I still wanted any answers she could provide. *"Then tell me."*

"Then watch and know."

My reflection faded into a forest clearing that I viewed from above. The forty-two-point circle glowed with power as life aura seeped into it. I could sense that the sacrifices would fall over at any minute, having surrendered their essence. I held my breath, waiting when everyone suddenly ran in every direction. Bright aura trails flowed back into their destinations like running paint on a design. One by one, each of the paths stopped flowing and glowed brightly as a single point until the circle was completed. The ring of aura spun into a cyclone seeking the right soul until the hint of one of the Dahomey descendents flowed on the wind. The fierce warriors would have wept that their child ran into the woods like a coward. The child was not worthy, yet there was destiny surrounding them.

I watched as Oya followed the scared women through the woods and to a lot full of cars and frantic people—Obscura personnel. The woman appeared to give orders, and they scrambled to follow them. My heart sank as I realized the identity of the "descendent." It was Lauren.

"What does she have to do with this besides helping to summon you?"

The reflection pool's scene shifted to Lauren entering a conference room early in the morning. She appeared cagey and annoyed as though she had to get back to something—work most likely.

A woman in a gray business suit ushered her into a room where a couple stood. The wife held a baby swaddled in blankets. The baby appeared to be a few weeks or months old. The husband rubbed his hands together in a way that, when coupled with his wild gaze, bordered on anxiety. He kept his eyes on Lauren while he remained close to the baby and wife.

"Why are they here?" she asked. "I thought I was supposed to be alone."

"Ms. Truman," the woman in the suit began, "because of the nature of this adoption, I thought it best that there be no question about the validity of the paperwork. I tried to inform you of the change, but your phone—"

She nodded quickly. "Yes-yes. I lost my phone and haven't replaced it. Let's get this over with so I can get out of here."

The lawyer continued in a business tone, "The Hardys have already signed the documents accepting parental rights and power of attorney. Their name will be under yours on each of the pages that require a signature—"

"And what about the NDA?" Lauren studied the document without connecting with anyone in the room.

The lawyer pointed to one of the documents waiting for Lauren's signature. "Yes, Ms. Truman. I have prepared that as well so you can witness them sign it. Once the adoption is complete, they are not to contact you, nor will you contact them."

The woman placed the pen next to the paper Lauren studied. She took it and began scribbling her signature on the documents set out in front of her. Once she started, the couple's rigid posture eased when she paused.

"Is there something wrong?" Mrs. Hardy clutched the bundle closer to her, and the baby began to fuss. She cooed as she rocked the child in her arms. "Shhh. I'm sorry, love."

"What's her name?" Lauren asked.

The Hardys stared at one another, then their soon-to-be child.

"I haven't changed my mind," she replied. "I selected you if you remember."

"Adora," they said in unison.

She watched the family for a few breaths. A longing expression on her face, then sighed. "Nice name, and I trust this is the last I see of you three."

Lauren folded her hands behind her back in a gesture I'd seen Matt do when he behaved condescendingly.

"Yes, never again." Mr. Hardy kissed the baby's forehead then signed the paper—the NDA—laid before him. When he finished, he took Adora so his wife could sign. Lauren left the room the moment it was done.

"Are you trying to say Lauren is my mother?" The idea of that was horrifying and wrong. Even crazier, who was the father? Thank all that that was holy, she gave the baby up, but the Hardys were not the Spellmans. And Matt for damn sure wasn't the father, she would have trapped him with that. *"Well?"*

Oya ignored my question.

Adora cooed and grunted as aura seeped into her open mouth, then giggled. Her parents smiled as they kissed her and cried in their joy.

The baby was a witch and the Hardy's were practitioners too. That must have been why Lauren "selected" them. It made sense. She had access to magical technology and was part of Matt's brain trust. It wouldn't surprise me if she found the most obscure magical family she could and placed the baby with them to keep anyone from finding out. It wasn't like they would complain. Magical couples were often childless for decades. *This is crazy.*

And Oya possessed the baby anyway.

"More like we waited."

My blood chilled. The ache in my chest changed from one of agony as I healed to the heartache of dread and sorrow when the pool changed to the image of my father as a young man. Not that he was old, to begin with, but seeing him as a twenty-something was different.

"We will spare us the visual of this one given our bond. Adora was our host. She wanted our father for her own, but he had eyes for Georgia. So she concocted a plan to get him drunk during a coven celebration. Georgia was sick and unable to attend, but Adora talked him into going anyway. They ended up lying together. Then we were born."

"What?"

The reflection pool showed a lovely woman that resembled Lauren arguing with my father. I knew the look. He was ready to blow his top. I could relate.

"You think you can have a life with Georgia?" Adora snapped. "I may not have as much talent as you, but at least I'm a witch. You know how hard it is for practitioners to have children, and we got it on the first try. It's destiny."

"Georgia is my fiance. You were supposed to be our friend. We practically grew up together. Our families were neighbors. Then you…"

"Maxwell, calm down. It was an accident. I—"

"You're lying," he said. "You know I can tell when someone lies, and you do this to me? To me, Adora?"

"Maxwell, please, I love you." She grabbed his arm. "Think of how strong our baby will be."

His eyes hardened. "And there's the truth. You love power, and I was the only one available. So you tried to destroy things between me and Georgia. No more."

He slipped out a small bottle from his pocket. It was a tubelike style that practitioners favored for potions. He uncorked it, swallowed the contents, then tossed the glass in the fireplace next to him.

"What did you do?" She rushed over to the fireplace, attempting to examine the potion.

"Georgia and I are leaving Fairy Stone. We'll start our lives together as mundanes far from you and magic. Power will never come between the two of us again."

"And what about me?" she asked.

"My lawyer will be in contact about the terms of custody," he said, then turned on his heel to leave.

"I've seen enough." I turned over and lay on the cloud raft to stare at the starry night sky. Lauren Truman—even her loyal surname fit her personality—was my grandmother. Daddy was my biological father, and like my birth mother, I lied to the man I loved to get what I wanted.

"That does seem to be a tragic trait that our line seems to share, but we can break the cycle. Don't take the easy way out. We own up to our mistakes and correct them. It's time for us to become I."

267

Stars swirled together into a large constellation of a woman holding out her hand.

"As long as we are at odds with ourselves, the destruction will continue. A merge will destroy the Sphinx—our anger at uncertainty—then we can take care of the infidel."

"You can justify killing Matt but not yourself?" The constellation sighed but kept her hand outstretched.

"Killing him will not solve the problem, much like ending our life will not absolve us. The infidel has followers, of which our ancestor is one. His death would harden his followers' hearts and create a power vacuum for others of similar ilk. They would carry his plans off in his name, and nothing would be corrected."

It went to show how naive I was. Matt's death was a means to an end for an emotional person. He pissed me off, and I wanted to be rid of him without considering what that would mean long term. I was such a spaz. It was stupid.

"Unwise. We have allowed our passions to dictate our actions for far too long, and we must atone. We will bind his powers then help Quyen dismantle his influence. The infidel will either fall in line, or he will wither away, but he won't have the power to manipulate events the way he did in our past."

It could work if I existed past whatever decision point caused Quyen's diary to add pages. *"If we merge, will I still be myself?"*

"No. We will be more."

Her tone was neither condescending nor treacherous, and with veritas, I could hear the truth in her voice. She didn't lie. I didn't know what more meant, but I believed it wouldn't kill me, though I would change. *"Why aren't we merged already? You were with me since the beginning."*

"We were angry and wanted revenge, so we waited. Even when I unleashed my wrath through the Sphinx, the satisfaction never came. Living as us was more satisfying than the vengeance, and we cannot have Quyen while trying to seek it."

"So for a man?" I snorted. My chest ached from the nearly healed wound. Every woman in my line seemed man crazy—to the point of self-destruction.

"For us. We cannot continue this way, mate or not. He pleases us phys-ically, emotionally, and he returns our feelings. How is letting him go not a foolish choice?"

It also made the situation different. Except I doubted Quyen would have anything to do with me—cycle broken. No more destructive path. I would merge with Oya. Before entering the godscape, I demolished most of the building, and only Oya knew what else. She was right. It was time to face the situation and fix it. Not having to worry about the Sphinx anymore was step one. The rest I would figure out as I went.

I held out my hand toward the constellation. The figure faded then my breath left me. I grasped at the cloud raft in panic as images, memories, and sensations downloaded into my brain.

Quyen held me to him in my hallucination.

"Heal yourself, damn it," he muttered. "I'm not going to lose you."

I gasped for air. He held me tighter. The cool sensation of his magic alerted me to my return to reality. I was back. "Too tight."

"Don't scare me like that ever again." He released me then covered his lips with mine.

I wrapped my arms around his neck.

"Now is not the time. We have dangerous company," Matt said.

"ATF. Drop your weapons and put your magic away, or we will shoot."

uyen

I pulled Pandora to her feet as I stood. She wobbled in my arms. I wanted her close to me. However, we had other issues.

"I said freeze," the officer in charge barked.

"You also said to put away our weapons." Matt raised his arms and stepped in front of us. "This is private property, but I also recognize that you are doing your job. Which would you rather?"

"Sir. Step away from the man and woman. Slowly."

The air was moist from Pandora's loss of control over Oya. It wouldn't take much prompting to lay cover fog and start a storm. That was the one blessing about finding out that she lied to me. I wouldn't have to exhaust myself trying to escape the damn ATF.

"I am the Grand Magister of Obscura. You are trespassing for what reason?" Matt asked.

He didn't move an inch. We need to get Pandora away from the

ATF. I didn't want to consider what would happen when her identification didn't come back on any country's registry.

The air thickened as I gathered water vapor to the lobby wreckage. "What are you doing?" the commanding officer asked.

A wall slab fell over as Bane staggered forward from the rubble for an answer. That ass was beyond fortunate that Pandora didn't kill him in her transformation rampage. If I hadn't—I didn't want to think about it. That problem was over.

"They're attacking," someone yelled.

Automatic gunfire sprayed around us and flattened against Matt's shield. Mud along with cement dust mixed in with the fog. "Get down."

Bane's attention focused on his environment too late. Bullets tore through him, causing him to spasm in an awkward rictus of physics before falling over. Shouts from outside the immediate war zone rang out as craft answered the attack. I covered us in mist.

"Get her out of here," Matt yelled as power and ammunition sparked and flattened on his shield. He wouldn't be able to hold it much longer. Camera's attack, followed by Oya, and then the ATF put us at our limit—me anyway. I was not a combat wizard. My defense was for minor skirmishes and personal safety, not war.

We had cover, but escape would not be so easy. The lobby and several other sections of the building were closed off to us. Making a run for it was the only option, but I was too tired to flood the area with fog. I doubted the ATF force in front of us were the only ones. It didn't look good.

"Hold on to me." Pandora wrapped her arm around my waist. The world melted away like steam from a pot as a new reality took place. She dropped to her knees, panting. "This is as far as I could go with the two of us. I'm low on magic."

I surveyed our surroundings. Debris and distance muffled the shooting and yelling. We were in one of the corridors. Emergency lights blinked as dust drifted from the ceiling. Broken walls and a partially collapsed roof sealed off the corridor leading toward the lobby. It was a miracle that we could shimmer to an area that was whole. We had a chance to evacuate the same way the non-combatants did if we hurried. I didn't put it past the ATF to seal any other exits. I knew enough tactics to know that.

I urged Pandora to her feet. "We have to get out of here."

"I know." She leaned on me for a second, then took a deep breath. "Let's go."

She staggered forward. I caught her arm to pull her along faster. It must be the wound. She may have healed it, but she still needed time to recover. I caused it. I would deal with it. There were other ways to stop her from changing. I could've...

Nothing came to mind.

All I knew was when her eyes glowed crimson and she began talking in the plural, I would lose her. She absorbed magic. The over-saturation led to a loss of control. It made sense to make her use enough power that she couldn't let Oya loose. It was a hell of a gamble.

What if I lost?

"Pan, I'm—"

"Drew," Tonya cried out as she crushed the two of us in a bear hug.

Max and Trina followed in pursuit.

"Thanks for the love, but the ATF is raiding the place. We have to get her out of here. Tell me you have a plan."

She released us. "We have a plan."

Her quick answer threw me. I didn't know whether she said that to break the tension or she was serious until she held up five vials. "We were going to use a summon, but the Obscura assholes have the place warded against it. However, we found these in the arsenal."

The labels on the tubes read escape. "And where will these take us?"

Using their potions was beyond risky. In my time in Obscura, the escape potions led back to the summoning circle in the Richmond building as a fallback point. Who knew what was in place since I left. They could lead anywhere – DC, even oblivion. Even if we arrived safely, Obscura might be waiting on the other side. Matt wasn't the most merciful, and I doubted that most of his personnel remembered me. We would be leaving our lives in Obscura's hands.

"It would be away from here," Tonya answered. "It's this or a detention center."

She had a point. Beggars could not be choosers. We all took a potion. "See you on the other side."

The drama was making me punchy. So many things went wrong, and most of them were due to my miscalculation. We each threw a potion on the tiled floor. Five large wisps of mist surrounded us as the pounding of dozens of boots on the hard floor edged closer to us.

"They're using a smoke cover, grab them," was the last thing I heard before I faded out of existence before popping into the center of a large circular dais. A contingent of battle mages glared with their hands ready to blast us. At least I recognized the large amphitheater. The stone walls, glassed-in observation area in the upper portions of the room, and stage were the same as I remembered. It was the Richmond tower.

"We just came from the research center. The ATF stormed the place." We didn't need Pandora to lose control of Oya again. With so much magic, anything was liable to set her off.

No. If that were true, she would have changed in Fairy Stone. That place teemed with magic.

I didn't know what the rules were about her powers. I also didn't want to take chances.

"Where is the Grand Magister?" Lauren asked from behind a ring of guards.

"He confronted the ATF. They probably have him in custody," I answered.

"You left him," she screeched. "And brought that monster with you?"

Pandora flinched. "No need to call names. It didn't turn out as you hoped. An NDA cannot stop a goddess, but it is I, ancestor."

Lauren's brown skin dulled. "Get them out of here. Be discrete."

"Magia Lectore, the Grand—" one of them began.

"I said do it," she snapped. "Then break the circle. We don't want more non-personnel in our inner sanctum."

I glanced at Max as they closed in on us. He wasn't happy about the situation. However, he didn't have that twitchy expression he got when he heard a lie. Lauren's intention to let us go was honorable. I wanted out of there before the ATF decided to raid Richmond, seize everyone, and sort it out later. Many questions were mounting that Pandora needed to explain—Obscura's headquarters was not where I wanted it to go down.

It took fifteen minutes for the guards to lead us from the bowels of the building with slight hallways of white, cream, and alabaster mixed with the occasional gray—nothing changed about the starkness since I was last there except the addition of checkpoints.

Matt was always a quick study. I thought as I stood in front of the glass and metal doors of a side entrance.

And of course, Lauren was smarter.

"I'm sure this should be obvious, but just in case it isn't, don't come back," the leader said.

I shrugged, not in the mood to say anything clever to anger the automatons that Matt recruited while I was gone. Walking from the amphitheater to the lobby floor, we crossed paths with no less than a hundred people watching us in curiosity and some hatred. We were intruders being escorted out of the building, after all. To them, nothing good would come of our presence. A few in there gave us the wide-eyed look of what I assumed was recognition, not that it would do me any good at the moment, but it forced me to consider the level of effort to dismantle Obscura once I removed Matt from power.

I would have to do more to groom Tonya to handle both Camera and Obscura. "Let's go."

We walked down Eighth Street until we were out of Obscura Tower's shadow then down Marshall toward a parking deck. We reached the cement building a few blocks away with the blue and white "P" sign. We ducked inside then walked along the pedestrian walkway of the multilevel garage. I motioned toward the stairwell. It was empty.

"Okay. We have some privacy to get some plans. Does anyone have any money or a prepaid credit card?" I asked.

Max shook his head. "I only have a few dollars—"

Trina signed.

"We have about $1200 in cash. It was all I could withdraw

without making Betty more curious than normal, and I have my gift cards," he translated.

"I know it's not the time, but I got to ask," Tonya said. "What's the deal with the gift cards?"

"Max and I give each other gift cards to go into town and pamper ourselves when we have a day off," she answered. "Hopefully, we won't have to go to jail. I don't want to have my baby in prison."

"Your baby?" Tonya hissed. "Why didn't you mention that earlier?"

"I'm not that far along. Besides, I wasn't about to be left home to worry," she signed. "Stress is just as harmful to pregnancy as combat."

"But—" I put my hand on Tonya's shoulder.

There was no point arguing with Trina especially through Max. I agreed that leaving her home would have worried her. The combat comment was another battle that was out of scope for the moment. "Tonya, do you still have your bug-out kit?"

"In my stomping grounds, please. You should know better." She elbowed me lightly. "I've been your partner for the past couple of years. I have a couple of them in different places in case I'm on the run. You'd never let me hear the end of it otherwise. I just need twenty minutes to get the one closest to here."

"Good, that leaves my Richmond one and one other I have tucked away." We could easily hole up out of sight between the four of us until the Senate vote if necessary. "We should be good."

I turned to Pandora. She would have been left out of our resource conversation, but there was no reason she couldn't be in on the planning. She rested her hand against the cinderblock wall. She had drawn a summoning ring on it and retrieved her bag. The effort exhausted her to the point that fine sweat covered her forehead as she attempted to catch her breath.

I went to her side. The moment I touched her hand, that euphoric sensation rushed over me. I got hard, and I understood a few more things about us. Touching her was about more than lust. She took some of my magic. "You're like a vampire."

She met my gaze, no longer looking as though she were about to fall over. "In some ways."

She slipped the strap over one arm. "I don't have anything to contribute except magic."

"We figured, considering where you're from," I added as we joined the others.

"I hope this plan goes better than the last one," Max quipped.

Me too. "I will take a play from your book and keep it simple. Two of us rent a room while the rest lounge in the lobby casually, then make our way to the room while we gather information."

Trina signed.

"This is a nice hotel," Max translated.

"And it's in plain sight," I added.

"I think she's talking about our clothes." Pandora gestured toward the two of us in particular.

Dust and dirt covered us from the attack, along with rips in our clothing. I studied the hole in her bloody, ripped shirt then moved immediately to Tonya. "Trina and Tonya will have to rent the room then come back here so we can plan our approach. We still have one thing on our side—the ATF doesn't know we're in the Richmond area. They saw Matt, Pandora, and me, so long as we keep a low profile, we should be fine. I won't know how bad it is until we dig for information. Phones off and cash or prepaid cards only."

"Gotcha," Tonya said. "Then we can find out what the hell happened. We'll get two rooms then—"

Trina put her hand on Tonya's shoulder, causing her to frown, then she glanced at me. "Oh, I see."

Her tone held shock more than anything, but the moment was still young. I was confident she would want an explanation. Pandora took my hand in hers but remained silent. The gesture said it all.

"Well, okay. I room alone. It's better for my sanity anyway. Let's go, Trina." They started up the cement stairs to the hotel entrance level.

"Okay, then what about you two?" Max said. "I look like I escaped from a hospital at best, but you two are covered in blood, dust, and mist. If it weren't for the fact that it's the middle of the day during a workweek—scratch that, I don't know why we haven't been stopped."

"I've been veiling us." Pandora squeezed my hand.

"That's why you're so tired." I brushed my lips with hers.

"It's the adrenalin," Max muttered. "Hold it until you get to the room."

I wanted her. It wasn't just coming down from the flight or fight. I hurt her. I had to know if she was okay. I wanted to be as close to her as possible—to make it up to her. The kiss was as much for my sake as it was for practicality. "I'm sharing my magic with her so she can keep the spell going."

"That's what you're calling it." Max snorted.

"G-Max," she sighed. "Don't worry. I'm using an active power since it's easier to compensate for minor environmental changes versus coming up with a spell that fits all occasions. I can hold out for another twenty minutes."

He ran his hands through his hair. "This is too much. You were in the hospital less than five hours ago. We never did get lunch. You're exhausted."

I squeezed her hand. There was her conversation with Oya too. We had a lot to talk about.

"I'm fine," she said.

"Half-truth," Max snapped.

She kissed me. My head buzzed from the sensation as she absorbed my magic, lust, and calming down from the attack. When she released me, her eyes shined—not like they did when she transformed—the memory of having to hurt her deflated the mood. An odd expression passed over her features then she turned back to Max.

He rolled his eyes. "I'd say get a room, but we're already working on it. Come on and do whatever you're going to do to hide us. The girls should be ready by now."

I took Pandora's hand. There were other ways to lend her energy besides methods that gave up focus. Besides, we had several things to hash out before we got to personal issues. "Let's go."

We started for the double doors that led to the lobby. Nothing seemed odd as we walked, but I noticed that the world seemed darker, as though a cloud had passed overhead. It explained several things when knowing what to look for. When we left Obscura Tower, it was the same. However, going into the shade of the garage made it less noticeable, or perhaps I was overthinking it. I'd ask her about it later.

The double doors opened for us, and we slipped through before anyone had a chance to become curious. Inside the lobby, there were a couple of dark blue couches and cherrywood desks for guest services, all bathed in the golden light of a crystal, tiered chandelier. The way the concierge and front staff looked up when the doors opened, they would have greeted us with big smiles as we entered—if they could have seen us.

"I think we may have tipped them off, not waiting for someone else to trigger the door."

She squeezed my hand. *"Everything is solid. I promise."*

It appeared to be the case. No one approached us, and there were few enough people in the lobby that we didn't have to worry about bumping into people. Tuesday afternoon was not a prime time for travelers. At least we had that working for us.

Trina and Tonya left the registration desk then walked to the elevators. We trailed them close enough to alert them to our presence wordlessly. Tonya didn't even flinch when we got into the car, but Trina squeaked. Pandora unveiled us once the doors closed.

"Ow," Max said, then he signed without translating for the rest of us.

Trina glowered at him then signed back at him.

"You don't want to know," Pandora muttered when I looked at her for help.

"Okay. We got three rooms." Tonya faced the keypad. "We got them next to each other by telling them it was for our boss."

"That was an unnecessary story." I ran my hand through my hair at the complication. "Now, they will be expecting one of us to fulfill that role."

"You try and book three rooms in person as two black women then," she said. "The look the guy at the desk gave us said, 'sex workers trying to find a place to work,' even though we look more like the fashion swat team. So before he went there, we cut the questions by throwing in a comment about our CEO boss coming in on the late flight from Hanoi at the last minute, and we didn't want to lose our jobs."

Black jeans, a shirt, leather jacket, and boots did not immediately connote prostitution or business for that matter. All of the items were difficult to remove even when adequately motivated. The guy was an asshole. I hated biased behavior. It made things complicated. The only plus was it made those who operated that way predictable. "We'll figure something out."

The doors opened, and we stepped out. Pandora didn't veil us when we left because Tonya held out a card to me. "You're 3246. I'm going to grab my bug-out kit, some food, and your supposed dry cleaning. Then I'll fifth-wheel back here so we can plan our next moves."

Tonya had a strong guilt game. Part of me wanted to apologize, but I did nothing wrong by moving on. She would too. I just didn't want it to affect our friendship. "Sounds like a plan. Two hours?"

She nodded. "It should take about that long. The usual applies."

"Be safe."

She smiled. "Always. The same to you, or you'll end up like those two." She thumbed towards Max and Trina, waved, then left me in awkwardness.

Max shook his head. He signed to Trina then unlocked the door. They went inside, but a giggle escaped before the door closed, and the silence blessed us.

Pandora opened the door to our room. It had to be the adrenalin. The downgrade from danger to less danger to—I don't want to think —was messing with all of us in different ways. The nervous energy needed somewhere to go. We wouldn't be able to think straight until it did. So the moment we were alone, I pounced.

39

andora

The euphoria of Quyen's kiss was a balm to my soul. I wanted nothing more than to be close to him after exposing my secret to him. His tongue rubbing mine as he hungrily explored my mouth pushed away the fear and allowed me to bask in lust for the moment. I didn't doubt there would be a reckoning. He was too shrewd not to call me out.

For the moment, he was mine. I was free to love him.

"Yes," I sighed as he kissed the side of my neck.

The crush blossomed into much more when I saw that his thoughts and his personality in real life were a match for me. I always knew. The merge made many things clear. I'd been around too long not to know what I wanted.

Judging by Quyen's pants and hand—everywhere on me, I wasn't the only eager one. We quickly rid each other of our offending raiment. I had one leg out of my jeans when he lifted it to his shoulder and sheathed himself inside me. The delicious friction between us coupled with heady magic sent fireworks of sensation all through my body. The stress and anxiety of the past hours melted away as we moved together.

I couldn't help myself. I pulled his head down to meet mine so we could connect at both ends. There was nothing I wanted to hold back. He had to have everything, and I wanted just as much in return while we were one.

His pace quickened with a satisfying roll of his hips. Every time he did that, it drove me a little crazy. It made me want to chain him to my heart, my bed, have him be forever mine. I would be his. All he had to do was ask.

If he still wanted me.

He eased out of our lip lock, peppering the side of my mouth.

"You make me crazy," he said in between thrusts.

"Same," I moaned when he rolled his hips again.

"Then show me."

That was my only warning. He quickened his pace from long deep thrusts to a drizzling, drill-like rhythm. Thunder boomed overhead as I shuddered through my climax. The loss of control should have mortified me. Instead, I wanted his completion inside me. It was similar to my view of him in the River of Reflection, unabashed and pleased based on the tension in his neck as I wrung out every bit of ecstasy from him.

But it was the long, slow kiss afterward that did it for me. He didn't simply take his pleasure then roll off me, but enjoyed the descent as though we were drifting leaves in the breeze. When my body met the comforter, I realized I levitated us during sex.

"Talk about getting high," I quipped.

He released my leg then lay beside me. "I can dig it."

I slapped his shoulder gently. "There's no need to make fun of me. The experience was pretty far out. I'm not afraid to admit it. You pleased me."

"Why, thank you." He trailed his hands down my arm.

I shivered when he touched the tattoo of my symbol. It was a faint outline of air currents that were barely colored in. I hid it from sight.

The pupils of his brown eyes went from languorously large to smaller as their intensity changed. He propped himself up by his shoulders. "Why didn't you tell me about Oya?"

I held his gaze. There was no censure in them. It was worse, disappointment. I betrayed him by not coming clean. My instincts had been right. Deceiving him led to trouble. "Quyen, I..."

I sat up. His gaze burned too much. I focused on my partially dressed state. My bra bunched up under my sweater, which the rebar ruined. I slipped the garment off, poking my finger through the hole as a distraction.

Facing him shouldn't be that hard. I was a goddess. In the thousands of years that I lived, I had many lovers, divine and mortal, but this one humbled me.

I tossed the sweater in the trash, thought better of it, and placed it in my bag. When I pulled out a new sweater, Quyen began muttering to himself.

Okay, that's worse.

I turned to face him. He slid his jeans over his hips, and he wouldn't meet my eyes. I slipped my panties and jeans the rest of the way on, lest I continued to look like a goof with one pant leg, dragging denim and silk behind me. I tugged the clean sweater over my head, then broke the silence.

"I can't do the right thing when you're around. Oya's powers are dangerous, and I can't separate you from them. I think it's best that you go back to your time, and we settle things here." He scrubbed his face with his hands.

That was a bummer. My heart became cold in my chest. He wanted me to leave? I wouldn't believe that he just needed to cool off. "You're right. I am dangerous, more so since I am complete, but don't give up on us because it's complicated."

"Complicated is being part of a love triangle while trying to keep Camera from incurring the government's wrath. This—" He gestured between the two of us and then all around. "—is the end of the world. My girlfriend could jump-start the apocalypse, and I don't want to think about the other consequences of being here. Will you still be born? I heard you mumble about Lauren when I...stabbed...you."

I reached for him, and he raised his hands. I hugged myself to cover the moment. He rejected me. "The timeline is still intact, or I would disappear. If we checked your journal, I'm sure we'd see new entries each day as the time stream course corrects."

He studied me. "Since when have you been so sure?"

"Merging my soul gave me knowledge."

He grabbed me by the shoulders. "You what? When?"

I wanted to shrug him off of me. His hold was not loving. The aggression of it was not of lust but anger. It was as if he sought to coerce the answers out of me. "Release me."

Quyen blinked, then relinquished his hold. "Your eyes are different. Is that what she did to you?"

"I am whole," I assured him. "Quyen, I am the same."

He kissed me.

I yielded to the moment as I projected all of my feelings into the act. A breath later, it ended. His eyes had the same dark, lusty shine they did whenever he kissed.

"Far out," I whispered.

"Why did you keep this from me?" He rested his forehead against mine. "It changes things."

I didn't want it to change. The fear of him becoming like Jannes and Matt drove me so hard that I missed the possibility of his fears of me. "It doesn't have to."

Silence hung between us. "Pan, I—"

The insistent *knock-knock-knock* at the door ended the conversation. This round was lost to me. He needed his space. I would honor that. I went to the door. Tonya stood holding out a paper bag with *Portents* written on the side and a suit bag while she squeezed her eyes shut. The amusement was bitter but a balm to my aching heart. "We're decent."

She opened her eyes. "Cool. Here's some food and a costume for our 'boss' cosplay. We think it will come across more impressive if the boss character finishes a stressful international business call and we all break into Vietnamese to make the front nervous."

It was a viable social engineering plan for the area, and it was something almost all of us could pull off. The staff wouldn't expect a foreign business person and his team to be witches. When in doubt, cater to expectations.

Which is what I should have done with Quyen. He respected honesty above all else. It would be challenging to recover ground.

If I could recover.

The pessimist side would not win. He was stressed and disappointed. Rest and space would fix the situation. "Sounds like a winning plan."

Tonya grinned. "Don't you mean you can dig it?"

I wanted to roll my eyes. There was no reason to point out my slight differences as my whole self. "Really? You're jivin' me?"

"Hey, it's what I do." She shrugged. "Oh, and take care of him."

My heart sank. "If he lets me."

She furrowed her brow and opened her mouth when Max opened the door and stuck his head out. "You two need to turn on the news."

We hurried inside the room. Quyen already had the television on. He folded his arms across his chest as he watched a newscaster report the Morgan LeFay Nature Preserve and Research Center disaster.

"—terrorist activity has been as ATF and the Agency investigate the Obscura owned facility," the newsman reported. "According to witnesses, there has been suspicious activity going on since the unnatural storm that killed fifty people last month. Some locals believe that witchcraft may have been involved. When confronted, the conflict unfolded, leaving many injured, one dead, a 'Bane James Clifford' a possible terrorist, and several others in custody, including Obscura's Grand Magister."

The shot changed to a dark gray one-story building as a black SUV pulled up in front of the entrance. Reporters and protestors descended on the vehicle as uniformed security held them back. Matt stepped out of the car in handcuffs with tape across his mouth. His eyes searched the crowd as though he were a terrified deer in the forest as officials ushered through the door. Gagging would not stop him from spell casting as long as he could think the spell. If I hadn't known better, I would have been angry on his behalf. He was dangerous, but I knew Agency's tactics had more to do with fear of magic than his actual potential villainy.

"Burn the witch," several chanted while counter-protestors chanted, "Free the wizard."

"Counter protestors. That's new," Tonya muttered.

"Yeah, he's milking the sympathy," Quyen added.

"With the civil unrest over craft users fueling conflict around the country, the Senate will gather on Thursday for an emergency vote. For commentary on what the Witchcraft Act means for the American people, welcome correspondents Adrian Brown and Nelson Du Bois—"

Quyen muted the television. "This went from bad to worse. Bane's dead *and* a terrorist."

"What?" Tonya asked.

"The ATF got trigger happy and shot him." Good riddance as far as I was concerned since he tried to kill me, but initiated a transformation instead.

Tonya paced. "This is bad. The gun nuts in the NoVa cell will go HAM when they hear about this. They'll do something rash."

"They were already planning something rash. That's why we tried to stop you and Trina from doing what you did." Quyen ran his hands through his hair.

"Yeah, we thought that was a trick, and—never mind, everything went sideways. Bane was supposed to cause a distraction, but then fullscale shit went down." Tonya sat on the edge of the bed then jumped up as though it were hot. "I can't believe he is dead."

"Were you two close?" I asked.

She shook her head. "We talked off and on, but he was spun up the last few months. He was hounding me to join the NoVa cell, then he asked me about Quyen, and Camera became…intense."

The last few months. And when Bane saw me, he panicked and attacked. That confirmed that he was from the future too, but how? And were there any others?

And who else?

"Okay. Here's what we have—"

The knocking at the door interrupted his flow briefly as he opened it and ushered in Max and Trina. Once he shut the door, he continued. "The ATF and Agency are watching Obscura and will soon track

Camera members if they are not already. The Senate votes have been moved from next week to in two days. Matt's in jail, Bane is dead, and the media is having a field day covering it all."

"It's a pickle for sure." Max hugged Trina.

"This is my fault," she signed.

It was mine. I should have remained on guard. Matt was not the only one who visited in the future. Of course, Camera would have their efforts. I wondered how long it would take them to accomplish it.

"No, Trina, it's not your fault," Max said aloud. "The plan was destined to fail once we got new information."

"And it was my plan, my fault," Quyen said. "None of us counted on him having a legitimate reason and being heavy-handed about it."

"Heavy-handed, my ass," Tonya said. "He kidnapped you to win you to his side. Y'all are lucky that Bane got overzealous and half-destroyed the place."

Again my fault. "I'm pretty sure that was Bane's plan from the start. He's Camera from my—"

"Excuse me?" Tonya put her hand on her hips. "I'm Camera, too. So is Drew. All of us came to the rescue, damsel. The Grand Magister grabbed them because they were with *you*."

She jabbed a finger toward me.

"I am not a damsel." I met and held her gaze. The mortal didn't scare me.

"Hmm." She gave me the stink eye.

Quyen stepped between us. "We need to focus on the problem."

Tonya moved around him. "I agree. Miss Thing here is wanted by Obscura, and when the government finds out, they'll be after us, too. We should send her back. She's nothing but trouble."

"Hey. Hey," Max said. "Hold on now. I get the three of you have some romance troubles that you need to work out, but don't go pinning it all on her."

Trina stood her ground beside him as she read everyone's lips. She nodded. Both appeared prepared to defend me.

Tonya rolled her eyes. "Look. I get it. She's your future grandkid or whatever, *if* everything plays out. She's not even a blood relative."

"Doesn't matter," Max said. "She's ours regardless."

I put my hand on his shoulder, then kissed his cheek. "Thank you."

He nodded.

"We need to focus on the real matter," Quyen said. "We do not have time for in-fighting. Regardless of how everyone feels about it, the Senate is voting Thursday, and there's a strong possibility that Camera will retaliate. We have to get to DC to stop them."

"What makes you think Camera is going to do something?" Tonya asked. "I haven't heard anything about any attack or even a DC counter protest."

"Are you sure?" he asked. "You did mention that some aggressors stirred things in the cell—and the increased activity with other cells."

Tonya nodded her head. "That doesn't mean they are terrorists or bad people."

"Then how about the fact that Bane knew me," I said. "Everyone was down, and the fight was over. He saw me, then ordered everyone to shoot at *me*."

"So you are bad news," she sneered.

I ignored the comment. "Bane was from the future. He recognized me from my time at Obscura."

"But he didn't know you would turn, or he wouldn't have used magic," Quyen remarked. "Who else may—"

"Wait, what do you mean by turn?" Tonya asked.

She *would* catch that. "It doesn't matter."

"It does matter," Quyen replied. "There have been enough secrets, and this one could kill us all. Pandora has Oya's powers."

The silence filled the room. Everyone stared at me with degrees of judgment and censure. It was evident that bridges were burning with each breath, the likelihood of Quyen and I making it through this snag in the relationship cloth unraveled before my eyes.

He was so mad.

"Since it's out there, yes, I lied. I'm Oya. Everything else I said was true. I believed I was adopted. It turns out that I wasn't. It doesn't change that Matt still needs to be stopped."

"No, *you* need to be stopped," Tonya replied. "You destroy everything. The way I see it—"

"Enough."

The building shook with my anger. A watercolor of a landscape fell off the wall while the muffled sounds of panic in the hallways made me regret my temper. Everyone cringed, including Quyen. I took a deep breath to center my emotions, then stepped forward. "I'm sorry."

He watched me, then looked away. "I don't think this is going to work."

I wanted to ask what he meant, but his body language told me the answer. None of it. For the moment, we didn't work, and I caused too much of a distraction. To get through to Camera, he'd need Tonya, and she was too jealous to stand me.

Then fine. *I* would take care of Matt. Then I would see if Quyen's heart remained hardened. We were meant to be, but we both had to want it for the relationship to thrive. It was my chickens of deceit roosting, so I would take the high road. I grabbed my bag and slung it on my shoulder. "I betrayed your trust. Don't betray my love."

I wouldn't waste time while I waited for him. Binding Matt would take hours to prepare. The least I could do was prevent disaster by removing his power and influence then allowing the chips to fall where they may.

I opened the door and let the chaos of the other guests swallow me.

40

*M*att

An arrest was not all that it was cracked up to be, but I was in good company. It seemed to be a rite of passage for revolutionaries if history books were to be believed—which some weren't. At least there was no physical torture. The ATF handed me to my jailers and merely held me for the night in a cell with my wrists cuffed together—no food or drink, just a toilet, cot, and silence. If it weren't for the fact that I knew they were terrified of me using my craft, I would be incensed by their uncharacteristically heavy-handed treatment.

It was additional ammunition for my legal counsel and PR to use.

At least they cuffed my wrists together so I could relieve myself.

"Grand Magister?"

I opened my eyes from my meditative state. Chambers, my council and public strategist, stood in front of my cell in a blue power suit and heels that put her at eye level with most men. She gave me a once over, frowned, then schooled her features. Her dark eyes were hard as she turned toward a wary agent that hung back from the bars as though I planned to walk through them.

"I want those cuffs off him, Agent Park. As his legal counsel, I can guarantee that the Grand Magister will not take retribution nor will he attack other than for the defense of his person."

Agent Park furrowed his brow, then watched me. "Nod once in agreement."

I nodded.

"Put your wrists close to the bars," he said. "I'm going to remove the cuffs and unlock this door. Don't cause trouble."

I complied, and Agent Park did as he stated. Once free, I pulled the duct tape gingerly off my mouth. Glue from the tape lingered on the edges of my lips as I worked them. It was a necessary evil to set the stage. Allowing the government to take me and appearing as harmless as possible would go a long way to swaying the sympathetic mundanes to my side. It was worth it to spend the night in a holding area while the crowds raged outside.

Leaving too soon would cause suspicion, and staying too long would suggest evidence against Obscura. Wednesday morning was perfect.

"I wish to speak to my client for a brief moment," Chambers said.

Agent Park took up station next to the door leading out of the holding area.

I scrubbed at my face when Chambers handed me a wet wipe.

"Don't make yourself too presentable. We want the media to see you at hardship," she advised.

I cleaned the edges of my mouth. "Is there anything I need to know before we leave?"

She gave me another once over. "We should be fine. There is press in the lot. I want you to keep playing the harmless, misunderstood magic-user. We're not ready to address the press. However, I'm working with Robert to set up a press conference at one today."

That would serve multiple purposes. The Witchcraft Act vote was tomorrow. Anything to sway the Senate was beneficial. My lobbyists were already on it, but public opinion would help persuade those on the fence. The vote would be close. However, I was confident that it would go in my favor. Even Camera's meager attempts at first amend-ment rights wouldn't thwart me. Obscura would sweep in, save the day, and prove that we could handle our issues. I would crush Camera in the public eye *and* gain Quyen to my side.

Then there was Pandora.

"Ready, Grand Magister?"

Chambers gestured toward the door where Agent Park waited. She wore her blue and cream power suit and black heels—the uniform of her legal work. She was an enchantress with the acumen for empathic manipulation and law. Chambers would work the crowd to whatever spectrum of emotion I wanted without any effort. However, her magic didn't extend to mediums. There would be plenty of press, so I'd follow her instructions until we got to the car. "Chivalry, Chambers. It's a dying art. However, it's not dead yet."

Her lips twitched when I opened the door.

"One moment." I tossed the cleansing cloth into the trash "Ignis."

I watched Agent Park flinch with his hand at his side but with enough trigger discipline not to draw his weapon as a small blaze flared up like a geyser.

He trained his eyes on me as the cloth sizzled. I removed the air inside the receptacle to drown the fire while I held his gaze until he gave me a single nod.

Destroying the cloth served two purposes. If there were any practi-tioners that aligned themselves with the government, they wouldn't have any means to trace me. A paranoid precaution that has always served me well. And I earned an enemy's respect.

As she proceeded forward, the agency personnel watched us. The silence in the room was deafening. There were few allies in the build-ing. I knew them by the lack of fear or hate in their gazes. I took comfort in knowing that I wasn't entirely surrounded by vipers, not that they would do anything overt to show otherwise. They served me better in the shadows anyway.

"This way," Chambers advised as we left the holding area.

The building was only one story above ground. Our egress wouldn't take much more than a moment or two from where we were. Though in the silence, it seemed like forever.

"Burn the witch," someone hissed.

"Quiet," another shushed.

I didn't respond. If I addressed them in any way, they would find themselves knocked through a wall. Then my PR efforts would be wasted. It was petty.

They were nothing.

My real problem was how to separate Quyen and Pandora while keeping them both. Their touches and glances were more than play-acting. The way he looked at her—

I knew the look. It was possession, except Pandora belonged to me, not him.

Chambers stopped in front of me. "You look angry. That bigot is nothing. We will be here long after his great-grandchildren die. You can't show them that they can get to you."

She misread my thoughts, but Chambers was right. I needed to put on a solid front. Mooning after Pandora would not serve my interests. It was an issue that I would see to when I could afford to do so. *Relax. Think about them later.*

I took a deep breath then we waded into the sea of reporters and protestors that my people held back. Chambers rushed me to my car. She pushed me inside then then slid in beside me.

"We survived the gauntlet. Excellent job," I said as we drove away.

"Thank you, Grand Magister." She dipped her head and then pulled out her phone. She smiled. "The press conference is a go, and we're trending on social media. Twenty minutes before, I want to brief you. Until then, I will take care of the comments. You can't buy this type of publicity."

One more thing to do. "If it advances the agenda."

"It does. I promise you." She swiped at her tablet. "In a few months, we will have the mundanes so divided it will be impossible for the President to sign the Witchcraft Act without political suicide."

I leaned my head back to let Chambers work her magic. "Peters?"

He turned in the passenger seat. "Yes, Grand Magister?"

"Fill me in on everything that has happened since they arrested me."

He nodded. "James and I absconded with as many of our people as we could, as you directed. The ATF arrested only our most trained mages."

"They will be released tomorrow afternoon," Chambers chimed in.

Good, everything appeared to be following expectations. Quyen was such a bother sometimes, him and his morality. However, his acquiescence was key to my plans, though the media face-time and ATF intel didn't hurt. "Debrief them once they are back with us. I want a nice warm meal waiting for them."

Chambers nodded in approval. She understood the importance of interrogation in comfort better than anyone as one of my most prolific spies.

"The women and Quyen came through the escape portal during the raid," Peters continued.

Good. I wouldn't have to locate them again. "I assume they are waiting for me to plan the counterassault on the Senate with them."

Peters paled. He wore dark glasses to hide his gift. The sclera of his eyes turned black when he listened to others' minds. Naturally, the small-minded mundanes of his town imprisoned him for being a demon. I rescued him from their execution. He owed his life to me, so I knew he failed when he shook out of past trauma. He expected me to rage, to behave like the ones that tortured him.

"What happened?" I kept my voice calm.

"Grand Magister, they left. The Magia Lectore ordered my men in my absence, and they were veiled the moment they left the building. I apologize."

I waved my hand—he flinched—I put my hand at my side—poor choice of action. "The fault does not lie with you. I know where Quyen will be on Thursday. I can start the trail from there. The lovely witch with the red eyes is cunning and powerful. Now she knows we're on to her. I'm the only one who can catch her."

Peters relaxed. "Yes, Grand Magister, we will be ready to assist."

"That's all I can ask," I said as we arrived at Obscura tower.

Reporters waited for me in front of the building, as expected.

"Showtime." Chambers got out first. She wore a somber expression as she met the press. "The Grand Magister has just been through an ordeal after his night in holding. You saw the inhumane way the

Agency brought him in. They treated him as though he were a criminal and not an upstanding American citizen. We humbly ask for your patience as we see to his needs."

She urged me to go with Peters and his team.

"We will take your questions at two p.m. Please be ready to hear the entire story with open minds—"

Once I was out of earshot, I said, "Make sure someone is with Chambers when she is ready to make her exit."

Peters motioned to one of his people, and they peeled off from my detail and went back to Chambers. Inside my tower and behind my security wards, I let my genuine emotions seep into me. Lauren did it again.

And said person rushed towards me with all concern and misty eyes. The crushing weight of my anger was more than I wanted to dole out. If I started violence against my allies, my organization would crumble. A dog kicked so many times was bound to lash out eventually, and if there were several of them together, my empire would never be built. Every leader that went that route fell horribly. Lauren had it coming, but I wouldn't let others see me. "My office. Now."

Peters's people fell away from me as I ushered Lauren into a waiting elevator car. I punched the eighth floor but did not release her elbow from my grip.

"What's wrong?" she asked.

I did not engage. Keeping a lid on my ire was difficult enough. I would not lose control in the elevator for all to see, or worse, get to a point from which I could not come back. "In my office."

She flinched at my tone while giving me dewy looks of disapproval, but she didn't push. Moments later, the ding of the floor alarm reoriented my focus, and I urged her to my office with a little more force than necessary.

"Why did you send Pandora and Quyen away when you knew I needed them?"

She took a deep breath. "You don't need them. We can handle everything ourselves, and that woman is a monster. She'll turn on us first chance—"

I slammed my hand on the wall next to me. She jumped. "Why are you not following my orders?"

Her eyes flashed with the familiar defiance that I loved in Pandora. The eye color was wrong, but the expression was correct. Why didn't I see it before? More importantly, why didn't I know about her having children?

"I'm your Magia Lectore. I know you better than anyone, at least I used to. *My* Grand Magister trusted me. What went wrong between us?"

You.

"Lauren, I asked you if you had any children." I had to tread carefully. If she was pregnant, I didn't want to harm my future. "Are you sleeping with anyone?"

"Not that it's any of your business, but I haven't had a lover in a year." She crossed her arms.

There was something that I missed. I wracked my brain going over events that were more than fifty years old to me, trying to recall if I ever saw Lauren with someone. Nothing jumped out at me, but I remembered Lauren going on a vacation to reset her creativity. I didn't think anything of it at the time because she became insufferable with her frustration summoning Oya. She lost her temper several times, trying to make strides with the ritual. It was nothing of note to me because she returned renewed and with a plan.

"Where did you go on your vacation in December again?"

Her spine went rigid. "Aruba and Bonaire. It-it was all of the ABC islands. Curacao, too. I told you about it. I even bought you that Dutch clock."

I glanced at the white timepiece on my shelf. It was shaped like a windmill with blue tulips along its bottom. "You did, but we never talked about what you did while there. What was the first day like?"

Her eyes danced around. "That was months ago. How would I remember?"

The panic response in her eyes and the uncharacteristic nonsensical response showed me that I was on the right track. Lauren hid something from me. "In all the years that I've known you, I've never seen you take a vacation away from Obscura. Even when you married Henry, you—"

She stiffened at his name. In my previous history, she married him fifteen years from this point. They never had children. He was a wizard, so I expected the possibility, but it wasn't surprising that they didn't. Our scientists were fairly certain that magic was passed from mother to child, but it was still up for debate. My people struggled with having children, which is why I didn't want to waste any more time before getting with Pandora.

Lauren and Henry had a high probability of having a mundane child. It was her life. I didn't interfere. He died a few years before Pandora left Obscura, and Lauren had become increasingly sentimental. While Henry had her focus, she had her best years as my Magia Lectore.

"—two didn't have children."

"I-I married Henry?"

There was an unexplained emotion in her voice. It was difficult to tell if it was shock, sadness, or both.

I hadn't introduced them yet, but she appeared to know him. Or she knew another Henry. The name wasn't as popular as it had been in the seventeen hundreds. Perhaps I didn't deserve the credit of matching them in the first place. "Yes, sorry to spoil it for you. It slipped out. But yes, you'll be happily married one day, but remain a workaholic."

"Sounds like me." She sat down absently in one of my chairs. "The workaholic part."

I kept my tone conversational. "You're dedicated to the cause. Where did you really go in December?"

I knelt to her eye level.

She bit her lip as she wrung her hands. "It was one time. I loved you, and I know that I'm not a witch. I have come to accept that." Tears filled her eyes. "He was right there, and we were drinking at the Solstice Banquet. He said I was beautiful, and being a mundane didn't matter to him."

I patted her hand. "You and Henry are adults."

"But I wanted you." She wrapped her arms around herself.

"It was all for nothing. I found the Oya summon so I could be the witch you wanted, but it wouldn't matter if I couldn't manage the ritual, so I gave myself over to misery with Henry, and he got me pregnant, and all you can say is I'm an adult. You don't care. You used to care about my feelings."

I placed my hands on either side of the armchair, caging her. "That me is dead and gone. It's past time that you deal with your little crush. Marry Henry and capture whatever you wish to pass for happiness, but I will never be yours."

Her lip trembled.

"Now tell me where the child is, and how did you keep it from me?"

"I don't know. I gave her up for adoption. The family is not to contact me or me them," she answered.

"You are *my* assistant. How did you keep it from me?"

"I used a perception spell thread woven into my clothes, as we use in the wards. Everyone saw what I wanted them to see, a devoted Magia Lectore and not a heartbroken pregnant woman."

If her insolent actions had nothing to do with Pandora, I could appreciate her ingenuity. It was why I made her my assistant. She was a genius at the craft without being a practitioner. The fact that she fabricated a deception using her access to magical implements already powered by a practitioner was inspired. However, the fact that she used it on me meant she would present a problem if not corrected.

"You're never going to learn, are you?" I met her gaze.

Her eyes widened. She shook her head fast. "No. No. No. Please."

I held up my hand. "You need a vacation. Take a scrying crystal for when I need to find you. There's a press conference at one. After it's over, I want you gone. And do not try to sabotage the conference, or I will treat you like an enemy."

I stood so she could exit.

"For how long?"

Her voice quavered.

"Until I decide you won't interfere in my agendas."

"But I—"

"Lauren, up until now, all the missteps in my plans were because of you and the decisions you made without telling me. Your child becomes Pandora's parent, and she has Oya's power which I find you wanted for yourself and not for me, as you previously explained."

Her eyes widened, then narrowed. "That monster is Oya?"

I gripped her shoulder hard. "Never disrespect Pandora. She's to be my Grand Mistress."

She cried out, and I released her. The betrayed expression stirred bitter remorse. We both needed the time away. Once my plans were back on course, I would ease Lauren back into operations until then she was a dangerous liability. "Leave."

 andora

I waited for signs of Matt's arrival in a coffee shop across from Obscura Tower called *Portents*. After I left Quyen at the hotel, I roamed the streets of Richmond, clearing my head before I was in a calm enough state to gather what I needed to bind the Grand Magister. There were many practitioners in the area. The coffee shop seemed to be a central collecting area for magic users. A good portion of them had spell gardens for potion work. I bartered everything I needed without issue.

When I put aside my problems, the collection of practitioners made sense. Obscura Tower was located near the IRS building, a place of government power. Magic, especially for those with active abilities, was primarily based upon the user's will. We drew to those in positions of power. It was natural for a magic power to be nearby and others to gather near.

Portents catered to practitioners, but there were primarily mundanes in the shop. A barista with piercings, tats, and wearing a yellow apron with cranberry stitching greeted customers. The rest of the decor sported geometric patterns, coffee cups interspersed with protection spells.

Anyone who entered the space was encouraged to be calm and enjoy the relaxing atmosphere as they listened to covers of popular music. The coffee was rich, and my cinnamon roll melted in my mouth like mana—all in all, an excellent stakeout point. From my perch by the corner, I had a full view of the shop and the surrounding area outside Marshall Street. I witnessed the chaos of Matt's release as reporters, and protestors vied for attention. With him back, I was free to make my move.

I slipped the novel I was using as part of my cover back into my bag and tossed a few bills on the table before slipping my arms through the bag's straps.

"Come again," the barista called as I left.

I waved, then negotiated my path across the crowded way. Traffic on 8th Street slowed due to chanting protestors marching up and down the sidewalk while chanting. The police presence on either side of the eight-story building appeared to keep the demonstration peaceful, well, as peaceful as one could get chanting "ding dong the witch should be dead."

Going in the front door was a no-go, as was using magic. My reconnaissance from earlier revealed a greater circle around the building that warded it against magical intrusion. I would have to use another physical entry. I could even do it veiled since they designed the ring to deter summoning magic and bilocation. Veils, on the other hand, were a different problem. That was what the battlemages and aura readers were for—any aural signature not cataloged would set off an alarm.

I watched a couple of foolish reporters try to sneak in last night. If I went through the doors, they would know I was there. The question was, how would the battlemages react? Lauren didn't imply we would be welcomed back when she kicked us out, nor did she specify how thoroughly she exiled us.

I rested the palm of my hand over the pocket of my hoodie. The potion I brewed in the early hours of sunlight remained warm against me. I had two vials—two chances. Once I got in the building, which I still struggled with doing, all I had to do was perform the monumental task of getting Matt to drink it. From there, as long as I limited my time around him, the potion would hold. Being around me would weaken the effects, which I suspected happened to my father. He became so unbearable once I turned thirteen. His powers must have slowly come back, and then he could hear every lie he told me, *and* the ones I told him.

I wish I'd known.

What's done is done. It was a bummer but accurate.

Once Matt consumed the potion, I'd collect enough materials for two to make the trip back to my time.

Quyen was right. I couldn't stay. Matt would figure out that proximity to me would undo the potion. He would cause problems. With his powers bound, he'd grow old at the mundane rate, which must have happened with my grandparents. They must have taken the potion with my father. Given how hurt and angry Daddy was, he probably made them take it if they wanted to see me. It was trippy stuff. Becoming my whole self filled in the gaps of my craft knowledge. I still didn't know the skinny on what happened with my family, but I knew enough.

That was another lifetime. The new one would hopefully be better with Quyen at my side.

If he comes.

I didn't want to give in to doubt. There was a possibility Quyen wouldn't be able to move past me being one with Oya. If he couldn't... I'd face the consequences then and not before. It was the fears of my past that created this situation. I would have to wait until his decision killed our future or made it a reality.

"—me go," a brown-haired woman twisted in the grasp of a battlemage at the delivery entrance between the tower and another office building. "Ever hear of freedom of speech?"

"Yeah," the stout female battlemage shoved the reporter outside the perimeter. "That's not the same as trespassing. Now observe my right to say 'get lost' and then do so."

The woman straightened her button-down shirt and then gave the battlemage the finger.

"Lady, you're not my type," she replied, then slammed the door.

The woman stomped away, giving me an idea. I could use her as a distraction. She was my way into the tower!

My aural signature was in the database—its status was another concern—but it was there. Lauren was a creature of habit. She guarded Matt's interest first and foremost. Nothing would come between her serving him, including petty jealousies. It was a gamble, but I was sure she hadn't removed me.

I would use the reporter as my distraction and get past them while they dealt with her.

"Stop." Power flared in my throat as I compelled her to do my will. Compulsion was an annoying ability. It was a study in semantics. It wasn't enough to tell someone what to do. They had to understand the goal, which meant I had to keep the instructions simple or know the subject well enough for them to interpret my desires as *I* wanted. "That witch can't tell you what to do. You have an assignment."

The reporter's eyes narrowed. She pushed back an errant lock from her braided ponytail, then turned her booted heel back toward the delivery entrance. I fell in step with her, hidden from sight as she whipped out a small case. It was fascinating to watch her work on the steel door lock. Her determination was a little eerie in its single-mindedness.

The delivery entrance consisted of two bay doors on a cement dock and a metal door with a com for requests. I glanced up at the camera in the upper corner. Because of my suggestion, her anger was stoked to the point of the idiocy, judging by her lack of discretion in her repeat approach of Obscura Tower. If she wasn't careful, the battlemages may ignore her or take other precautions without opening the door. I may have gone a bit too far.

Compulsion was delicate magic. I needed more practice with modern minds. In the current century, they were too rash, leaving me few options. Soon I would find out if my gamble with the reporter would serve me or not.

My accomplice unlocked the door as the corrugated metal door of the first bay raised.

It would serve. I slipped in as two battlemages engaged with the angry mundane.

"Don't make a scene. That's what *they* want. Detain her in holding and call the police," I said to the guards before leaving.

I left the battlemages to their prisoner. I didn't have a lot of time since the reporter was part of my exit strategy. With the chaos outside and the wariness of the craft users, a non-emergency would take about thirty minutes for police response. During that time, I had to get to Matt, force the potion on him, and get to holding so I could follow the reporter out with a police escort. It would be tight, and the possibility of failure was high.

I wished compulsion worked on Matt, or I should say worked well. Suggestions on him would be just as tricky. I might get him to drink, but I would have to sleep with him to do it. That was something he wanted besides my power and I wouldn't give him that either. The vote was tomorrow. I may have been desperate but not that level. Besides, that would likely make him more suspicious since he knew my feelings. Then there was trust.

I wouldn't be surprised if he planned something to gain an edge over Camera. He knew my history with events like that. He might kick off a rampage thirty-five years early.

Never again.

I came to the door that led to the office, judging by the aura crystal next to it. I would enter and proceed at my own pace or like a bat out of hell when it read me.

Lauren, do me a solid for once in your life. I pushed the door open. Silence.

Not complete silence. The hum of fluorescent lights in the empty corridor buzzed around me and three elevator doors shined, but no alarms betrayed my presence. My first hurdle was complete.

I hit the call button for an elevator. The bing of the alarm as the middle doors opened was like a reward for making it to the next checkpoint. The bright lights of the car encouraged me. It was stupid to use that. However, it still calmed my nerves, and I hit the black enameled button for the 8th floor.

My sister goddess, Fortune, smiled upon me. No one called my car. Everyone was likely watching the windows to see what the protestors were doing or remained on watch for intruders—something I noticed the moment I stepped off the elevator. I ducked and dipped to the side of the hallway as he walked past me.

A battlemage studied the vacated car briefly, swiping his arms back and forth. Timing was everything and at this moment, mine was perfect.

"What are you doing, Pringle?" The battlemage straightened as Peters walked towards him.

I quieted my thoughts as I edged away from him. Peters's listening ability could detect me if my concentration wavered.

"The elevator opened," Pringle explained as I moved quickly and quietly over the tiled floors of the elevator lobby to get out of earshot.

Matt always preferred the top floor of a building with eastern-facing windows. With his affinity for air magic, it tracked. I could dig it, considering it was an element I favored too. It was another thing that drew me to him. I should have known too much of the same would lead to disaster, but then I wouldn't have found Quyen.

"What was that?" Peters asked loudly.

He looked around wildly.

Even though a veil hid me, I plastered my body against the wall at the end of the elevator lobby. I hadn't yet made it around the corner.

"I don't see anything," Pringle replied. His hands were raised with this index and forefinger extended, another air user most likely. Any sudden movement would give me away to Pringle and panic would betray me to Peters. I centered my mind as I slowly scaled the wall until I made it around the corner. The offshoot corridor branched in three directions, each ending in a suite. The suite straight ahead was the eastern side of the building. I strode toward what must be Matt's office before Peters decided to check on him.

A couple of steps in, someone came around the corner and hurried past. I pivoted to keep them from running into me.

Peters's shoulders relaxed, and he motioned for Pringle to stand down. "Where's the fire?"

"The Grand Magister needs me to bring him some notes from his office," the harried man in a lab coat replied. "He's in a mood, and Magia Lectore is nowhere to be found. I don't have time to wait."

He didn't wait for a response which was just as well. His hurry made it easier to shadow him while Peters was on alert, and the tech mage—judging by the lab coat—saved me the added effort of searching for Matt. I had assumed Matt was in his office since he always worked on something, but then this wasn't the Obscura Tower he had in the future. That must have some bearing on his habits that hadn't been accounted for.

The lab tech rushed into the office and back out a moment later with the grimoire. My heart raced. Matt was up to something if he needed his journal. The tome was where he kept his finessed spells for posterity, not his everyday spellwork. It had to concern my summoning. He couldn't have rounded up forty-two powers again so quickly. How would he power the circle?

Several flights of stairs later, I still didn't have my answer. The lab tech didn't believe in elevators, and the echo in the stairwell covered my descent as we passed others that also chose to hoof it instead of using technology. At least it was an excellent way to burn the excess nervous energy as I followed the tech to the bottom floor. He flew out of the exit and stalked to the eastern part of the building, where they kept the escape ring. It was full circle for me, considering I left there almost twenty-four hours ago.

"Here it is, Grand Magister." The tech bowed his head and held out the grimoire to Matt with a touch of awe. "Is there anything else?"

Matt took the book. "Notify me an hour before the press conference. Otherwise, I wish not to be disturbed."

The tech nodded and then hurried off, closing the doors behind him.

We were alone in the Craftorium. I recognized the setup from my time. It was a theater where he did large-scale craftings for demonstration. In my case, Lauren drilled me in the Craftorium for the masses when my magic theory was weak. Once I got better, she hid me away, and on the spot, sessions miraculously stopped. It was hard to believe that bitch was my grandmother and that she saw me as competition.

She could have him.

Matt studied his notes as he walked towards the dais with the circle. The raised platform made it easier for those inside to observe the spellwork while remaining somewhat close. Whatever he was up to, he planned an audience or needed the extra energy without going off-site. It made sense. The ATF and Agency were after him. They would watch every move he made outside of the building.

I doubted his intentions were furthering world peace, which was a shame because he was the type of historical fulcrum that could achieve it. He and Quyen were unstoppable together.

That's why he's trying so hard to get back in Quyen's good graces.

All the more reason for Quyen to come back with me. Matt would be less of a threat as an old mundane.

Getting the potion into him would not be easy. There were only two ways, seduction, or a fight. He'd never believe my sudden change, and I'd have one shot to catch him off guard. One attack had to stick, preferably knocking him out. Having him in a confused state would be unpredictable, and his disorientation wouldn't last.

I reached into my pouch. My fingers brushed the vials and cushioning I used to keep the glass from clinking together. They were poly-filled bean bags. On their own, they were a joke as a weapon, but when aided by air magic—I hurled the small sack at Matt. He grunted as the bag beaned him in the back of the head, then crumpled to the ground.

Yes.

I dropped my veil before scrambling over to him. Matt lay sprawled face down on the dais. I checked his pulse. He was still alive. I turned him over with the vial readied in my hand when he grabbed my wrist and flipped me. There was a brief flash of agony from my wrist and back, but overall I landed well.

I guess I could thank James for that, except he drilled Matt too. *The jerk.*

"There you are, Kitten." He straddled me while holding my wrist above my head. "If you want me on top, you need only ask."

I rolled my eyes. "I have a boyfriend."

His eyes narrowed as his grip on my wrist tightened. I swung with my free hand. He blocked me before cuffing my wrists to the floor using his active power. The energy from his magic wasn't much. I absorbed it and prepared for another attack.

"Do you want me to use a more powerful spell on you? A rampage would suit my purposes better than a wine and dine with those Washington fools. Keep that in mind."

I relaxed.

He puckered his lips in an air kiss, then studied the vial he plucked from me. "Now, what's this?"

"A potion," I answered.

"That does, what?"

"Doesn't matter. Get off me."

"You are going to make me do this," he sighed.

My blood chilled. What did he mean by that?

I pushed him off of me simultaneously as a collar fastened around my neck. I tugged at it, but it would not release. "What did you do?"

"Rest."

My body grew weightless, and my eyelids were heavy. I fought to remain awake. Was I going to sleep on Matt's command?

"Calm. I want you to remain calm. I'm not in the mood to fight, but I don't want you to sleep just yet," he added. "The collar will take some getting used to."

My body relaxed while my mind raged. It was as though—I wasn't in control. I clawed at the collar. My neck stung from attempts to take it off, but it remained.

"It's a spell of binding. I had it developed for outsiders. Demons are dangerous as they are known to turn on their summoners, but then another thought came to mind with yesterday's little incident. I could also use it if the Sphinx took control without my direction. Bane nearly put us in a bind. If the ATF hadn't shot him, I would've."

"You took my will."

He caressed my face. "I didn't want to, Kitten, but you have too much of your grandmother in you."

He kissed the side of my mouth. "It's temporary. I promise. I'll even wipe your memory so it won't leave a bad impression. That is what I was working on before you stole into the Craftorium. Did you think I wouldn't sense your power? You have a subtle draw that is more than just your beauty."

Damn. I hadn't thought of that. I always sensed magic, but I hadn't considered that others could perceive me and mine.

"You." I tried to lunge at him.

My body refused to take any real action. I wanted to relax on the floor.

"There's no point. As long as I live, you belong to me." He leaned close to my ear. "And I will never let you go."

I wanted to head-butt, bite, or do something violent to him. However, my body wanted to lay under him. To enjoy the weight of him on top of me. He wouldn't have me again if I had to destroy both of us to stop him.

He pulled the cork out of the potion and then waved the contents past his nose. "I know what you're thinking, and as much as the fantasy of taking you while you wear the collar is tempting, I won't. You'll never forgive that. But I can't let you go on with your short-sighted attempts at stopping me either."

He poured the potion out on the floor. "I want—"

I gathered the potion particles and shoved them down his throat with one burst of mental strength. Matt sputtered and coughed, then yanked me close to him.

For the first time, there was no cool heat. The potion worked. It bound his aura, but it would weaken if I remained close. I had to get the collar removed and get away.

"What did you do?" He snarled.

"Remove the collar, and I'll tell you."

He raised his hand. Nothing happened. The color drained from his face as he realized his power was gone. "You *bound* me?"

"Apparently, we had the same idea," I answered. "You are done."

His eyes widened. I could see the cloudy despair in them. They darted back and forth several times before they rested on me. "Not as long as I have you. Your power will fix this eventually. You and I will—"

BAM.

Matt frowned. Blood dribbled from his lips as the lethargy that held me in place lifted. I shoved him off me and then scooted further away from him. I snatched the collar off and set it on fire. No one else would do what he did. I watched the metal melt as the leather burned.

Never.

Lauren stepped onto the dais a breath later with her arm held out and her finger still on the trigger of a gun. Her blank stare chilled my blood when she blinked once. Her eyes widened as she whimpered at what she had done.

She hurried over to him and held him in her arms tossing the gun beside her. She made shushing sounds as she rocked him. I moved further away from them. Shooting Matt didn't make her an ally. If anything, it made her cuckoo. There was nothing copacetic about the loving way she held Matt's cooling body when she was the one who shot him.

"He's not the same," she said finally. "He shouldn't have gone through time. If I hadn't called Oya, he would have been mine and NOT YOURS."

I raised my hands when she screamed the last two words. Crazy or not, I would not allow her to take me out. I preferred a non-magical solution since I still had to get out of the tower. "He's not mine."

Lauren glared at me. "Get out or die. I won't let you steal his legacy."

Then alarms shrilled throughout the building. I recognized the evacuation protocol. Lauren was going to destroy the tower. Safety protocols would protect the majority of the personnel, hence the aural signature database, but I was not so sure about the reporter or me—more on my plate.

She didn't have to tell me twice. I ran.

42

uyen

"Anchoram habemus." A sensation of completeness settled in me as the anchor dropped in the eighth-floor stairwell of our hotel, followed by a heavy heart. I wouldn't know this spell or have this option if not for Pandora. It didn't seem right to do it without her. I knew that was sentimentality eating at me, but I couldn't help it. I fell hard and fast for her. It was scary how much I wanted to be with her.

That was not how I worked. I was in the lust phase, albeit an intense one. What would have made sense was that we dated another few months, she lived with me, and then I'd formally ask her to marry me. It may have been born out of horniness, but my feelings were real. She was the one. Oya messed it all up.

She and Pandora were one—I loved her too. That was the part that terrified me. Oya was a goddess. Already in the timeline, they accidentally made Matt a dictator demi-god. What could happen *on purpose*? Matt I could deal with, but her....

No.

I already stabbed Pandora once to stop the transformation. There was no way I could do it again. It nearly killed me seeing that rebar sticking out of her chest while her life's blood gushed—the stillness of her body when she stopped breathing and the joy when she healed herself. I couldn't.

I'd rather watch the world burn. And that was a problem. Matt's way was the same as the non-tolerant mundane's, save we were the victors. It wasn't right. Matt had to be stopped. Then Tonya could take over Camera.

And Pan…

Our time was over. I would have to send her back. Maybe there would be enough change in the timeline that Oya would remain dormant.

"Are you sure about placing it here?" Tonya touched my shoulder. "You look like you are reconsidering."

"No. It should be fine." I doubted anyone would stumble across the bridge once I dropped the other side. Most people took the elevators when they had to travel more than a couple of floors, and for the magical adventurist that stumbled across it, there was a password, *trái táo*. Apple was a random enough word that it was unlikely someone would use it while also standing in the doorway *and* speaking Vietnamese. "That's what passwords are for."

She grinned. "Love the password, by the way. It's one of my favorite words to say."

With her mercurial mood the last couple of days, I wasn't sure if she meant it or not. "Then it should be easy for you to remember. Just don't forget the article, and you should be fine."

I let the door shut and started for the elevator landing. After Pandora's tantrum shook the building, everyone was on high alert for anything odd or anything construed as shady. For the sake of appearances, I'd ride the elevator and let the staff see us leave.

"Okay. What is it?" she asked.

I adjusted my tie. I hated wearing anything so close to my neck. It was my plan to change the boss in the plan to Max since a White male would make a better cover, especially in the south, until the argument separated us. With Max and Trina looking for Pandora, it was up to me to play the boss in our cover story. Tonya would be my assistant since that was what she established when she checked us in.

"Nothing is wrong, except this damn tie choking me, and we're down to half our team." I switched to Vietnamese when a couple of suits from Texas joined us in front of the elevators.

"Howdy, Miss," one of them said to Tonya.

The other nodded his head while giving us both flat eyes.

"Are you and that Dong fella headin' to a meeting?" the friendly one asked.

I kept my face blank and spoke, *"So he's going to ignore me blatantly?"*

Tonya nodded and then replied in Vietnamese, *"It's not like he wanted to make nice anyway."*

"What did he say?" The friendly one asked while his companion sucked in his cheeks as though he sucked on a lemon.

"Mr. Duong was curious about why you didn't address him," she answered.

The friendly one turned pink. "Tell him my apologies and konnichiwa."

I fought not to cringe. Some people were antagonistic to those who spoke multiple languages in public. If they discovered I was a native speaker, they'd cause issues.

"You heard what he said," Tonya replied. *"I'll leave the response to you."*

"Chào buổi sáng ban." I held out my hand to go with my good morning.

"He said Good morning," she translated.

"Well, hell, I don't know how to respond, but ciao boo sang bun to you too." He pumped my hand twice, and the elevator car thankfully opened.

We all went into the elevator, and the two Texans fell into a private conversation. I never understood why people clammed up in elevators. It was terrible enough riding with strangers. The crushing silence was worse. The entire ride was like the world stopped. Even the insipid going-ons of strangers were better than leaving me to my thoughts.

I knew what it meant to be empty. Pandora and I didn't have long together, but I knew chemistry with another when it happened. There were so few that I gelled with on a social level that I tried to keep them close. It was why it was so hard to let Tonya go, and Matt had an opportunity to create a temporary alliance with me.

It was a weakness of mine.

Pandora's absence hit harder. I kept dreaming about her the entire night. Each time I reached for her warm body, I found cold, lifeless, empty sheets. I meant everything I told her in the hospital. What my brain didn't catch on to until yesterday was what that meant.

She lied to me.

We would hash that out once we resolved the immediate situation, but Pandora was a goddess, and that "complete" comment churned my insides. It sounded as though she had changed.

I knew she did.

That kiss—it was the same if not more intense. With it, I wanted to kneel at her feet and ask for forever.

That was reckless. It had to have a magical reason. Perhaps her presence had a compulsion attached to it if someone knew the truth. Except the others didn't react any differently. I was the only one that wanted her more.

I was just as stupid as Matt. Maybe it was best that she left.

The Senate vote would be tumultuous without the added danger of us losing control. A magical attack of the magnitude that Oya's powers could pull off could easily set Matt's plans in motion fifty years early. That might have been his intention.

I shivered as the elevator doors opened.

"You alright?" Tonya put her hand on my arm.

I patted her hand then nodded.

"Looks like lemonade enjoys brown sugar," the unfriendly businessman muttered. "Explains a lot."

Tonya narrowed her eyes. I held up my hand in an "I got this" gesture.

I gathered a fine layer of moisture from the vase in the landing and then slid it under his foot as he joined other businessmen in their party. He went down, hard. After he collected himself, the jerk rested against his companion for a moment and stood straight only to wince in pain. He hopped over to one of the lobby armchairs as several watched. I held my satisfaction until we reached the valet station.

"Mr. Duong, your car is ready." The valet dropped the keys into my hand before he opened the door for Tonya. Once she settled in the car, he opened my door, and we left the hotel driveway.

"You are so petty. I love it." Tonya clapped her hands together.

"Damn right. We have the same right to stay in the hotel as he did." I turned down Eighth Street and then on to Broad. "If I didn't want to bother with witch cracks on top of his racism, I would have laughed."

"I know, right." Tonya leaned back in the chair. "It's nice to see you smile again."

The incident was mildly amusing—hell, it was satisfying even if it was wrong. However, it hardly qualified as a life-altering experience, nor did it fill the void.

"There you go again with the hangdog look for the ages. Out with it."

We merged on to I-95 toward DC. The plan was to scope out the terrain, see what new security measures were in place, drop an anchor, then head back to the hotel—total deniability since they would not see us leaving the hotel tomorrow.

Tonya sighed. "You know."

"No, I don't."

"Fine." She threw up her hands. "I'll start. What's really going on between you and the goddess girl?"

"Goddess girl?"

"If you keep asking questions and don't provide some answers, you'll regret it. Out with it."

As if talking to her about my sex life wouldn't be weird. "We don't talk about sex with other people."

"We didn't need to until three months ago," she replied. "Look, you and I *used* to sleep together. You're the one making it weird."

"I'm making it weird when you act as though you pissed a circle around me and no other females dare cross."

"Damn right. I can't make it easy for some random heifer to slide in your sheets. It's a moral imperative."

"A moral imperative?" I barked a laugh. "That's rich. I suppose I should do the same for you then?"

"Hell yeah. It'll make the guys think twice if they want this kit kat. My friend is ready to pounce on anyone who doesn't come correct. It's best friend code."

I glanced at her. While her tone was pleasant, her face was severe. "The whole time, you were hazing Pan."

She shrugged. "You call it hazing. I call it testing her worthiness. Tomato, tah-mato."

"I can't believe you."

"You know me inside and out. I guess you weren't paying attention," she said primly.

"I'm a guy. I was enjoying the kit kat while trying to figure out how not to hurt you." Tonya was a piece of work. "Pandora and I were complicated."

"You mean she scares you," she said.

Pandora didn't. My reaction did. I would let her burn the world if she wanted. "I love her."

Her breath hitched slightly. "She turned you out, huh?"

Technically. "I'm serious here."

"Sorry. I'll behave. You want to worship at her temple. I get it. And she wants you, too. What's the problem?"

"I'm in love with a goddess. A woman who's thousands of years old and can turn the world to ash. She's the one who will destroy the east coast in the future we know." Not on purpose, but that didn't change the fact that she did it.

Tonya shivered. "Thanks for reminding me not to go too far antagonizing her. Shaking the hotel was a little scary. So you have a powerful girlfriend. Congrats to you. I don't see a problem."

"What if she decides to take over? We've been worried about Matt and Obscura. She's as—" My almost words brought a chill over me. I gripped the wheel to contain the tremors. It was out there, my fear. Pandora lied to me. She had the power to do whatever she wanted. "I need to concentrate on the road."

I turned on the radio.

"So it's like that, then?"

I turned up the volume. Tonya didn't say anything else. She crossed her arms. Her forefinger tapped her bicep in an angry tattoo. Judging by her body language, I'd have to come up with something else to distract her, or she'd explode long before we got to DC in a few hours.

Diva's latest song, *Lie*, played on the radio. The smooth strings settled my nerves as her sultry, melodious voice sang. "Caught in a lie. I'm begging you not to go. I love you so much. Craving your touch. I can't go on this way."

A vision of Pandora's haunted eyes flashed into my mind, and I stomped on the brake. Horns blared as a couple of cars zoomed past me.

"Go. Go. Go!" Tonya yelled.

I floored it, wheels screeching as more horns blared around and behind us. My heart thrummed against my ribs, but there was no bump from behind. Tonya reached over and changed the station as Diva continued to croon about her mistakes and hurting her man.

"It's too soon," she muttered.

I couldn't argue, considering my breath still puffed out of me as though I had run a marathon. The song was too on the nose. Pandora didn't beg to stay because she knew I needed her gone. I was the one who loved her and craved her touch.

I am so whipped it's not even funny.

"Okay, I can't stand it anymore. You almost killed me back there with a love song. That girl has you wrapped around her finger so tight you might as well put a ring on it." Tonya pointed to a rest stop sign. "Pull over. We won't die if I'm driving."

She exaggerated. It was one moment of weakness. The near-accident focused me. I doubted we would have any more trouble. "I'm fine."

"Quyen Andrew Duong, if you don't pull into the rest stop, we will have a problem."

I rolled my eyes at her but signaled to get in the right lane."

She crossed her arms. "That's what I thought."

"You didn't have to break out my entire name like I'm a kid or something." We rode down the entrance lane to the brick rest stop with a LOVE sign for visitors. All the rest stops in Virginia reminded me of houses with their friendly layout and archway portals.

Love.

This place was the last location I needed to be. "Let's just switch and go."

I parked the car.

"At the risk of being the sassy Black friend, what the hell is your problem?" Tonya was wound up. We were still in the car, so her neck was the only part of her bobbing in rhythm to her statement.

We had someplace to be. "I don't want to talk about it. We're in a time crunch."

She narrowed her eyes. It was all the warning I received before she grabbed my wrist and bent it in a direction that ensured compliance.

"Try again. *We're in a time crunch.*"

"Ow—okay."

She released me.

"I don't know what to do, and I miss her." I rubbed my injury. She didn't break anything, but my hand did smart. "Happy now?"

Her eyes flared then she shook her head. "Hardly. This is what we're going to do. We're going to go to DC, solve the immediate problem, and then look for Pandora. Then you can talk, have makeup sex, and get your head back in the game."

The sex part appealed to my base instincts, but that would just dig me in deeper. Thoughts of being inside Pandora aside, one discussion would not solve the issue. "I can't."

"How are you so complicated?" Tonya threw her hands up. "You're cool with the friends with benefits thing, but you fall in love with a girl and punk out? Get out of the car and let me drive."

I did. The conversation made me doubt we would make it to DC in my current state. As we passed each other, Tonya embraced me. I held her for a moment then she released me without a word. Her silent support eased my heart somewhat.

And it was better than her interrogation tactics. I opened the passenger door and got in. I buckled my seat belt as she turned on the car.

"—tower has been destroyed. Downtown Richmond is in chaos due to protests in the street. City officials ask residents and workers to stay inside so investigators and first responders can assess the situation."

My heart sank.

"Again, Obscura Tower has been destroyed. Downtown Richmond—"

I opened the door. "I have to get back."

"Whoa. Whoa." Tonya tried to grab my arm.

I slipped out of her reach and was out the door. She cursed as she shut the car off and took after me. The rest stop was by no means empty on a Thursday morning in March. The March weather made some travelers linger on the Welcome Center's benches in the balmy sixty-five degree sun. Those were the people who watched us. Their too eager eyes focused on us as though they were about to enjoy a show. It was the moment of clarity I needed.

"You're right." I held out my hand to her, to the apparent disappointment of many since their attention instantly waned. One gossip still held their phone as though they were ready for the slightest turn in the situation. I knew how to squash that.

"Thanks?"

Tonya took my hand, and I drew her into a hug. "Does the guy with the brown hair and green t-shirt still have his phone out?" She squeezed me once, then released me. "Let's get something to drink, then stretch our legs. I think this trip has us both crazy."

We walked through a brick archway. Automatic doors parted for us. We walked past the touristy information, holding pamphlets about the area below a giant map of Virginia. On either side of the large room were entrances to public restrooms, and past them, the vending area. Machines with food and drink lined the walls leading to another archway, the RVs' entry, and large trucks' entry.

I went to the one with iced green tea. "Want one?"

"Yeah. Make mine a diet. I need to lay off the sugar." She slapped her butt.

"I know I have no say in the matter, but you're fine the way you are." I put money in the machine. A man sitting at a table near the machine glanced at her behind, gave a thumbs up, then left. "Apparently, others agree."

"Hazard of living in this society. As long as he stays quiet and keeps his hands off, that's his business. Now, what's the plan?"

I wanted to hug her again. "I will return to Richmond and catch up to you if I can."

"Or *we* go back to Richmond, ensure everything is good, and Pandora is safe because that has goddess retribution all over it. Obscura Tower's destruction is a bit of a question mark. I'm not down with the innocents dying, but the organization could burn for all I care."

"It has its purposes. Our people need a coven to liaise with the government and all the more reason to go to DC. We may have to contend with angry Obscura *and* rogue Camera. DC is important."

"So are you, and so is this. You freaked out twice today about Pandora. She means a lot to you. I respect that, so no more trying to murder me. Now let's do this." She smirked. "Seriously, I'm a badass, but I can't stop Camera alone. I at least need a hype man as I confront the NoVa cell. And for this part, you need a hype woman."

I reached into the breast pocket of my blazer to pull out the tiny piece of cement I chipped out of the hotel stairway. "Then we drop the anchor here and figure it out."

She put her hand over mine. "Or *we* go back to the car and drive back. It's the lesser of the two evils. The ride will give you time to figure out the next moves since we're only thirty minutes away. If we're seen in the hotel again so quickly, they will out us, and we won't have options. In the car, we can join the mass hysteria."

Tonya was my rock. She had a valid point. The least I could do was pull it together and stop acting like the worried boyfriend. The tower would be considered the second incident of "crazy devil magic," as I overheard one of the staff say in the hall last night. Coming in by car would make sense. There were protestors in the area, so the damage was likely the self-destruct mechanism Matt and I built into the foundation before I left.

That meant the casualty count was low or non-existent as long as he didn't change it. I designed the spell to transport everyone away and destroy the building without affecting the surrounding ones. It was a failsafe to protect us if we ever became enemies of the state. We didn't want our knowledge and craft used against other practitioners.

It was the only scenario that made sense. An anti-magic organization would have collateral damage. The news would report deaths. The area would be locked down instead of the news asking people to stay indoors. The city didn't want it to get bigger than it already was. If Pandora has something to do with the self-destruct—which I suspected—she was okay.

She had to be.

Why did I have to think of the worst?

"Because losing her is easier than fighting for her," Tonya replied.

"What? Why did you say that?" I stopped.

"Sorry. I was looking at that poster for a Romeo and Juliet remake at the Aria Theater." She pointed to a lacquered 11 x 17 poster of a couple performing on stage. Their expressions were tragic, and sure enough, the tagline underneath was, as Tonya said.

I lost it.

"Oh," was all I could get out of intelligence as we headed to the car.

Tonya drove. We both knew I could not be trusted. I wanted to use magic to arrive, but that was the last thing we needed to do. DC still had to happen as there was no telling what the situation would be when we arrived at the hotel. I selected it for its proximity to Obscura so we could monitor it from a block away without appearing out of place. It was time to act on the forethought.

We'd park in the garage and do street surveillance when we arrived. Just like the Vernon Street disaster, there were people who mouthed off about what they saw and what they thought for the two of us to overhear. We could sift out fact from fiction. There was a coffee shop across the street. It would also be a wealth of information if it weren't damaged.

"You've got your game face on. That's the Drew I know. Or is it Quyen these days?" She teased me, but I knew what she asked.

"Drew's fine. I prefer Quyen. I use Drew around people who can't say my name right and people I don't trust."

"That amounts to the same thing in my book," she replied. "Quyen. I like it. It's real, and I don't have a history with it."

Point. Using my first name did kind of clear the past away. I could look at it as my past. It was a line of demarcation. "Less drama."

"Nah. Pandora knows we're a package deal." She smirked. "And yes, I will be on my best behavior unless she acts crazy...or you do."

"Anyway," I stared at the interstate. We weren't far from our exit. "Park the car in the garage. Then we'll go on foot."

"Recon. I like it. I'll hit the coffee shop. I could use a snack, and I know the barista there. Her name is Mara."

"If it's still there," I remarked.

"It is. The protection spells were laid by over a hundred kitchen witches when the place opened. We wanted a safe space for kids coming into their power until they could be placed somewhere."

"I didn't know that."

"Not all of us come from secretive magical families. We have to learn the long way."

The jab stung, but she had a point. I grew up knowing and studying. If I hadn't broken our rule of secrecy, I'd probably still have some of them in my life. The ones that I didn't side with chose Obscura or weren't scared of me anyway. "It may be a target if it's untouched."

"Oh, we warded the whole block and the Laveau building. *Portents* is the keystone."

"Is there anything else I should know?"

"It's Richmond, and I'm the HWIC. Head Witch in Charge."

"You never lack confidence, do you?" I laughed. It warmed my otherwise numb body. I didn't know what waited for me in Richmond. Was Matt dead? Was Pandora? My throat tightened at the last thought.

No. Pandora was powerful. She had almost all of the forty-two powers along with Oya. The likelihood she didn't escape, or Matt, was low.

"Obscura Tower was warded too, but when we set it up, I focused on member safety rather than the building's integrity."

We pulled into the parking garage.

"So then Pandora's safe?"

"I don't know what changes Matt and Lauren made in evacuation protocols, and they took months to set up. Kitchen witches and heavy lifters."

Tonya put her hand on my shoulder. "That's the difference between you two. You try to preserve life, and he preserves his interests. No matter what, you're going to do the right thing."

"What makes you say that?"

"Because I know you." She winked. "Game face on. Gossip about goddess girl later."

I shook my head as we exited the car. We entered the fray on Seventh Street, which was a little congested. A block ahead on Eighth street, everything was in chaos. People flooded the sidewalk and asphalt to the point that the roadway was barely walkable as they crowded around pockets of protestors. A news van with a camera operator on the roof swept the area sniffing for a story while their next big break roamed below.

"Stay close to me," I said into her ear, then pointed in the general direction Obscura Tower used to occupy. The eight-story, gray stone building used to stand stately amongst the other properties. It was our first headquarters once we decided to make our presence known to the world. Seeing the tower missing from the familiar skyline spurred me into action. I needed to see with my eyes if the situation was salvageable—more importantly, could anyone have survived.

I shoved past a group of loiterers.

"Watch it, Bitch," some yelled out.

"Asshole," another muttered as I moved through the sea of onlookers and hate. Once past them, their rants were swallowed by the general noise and collective screams of nonsense.

Tonya's grip on the back of my blazer remained strong. For her to stay so close, she must have elbowed and shoved several people. It wasn't an impossible task maneuvering through the crowd if one enjoyed swimming in molasses. We took every foot we gained, and it was only a matter of time before someone shoved back. If that happened, a mass fight would break out with so much tension in the air.

Eventually, we spilled out onto an even more crowded section of Marshall St. unable to get any further. We had a block to go to get to Ninth. We wouldn't get anywhere when it took fifteen minutes just to get half a block. The density of people would only increase.

"We can't see anything with this wall of people. Let's try to go through the back," Tonya suggested.

"What about *Portents*?"

Going to Seventh Street and using Traveler's Ally was a better plan. Everyone was there for the drama not to necessarily get to the site. We would encounter less resistance approaching from the other side. It was why I chose that path for my exit months ago.

It feels like years.

The irony of being back in the same place again after my escape months ago was poetic. I wanted to bring Obscura down. Somebody did. And I was still in the same place.

"Right. Except for the back of *Portent*s is on Ninth too. We'll never get across in this crowd."

She stared at the crowd from our pocket oasis. Traveler's Ally was by no means empty, but at least we could get our bearings without being accosted. "But I guess we were committed when we came out here."

She was right. I had to know what happened before I went to DC.

"Ding dong, the witch should be dead," the crowd chanted.

Tonya frowned and shook her head. "They are ruining my childhood."

Both paths were complicated. We were damned if we did, damned if we didn't. *We might as well keep moving forward.*

I motioned to her to come with me. She grabbed the back of my blazer again as the boiling crowd absorbed us. In the center of the chaos was a mix of several chants that were mostly indistinguishable from "ding dong, the witch should be dead."

The closer to the chanting bigots we got, the thicker the crowd, until we reached a wall of counter-protestors yelling obscenities and their own chants. I collided with someone when Tonya stumbled against me. The low buzz of magical energy made me and the person pause. An African-American man lifted his chin and then went back to screaming at the ding dongs. There were three people between us and the opposing people-wall of hate. The tension in the air would ignite at any moment. The police stood on the sidelines, most of them with stoic dismay. A few of them betrayed their views by either focusing on the ding dongs or us.

It would be a slaughter.

Someone needed to do something fast—

"He has a gun," a voice sliced between the chants.

There was a brief silence before people began to dodge, run, and push forward. The wall of bodies that separated us opened with a scream.

Several "Oh, Shit!" sounded near me.

BOOM.

"No!" I covered Tonya as I called water from the surrounding buildings' hydrants and fire suppression systems. I surrounded us with a water bubble while putting up a wall where I last saw the division of mundanes and practitioners, then dropped it on everyone.

The stagnant water from the suppression systems reeked of old socks, but the dowsing did the job. Everyone stared at each other, drenched but not fighting. It wouldn't last, but at least there was an opportunity for the authorities to defuse the situation.

"It's the witches," a man yelled, pointing at Tonya and me.

We were the only ones standing and dry. Great, I made us targets.

"Yes, we're witches," I yelled back. "We're also people. We're your brothers, sisters, lovers, and parents. Keep that in mind when you aim at us."

Tonya put her hand on my shoulder. "And that you shot first. Magic is not about violence. People are violent. If you are so afraid of violence, perhaps you should look in the mirror and start there."

The man stood waving his gun.

I kept a moisture layer around the weapon. With all eyes on me, any more overt magic would spook another crazy to attack. The insane mundane was too drenched and hopped up on adrenalin to notice that I disabled his gun, but that wouldn't last if someone didn't step in.

"We're going to burn you at the stake like the good old days. Ding—"

"We're only human," I yelled over him. "We're only human."

Tonya joined me in the mantra, which spurred others to chime in. I didn't intend to join the protest, but I couldn't let that nutcase churn the crowd again. He didn't see us as people, and nothing would change as long as the authorities remained on the fence. It didn't matter that there were some sympathizers and maybe even some practitioners among them. Someone had to do something. Magic would not solve the mob problem. Even if a practitioner were powerful and subtle enough, which Pandora was, it wouldn't work.

Besides, she wasn't here.

I owned that.

"This is the Richmond Police. We order that this crowd disperse and allow us to come through." A voice boomed over a loudspeaker. "Again, this is the Richmond Police. Clear the way. This is an illegal gathering, and you are disturbing the peace."

I watched the man who tried to stir the ding dongs. He put his weapon away, smiled, and ran his finger across his neck. There was at least a centimeter of water in the street. It would be nothing for me to dole out petty justice. I wanted to trip the guy or throw rank water down his throat—filthy water for a foul mouth. Except then I would be like him, and those watching wouldn't understand.

Violence and fear gained temporary peace until the opposition weakened and one or both sides were eliminated.

That was Matt's way of doing things, but not mine.

"Sir, we need you to stand down, and no funny business like you did before," the loudspeaker—megaphone advised.

It was more apparent with them closer. The officer wearing a black kevlar vest pointed to me. A phalanx of officers in full riot gear and assault rifles flanked him while others focused on the crowd.

No good deed goes unpunished, just like always.

The chanting on both sides dimmed so that I heard it from the back of the crowd.

Tonya and the guy I bumped into earlier stepped in front of me. They briefly exchanged a nod. She eased her stance. Even in a business suit, she made an intimidating figure, and with the three of us together we appeared like the leaders of the protest. Everything was going sideways. We were supposed to be recon—hell, we weren't supposed to be here at all. They might shoot her and our new ally. It wasn't like everyone was in the calmest state of mind.

Then I'd have to lead.

I stepped in front of them with hands raised, palms out in the universal sign for surrender to the police. "I will cooperate."

"So will we," the man said.

"Thanks, friend. I'm Quyen. What is your name, by the way?" I watched as a couple of the officers peeled off to approach us.

"Nelson," he answered. "I'm a civil rights lawyer. This will not stand."

"Welcome to the coalition, Nelson," Tonya said as the police grabbed us and wrenched our hands behind our backs.

The ding dongs cheered while our side closed in around us.

"No." I raised a short water wall between the crowd and us. "Work through the system, don't become vigilantes. Write your leaders and hold them accountable. Show them your power as a citizen, just like they used theirs to cause this. Let them see the power of the coalition. We're only human."

The chant started up again as the police yanked us through the crowd. They pushed us into the back of a truck. It was the kind of police van one saw in films. In real life, it wasn't dispassionate or even amusing. My heart raced. They were arresting us. I still had to find Pandora and keep Matt from enacting his plan. He was probably orchestrating the whole thing. I would potentially owe him a favor, and we'd have to work together for a while longer.

And what about Pan?

I stared out the open doors as they shoved Tonya into the truck after us when I met Pan's crimson gaze. She pushed through the crowd heading toward us. She was alive, whole, and pissed. Part of me wanted her to be the calvary, but the cost was too high. She'd be exposed, or worse, one of the ding dongs could attack. A battle would begin—magic was sure to be involved. Pan might lose control. They might kill her—no.

I wouldn't let that happen.

I shook my head. Pandora paused in her progress. I mouthed the word "no" as the officers shut the doors. One of them slapped the door a few times, and the truck pulled away from the dispersing crowd.

Through the small windows of the vehicle, I saw her melt into the shrinking mass.

One less thing to worry about.

First, I would deal with the immediate situation, then she and I would talk.

43

andora

I stood on the porch of my father's ancestral home in Stuart, Virginia. For some reason, I couldn't bring myself to knock and intrude on my grandparents' lives any further. They'd also want to know what happened with Quyen, Tonya, and the vote. I was sure that the media had so many spins on their take of events that it created confusion even for those in the know. If I weren't there in Richmond, I knew I would be confused.

It had been difficult allowing the police to take Quyen during the protest. Freeing him would have made it worse. The tension had been high—it still was two days later. My intervention would have stirred the crowd, and he probably feared that I would lose control. He didn't have to worry. The Sphinx was no more.

When I became my whole self, the beast side of me—my wrath—died with it. Too much magic absorption would lead to an entirely different scenario if I were overloaded. It would be volatile still, but not apocalyptic. It was the balance of a goddess living a mortal life.

Restraint was to become my mantra. I used most of it when Quyen told me not to help him. He was my mate. It was my duty to protect him as it was his to protect me, though he impressed me with his ability to rule. He wooed the crowd with his charisma and action. Otherwise, there would have been fatalities besides Lauren and Matt.

Reports of their deaths set many practitioners on edge. Most of them did as Quyen asked and went through official channels. The rest turned up at the Capitol for the vote the next day—with Camera. I was there as well, in the shadows. Quyen wanted to prevent Camera from turning the mundanes on us. I ensured that the masses remained a movement and not a riot since he could not lead them personally.

No lives were lost as my mate desired, and no Sphinx appeared to kick off the apocalypse or to unleash the nation of Obscura. Once done, I made my way back to Fairy Stone. Quyen would want to link up with everyone once he was out of jail. We would have to decide what to do about Obscura and Camera with both covens now leaderless.

We could reconnect.

With that thought in mind, I rang the doorbell. The curtains in the small side window stirred slightly before an audible "Oh" sounded through the door.

Trina drew me into a fierce bear hug. Max stood behind her for a moment, then joined us.

Her thoughts flowed into my mind like a tsunami after an earthquake. There was too much to process. I eased out of her embrace—their lock on me—then sighed. "May I come in?"

For an answer, she furrowed her eyebrows and yanked me into the house as though I planned to escape. Once I was behind the closed door, she visibly relaxed.

Really?

"We were worried. Where did you go?" She signed.

"I went to gather some ingredients, then to Obscura Tower to take care of Matt." It was an oversimplification. Hopefully, they wouldn't ask about details.

"Then you did kill him," Trina signed.

"That explains the crater we saw on the news," Max signed. "I don't approve of killing, but that guy was out of control. I gotta ask though, weren't there subtler means?"

"I didn't kill him. Lauren did, then activated the building's self-destruct spells. I bound his powers, then she interrupted." The memory of him using that collar on me elicited a chill down my spine. Quyen's power saved me. The symbolism was not lost on me—the moment I settled on the diplomatic approach, violence destroyed Matt while my mate's power protected me. There was no doubt that we were destined for each other. I knew it the moment I read his journal. It was all that I would have as I waited for him to get out of jail and forgive me.

"That's crazy. Wasn't Lauren in love with him or his assistant or something?" Trina signed. "It's hard to keep thoughts and dreams straight when someone is unconscious."

That's right. She listened to my mind when I was out, probably more than once. "It's less crowded in there than last time, but more is going on."

"What does that mean?" Max signed. "Is Oya about to take over?"

"No, I am not taking over because I am now whole."

They both blinked at me for a few moments. Would they panic or reject me? I prepared for either. I knew rejection was a possibility when I set out on my quest. I could cope if they didn't dig my new situation.

"So you're safe?" Trina asked.

I nodded,

They both let out a sigh.

"One less thing." Max shrugged. "I don't know if I can take all this drama. I thought those Camera nuts and Obscura fools were going to blow up DC when the news of the Grand Magister's death spread."

"Quyen's speech in Richmond calmed most of it."

Trina nodded. "I didn't know he was so passionate. He didn't seem like the same guy that sat in our living room days ago."

"That feels like a lifetime ago after being kidnapped and escaping the ATF. Speaking of which, we appear to be in the clear, but you need to keep a low profile for a while. They had a sketch artist draw a picture of you that was fairly decent, but they think it was Tonya, so they have 'you' in custody already. Deputy Wright came by, but we haven't seen hide nor hair of him since yesterday. I think we are in the clear."

"He may be back when Quyen comes back to link up with us."

My heart fluttered at the thought. He shouldn't be in jail for long with the publicity he got. Then he could use the bridge to come back to Fairy Stone under the authorities' noses. And when he forgave me, I would convince him to return to the future with me.

"You're going back, aren't you?" Trina signed.

Her face held resignation and sadness. I could relate. There was no telling what my new history would be or if I would truly experience it. Stopping Matt would not end all of my sadness. I didn't expect it to change my past outside of the Sphinx attack. Max would live. I may still lose Trina but keep my parents.

I hugged her tight.

"I'm not leaving right away," I said into her mind.

I figured a year, perhaps a year and a half tops. It would be enough time to search for any other time travelers, help dismantle Obscura and for the coven to stand or fall. I wasn't sure if it was a good idea for the organization to continue, but it was part of Quyen's legacy. Working with him, we could accomplish everything faster, and if he wanted—no, I couldn't stay. My soul was always present, but I could not risk splitting myself again, nor would I want to become a child and make Quyen wait until I reached the appropriate age.

I had to go back.

"The lack of an answer makes me think that is a yes," Max signed. "How long will you stay?"

"In theory, I have until my birth, but it would be too destructive for me to stay more than a year or so. I don't want to influence Dad or my birth mom—their relationship may not be solid as a rock, but I want that to be their choice. I also don't want to lose my mom." The sooner I left, the better.

"What about Quyen?" Trina asked. "A relationship across time is a lot."

"I want him to come with me." I took a deep breath to soothe my heart. "He will be angry for a while, but we can work it out when he returns."

"And what makes you think he'll come back?" Max asked.

"He's coven, and we have a destiny." It was a sentimental answer but no less accurate. He was my mate. I crossed time for him. It would only make sense that he would do the same.

44

 uyen

1.5 A.Q.

I leaned against the boardwalk balcony outside The Gaylord National Hotel. There was a chilly January wind across the National Harbor. Usually, the DC weather, while mild, was colder than the fifty degrees it was outside. Even if it was thirty degrees, the fresh air did me good. It was a break from the Secret Service and Obscura battlemages in my security detail.

Security.

I had people to watch my back, ones I paid as Grand Magister. The past nineteen months after Obscura Tower's destruction and the Senate stalemate vote had been surreal. Tonya assumed leadership of Camera. We changed the cell style organization to covens.

Nelson turned out to be a more significant ally than we thought. He became chief legal counsel of the Magical Consortium, our party within the government. Both of us worked closely with him—her more so considering I was Tonya's Man of Honor at their wedding two months ago.

The world wasn't perfect. The ding dongs sent a pipe bomb to my office last week, but there was a promise with the WTCH Bill, Working Towards a Coalition of Healing. In it, there were several statutes to protect both practitioners and mundanes. Public opinion was overall positive. We still had more details to iron out before it would go for a vote in the spring, which meant Tonya, Nelson, and I were schmoozing at events garnering support, being seen, and being palpable to those who might fear us and those who were allies.

It was a strange time. My family still wouldn't talk to me—except Thuy. She came by the office a year ago with a check to pay me back and left a picture of my new little cousin. I ended up hiring her as my investigations lead. We spent Tet together last year, and we planned to spend this one too.

Except it wasn't enough.

I missed Pandora. She was still in the past, in Fairy Stone. My private investigator in the area gave me weekly reports. I emailed Max occasionally, but his emails didn't say much and nothing about Pandora. He was probably angry with me. I meant to return to Fairy Stone, but the press and the government closely watched me the first few months. Then Obscura's replacement leader contacted me asking me to take over. I wouldn't leave them to their own devices. The next thing I knew, almost a year had gone by, then another six months.

"This is a private area, ma'am."

James, ever glued to my side, hovered at my elbow. "It's Pandora, Grand Magister."

I whirled around. She stood in a floor-length dark blue gown with a black swirl pattern, one of those one-shoulder dresses that drew my focus to her neck and chest until a shift in her stance gave me her entire leg to fantasize about.

"She's fine," left my lips instead of "it's fine." The sentiment was the same, even if my brain was muddled in fantasy. James moved to his idea of private distance from us.

"Keep in mind, she was the last to see the previous Grand Magister and the Magia Lectore."

"Lauren shot him and then initiated the evacuation protocols," Pandora said.

There was no tact or softness in her tone at dropping the horrific news. I couldn't blame her after James accused her of murder and warned me in the same breath. "So that's what happened? I will make sure everyone knows the truth."

"Lauren wouldn't—" James bristled.

Pandora stared at him hard. "Surely you noticed how different he was. I bet he trusted you more as though *you* were his lead and not Peters."

He adjusted his tie as though he considered his words.

"There was a reason for that," Pandora continued. "I'm not going to get into it, but when she found out, she killed him to protect his legacy."

It was a vague explanation. However, I could fill in the blanks. Lauren must have discovered that Matt was from the future and did not like the man he became, or maybe it was out of jealousy. It could be any number of explanations that his former assistant had. She worshiped the ground Matt strode upon. I would never have thought she'd go so far as to kill him.

I couldn't help but linger over the vision of Pandora in that dress. *How would Lauren compete with her?*

My heart ached to hold Pandora and do much more. After abandoning her for nineteen lonely months, I didn't deserve her affection, even assuming she would give it.

"As if anyone would believe you," James sneered.

"I believe her." I met his gaze. "Something happened with Matt that I have not disclosed because it would disturb some people. Lauren was loyal to a fault. We both know that. If she believed he strayed from his purpose, she might have snapped."

James's anger subsided then turned to grief as he nodded. "Thank you for giving us closure."

He didn't look at Pandora. It was as if he said it to the air. Then he withdrew his attention from our conversation. Watching him in his protective mode was eerie, but I knew he used his powers because the skin on the back of my neck tingled and he went still as stone.

"I won't keep you long," Pandora began. "I haven't spoken to you in months. Maxie—that feels so weird to say that still—is almost one, and he's already walking. He started calling me Dora, and I knew my time was up."

"You're going back? How?" My heart thundered in my chest. There was no telling what would happen to her.

"I will use the spell you wrote to summon me," she answered. "Oh, and Max and Trina have your spell diary. I didn't trust a package service to get to you."

"You can't."

"I've changed history too much—that's the wrong wording... I fulfilled my destiny and closed the loop. There's nothing left for me here, and now I have to go back."

The "nothing left for me here" comment slapped me. Was I nothing then? It made sense. I was gone for over a year. Pandora got over me. She would return to her time and hopefully merge with the timeline. There would be no us. She'd find someone without fear and be with him.

"I just came to say goodbye and congratulations on your accomplishments. You've done well. Leadership suits you." She leaned in and kissed my cheek.

My body heated from her touch as though I jumped into a jacuzzi in cold weather. The rush of sensation shocked me. All I could do was stand there like an idiot as she pulled away, waved, then walked out of my life.

It was James that brought me back to common sense. "Should I have someone bring her back?"

"...*nothing left for me here...* "

"No, it's fine." I faced the harbor.

"The Coven Leader and MC Council approach." James wore his ubiquitous dark shades, but the slight roll of his head let me know that his eyes matched his head movement. "She is fired up for some reason."

Tonya and Nelson burst onto my area of the balcony—Tonya

more so. Nelson likely hung back in case she needed backup. He was the yin to her yang.

"What the hell, Quyen?" Tonya had her hands on her hips.

"Baby," Nelson warned.

She signed. "Hey, Quyen. What the hell were you thinking?"

Tonya glanced at Nelson, who gave her the thumbs up. She wasn't giving me much to go on. I honestly thought she did that so that I would tell on myself.

"Hi, Tonya. Hi Nelson. What are you so riled up about?"

"I don't have time for games with you today. All three of us can't hide out here during such an important event," she said.

"It's an inaugural ball," I said.

She gave me the stink eye while Nelson gave me the "cut it out" sign. Tonya must have been super annoyed, which meant she thought I hurt myself.

"We saw goddess girl walking through the lobby like she was leaving the hotel."

"Don't call her that," I snapped.

Tonya held both hands in the air, then turned her wrists downward in a celebratory checkmate. "I knew it. You still love her. Why in the hell aren't you heading to your suite. No. Please tell me she's going to double back, and the two of you will ride into the morning. Nelson and I will be glad to make your excuses.

"You know it," Nelson put his arms around Tonya. "You're backed up, bruh, and after seeing her, I'm not mad."

"So?" Tonya asked.

"She's going back to her time." I held steady for her wrath. Tonya cared about her friends. We were family to her. Nelson mellowed her out in some ways but not enough that I wouldn't earn a headlock until I agreed to self-care.

She did nothing.

I checked to see if Nelson held her back. He didn't. His grasp on her was loose. "In light of new information, I'm going to turn over a new leaf."

Nelson kissed the side of her head, and I got it.

"You're pregnant?" I stated more than asked. It was monumental.

Our people struggled with infertility. Some couples took decades to get pregnant, and then some were lucky. "Congratulations."

"Thank you," Nelson said.

"You're the godfather, so you better be." Tonya smiled, then returned to her stern expression. "Don't sidetrack me with baby talk. You are letting the love of your life get away."

"I'm not so sure. Pandora made up her mind. She told me that nothing was keeping her here." I ran my hands through my hair.

"Bruh, come on, that's woman-speak for 'spill your feelings for me,' I thought everyone knew that."

"Let 'em know, baby," Tonya encouraged him.

"She wants you to go after her," he continued.

"That's right," Tonya added.

I stared at the two of them then my brain began to process. Why else would she come to DC? She didn't need to see me after I stupidly hid from her for the last eighteen months.

And certainly not in a ballgown that I could happily remove from her.

And I just let her go.

"I need to get out of here. Give my regards to Senator Kelly."

Tonya held out two fingers in a reverse peace sign. "We got this. You grovel. I don't expect to see you for at least eighteen days."

I planned to do better than that. James fell in step with me as I went back into the hotel. It was easier to get to my car through the lobby than it would be navigating from the outside. There was no he'd let me go on my own and I didn't have time to argue. Pandora had a head start on me. I was already about thirty minutes behind if she drove. Shimmering would only take several hops for her to get from DC to where Max and Trina lived near Fairy Stone, but that was too much magic and inefficiency when she could drive.

Pandora would need all of her magic for the spell and the new moon. It was the strongest of the year since it was the first one. Each day it would get exponentially weaker. I summoned her from the future on the second new moon—which I think was more of a perfect story from the combination of residual energy and leylines. Even if I didn't convince her right away, stalling her would buy me a few weeks and I could possibly spend the next year making it up to her.

I took my cell phone from my pocket as James ushered me to my car. It waited for me as I dialed. "I need to get to Stuart, VA. I'll give you the address when we get on the road."

I hopped into the car, and James followed me. I scrolled to Max's number and hit send. The phone rang several times.

You made your point, Max. Pick up.

"Long time no hear," he greeted.

"Sorry about that. I shouldn't have hidden from you and Trina."

"You weren't hiding from us," Max said. A squeal came across the line then he grunted. "You caught me, Son. Good job."

"Sounds like fatherhood agrees with you." I gripped my phone. It wasn't Max's fault that he was happy and moving forward with the woman he loved. We both had the same chances. He took his, and I chased mine off.

"Max. We need to talk later. Right now, Pandora is on her way back to Fairy Stone. It's the closest confluence of ley lines. When she gets to you, stall her. I'm—"

"She's already gone," he replied. "We said goodbye to her yesterday. She wouldn't let us see her off."

"She's not gone yet. I saw her at the Inaugural Ball less than an hour ago. Please go out to Fairy Stone Park, where we did the summon, and stop her. I can't lose her again."

"Alright. I'll meet you—we'll meet you out there. Apparently I'm bringing an entourage."

"Thank you, man. I will be there as soon as I can. I should be right behind you."

"She missed you, you know? I want her to be happy. You too. See you in a couple of hours."

We hung up. I watched the city lights and cars streak by as we moved down I-95. DC traffic was always a beast, but fortune shined on me, and it didn't delay us much. The only saving grace was that Pandora wasn't that far ahead of us. She battled the same time constraints, traffic, and travel like me, except I had the added anxiety of chasing her.

What would I say to her? It had to be epic. I kept her waiting for over a year and passed up her last chance. Groveling didn't cover the level of ass-kissing I owed her. Whatever I came up with, it had to be good.

~

When I arrived at Fairy Stone, my heart raced, my body shivered, and I was nauseous. It was dark, so we couldn't approach by conventional means without a cabin reservation. I directed my driver to the same access road I used the other times I slipped into the park. Hopefully, the Park Rangers didn't guard it.

We reached the little pull-off and encountered an SUV. I recognized the license plate as Max's from his previous pickup truck. A quick look once we exited the car confirmed my theory by the car seat in the second row.

"This way," I called to James. We stalked through the forest in January in tuxedos. I was overdressed. Perhaps that would impress Pan when I caught up to her—anything to gain an advantage.

It took twenty minutes to get to the amphitheater by flashlight. By then, the chill had set in from the cold. My heart seemed to stop. Pandora wasn't there.

"You made it." Max melted into view. He rubbed his hands together. Trina stood beside him with an all-terrain stroller covered with a blanket.

"Yeah, I did. Where is Pan—"

Trina punched me in the gut.

James restrained her.

"Get your hands off my wife," Max growled.

"It's fine," I gasped while doubled over. "I deserved that."

I stood when the pain subsided. I signed, "Were you able to stop her?"

Trina's narrowed eyes widened. Learning to sign must have impressed her, or it would have if she weren't so pissed at me. She gave me a nod and then signed. "Kissing up. It's a start."

"We've been here an hour, and we haven't seen her. Are you sure she's going to come here?" Max asked.

I wasn't anymore. It was pure intuition. I assumed the amphitheater because of the summon, but any part of the park would serve her needs. "I have to find her."

Max signed to Trina, "Go back to the car, please."

She frowned and then pushed the stroller in the direction of where our cars were.

"James, go with her. Max and I are fine on our own."

"Grand Magister," he protested.

"Their safety is important to me." I turned to walk in the direction where I saw a trail once. He didn't follow me.

"Thanks," Max said as we walked through the leafy grass on the packed earth trail.

I noticed he didn't ask me where we were going. It wasn't like I could answer. It was more of a feeling. Pan absorbed magic, and her touch as she took mine made me hyper aware of the power in others as a side effect. The skill had been instrumental in identifying potential allies in the government that hid or did not know their talent. Fairy Stone teemed with it, and there were areas of greater concentration than where the summons took place. "You didn't have to continue with me."

Max snorted. "You're coven, remember?"

My throat tightened. I should have. I screwed up all around. "Max, I—"

A column of light shot into the sky. Clouds gathered around it and swirled as though an eye opened in the night. It was her. I took off in the direction of the light, trying not to kill myself on the branches, roots, and the occasional park bench.

Running in a state park wasn't like a city park. Thousands of feet trod the trails, the grass grew wild, and there were more trees than clearings, which was why I failed to make it to her in time.

When I reached the clearing, the afterglow of the summoning was growing dimmer and dimmer. My blood rushed in my ears, and my lungs burned. Neither compared to the heartache of knowing that I just missed Pandora.

I doubled over for the second time that night, full of grief and not enough air. She was back to a future that I was not sure was better.

There was only one thing left: follow her example and wait. I missed our opportunity to reconcile. I wouldn't miss the next one. I had fifty years to plan, and I would use every bit of it. In the meantime, I would create the future that she deserved.

45

andora

50 A.Q.

My world was in darkness. Not the starry night sky I left moments ago but oblivion and air. That was something. I would be able to breathe while I surfed the void with my leaden limbs and silence.

"Baby, please wake up."

I was not in a vacuum if I could hear, but there was no sensation. The voice that wanted me to wake was distant. Based upon the frantic request, my body was somewhere, and my mind was in oblivion—that made sense. My physical body did not exist in the past. However, part of my soul did. Returning to the future where my body lived meant leaving my old one behind in the time dimension. That was freaky deaky in practice. My former life, along with any possessions that did not have a match in the timeline, were gone.

Basically, I was dead and in the process of reincarnating into myself.

That was disconcerting even for me, and I spent a thousand years as a soul in the godscape. However, it was not the same as negation.

"Max, I think she needs a hospital," the frantic voice replied.

The owner's voice was closer. It was on the tip of my tongue. I should know it.

The darkness remained but seemed less all-encompassing and like a shroud of dull sensation. My limbs weren't cooperating, and my head was muddled. I knew the theory, but it wasn't as though I had ever attempted it. There was a reason it was forbidden art, meddling with events aside. The experience was not something I would ever repeat.

"Stand back while I examine her," another voice much closer, in fact, over me.

My skin tingled as someone touched my wrist and neck.

I knew the last voice. I opened my eyes. "Max."

I sat up. He should not be here. How did I mess up the spell?.

"Whoa there, Pan. You gave us a scare for a minute. Relax." He put his hands on my shoulders. Max looked the same as when I left—which was last night. I must have passed out in the park. "I'm fine, but I have to figure out why the spell pulled you in. It should've—I must have been too distracted."

My mother and father watched me with worried expressions, then glanced at each other.

Or did it go the other way? Did my regret with Quyen, bring them to the past. That was worse.

"No. No. You shouldn't be here. I made a mistake, but I will fix it." I wanted to hug both of them. The ramifications of their presence in the past aside, I missed my parents.

My father nudged my mother, who touched the back of her ear. "Nine-one-one. I need medical assistance at TiroSidhe Memorial Gardens. My daughter…"

"I'm fine. Confused but fine. Max tell them," I stared at him, looking for corroboration. The quicker they believed me, the faster I could figure out how I pulled them from the future to the past.

"Grandaddy," he corrected. "I finally earned the title, or you could go back to G-max until everything in your head gets straight again."

It can't be. This was the future? It looked nothing like I expected. I knew I set out to change things, but I didn't expect it to be—I thought I would have to deal with a fractious government or some other organization that rose in place of Obscura. Did Matt's death make that much of a difference?

"You need a moment. I get it. It was kind of like that the last time too. Except no one was thrown up into a tree or put into a headlock." G-max winked at me and then walked over to my mother. "Georgia, tell them we have it under control."

"But she—"

"Trust me. It's a long conversation, but it's one pickle I know how to solve," he assured her.

She apologized and ended her call. I stood, my father, rushed to my aid. It wasn't necessary, but I appreciated the concern. It also gave me a moment to course correct. I poked around in memories from before I went back. The last thing I remembered was being at Fairy Stone State Park at night—no, wait, I went to my birth mother's grave at TiroSidhe Memorial Gardens.

We went every year since I turned twelve. I brought her favorite flowers, white pandoras, my namesake. Hope was all she had left when she had me. They co-parented me until she died in a car accident. I gripped my chest.

There was more, Trina—Grandma stayed home with Uncle Tony because he had a hundred-degree fever, and she didn't want to take any chances. I had an uncle now. He was fifteen, and Daddy always grumbled that Uncle Tony was younger than his niece.

"Are your memories catching up?" Grandaddy asked.

I nodded. Oh, were they.

Both timelines existed in my head like elaborate dreams. They were equally real to me, or was I cracking up? I couldn't be. Grandaddy knew that I went back in time. He looked the same as he did in the past instead of his older version—another change from my past. My father never hid magic from me. My mother—Adora—had the same power as me, except she could not recall the magic once she absorbed it.

345

"What are you talking about, Dad?" My father asked. "Do you know something?"

"It's one of those grandfather-granddaughter secrets that you're better off not knowing, Son. Trust me. There's not enough beer in the world."

"Truth." My father sighed. "I'm going to take your word for it this time. I don't think my home insurance ever forgave me for not listening to you the last time."

"What in the world are you—?" I began when the memory came to me.

My father tried to force answers from me about my dreams of a past life when I was fifteen when I lost control and blew a hole in the roof.

"You do have to admit the sunroof is pretty far out," Grandaddy said. "I don't have one of those."

"It is," My father admitted.

"So then Pandora is okay." My mother's hands shook. "I just knew something was wrong with her, and I—"

"I'm fine." I hugged her with the intent of reassuring *her.*

As her nurturing warmth seeped into me, tears flowed. The nightmare was over. It really was. There was no destruction or lawless zones throughout the world. Wars still happened, but not Obscura or Camera driven. The Pandora's Box Act passed twenty years ago, and practitioners were treated with equality—for the most part. We could openly practice our craft for personal use or with a license for other applications.

With all the evil that can be done, there's always hope and love—the slogan used by the Magical Consortium to push the bill.

I had the same name as the law. Kids teased me in middle school about it. I thought they were jerks because it had nothing to do with me.

What if it had everything to do with me? I poked my memories for anything about Quyen. Televised speeches and articles online were all I remembered about him. We never met in the current time, and I watched every speech he made. He even spoke at my graduation from Hampton University, his alma mater. I went there because he did too.

I studied political science and was an HR consultant at my firm. That was a far cry from beating slavers or becoming Grand Mistress of Obscura. I recalled my life, but I barely recognized it. Still, there was one consistent thing. I wanted Quyen.

My mother squeezed me. "Baby girl, is something wrong?"

I kissed her cheek. "No, there's something I have to check out. I have to go. It's a long drive, but I will call you, and we'll catch up." I hugged each of them quickly.

"The bridge is faster," Grandaddy advised. "You two have waited long enough. Oh, and tell your grandmother I'll be along."

My heart raced. The bridge was still intact after fifty years.

Hold up. He hid his relationship with Quyen from me? He made it sound like he met Quyen once in passing and—wait. I will sort the timestreams later.

I hugged him tighter, then shimmered to the cabin. I didn't trust myself to drive. My limbs were too jittery as I appeared in the kitchen. A young carbon copy of my father jumped then held a finger to his mouth, not that it mattered since Grandma wouldn't hear him yell.

He realized that a breath later and then scowled at me.

"Don't scare me like that. I'm supposed to be in bed resting." He adjusted a plate with three sandwiches on it.

"I'm not going to ask," I muttered, then went to the pantry. "Tell Grandma that Grandaddy is on his way."

"Love you too, Niece," he called, followed by an "Oh, shit, Mom," as I opened the bridge to Quyen.

"Pop-pop."

The dim interior of the pantry dissolved and a lit basement formed around me in its place. I stumbled into a bookshelf knocking it over. If Quyen weren't the owner, I would have a lot of explaining to do, and if he did…?

I still would need to explain.

The stupidity of rushing into the house weighed on me as steps thundered towards the door. I set up the bookshelf before waving my hand to gather the books and knick-knacks scattered across the floor back onto the shelf. Insanity made me use the bridge spell. I would invoke that as my reason, but either way, I had to know if—

Quyen stepped onto the landing of the basement stairs and then froze. It was him. The same sexy, dark eyes, gorgeous black hair. Not exactly the same. He'd grown it out a little from the clean, businesslike cut he usually wore. Bangs lay on his forehead carelessly, daring me to touch them. Despite my new memories of him always in a dark suit and gold tie, the colors of the Magic Consortium Party, he wore a t-shirt and jeans. His feet were bare.

I kicked off my shoes. The act gave my brain something to do besides stare at him like a stalker. I looked up.

"Do you—" In my distraction, he'd closed the gap between us. A mere eight steps were all it took to fill my world. "—remember me?"

For an answer, he cupped my face and kissed me like a man whose life depended on it. My body melted against him—eighteen months since I last touched him like this. My body craved him as much as he did me judging by his ragged breath and his need poking me. I wanted to celebrate our reunion by taking him right there. However, there were matters unsettled. I hated to do it because it was the sensible thing to do, and my emotions wanted intimacy.

Quyen may have belonged to me, but I needed to hear the words and, more importantly, know he was available. "I-uh," my voice rasped as I broke our soul-searing liplock. I stepped back when he caught me by the elbow. No ring. "I..are you still mad?"

He shook his head. "I've had time to see the error of my ways. Forty-eight years, six months, and ten days," he glanced at his watch, "eighteen hours, and thirty minutes worth of time.

Far out. It was hard not to jump him when it was clear that he missed me as much as I did him. "You waited the entire time?"

He took my hand and kissed my knuckles. "I had much to atone for, but I kept busy while waiting."

He moved up to my wrist. Each kiss sent pulses of pleasure down my spine as our auras mingled. "I may have been a fool, but I meant what I said about wanting you for myself. I didn't understand what it meant or that I had to become a man worthy of a goddess."

My heart raced with the trail of kisses on my neck. "You're not scared of me?"

"It was never you but what you meant to me."

I melted with the touch of his lips on my ear. My knees nearly buckled.

"I would scorch the Earth if you wanted me to, and I knew it. What I realized was that you wouldn't ask. Being without you forced me to realize that love would never do without you, so I spent the time preparing my love letter for you."

He scooped me into his arms, then laid me down on the bed in the corner—not the cot. He upgraded.

"Love letter?"

Quyen placed his hands on either side of my shoulders as he leaned next to my ear. "Your world was destroyed. I kept this one safe and whole for you. It's been decades since we've been acquainted. I want to give you a taste of the next hundred years. Then I plan to bind myself to you before you come to your senses."

That was his proposal?

"If that is supposed to be a marriage proposal, you're a goof."

"It was and I will take that as a yes then." He smirked, then peppered my face with kisses. "And. I. Am. Yours."

"Yes."

Then he covered his lips with mine, and we reacquainted our bodies until the next day when my mate kept his promise.

We were forever intertwined.

The End

I hope you enjoyed Quyen and Pandora's epic. Please leave a review or a rating and tell all of your friends. It lets me know what you're thinking. Who knows? Maybe there will be another book where decisions were different and another timeline emerges. There are lots of possibilities in the multiverse.

Oh, and for those who love maps and more, keep turning or scrolling.

Keep slaying.

MAP OF DOWNTOWN RICHMOND

Map of Downtown Richmond

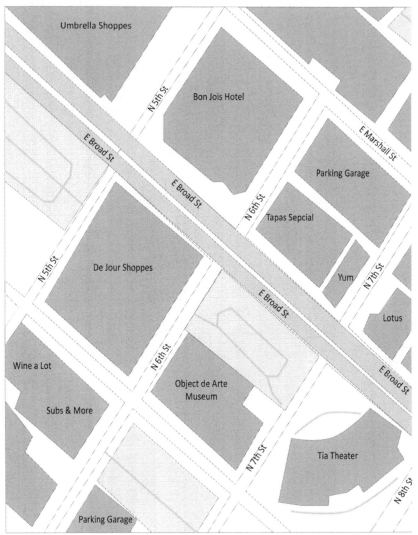

(c) 2022 by T.B. Bond

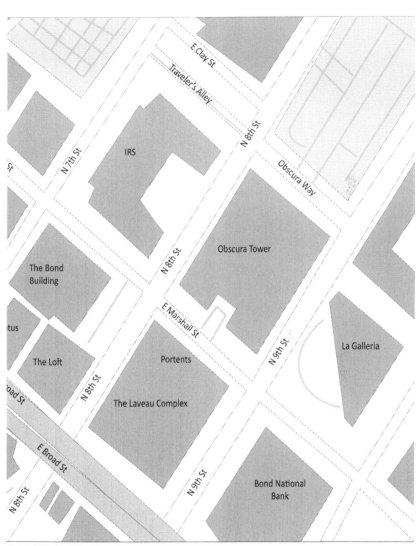

SPOILER ALERT! - SPELLMAN FAMILY TREE

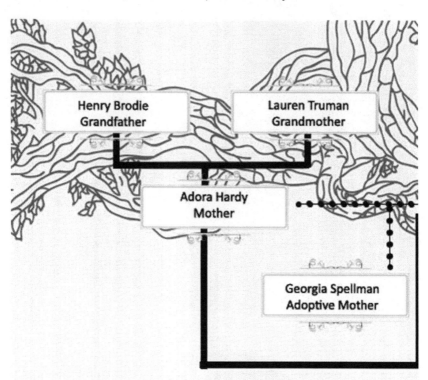

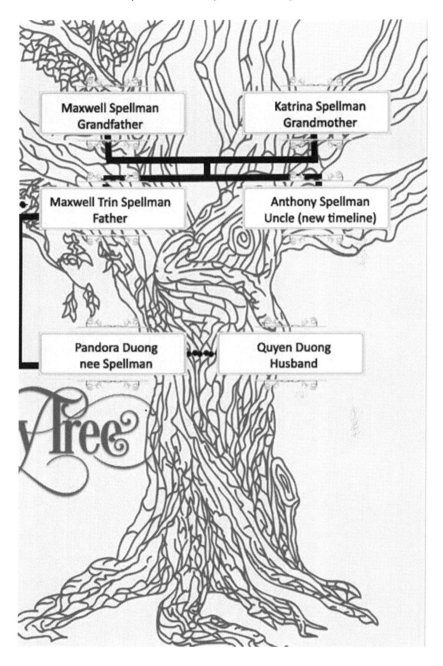

ABOUT THE AUTHOR

TB. Bond has been writing, drawing, and web designing for years. When she is not doing one of those things, she's reading and watching anime. Nerdtastic to the core she's a Whovian, Trekie, Otaku, and probably a whole host of other things.

Currently she lives with her husband, a fellow nerd, in Virginia.

Join the League Extraordinary Romance - https://www.facebook.com/groups/1031410217264327

Join T.B. Bond's Martinis - https://www.facebook.com/groups/1592694411043371

facebook.com/tbbond

twitter.com/neverstirred

instagram.com/neverstirred

bookbub.com/profile/t-b-bond

OTHER WORKS

Love, Sex, and Magic series

Novels

Shenanigans

Debacle

Short stories

Brave Little Taylor

Paris in Springtime series

Novels

King of Wishful Thinking

Ursa Major

Basis of Comparison

Hunter's Creed

I Gave You My Heart

Friends with Benies

Short stories

The Sweetest Thing

Rezoned *

Kiss of a Shifter *

Just a Taste

Anthologies

Irreplaceable - The Luck Bucket Anthology

Stand-alone Stories

Pandora's Kiss

*These are side stories in the world of Paris Springtime. They are related to a client of the agency.

Made in the USA
Middletown, DE
23 January 2023

22200855R00217